RED EYE

FULDA COLD

REDEYE

FULDA COLD

A RICK FONTAIN NOVEL

BILL FORTIN

Published by Cold War Publications
June 15, 2015

www.billfortin.com/book

TABLE OF CONTENTS

TABLE OF FIGURES & PICTURES

Special thanks to Ellen Lindenbaum for her guidance and provisioning with the logistics in setting the tone and assisting with laying out the storyline. And thanks to my Mom, Dorothy Fortin, and my brother Mark, who helped me immensely during the entire project.

Thanks to Larry Stockert and Jack Swanson
for sharing Ken's photos.

I would also like to recognize three individuals who provided both strength and words of encouragement throughout the initial marketing process.

- 1st LT Martin Milco, who served as a Platoon Leader, 1st/48th Bravo Company, the year before my tour started. I have included in this story several of his event descriptions of 3rd Armor activities in and around Gelnhausen and the Coleman Kaserne in 1968. His eye for detail was invaluable for sharpening the technical elements of Redeye in this final revision.
- COL James Pittman started his military career around the same time as my tour in West Germany. I met Jim through the 'Together We Serve' site. I have used his comments to start the conversation in the Redeye Prologue. I'm honored to have made his acquaintance.
- And last but not least, LTC Luke Lloyd, who took over command of the 1st/33rd Armor Battalion the year after I rotated back to the land of the big PX. His counsel and friendship have been the best part of this journey.

Finally, on a professional level, I want to express heartfelt gratitude to my editor extraordinaire, Donna Foley, who went the extra mile and made RedEye better!

And a special thanks to Stephen Walker --S. R. Walker Designs – who redesigned the Redeye cover with professional speed and dexterity.

*In loving memory of **Sergeant Ken Clark**, 1st/48th INF, HHC, 1969 - 1971, who used his camera to record for all of us important moments in history long since forgotten. The entire Redeye team owes our very lives to him. Ken passed away on May 11, 2007.*

This story is dedicated to him...

LTC Thomas Brogan *born May 2, 1930, to Harriet and Tyler Brogan in Los Angeles, California.*

Survived by his daughter, Lisa, and son, Tim. Tom passed on July 13, 2010, in Tyler, Texas. Tom was an extraordinary human being and a true American hero. "Blood & Guts, Colonel."

"Joining is hard, belonging is earned, and committing to those you serve with will define you forever."

CHARACTERS, PLACES AND TERMS

London

- **Staff SGT E-6 Joe Benson** –– COMM Center – supported David James
- **Alex Dobbins** – CIA alias. Real name: Bill Douglas. CIA GPC – Global Projects Coordinator
- **William (Bill) J. Douglas** - CIA aliases Major Bill Carlstrum and Alex Dobbins. CIA GPC – Global Projects Coordinator
- **David James** - U.S. Cultural Attaché to London Embassy - March '68. Actual position - CIA Station Chief in London

Netherlands

- **Technische Hogeschool Eindhoven** - University campus called *"THE"*. The **think-tank** for Philips Research, Bell Laboratories, NATO, and select members of the International intelligence community
- **Dr. Kevel Natton** - Academic. NATO expert on the Russian mindset; was the chief architect for MC 14/3 C
- **1st LT, now Captain Jim Pezlola** - CIA area operations control for surveillance in East Germany and Czechoslovakia

Germany

- **Specialist5 Larry Anderson** - Gunship Crew Chief
- **Captain William J. Beck**—1st/48th Battalion S-3
- **Lieutenant Calvin Berkline** - Section Leader took over RedEye in February 1970
- **Spec5 Carl Blubaugh** - 1st/48th Battalion S-3 Clerk

- **Command Sergeant Major David Bost** - Top NCO of the 1st/48th—a very large presence and command influence who stood at 6' 7" and weighed in at 270+ pounds
- **Lieutenant Colonel Thomas Brogan** - Battalion Commander: 1st/48th Infantry
- **Sergeant Von Boyd** - RedEye Team Leader, 1st/48th HHC; call sign Sparrow22
- **First Sergeant Ernie Bumpus** - number one NCO of the 1st/48th Headquarters and Headquarters Company
- **Staff Sgt. Tom Burgraff** - Maintenance Supervisor 1st/48th HHC
- **Major B. D. Carlstrum** - The name CIA agent Bill Douglas aka Alex Dobbins used when posing as a member of the U. S. Army
- **Spec5 Jake Carson** - Battalion Commander Security Coordinator: 1st/48th
- **SGT Jimmy Carson** - HHC maintenance: 1st/48th
- **First Sergeant Jake Carstairs** - First Sergeant Bravo Company: 1st/48th INF
- **Spec4 Gary Cisewski** - HHC Driver/Medic: 1st/48th
- **Sergeant Ken Clark** - RedEye Team Leader: 1st/48th HHC; call sign Sparrow25 - Photographic expertise
- **Specialist5 Bernie Costa** - Company Clerk: 1st/48th HHC. A good friend and supporter of Rick Fontain
- **Staff Sergeant Elton Covel** - Section Sergeant - RedEye - February 1970
- **Captain Steven Davies** - Charlie Company Commander and acting FO – Goldenwire - Operation Synchronized Sparrow: 1st/48th
- **Sergeant Dan Elven** - 1st/48th Bravo Co. - assigned to RedEye Security in Sparrow Hawk
- **Spec4 Jason Farmer** - NATO Canine Guard Kennel Cadre
- **SGT Rick Fontain** – Redeye Fire Team Leader: 1st/48th HHC; call sign Sparrow6
- **Lieutenant General N.G. Galaiologopoulos** - Hellenic Army -International Military Staff
- **Lieutenant Justin Gambeson** - Fargo4 HHC Company Commander
- **Gehlen Organization** - intelligence agency established June 1946 by U.S. occupation authorities – referenced in NATO document MC 14/3

- **Andrew Jackson <u>Goodpaster</u>** - NATO's Supreme Allied Commander
- **Sergeant Joe <u>Gordon</u>** - mechanic extraordinaire 1st/48th HHC
- **Max <u>Gresonine</u>** - Hotel owner; Jim Pezlola contact/coordinator with the Bundesnachrichtendienst - Federal Intelligence Service (BND)
- **Major Daniel <u>Gustafson</u>** - [Chaparral] advanced team - Sparrow Hawk/2nd Cavalry Regiment (2 CR) Squadron 3/Fargo4
- **<u>Headquarters and Headquarters Company</u>** - company sized military unit – usually positioned at the battalion level or higher; abbreviated HHC
- **Retired SFC Jimmy <u>Hansen</u>** - proprietor of the Gasthaus "Twenty and Out"; retired 3rd Armor Division
- **Gustav <u>Heinemann</u>** - outgoing West German President of the Federal Parliamentary Republic; appointed Ambassador to Washington, D.C. 1970
- **Staff Sergeant Wally <u>Hoffenburger</u>** - NCOIC HHC Facilities; Supervisor Fargo4
- **CSM Dennis <u>Houseman</u>** - Sparrow Hawk/2nd Cavalry Regiment (2 CR) Squadron 3/Fargo4 - advanced team
- **Captain Donald <u>Jamison</u>** - Grafenwohr Plans and Training Officer; call sign Graf Train6
- **First Lieutenant Walter P. <u>Janzen</u>** - took over for George MacKennia as Company Commander: 1st/48th HHC
- **Corporal Elmer <u>Jenson</u>** - member of the Headquarters Company at Fargo4
- **Sergeant Stan <u>Johnston</u>** - 1st/48th Bravo Company; RedEye Security – Operation Sparrow Hawk
- **Staff Sergeant Zach <u>Jorgensen</u>** - Section Sergeant NATO Canine Guard
- **Lieutenant Carl <u>Key</u>** - 1st/48th Battalion S-2/S-6
- **Bob <u>Ketter</u>** - Rhein-Main AFB Flight Operations, Chief Warrant Officer; Operation Sparrow Signature; call sign Birdview6
- **Lieutenant Colonel David <u>Kingston</u>** - Regimental Commander advanced team: Sparrow Hawk/2nd Cavalry Regiment (2 CR) at Fargo LODs 2-4 - Chaparral/Vulcan
- **Staff Sergeant Scott <u>Kirtwin</u>** - Arms Room Supervisor: 1st/48th INF HHC

- **SFC Gary Lawson** - COMM Center Supervisor – reported to Jim Pezlola
- **Dr. / Colonel James D. Lattermire** - 54 years old; Commanding Officer of the Nuremburg Hospital Center; CIA's Chief Forensic Psychologist in Europe
- **Captain George MacKennia** - Incoming Company Commander: 1st/48th HHC; promoted to Major, January 1970
- **Nathan Pebble** - Spec4 Transportation Section; 5th floor of the HHC
- **LTC Arthur J. Peck** - Battalion Commander: 1st/33rd
- **Dr. /Captain Janice Prasonio** - Nuremburg Hospital Center; trained University of Maryland School of Medicine
- **Maj. Gen. M. Roseborough** - Commander 3rd Armor Division - August 1969-May 1971
- **Captain William Sager** - [Vulcan] advanced team for Sparrow Hawk/2nd Cavalry Regiment (2 CR) Squadron 3/Fargo4
- **Willie "Slick" Sanders** - Spec4: 1st/48th Line Company
- **Spec4 Bob Saur** - 1st/48th Bravo Company; spotter to RedEye during Sparrow Hawk
- **Hanna Gresonine Schmidt** - Owner/Hostess "Dining in Paradise"
- **Heinrich Waldemar Schmidt** - Serving West German Minister of Defense; West German Chancellor 1974 to 1982; Social Democratic politician
- **Karl Guntur Schmidt** – deceased husband of Hanna Schmidt; agent for the West German organization known as the Bundesnachrichtendienst, the Federal Intelligence Service or BND; killed in the line of duty
- **PFC Fred Simpson** – 21 years old; Special skill in RedEye guidance electronics; assigned to RedEye for Operation Sparrow Hawk; call sign Sparrow211
- **LTC Richard "Dicky "Stern** - 1st/14th Armored Calvary; call sign ACR6
- **SFC Donald Stebbins** - advanced team - Sparrow Hawk/2nd Cavalry Regiment (2 CR) Squadron 3/Fargo4
- **SGT Larry Stockert** - RedEye Team Leader; call sign Sparrow24
- **Staff Sergeant Malcolm Summering** - 1st / 48th HHC - S-4 NCO

- **Jack <u>Swanson</u>** - RedEye Team Leader –Call sign Sparrow23
- **Spec4 Jerry <u>Terrell</u>** - -1st/48th HHC
- **SPC4 Glen <u>Towson</u>** - 1st/48th Bravo Company; nickname "camera guy"; RedEye spotter - Operation Sparrow Hawk; promoted to Sergeant E-5, January 1970
- **Spec4 Jerry <u>Wilson</u>** - Battalion EXEC Security / driver: 1st/48th
- **Lieutenant Dave <u>Wirth</u>** - Battalion S-4: 1st/48th
- **Markus Johannes "Mischa" <u>Wolf</u>** - Hauptverwaltung Aufklärung, Department Head, Foreign Intelligence Division for East Germany's Ministry for State Security, commonly known as the Stasi

United States

- **PFC Jake <u>Ashcroft</u>**—Company clerk AIT Ft. Dix
- **Les <u>Baxter</u>—Director** Bell Labs: Electronics / Software Design
- **Maj. Richard I. <u>Bong</u>**—the USAF's all-time aerial victory leader
- **Sergeant First Class Tom <u>Burlap</u>** — Section SGT [SFC] - 6th CAV - Ft. Meade; call sign 'Burlap'
- **Lt. Gen. Gerald <u>Bushman</u>**—Deputy Director of the CIA
- **William Egan <u>Colby</u>**—(January 4, 1920-April 27, 1996) spent a career in intelligence for the United States, culminating in holding the post of director of central intelligence
- **PVT Robert <u>Coons</u>** - Basic and Advanced Infantry training with Rick Fontain
- **Don <u>Coover</u>** - Director, Research and Development: Bell Labs
- **Brent <u>Cummings</u>** - CIA East German INTEL Desk at Langley
- **Barry <u>Flax</u>** - Vice President, Research and Development: General Dynamics
- **Matilda G. <u>Hodges</u>** - President, Selective Service Draft Board - Ellicott City, MD - 1968
- **Roger "Kelly" <u>Johnston</u>** - Chief Engineer: Lockheed Skunk Works

- **Ed McCall** - CIA Field Support Analyst - direct report to Joe Wilson at Langley
- **Major Thomas B McGuire, Jr.** - Medal of Honor recipient; the second leading ace in American history
- **LT COL Milision** – Pilot in Command – Operation Sparrow Signature
- **Daniel and Mary Prasonio** - the parents of Dr. Janice Prasonio
- **Daryl Russell** - CIA, Russia INTEL Desk
- **Spec4 Hal Stacy** - Vietnam Vet; assigned to the 6th CAV- Ft. Meade
- **Joe Wilson** -Department Head Central Intelligence: Office of Russian and European Analysis (OREA)
- William P. **Rogers** - U. S. Secretary of State: 1969 – 1973

AUTHOR'S NOTE

Many people forget that during the Vietnam War era there was another war going on -- one that had been raging since the 1950's: The Cold War. While brave men were dying in Vietnam, equally brave men were facing an enemy much more threatening than those in Southeast Asia - namely the Soviet Union. Redeye Fulda Cold brings to light the rigors and experiences of those in the 3rd Armor Division, as well as humorous anecdotes of life in the U.S. Military in Europe in the 1960s. The Cold War, as played out in places like the Fulda Gap, and the threats and missions our soldiers faced in this environment, is all but forgotten in our history except by those who served in it.

PROLOGUE

Putting a chink in communist doctrine may not have been the primary motive of the reform movement called Prague Spring. However, it did provide the people of Czechoslovakia with a brief view of the concept of western capitalism -- and its potential value. Czechoslovakia's newly elected First Secretary of the Communist Party would introduce some radically new ideas to his people and his party. Reformist Alexander Dubček, on January 5, 1968, released his vision of what he considered to be the future success for his country. However, this breath of spring, and his dream, came to a screeching halt on August 21 of that same year when the Soviet Union and the Warsaw Pact invaded his country and halted any and all reforms that were thought to be detrimental to Mother Russia and the communist party. Romania and Albania were the only Pact countries that did not participate.

History would show that the Czechs attributed the invasion to the "Brezhnev Doctrine", which stated that the U.S.S.R. had the right to intervene whenever a country in the Eastern Bloc appeared to be making a shift toward capitalism. In fact, Brezhnev's Soviet foreign policy specifically stated -- and I quote: "When forces are hostile to socialism, and attempt to turn existing socialist countries toward capitalism, it will become a concern for everyone indoctrinated in the family."

Two months before the invasion, several members of the Dubček Cabinet defected to the West. They took with them several interesting documents from the safe in the palace in which the president of Czechoslovakia resided. These official papers clearly outlined a Soviet war plan with intent to fake a NATO first strike invasion of the Eastern bloc countries. What really surprised the NATO intelligence officers, and caused major fallout within the intelligence community itself, was the amount of detail in the plan that specified the immediate use of nuclear weapons. Most everyone just plain refused to believe what they had been handed.

The Langley interrogators, however, took exception to this stance and requested an additional analysis be conducted by the Hilversum Group in Holland. What caused the CIA men great concern was the level of detail used to describe the nuclear strike and the interesting list of the countries that were not to be harmed in the proposed

21

missile barrage. These named countries were the nations of Great Britain, Spain, Norway, and France, with a special notation for the protection of the city of Paris.

The CIA Station Chief in London was directed by the U.S. President to immediately respond to this clear and present danger. The highest levels of the U.S. and West German governments were summoned to meet in The Netherlands. After much discussion, a complete re-write for the response to invasion, titled MC 14/3 C, was sanctioned. If Russia was indeed going to attack the West, buying time to prepare was the order of the day.

The term MAD, Mutually Assured Destruction, was always considered to be the most distinguishing of all factors blocking a Russian invasion. But by mid-1968, it seemed that was no longer the case! The alerting term, created in the early 1950s, was called DEFCON, which stood for Defense Readiness Condition.

The enhancements to the NATO war plan, MC 14/3 C, would mandate an instant escalation to the second highest level, DEFCON-2, for any invasion attempt. This would be followed by an immediate call for a DEFCON-1. The key word in this new policy was "immediate", with an absolute no-pause-for-diplomacy mandate. Not since the end of WW II in the Pacific has this God-like power been authorized. This resolve, known only to the U.S. President, the German Chancellor, and a few high ranking officials in the NATO command, would be carried out by the American CIA and the U.S. Army's 3rd Armor 1st/48th's "Blood and Guts" Battalion. Specifically, the expertise of the RedEye fire teams would initially position this new strategy.

The general consensus in the CIA was to buy as much time as possible so that the second part of the new NATO war plan could be made ready and implemented. A complex set of military exercises were hatched and submitted for approval by a secret NATO think-tank. These carefully crafted series of maneuvers would be specifically designed to influence the Russian military mindset. The first set of operations would seek at the start to delay the Russians from coming across the border. The final strategy would deliberately draw the Russians to a predetermined point well inside the Gap at Fulda. The world was about to change, and its entire future was now in the hands of a new defensive posture known as **Fulda Cold**.

PART I

"AN HONOR AND A PRIVILEGE"

"We all take different paths in life, but no matter where we go, we take a little of each other everywhere."

—Tim McGraw

I

THINGS ARE SELDOM WHAT THEY SEEM[1]

LONDON
0515 HOURS FRIDAY 7 FEBRUARY 1969

It was early February 1969. I was on a three-day pass in London -- the first chance I had had to travel outside of Germany since I'd arrived in December 1968. I had left the barracks early to bum a ride to the airport with the duty officer, Lieutenant Key, who was driving into Frankfurt to place our S-4 equipment wish list for the coming month.

I had planned on getting *space available* that morning with the scheduled *medevac* flight from Rhein-Main to Mildenhal Air Force Base in the United Kingdom. My first sergeant, Ernie Bumpus, had told me about this little known mode of transportation that was

---

[1]   Lyric from the Gilbert and Sullivan operetta "H.M.S. Pinafore"

available on a first come first served basis.

I got lucky, or so I thought. Not only were there plenty of seats available, but the flight departed on time with only six patients going to England that morning.

ABOARD US ARMY C117—SKYTRAIN
ONE "GOOD" ENGINE AND THE ENGLISH CHANNEL
0830 HOURS FRIDAY 7 FEBRUARY 1969

The most critical case on board was a patient who was in traction. He was secured on a stretcher attached to the right side bulkhead directly across from my seat.

The décor of the cabin indicated it might have seen service with Jimmy Doolittle[2]. We took off and everything was great for the first hour. It was just after the explosion that I realized that my decision to save on travel time needed to be re-evaluated.

The aircraft's sudden deceleration gave me that sinking sensation in my stomach one would get if one rappelled off a cliff without a rope. The plane turned suddenly and sharply toward the right, then over-compensated back to the left. My mind told me that our aircraft might have suffered a structural failure from which there would be no return. I looked out the portal next to my seat and everything looked normal.

I unbuckled my seatbelt and went across the aisle and leaned across the guy in traction to look out his portal. What I saw made me immediately mumble the words, "*Oh, shit*" under my breath. Right then, I made up my mind to book commercial for the return.

The right engine was stopped and smoking a smidgen. The propeller was no longer spinning. Plus, its position in the wing was awry: it pointed slightly downward. Immediately, I subtracted one from two and came up with the number of *good* engines remaining.

Right above my head was a disconnected intercom speaker sporting frayed and detached wires dangling at its side. "*Just as well,*" I thought. The information that could have come out of it we probably didn't want to know just yet.

Traction Guy seemed to be fully awake now. I suspected he

---

[2] Lt. COL. James Doolittle, in January 1942, planned for and led the U.S.'s first retaliatory attacks on the Japanese homeland during WWII.

could read lips and had read mine. I looked down at his face and whispered to myself, "*I didn't know anyone could open their eyes quite that wide.*" I reached down and took his hand. He was strapped in pretty well. He couldn't move anything but his eyes from side to side. I put my face about three inches from his and looked him straight in the eye and said as calmly as I could, "We're OK. The right side motor appears to have just backfired, I said. Perhaps 'detonated' was a better word, but I spared him that.

"We're over the Channel. Only a few minutes more before we land," I said. "*One way or another,*" I thought was more to the point.

I was surprised at the tone and calmness of my own voice. I wondered how many of his fingers I had broken. I think it kept him from hyperventilating because his breathing seemed to slow down and return to what I would consider to be the *normal range* of 200 to 300 BPS[3]. I stayed with him until the medic came back and took over.

We landed in one piece about 30 minutes later. You would not believe the number of fire trucks the Air Force has on call. It was an astounding display of runway teamwork!

THE DOUBLE DECKER
ROYAL AIR FORCE STATION MILDENHAL, SUFFOLK, ENGLAND
1240 HOURS FRIDAY 7 FEBRUARY 1969

Royal Air Force Station Mildenhal is an all-British operation in support of NATO located near the town of Mildenhal in Suffolk, England. I took a double-decker bus, which departed right outside the main gate to downtown London. And since this was my first ride on a double-decker I went directly up the stairs and seated myself at the very front.

Did you know they drive on the wrong side of the road in England? And, they also make use of a traffic control device called a *traffic circle*.

"*Big mistake sitting where I was,*" I thought later. I had planned to take in the countryside on the way into the city. All I remember to this day is the bus pulling out into traffic on the left side of the

---

3 Breaths per second

road and entering a traffic circle in a clockwise direction. It was about 30 seconds later that I made the decision to change seats and to make a blindfold out of my handkerchief. Still, it was not as exciting as the plane ride.

2ND FLOOR, ROOM 26 D, E, & F
AN ARMED FORCES HOTEL AT LANCASTER GATE
1600 HOURS FRIDAY 7 FEBRUARY 1969

I had an address in Lancaster Gate for an Armed Forces Hotel with an unbelievable rate of three dollars per night. A great deal, but I had to admit I was a little disappointed by not having my own room. There were three bunks in my room located on the second floor, but only one of them had any indication of being occupied. The Desk Sergeant commented that I had come at a good time of year because the hotel was practically empty.

The door to the room opened and this tall, well set up guy wearing suit pants, a sleeveless undershirt and a towel around his neck walked in. I turned to face the door as he introduced himself.

"Alex Dobbins," he said, and extended his hand. I would find out later that his real name was William J. Douglas. His accent was decidedly American -- probably the mid-west, maybe Chicago. We would meet again in Germany several months later and he would be introduced to me as Major Bill Carlstrum.

The clothes that were laid out on his bed looked brand new. The outfit even included a bowler hat and long black umbrella. Once put on, the clothes would provide the appearance of a well-tailored English businessman.

"I'm Rick," I said with my best first-greeting smile.

"It's good to meet you, Rick. What brings you to the city of no sunshine?"

"I'm a factory rep for Foster Grant[4]. I'm here to address the Association of Blind Fighter Pilots," I said with the most serious tone I could muster.

---

[4]   AAI Foster Grant, based in Smithfield, RI, is one of the leading brands of sun and reading glasses in the United States.

Alex cocked his head slightly and laughed. "That's funny, Rick. That's very funny."

We had dinner together that night. He said the food was OK in the hotel but he had found this Italian place on Anchor Street, which was directly across from the Ritz Hotel that he described as *simply brilliant.* I was not sure if that meant that everything on the menu was spelled correctly or that the food emitted a bright light.

That night, while walking back to Lancaster Gate, he gave me his business card, which had the name *Mr. Alexander Dobbins*, but no title. The address was Sir Isaac Newton House, 8 Jermyn ST, London, but there was no telephone number. *Ding, ding, and ding*, even at my young age, there were warning bells going off in my head. We went down the cellar steps into the hotel bar. The pricing in the bar complemented the extraordinary room rate of the hotel.

The *interview* lasted about 30 minutes. The conversation included questions on topics that ranged from where I was from to where I was stationed. My answers were brief and to the point. I answered the United States and Europe, respectively. Dobbins paused a moment, then continued, asking me if I had had a job before I was drafted. This was

> "*Capt. MacKennia*—
>
> CON GRATS—
>
> Glad u came thru—BD"

Figure 1 Business Card

an interesting query on his part because not many draftees would wind up in Europe during this time period. He also never asked my last name, but I had the feeling he already knew it.

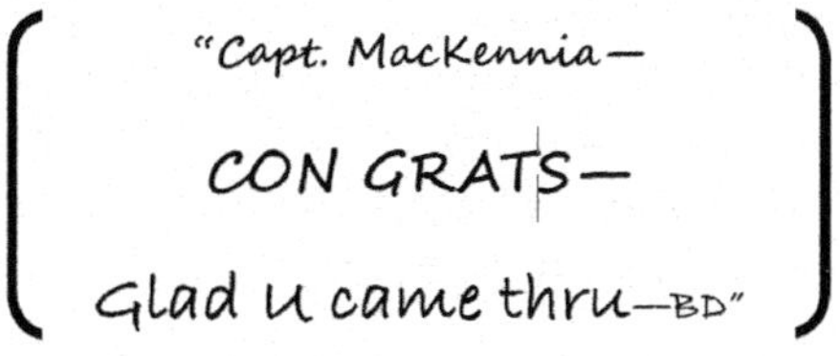

He asked me for his business card back. He wrote something on the back of the card and handed it back to me. We talked for a few more minutes and then he said he had an early morning meeting and that he was going up north to Manchester that night.

He shook my hand before leaving and said, "It was really nice meeting you, Rick. I hope we can get together tomorrow." He seemed quite genuine, and glad to have made my acquaintance.

"*Maybe we could link up tomorrow afternoon after he returns to London*?" I asked myself. He gave the impression that he knew his way around this city. After he left I looked at what he had written on back of the card.

CAPT MacKennia, Congrats, Glad U came thru, BD

"*I wonder who Captain MacKennia is....*" I didn't think I'd heard the name previously. Even by my standards this was one strange and secretive person.

Although I wasn't able to get him to disclose anything about himself, I did take him up on an offer to see some of London's more out-of-the-way sites. We met the next day at 1600 hours, had a quick drink in the hotel, and walked and talked for several hours.

**"MR. D" AND ABBEY ROAD
1815 HOURS
SATURDAY 8 FEBRUARY 1969**

Figure 2 - Abbey Road

We took in some of the lesser known landmarks of London. The one I remember most is Abbey Road[5]. This location was used by the Beatles for their album cover later on in 1969. Well, right around the corner from the street crossing he pointed to a house that he said was Paul McCartney's. I found out years later when I was based in London that it was actually the location of EMI Studios. When I asked how he came by the address, he said, "Oh, it's theirs, believe me."

"Mr. D" made sure I didn't take any pictures of him during our short excursion. To my knowledge, no one ever has.

I got an early start on both Saturday and Sunday mornings. It was a real treat being able to read English newspapers and take in the latest American movie releases. I attended several plays. I can only recall two however: one was *Hair*, and the best one, which I think about with great clarity to this day, was the production of *Mame* with Ginger Rogers at the Theatre Royal, Drury Lane, located in Covent Garden.

I kept my promise to myself and returned via a British Airways commercial flight. I was feeling pretty pleased with my decision until I pulled an information card from the seat pocket. The card said, "This aircraft can take off and land without the assistance of a pilot." That's brilliant, if only the trains ran a little faster.

---

5   Abbey Road is the 11th studio album released by the English rock band the Beatles.

MY NEW CO[6]
REPORTING THE INCIDENT
0815 HOURS MONDAY 10 FEBRUARY 1969

When I had come aboard in December, I was read the riot act to report any suspicious people approaching us, trying to solicit information or bribe us with money or gifts. I figured this mysterious "Mr. D" qualified, so I went to see the new company commander who had reported in during the weekend I went to London.

I went to the Orderly Room and pushed the door open.

"Hello, First Sergeant, is the CO in? I want to report a contact occurrence that took place in London."

"Yeah, he is, but he's just about to leave. What was her name?"

"No, it's not a girl, just a weird guy who asked a lot of questions."

"I'll see if he has a minute for you," replied the Top Sergeant.

"Thanks, Top," I said. Top Sergeant Ernie Bumpus went to the CO's door, knocked once and pushed the door open.

"A PFC[7] would like a moment of your time, Sir."

"Show him in Top, and call down to your buddy, Sergeant Collins in S-4, and see if he had any luck with finding me a refrigerator. Right now that's more important than a car."

"Yes Sir, I'll be glad to," replied Bumpus. He then addressed me. "The CO will see you now."

"Thanks, again," I said.

I walked to the open doorway, knocked once on the jamb and waited.

"Come," said the CO. I walked to within three feet of the desk, saluted, and stood at attention.

"At ease," he said and casually returned my salute. "What can I do for you?" I relaxed into parade rest and glanced for the first time at our new CO. He stood and reached across the desk to shake hands. He was about my height, of a stocky build, and he was wearing a flight jacket that had the wings of an Army aviator. He

---

[6]   Commanding Officer
[7] Private First Class

was also wearing the badge that indicated that someone had shot at him.

"Sir," I started to relate my encounter in London but I stopped in mid-sentence when I saw the CO's name plate located on the front of his desk: Captain George MacKennia. Instead of completing my sentence I handed him "Mr. D's" business card.

"So, what's this for?" he asked.

"Look at the back, Sir. Is he a friend of yours?"

Captain George MacKennia leaned back in his chair stared at the business card, and said, "We took a long walk in the woods together once. He saved my life. His name isn't Dobbins. It's Douglas, Bill Douglas."

"Small world, isn't it, Sir?"

II

THE BEGINNING - ZERO HOUR

NINE MONTHS BEFORE LONDON
INDUCTION CENTER, FORT HOLABIRD, MARYLAND
0730 HOURS WEDNESDAY 10 APRIL 1968

I'm Rick Fontain. At 20 years old, I had been out of high school for two years. After a full year of college at Loyola in Baltimore, and a full semester of ROTC under my belt, I joined the communications industry with employment in the Bell System. In April of 1968, while taking computer language and data programming courses at Catonsville Community College, sometimes referred to as the University of Southern Catonsville, I was drafted.

Even after all of these years I still have an intense mental picture of the head of Howard County's Selective Service Board, Matilda G. Hodges. From her commanding position on the front porch of the building, and with her smile blazing, she waved a final farewell to seventeen of Howard County's finest 1A classified inductees as we pulled out of the Board's parking lot.

The first destination of the day was to be Fort Holabird. I could

33

only imagine what gay adventures lay ahead. Jim Hutton later repeated these exact same words in the John Wayne movie called "The Green Berets."

Fort Holabird was established in 1917 on 96 acres of marshland in Baltimore City. NCOs, (Non Commissioned Officers), were screaming into their completely unnecessary bullhorns. The room was filled with individuals who obviously were perceived to have only a room temperature IQ. Clearly, the majority of us who were jammed into this small space were either deaf, or were about to be rendered so.

SEMPER BYE-BYE
COMPLAINERS AND TROUBLE MAKERS
1100 HOURS WEDNESDAY 10 APRIL 1968

As in any group assembled against their will, there were the usual complainers and troublemakers. My Dad imparted one piece of advice to me the day before I left. "Always strive to become invisible. Never volunteer under any circumstances for anything," he had said. In other words, remain silent. Anything you do, say, or look as if you would, will be used against you at the next earliest possible *change of station.* This, as it turned out, was sound advice.

The year was 1968. There was a little conflict called Vietnam raging at this time. Consequently, the draft boards were in a full court press. (I love to use sports analogies.) Little did I know I was about to meet a Sergeant who used analogies about lawnmowers and outhouses. He encouraged us to call our mothers to explain why there was no hope. He was a born salesman, convincing me right away that this was going to be a lot worse than I ever imagined.

Do you remember the scene from the movie "Animal House", where they administer the oath to the pledges? They said, *"I 'state your name'. . ."* and everybody repeated the phrase *state your name* instead of their own names. Well, I swear it looked like the same guy minus the white robe doing the swearing in.

I wanted to scream out, "Thank you, sir. May I have another?" But being intimidated by lawnmowers, outhouses and the dilemma over calling my mother, I didn't say anything but the words, "I do".

Apparently, the Marines were also attending the festivities this day. It seems they were not getting the required enlistment through the normal channels. *"Go figure,"* I said to myself.

So, if you exhibited any bad behavior, this assured you an all-expenses paid trip to Parris Island[8]. Of course, there were fewer and fewer occurrences of misconduct as the morning rolled on, once it became known who the guys in the different looking uniforms were.

Seemingly unperturbed by our sudden good behavior, the NCOs told us to line up and count off in groups of four. This confused quite a few of America's best, but we caught on only after a few tries.

Failure to perform a correct counting off, and/or receiving the number four, produced two distinct types of feelings: one was of great joy, the other of massive fear.

W.E.B. Griffin[9] wrote a series of books for the people who shouted out the number four. The series is called "The Corps". The reader travels through the early days before WWII all the way up to and including the Korean Conflict. What I like best about his storytelling is the insight he shows in describing some very young people who were able to grasp the big picture of how things work in the military at a very young age.

I shouted out the number two. My feeling of glee was short-lived when the bullhorn exploded with directions to proceed to the buses and, thence, Fort Bragg, North Carolina.

I will forever reflect back on that day. I know my life would have turned out differently if I had called out a four instead of a two. Understand, not for better or worse, but different.

---

8   Marine Corps basic training has the reputation of being the toughest of all the services. It most certainly is the longest, at about 12 1/2 weeks. It has been said time and time again by former Marines that Marine Corps recruit training was the most difficult thing they ever had to do in their entire lives. There are two locations which turn men into Marines: the Recruit Training Depot at Parris Island, South Carolina, and the Recruit Training Depot at San Diego, California.

9   The Corps, written by W.E.B. Griffin, is a series of war novels about the United States Marine Corps before and during the years of World War II and the Korean War. The story features a tightly knit cast of characters in various positions within the Marine Corps, Navy, and upper levels of the United States Government.

It has always been the natural born leaders who have made our military successful. I took a seat towards the rear of the bus and said a small prayer asking God for some of the same insights as had guided those leaders to guide me through this mounting adventure.

III

ZERO WEEK - PLUS EIGHT HOURS

FORT BRAGG, NORTH CAROLINA
0115 HOURS THURSDAY 11 APRIL 1968

It was 1:15 a.m. To set the proper tone, I think we should use military time from here on out: 0115 hours. We arrived at the gates of Fort Bragg Reception Center in the wee hours of the morning. The bus doors opened and, you guessed it, a guy with a Smokey the Bear hat and a bullhorn screamed, "Off the bus you *'XQFDSHGHGTEWASDF'.*" To this day, I still don't know how one person could fit that many marbles in his mouth.

I've racked my brain trying to recall what the rest of the night was like but I keep drawing a blank. I must have slept hard in spite of the stress. So, I'll pick it up at 0515 hours at the breakfast banquet. This was the first time I was introduced to the concept of *chewing your food on your own time*. We found out later that this was a lie. No free time was allocated to us for the next eight weeks.

ZERO WEEK TESTING AND TRANSFORMATION
1145 HOURS WEDNESDAY 17 APRIL 1968

It was called Zero Week. It started with the transformation of our hearts and minds. First, the interviews and testing took place over a two and one half day period. Drafted recruits who were assigned a serial number starting with the letters *U* and *S*, and had passed an IQ test with a score of twelve or higher, were taken aside and counseled on the many splendid benefits of the U.S. Army's "specialty" schools. The catch, of course, was the misrepresentation of the opportunity, which added one or more years to one's "time-in-service".

The Army calls their training skill sets MOS.[10] The Army has around 190 MOS's available for enlisted men. Related specialties are divided into "branches" or "fields." As it turned out for me, I got the coveted 11 Bravo MOS without committing to any additional time.

"*Eleven Bravo*" (Infantryman), shown on my permanent record as 11B, is the most popular MOS, and the easiest to get assigned. An Infantryman is considered the backbone of the Army. He is responsible for defending our country against any threat by land. In 1968, Eleven Bravo had the most vacancies.

OUT-OF-SCHOOL OXYMORONS
0900 HOURS WEDNESDAY 17 APRIL 1968

We all learned about the oxymorons[11] in school. But this was my first experience of actually living inside of one. Some of the ones with which you may be familiar are: *airline food, absolutely unsure, awfully good, clearly confused* and, of course, my personal favorite: *military intelligence.*

---

[10]   Military Occupation Specialties

[11]   An oxymoron is a figure of speech that combines contradictory terms.

DAY 2.5
ZERO POINT ZERO: THE EXIT INTERVIEW
1345 HOURS THURSDAY 18 APRIL 1968

I have always been taught to trust but verify. It became clear to me that the reason they were working on me so hard to extend my enlistment was that I must have answered too many of the test questions correctly.

The Specialist 5[12] had come into the cubicle and flashed what looked like a folded wallet to the Spec4 who was in the process of providing feedback on my testing. The Spec5 told the Spec4 that he would complete the interview. With that, we were left alone to discuss the results. He didn't identify himself, but his name tag displayed the name Henderson. I know now that didn't mean anything at all.

Henderson was dressed in what they call a class "A" uniform. He had interrupted the part of the exit interview during which the idea of enlisting for additional time in service is sold.

You remember Monty Hall asking, "Door #1, Door #2, or Door #3?" Well, this was really close to the same scenario, except you would substitute "door" with the words "asshole idea".

Henderson asked if I had been briefed with what the future would hold in the short term if I did not partake of any of the wide variety of Army MOS career opportunities. He went on to say that my decision-making would determine the quality and length of life I had left on earth. He then sat back in his chair, folded his arms across his chest and stared.

"Thanks, but no thanks," I said as I pushed my chair back and got up to leave this one-on-one sales presentation. Spec5 "Monty" slammed both hands on the table.

"OK. You're exactly as advertised. Here's another option to consider."

"Excuse me?" I said. *"Oh, great, door number four,"* I thought.

"You are exactly as your testing has shown. Here is what I would like to offer you. You are qualified for OCS[13]. No additional

---

[12] Specialist, often abbreviated as spec, is a junior enlisted rank in the U.S. Army. The number associated with it denotes the level of pay the soldier receives.

[13] Officer Candidate School or Officer Cadet School, a training establishment in

time commitment to you right now, same basic and advanced training for the next sixteen weeks, and then you go to Fort Benning to become an Army Officer."

"What's the catch?" I asked. I needed time to think.

"Officers are the Army's leaders. They plan the training, and lead soldiers all over the world." He then said, "I've witnessed your excellent evaluation skills thus far in our meeting, and I think you would be a good fit for OCS. It provides an opportunity for graduates who desire a challenging *management position* in one of sixteen career fields."

"Wow," I said, still perplexed. "I don't know what to say."

It appeared that the only thing that was going to get me out of this testing center would be my agreement to attend OCS after I completed the Advanced Infantry Training course at Fort Dix. The good news was I did not have to commit to any additional time at this moment. My time in OCS would be considered to be within the same two-year draft obligation. And, only at the successful completion of this course would a two-year reserve commission be assigned.

I estimated that would be in about nine months, "*Good Lord willing and the river don't rise,*" I said to myself. I was also told I could change my mind at any time before reporting to OCS at Fort Benning, GA.

THE HAIRCUT
1045 HOURS FRIDAY 19 APRIL 1968

The next few weeks were amazing. Actually, these initial weeks of training contained my very first near-death experiences. Soon I became entirely focused on survival and not so much on being homesick. Of course, there were the nightly bedtime stories by our drill sergeant on the topic of our present situation referencing, as ever, lawnmowers and outhouses. These stories revealed the little known fact that *mother* was only half a word.

The only other worthwhile experience in Zero Week (other than

---

many countries where military officers are trained

the interview with the Spec5) was the haircut. I had played drums in a rock & roll band for the last few years and my hair was a little on the long side. I remember being seated in the barber chair and, without a word of warning the barber ran the electric sheers straight from the center from my forehead to the back of my neck. He clicked off the sheers, spun me around to face the mirror and said, "How do you like it so far?"

I found out later this guy was a civilian. I wondered if he knew he was qualified to be a drill sergeant. Four weeks later we got our first pay of about $27.50 in cash, minus $1.25 for the haircut!

Our very first activity after arriving at our assigned barracks was a five-mile run around the training area. I made it, but it wasn't pretty. There were bodies all along the roadways. I found out later that this was done to identify who amongst us needed extra attention.

Four weeks later I was hospitalized with double pneumonia. But let me not get ahead of myself.

FALLING PINE CONES
FORT BRAGG: SOME HISTORY
0700 HOURS TUESDAY 24 APRIL 1968

Fort Bragg[14] is a large United States Army installation. One important note about the enormous campus called Fort Bragg is the necessary consumption of millions of salt pills that an individual must consume to stay alive. The other major concern is the sheer size and speed of falling pinecones. Truly, you should plan a family vacation to go and see these things. To this day I have no idea of how many guys were killed by them. Steel pots were mandated headgear for personnel walking outdoors.

Safety, as we all know, has always been an Army concern. It would usually take two of us together to pick up and remove the

---

14   Fort Bragg - Army installation, located in Cumberland, Hoke, Harnett and Moore counties, North Carolina, mostly in Fayetteville but also partly in the town of Spring Lake. The fort is named for Confederate general Braxton Bragg. It covers over 251 square miles (650 kilometers). It is the home of the U.S. Army Airborne Forces and Special Forces, as well as the U.S. Army Forces Command and U.S. Army Reserve.

pinecones from a walkway. They ranged in size from 12 inches to the size of a Ford Pinto.

Yes, there were some people who didn't like being at Fort Bragg, so they would go AWOL[15]. After two or three days of wandering through the endless pine forests they would surrender. This activity ranked right up there with hiking on *Bataan*[16], so most *AWOLie*s only tried this one time.

AVOIDING ENEMY FIRE
USEFUL TECHNIQUES
0630 HOURS TUESDAY 30 APRIL 1968

There was a sawdust pit located directly behind the barracks where we could practice a maneuver called the low crawl. We were told that there are times when you must move with your body close to the ground to avoid enemy fire or observation. It was in the second or third week that I realized our company commander's dog was using this essential learning tool as his personal toilet. I mean, come on, this had to be the biggest outdoor crapping area ever seen by any dog on earth.

Each day, some lucky private was awarded a special present from this rather large and well-nourished German shepherd. I found it extremely beneficial not to enter the pit first, but to be at least two or three persons back, and lined up directly behind the person in front of me. Any lucky winner who complained got to show us how to do 100 pushups.

JOYS OF AMBULANCE MAINTENANCE
0300 HOURS THURSDAY 30 MAY 1968

It was about week five when I started to get sick. An ongoing

---

15   Absent without official leave

16   The Bataan Death March, which began on April 9, 1942, was the forcible transfer by the Imperial Japanese Army of 60 to 80,000 Filipino and American prisoners of war after the three-month Battle of Bataan in the Philippines during World War II.

cold got progressively worse. Going on "sick call" was completely discouraged unless you were just plain dead. Next came a very sore throat and I finally had no choice but to cry "uncle." Actually, it was the guy on fire watch who called the ambulance at 0300 hours. I had a 106-degree temperature and was slightly delirious.

Fire Watch Boy got me up and dressed, the ambulance driver came up to the second floor where my bunk was located, and together they helped get me down the stairs.

I had recently been appointed squad leader. This award mandated that I move out of the general population to a semi-private room which I shared with seven other guys. It turns out that my roommates were all sound sleepers. Or, perhaps, they didn't want to witness when I stopped breathing. If it hadn't been for the fire watch safety patrol -- a great idea by the way -- boot camp and my time on earth would have been cut short.

The ambulance driver explained to us that he was by himself for this unexpected call.

"Bummer," I mumbled.

His colleagues were back at their motor pool preparing for a mandatory IG[17] inspection for their entire cadre and vehicles.

So, he had very little time to deal with me and get back to the ranch. He went on to say that I was in luck because he would pass very near the hospital on his way back to home base. I told him I was grateful for the limited amount of time he could allocate to my circumstance, but he needed to get me to a doctor before this fever set my clothes on fire.

When we got outside my barracks he then informed me I was to ride up front with him because he couldn't afford to mess up the back of the ambulance. Now, at this point you're probably saying to yourself, *"He's making this shit up,"* and I would ask you, *"Who in their right mind could make this shit up?"*

Fort Bragg's hospital main entrance appeared through the windshield as we approached the outpatient drop off point. I estimated the distance to be at least seven miles from the main road to the double glass doors off in the distance. As it turned out, the driver didn't have any more emergency medical training than I did. Concern about my condition dampened his obsession for not being late for his equipment review. This triggered a humanitarian response deep within him to slow almost to a complete stop before

---

17   Inspector General

pushing me from the open passenger door.

With my right ear firmly pressed to the front sidewalk of the hospital, I watched the tail lights disappear into the darkness. This is where all of my training would pay off, especially my expertise with the low crawl.

In what seemed like hours later, the person seated behind the lobby counter looked up at as I tapped on the large, *locked* double glass doors blocking my entrance. He didn't see me at first until he stood up to look out into the courtyard. Apparently, this hospice was not yet open for business. I whispered through the glass, "I need some help here," and slowly dropped my head back to the concrete.

I don't think he realized I was just a lowly Private until he had already committed to assisting me. He summoned a medical team who took me to an ER[18] area. Everyone on duty that night came to see the dummy that had come through the front door. One of the doctors asked me later why I used the wrong entrance and I told him that's where the ambulance had literally dropped me off. Apparently, I should have by-passed the main entrance and crawled around the building to the emergency admission bay.

The diagnosis was double pneumonia. I was put in an oxygen tent with two IVs, one in each arm, in a room with a retired alcoholic sergeant who had lung cancer and smoked like a chimney. Remember safe medical procedures were in their infancy in the late 1960's.

I felt relatively safe from the second-hand smoke[19] as long as I remained inside my oxygen tent. I can still see the look on my roommate's face when I asked to bum a cigarette and his lighter. (A year later I would see the same wide-eyed expression on the face of a guy in traction on a medevac flight.) Three days later I was completely cured and I returned to face my drill sergeant.

A "DEE EYE" HOMECOMING
0930 HOURS TUESDAY 4 JUNE 1968

I was seldom surprised in those days, but this particular encounter did shock me. My DI[20] actually apologized for not being

---

18   Everyone Running
19   Second hand smoke wouldn't be invented for another 29 years
20   Drill Instructor

there when I went to the hospital. I suspected my doctor had made a few calls congratulating everyone on how well the emergency services had performed a few days before.

I asked for his forgiveness anyway, not hearing a word he was saying.

"Pay close attention, boy," he whispered about two inches from my ear. "Most of the physical training is about over." And as long as I "keep my feets moving," I won't have any problems completing the training[21]. It was the first normal conversation I had had with an NCO. It turns out that surviving sick call is a big deal.

I'LL TAKE BASIC TRAINING FOR A $100
FRIDAY JUNE 14 1968

United States Army Basic Training (also known as Initial Entry Training or IET) is the program implemented today for both the physical and mental training requirements of an individual seeking to become a soldier in the United States Army. Basic Training in 1968 was eight weeks long and designed to be highly intense and challenging.

The challenge comes as much from the difficulty of the physical training as it does from the required quick psychological adjustment to an unfamiliar way of life. Notice I make wide use of a writing device called the *understatement*.

One of the most difficult and essential lessons learned in BCT (Basic Combat Training) is self-discipline, as it introduces prospective soldiers to a strict daily schedule that entails many duties compiled with high expectations for which most civilians are not immediately prepared. Few ever are. I never thought much about being a civilian, but I knew that someday I wanted to be one again.

Out of the 257 draftees starting BCT in April 1968, 243 finished the program on time. I felt very sorry for the overweight guys, who really caught hell. Some did manage to get into shape and made it

---

[21] More than 200,000 young men underwent basic combat training at Fort Bragg during the period 1966-70. At the peak of the Vietnam War, in 1968, Fort Bragg's military population rose to 57,840.

through, some did not. Others struggled with the mental changes being forced on them. A few of these guys broke down and disappeared from the group. The entire DI staff was tough but fair, especially the ones assigned to my immediate group.

Now, if you think back to Zero Week, many of the inductees chose a new career path. So, instead of going with me to Fort Dix, New Jersey for the AIT[22], they had orders for Advanced *Individual* Training. This would be for the MOS they selected for the additional one or two years of service.

It's funny, but I remember thinking at the time how dumb those guys were for enlisting for the additional time. I now realize that most of them didn't have a job waiting for them when they got out. Maybe they saw it as an opportunity to get a skill set that would get them started on a new career down the road.

YOU WILL ALWAYS REMEMBER YOUR ARMY SERIAL NUMBER
FRIDAY 14 JUNE 1968

The Advanced Infantry Training[23] (AIT) at Fort Dix specialized in the development of men on the ground for combat. The 11 Bravo MOS consisted of eight additional weeks of specialized training in the specifics of combat arms.

Although many Advanced Individual Training schools don't center on combat the way ADV/BCT[24] does, individuals are still continually tested for physical fitness and weapons proficiency. And, they are subjected to the same duties, a strict daily schedule, and disciplinary rules as the BCT environment. However, being able to attend this type of training center would be virtually impossible if you had the letters U and S in front of your assigned serial number.

---

22   Advanced Infantry Training

23   Advanced Infantry Training: MOS examples include Human Intelligence Collector, which takes place at the Intelligence School at Fort Huachuca, Arizona and Army medic, which takes place at Fort Sam Houston in San Antonio, Texas. There are over 100 other courses, which take place at specialized training centers for specific specialties. AIT courses can range from three to 54 weeks.

24   Advanced Basic Combat Training

This, of course, meant that you were drafted, and the letters R and A indicated that you were in the Regular Army. I liked to think that the "US" prefix in front of my assigned serial number would indicate to those in charge of each change of station[25] that I was someone who continued to maintain his sanity.

Another fact, that fascinates me to this day, is a statement made by one of my DIs, who said the following: "You will forget a lot of numbers in your life, but you will always remember your Army serial number."

He was right. It's been 45 years and I can still recite it: US51672681. (You identity thieves out there: please write and tell me if you find this information useful. I've racked my brain but can't think of anything.)

I'll tell you later how I wound up at the White Sands missile range after my AIT courses. The Army always makes good on its commitments. However, there were a few complaints that I overheard during our final days at Fort Bragg. These complaints were from disgruntled enlistees who had traded the "US" for "RA" lettering in front of their respective serial numbers.

For example, an acquaintance of mine from Zero Week signed up for an additional two-year period to be trained in Radio Communications. His re-enlistment orders read, "due to insufficient seat availability, the following course will be substituted: Sanitation Disposal Management Engineer.

---

[25] "Change of station" indicates orders made by the Army to any personnel, directing them to a school or new unit/assignment.

IV

THE ADVANCEMENT

FORT DIX—EXIT 7
1145 HOURS FRIDAY 14 JUNE 1968

The transformation that took place in this wonderful group of guys who had arrived at Ft. Bragg eight weeks prior was extraordinary. The last day before leaving Ft. Bragg we were assembled on the parade ground in formation. We marched in review. The band played. And basic training was done. The majority of us were ordered directly to Fort Dix, New Jersey. The rest were loaded onto the base sanitation trucks and taken to their designated advanced individual training locations.

As you undoubtedly know, the standing joke for any destination in New Jersey is to say, "What exit?" Well, Fort Dix is located off the NJ Turnpike at Exit 7.

All of our physical training had paid off. I was in the best shape of my life. I was becoming a soldier, or at least *soldier-like*. There was one guy, Bob Koontz, who was inducted the same day I was. We were from the same neighborhood in Maryland and were being assigned to the same AIT group at Dix. So we made plans to travel home together at the first opportunity.

Both Bob and I were a little on the wild side before our friends and neighbors volunteered us for this great adventure. That's probably why we didn't try to restrain ourselves as much as we should have on our first trip home.

THE THREE DAY PASS
1845 HOURS FRIDAY 19 JULY 1968

Before I tell you about all of the killer training we received at Dix, let me relate to you what happens when you are let loose after 13 weeks of chewing your food on your own time. Bob and I got a ride on a Friday afternoon to a train station not far from the main gate. We changed trains a couple of times and finally got out in downtown Baltimore.

Bob's girlfriend admitted that she remembered him when he called to beg a ride. She picked us up and they dropped me off at my parents' house. The next day we decided to double-date and go to a movie. It was a drive-in movie and we had procured refreshments. Drive-in movies were very popular during my high school years, especially on Tuesdays when the sign would read: *$5 Admission, No Movie Tonight.*

I stayed at Bob's house that night after we dropped our dates off. I think we really had a good time and I thought we were successful in sneaking into his house in the wee hours of the morning. I awoke at 0930 to someone pounding on the bedroom door across the hall from my room. The loud and excited voice was saying, "Bobby, please come out here now and look at this." We both entered and walked down the hallway together to where his Mom was standing, peering out of the opened front door. She repeated, "Look at this."

The car was parked at a 90-degree angle in the driveway. The windows were up, and the doors shut. However, I failed to mention that Bob's Chevy was a convertible and the car's interior could only be protected from a severe downpour if the top was in a raised and locked position. What gave us away were the two Mallard ducks floating on four feet of water in the back seat area of the car. Never

49

lie to your mother and always use valet parking.

"I guess it rained last night," I offered, to anyone who was listening.

GI JANE, PATRON SAINT OF AIT
0745 HOURS MONDAY 23 JULY 1968

I felt really sorry for all of those guys who opted out of combat arms training in Zero Week. Advanced Infantry Training was a very methodical series of hands-on courses that literally included every type of small and crew-served weaponry[26] that existed in the Army at that time. I had a blast. Literally. There was a demolitions course in week eight that was to die for. You could do just that if you didn't pay strict attention to the instructor. My introduction to a plastic explosive called C-4[27] was fascinating. It was boyhood dreams come true. There is dialogue in the movie "GI Jane", in which Demi Moore's character is asked by the female medic treating her for the 700 abrasions suffered that day, "Why do you want to be a Navy Seal?" And Demi looks right at her and says, "What do the other guys say when you ask them that question?"

Of course, the proper response has always been: "We get to blow shit up."

---

[26] Crew-served weapons require more than one person to operate them. There are important exceptions in the case of both squad automatic weapons (SAW) and sniper rifles. Within the Table of Organization and Equipment for both the United States Army and the U.S. Marine Corps, these two classes of weapons are understood to be crew-served, as the operator of the weapon (identified as a sniper or as a SAW gunner) has an assistant, who carries additional ammunition and associated equipment, acts as a spotter, and is also fully qualified in the operation of the weapon.

[27] C-4 plastic explosive is a specialized form of explosive material. It is a soft and hand-moldable solid material. Plastic explosives are properly known as putty explosives within the field of explosives engineering. Common plastic explosives include Semtex and C-4. Plastic explosives are especially suited for explosive demolition as they can be easily formed into the best shapes for cutting structural members and have a high enough velocity of detonation and density for metal cutting work.

A total of eight weeks of specialized training would expose us to a long list of small arms weaponry. Our primary rifle training was with the M14. However, the M16 was the standard rifle being used in Vietnam at the time. The main Army-issued sidearm of the period was the (Colt) 1911 45 ACP, which was created for use in the campaign against the Moros in the Philippines.

The Colt Model 1911 was the product of a very capable person, John Moses Browning, father of several modern firearms. And, just as a bit of trivia, this particular sidearm, because it seldom hit what it was pointed at, would become responsible for the creation of the famous expression, "You can't hit the broad side of a barn."

The small caliber machine gun was the M60 and the large caliber machine gun was the 50 CAL. We also trained on hand grenades and on a relatively new invention called the M79 grenade launcher. This weapon was really cool. Ever since I was a little boy playing cowboys and Indians I had dreamed of holding a weapon such as this!

The training course for the M79 made use of motorized machines which controlled pop-up targets. As if possessed, I became proficient in finding the distance-to-target with my eyes shut. I would receive an *expert* badge with the M79.

I was a natural. It was like the launcher became an extension of my right arm. The added bonus came when I discovered the sweet spot of the linkage to the electric motor that controlled the pop-up targets. My instructor consoled me later by saying it was just dumb luck.

THE 106 RECOILLESS RIFLE THAT USED 105MM AMMUNITION
0845 HOURS TUESDAY 24 JULY 1968

Our platoon was divided up into eight four-man squads to train on a weapons system called the 106 Recoilless Rifle, or just M40. This U.S. made weapon was unusual because it could kill you from either end when fired. The M40 was a lightweight, portable, crew-served 105 mm weapon intended primarily as an anti-tank weapon.

The weapon is commonly described as being 106 mm[28], but in fact, 105-millimeter ammunition was used. The recoilless rifle of this caliber had been in development since the Second World War.

This weapon was hurriedly produced with the onset of the Korean War. The speed with which it was developed and fielded resulted in problems with reliability caused by trunnions[29] that were mounted too far to the rear. I had no idea what a trunnion was, but they were still an optional feature available on the Chevy Blazer until the late 1980s.

Amazingly, when the recoilless M40 weapon is fired it will remain absolutely still on its mount. This was accomplished by allowing a tremendous outpouring of gas through vents located at the rear of the weapon. I suspected this had something to do with the trunnions.

Anything and anyone standing in the M40's exhaust would suffer the immediate consequence of being disintegrated. The instructor used an empty ammo box to demo what happens if you stand at the rear during a firing. I was convinced after only one demo. The really cool feature was that you could sit your beer on top of the rifle during firing and not spill one drop.

REDEYE, THE "TIPPING POINT"
1540 HOURS FRIDAY 26 JULY 1968

As my short stay at Fort Dix was coming to an end, I realized my decision as to whether or not to attend OCS was looming. We were given most of the weekends off, but the guys who were conscripted

---

[28] 106-millimeter designation was designed to prevent confusion with the incompatible 105 mm ammunition from the failed M27 project that did not pass muster during the Korean War. The M27 recoilless rifle was a 105-millimeter weapon developed in the early 1950s and fielded in the Korean War. The M27 was also considered too heavy by the U.S. Army, and had a disappointing effective range due to the lack of a spotting rifle.

[29] A trunnion is a cylindrical protrusion used as a mounting and/or pivoting point. In cannon, the trunnions are two projections cast just forward of the center of mass of the cannon and fixed to a two-wheeled movable gun carriage. As they allowed the muzzle to be raised and lowered easily, the integral casting of trunnions is seen by military historians as one of the most important advances in early field artillery.

for special service, like clerks or drivers, didn't get much time off at all. I got to be good friends with a guy named Jake who was the acting company clerk.

Sometimes, on weekends, I would cover the phones for him while he took care of personal stuff. He had been held over from two classes before because he was good at managing the company's paper work and he understood how the game was played.

We were by ourselves in the CQ (Command Quarters) when he conveyed to me that in two weeks' time orders would be prepared sending our training group to our respective next assignments. I recalled my encounter with the Spec5 creepy dude at Ft. Bragg during Zero Week. I related the exciting story that had me marked for Fort Benning and OCS. Jake looked up my name on the roster and saw the reference to Ft. Benning. Next, he pulled my 201 file from the sleeve. Sure enough, there was a form indicating that a request for a secret clearance background investigation had been approved and completed.

"What in the hell is that all about?"

It turns out that to become an Officer and a Gentleman you can't be in the KGB. I sat down in the chair next to the First Sergeant's desk and put my head in my hands. "This is getting serious, isn't it?" I asked.

PFC Jake Ashcroft, holding my 201 file folder, said to me, "Do you want to go to OCS? Because, you should know, 2nd Lieutenants aren't faring very well in combat in the war against the Godless communists."

He suggested that I take a different career path. Understand I had resigned myself to the fact that I would be going to Vietnam, but I was having second thoughts about where I wanted to stand in a total rewrite of "The Charge of the Light Brigade"[30].

Jake went on to explain the many benefits of having a secret clearance. The types of schools requiring the student to have a secret clearance were fewer in number, but they were good schools in high demand. He went on to say that if I decided *not* to attend OCS he would fill out the proper form cancelling my assignment to Fort Benning.

---

30 "The Charge of the Light Brigade" is a poem by Alfred, Lord Tennyson, published just six weeks after the event at the Battle of Balaclava during the Crimean War, in 1854. It emphasizes the valor of the cavalry in bravely carrying out their orders, regardless of the obvious outcome.

The list of schools was short and sweet. I felt like John Yossarian in "Catch 22". Ostensibly, I had struck oil and fallen down the proverbial rabbit hole all in one fell swoop. I asked what the hook was.

REDEYE, THE RIGHT CHOICE
1600 HOURS FRIDAY 26 JULY 1968

Jake suggested that I choose a technical school requiring a secret clearance.

"Right," I said. "Did you notice that the letters U and S are located in front of my serial number?"

"That really doesn't matter anymore," he said. "From here on out you have the legendary *get out of jail free* card, at least for the next couple of months."

A request had come in the previous month soliciting applicants to attend the new RedEye Gunners course, located in Fort Bliss, Texas and the White Sands Missile Range of New Mexico. Besides the obvious heavy drinking requirement, it sounded like a good opportunity for someone holding a secret clearance.

The RedEye Gunners course sounded wonderfully dangerous. It turned out that the General Dynamics Corporation had developed the very first shoulder-fired, ground-to-air, guided missile system. The best news of all was that RedEye weapons were only going to be deployed in Europe. That night I said a silent prayer thanking God for watching over me, keeping me safe, and finding me a school with a really neat name.

First the earth cooled, and then the dinosaurs roamed. Jake was awesome, he filled out all of the required forms, and he made sure everything posted correctly. I thanked him profusely, gave him my last 20 bucks out of petty cash, (which almost covered what I had borrowed from him), to be used toward his mounting bar bill at the EM (Enlisted Men's) club. I sat back and waited for AIT to complete.

V

THE COLOR OF RED

FORT BLISS, TEXAS
WEEK 17—DIX TO BLISS
0030 HOURS SATURDAY 3 AUGUST 1968

The good news about Fort Bliss[31] was that there were very few pine trees on campus. Most every type of tree located around the ranges had been destroyed by the afterburners of fighter aircraft whose pilots had recently returned from NAM and various mental hospital facilities.

I went directly from Dix to Bliss. Literally! I was issued a prepaid voucher for a commercial flight to El Paso County, Texas. It was a late night departure time and a very early morning arrival. There were seven other soldiers who were waiting in the Ft. Bliss military pickup area in the airport when I arrived just after midnight.

There was one other PFC (Private First Class) in the group

---

[31] Fort Bliss is a United States Army post spanning the New Mexico—Texas border. An area of about 1,700 square miles, it is the Army's second-largest installation, behind the adjacent White Sands Missile Range.

besides me; the rest were SPC4 and above. I assumed we all weren't going to the same place. It turned out that three out of the seven were attending the RedEye course. I was the only PFC. We were met at the base drop-off point by the post duty NCO, and after several stops to drop the non-Redeye participants off we were then transported directly to the Redeye Training Center. The area that was displayed outside my bus window appeared to be an exclusive sector reserved for faculty only. What happened next blew my mind.

REDEYE TRAINING CENTER
0130 HOURS SATURDAY 3 AUGUST 1968

The Sergeant E5 (a sergeant with 3 stripes), who supervised our pickup, came back to our seats before we got up. I was in the habit of not moving a muscle unless told to do so. Consequently, I cringed when he approached. He said in a whisper of a voice, "This is the Mess Hall. Sergeant Davies kept it open in case any of you guys missed dinner."

I remember thinking that the plane must have crashed and this must be some sort of way station in the spirit world. The other two passengers and the bus driver followed the Sergeant off the bus and headed for the open doors in the building located across the parking lot. The Sergeant turned, re-entered the bus and said, "Are you coming?"

I said, "Yes, Sergeant."

I followed him into the chow hall. There was a guy holding the door open who had on a white jacket and chef's hat. He said something like, "Hey, Mic, we were getting worried." Then he welcomed me and said I could put my things down over against the wall and did I need any help with anything left on the bus.

"*Yep, I'm dead alright,*" I thought.

"No thanks," I said out loud. "This is everything."

That was the truth. Everything issued to me thus far, and all my worldly possessions, now fit in something called a duffel bag. I looked around the room. There were individual tables with tablecloths and condiments displayed on each one. The food line had two guys behind the glass-shielded counter serving what looked like a breakfast blowout.

56

Apparently there had been some mistake. I couldn't be in the right place. But before I had a chance to think what had gone wrong, I heard the fellow operating the grill say to the fellows in line.

"How do you want your eggs?"

"Well, this certainly is 180 degrees from the concept of chewing food on your own time," I thought.

I proceeded through the line. There were pancakes, bacon, grits, SOS (which is cream of chipped "something" on toast -- or more commonly called "shit on a shingle"), and all the juice, milk, and coffee you could drink. It was 0225 when the chef's hat guy came around to our table and asked if we'd gotten enough and that he would open up again at 0600 for breakfast if we wanted to attend.

"No shit," I said.

Next we went by the Orderly Room to pick up the bunk assignments. This turned out to be individual rooms containing two sets of bunk beds each. I was the sole occupant of one of the rooms at that point. The latrine was at the end of the hall. Mandatory formation would be conducted at 0800. As I fell asleep that night, I remember promising myself to write and thank Jake, who was still trapped back at Exit 7. Fort Bliss was well named.

GENERAL DYNAMICS
FORT BLISS
0900 HOURS MONDAY 5 AUGUST 1968

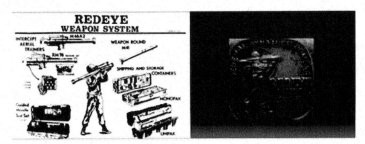

General Dynamics[32] delivers to the military establishment

---

[32] General Dynamics Corporation is a United States aerospace and defense company formed by mergers and divestitures. As of 2011, it is the fourth largest defense contractor in the world. It is headquartered in West Falls Church, Fairfax County, Virginia.

capable, relevant and affordable products and services. All are designed to scare the crap out of any Air Force pilot anywhere in the world of war. The RedEye missile system was being delivered to the U.S. Army for the first time in 1968. Thus, the rapid implementations of the hands-on RedEye course being held at Bliss and the White Sands Missile Range, respectively, later in 1968.

RedEye was a man-portable, surface-to-air, missile system. It used infrared homing to track its target. The whole firing system weighed only 18.3 pounds. Production of RedEye had reached 85,000 rounds by 1969. The FIM-92, Stinger, became the next generation weapons system that gradually replaced RedEye between 1982 and 1995.

General Dynamics spent millions on RedEye statistical data. Why, you ask? They needed to establish a DOD[33] requirement for a relatively new term called *kill probability.*

Literally hundreds of anti-aircraft systems were evaluated. For example, the Mikoyan-Gurevich MiG-22 was assigned an average kill probability value 0.403. Small to medium size helicopters, such as the Mi-6 and the Mi-25 and American manufactured H-13 and H-22, on average scored 0.53 kill probability. RedEye had tested the highest in its weapon systems category at 0.956.

I specifically reported these statistics to my friend and sister-in-law, Janet, who loves numbers with decimal points. Neither one of us would ever condone the shooting down of any aircraft regardless of the number of decimal points used.

I remembered from an advanced calculus course (I really only took Algebra II) that .9 was higher than .4. This was confirmed by Janet. However, we both entirely agreed that the data also clearly showed that even though a jet fighter goes faster than a helicopter, RedEye didn't care. This weapon was without a doubt extremely accurate and deadly, no matter what it was pointed at.

CATCH 23
FORT BLISS
0930 HOURS TUESDAY 6 AUGUST 1968

Reading between the lines of the statistics in the beginning of

---

[33]   Department of Defense

the RedEye manual, I started paging through it to see what data existed for the survival of the RedEye Gunner.

The pictures in the General Dynamic's documents and film clips depicted a long, thin, white vapor trail that is created by the rocket motor of RedEye. The trajectory of the vapor would lead a perturbed airplane driver right back to the point of origin and, hence, the shooter. This, I felt, was an important issue for discussion as we were driven out in the desert to be trained in the art of being strafed[34].

WHITE SANDS, NEW MEXICO
1140 HOURS
WEDNESDAY 14 AUGUST 1968

Figure 3- Vapor Trail

Toward the end of the second week we were bused into the desert to a specifically prepared range. The White Sands Missile Range[35] (WSMR) cadres had refurbished and specifically set up an environment for the newly developed handheld trackers. The range design would allow the jet jockeys playing the role of enemy aggressors to get down on the deck and get very close and personal. The experience of being strafed while providing close-in anti-aircraft support for an infantry combat unit was what it was all about for the RedEye gunners.

It took over an hour to travel the fifty-six miles out to the range. It consisted of ten firing positions: five located on each side of a short version of an air traffic control tower located at its center, which could only be described as target central. All ten teams could practice at the same time on one staffing aircraft.

We usually had to wait 30 to 50 minutes between shooting sessions. I climbed the tower stairs during one of these breaks to see what the surrounding area looked like. Suddenly, out of

---

34 being bombed and machine gunned

35 White Sands Missile Range (WSMR) is a rocket range of almost 3,200 square miles located in parts of five counties in southern New Mexico. The largest military installation in the United States, WSMR includes the Oscura Range, the Otera Mesa bombing range, and the 600,000-acre McGregor Range Complex at Fort Bliss to the south, which forms a contiguous and gigantic swath of territory for military testing. You'll notice that there in not one mention of the 120⁰ F temperature in any of the popular U.S. vacation guides.

nowhere, a Navy fighter jet passed by so low that when it went by the tower I could look down into the cockpit. The names "Maverick" and "Goose[36]" were clearly printed on the pilot helmets.

We were using a RedEye simulator, an XM76 that did everything but launch a missile. It had a battery adapter device used to spin up and cool the mini-gyro, a flip up sight attached to the missile tube, and, it also had a functioning audible speaker producing a tracking tone that confirmed missile lock using the IR (infrared) signature produced by an aircraft engine.

Clearly, this weapons system was going to work well in Antarctica, but with the exterior temperature of the desert being equal to the surface temperature of the sun, I suspected the IR output of a jet engine at full throttle would be cancelled by the heat being reflected up by the desert floor. This, I was convinced, would result in a missile boring itself into the desert sand, not an airplane. It turns out I was dead wrong. The IR seeker was incredibly sensitive and could detect sand fleas farting at 5,000 feet.

WEEK 3—LIVE FIRE
WHITE SANDS NEW MEXICO
1105 HOURS
FRIDAY 24 AUGUST 1968

Figure 4 - Redeye White Sands

The Grand Finale of the RedEye course was a live fire exercise. The top five students would be given the opportunity to fire a live round at a jet aircraft.

It's not every day you get to personally spend your own tax dollars, past, present, and future, so to speak. I could see that the grandstands were completely packed as we pulled into the parking lot.

---

[36] Top Gun is a 1986 American action drama film starring Tom Cruise and Anthony Edwards. Cruise plays Lieutenant Pete "Maverick" Mitchell. He and his Radar Intercept Officer (RIO) Nick "Goose" Bradshaw (Edwards) are given the chance to train at the Navy's Fighter Weapons School.

WHITE SANDS
PILOTLESS DRONE TECHNOLOGY
1115 HOURS FRIDAY 24 AUGUST 1968

All the days leading up to this live firing exercise had left me wondering whom they could get to fly the plane that pulled the target. After all, a missile has a mind of its own and, in the end, would go where it could do the most good.

It turned out that the target plane was a drone that was self-propelled and remote controlled. It was equipped with an elaborate tow array that had multiple heat pods, each with an IR signature and, in theory (not reality), four times the IR signature of the tow plane's jet engine.

The centermost firing position was being utilized today. All five firings would be conducted from this station. The location was 50 yards in front of the grandstands. I was to be the fifth shooter, selected at random by pulling a number out of a hat. I actually had the second highest course grade but tradition dictated that we draw numbers to establish the order to shoot. Of course, the person who pulled the number four was sent directly to Parris Island after firing his RedEye.

The way we practiced for this live firing was in two-man teams. The spotter would remove the RedEye from its weatherproof aluminum case. Then, the weapon would be handed to the shooter, who would rest it on his shoulder. Next, the round cylinder battery would be taken from the molded depression in the case lid and handed to the shooter. The shooter then would insert the battery into the front handle of the launch tube and twist it into a locked position.

The instructor observer would then replace the spotter assistant and step in next to the shooter. The instructor's hand would be placed on the shooter's left shoulder. This was done to insure that the final OK to shoot would not be misunderstood.

The instructor then signaled for the drone controller, who was located in the tower, to bring the drone into view to make a run from right to left across the range. You could only fire this system right handed.

The targets would pass about 500 feet off the ground, traveling at about 400 miles per hour. When the sound of the drone was heard, the instructor told the shooter to release the gyro and to start the sequence. The tone came immediately to life when the shooter pointed it at the rear area of the drone and the towed array equipped with six individual targets. As the drone got closer, the chirping sound turned into a solid tone, indicating that the target was locked to one of the IR pods. The instructor would then tap the shoulder of the shooter and say "Fire! Fire! Fire!"

The missile was blasted out of the tube. It would travel for about 30 feet before the rocket motor started on its journey to Mach 3 and the sturdiest of the infrared sources.

RedEye moves at incredible speed from the very beginning of its second-stage birth. Typically, the starting trajectory would take a path parallel to the desert floor. Once the aircraft's position was calculated by RedEye's onboard software, the gyro would call for a change in direction. Constant correction of the guide blades would hit the target within an inch of its life. This whole scenario took place in a matter of seconds. The first four demos worked flawlessly. It was now my turn.

WHITE SANDS, NEW MEXICO
BULL'S EYE MARKETING
1255 HOURS FRIDAY 24 AUGUST 1968

I was a little nervous. Each one of these missile systems cost over fifteen thousand dollars. My spotter and I carried the case to the staging area and unsnapped the locking tabs. I pulled the lid off to one side, gripped the handle and pulled the RedEye up onto my shoulder.

The spotter handed me one of the batteries. I pushed the battery into the handle and twisted it into a locked position. I walked to the firing line. The instructor stepped in beside me and ran his hand over the handle grip holding the battery. He asked, "You set?"

"Yes, Sergeant," I replied.

He placed his hand on my shoulder and signaled with a wave to the tower for the drone to be summoned. What happened next was surreal.

The order was given to start the gyro and the tone started to sound immediately. I pointed the weapon, using the foldout sight, directly at the approaching aircraft.

The chirping grew stronger with every second that passed. The drone was almost in range. Then it happened. The tone missed a beat, and then did it again. But then the solid locking tone returned to a constant signal with no more interruptions. I was waiting for the go ahead. Out of the corner of my eye I could see that the instructor was looking at the drone with his binoculars. Finally he tapped my shoulder and said "Fire."

After the missile catapulted out of the tube the second stage motor fired and shot it across the desert floor. As RedEye calculated its approach to a position directly underneath the target, the missile suddenly changed direction. Moving forward at a 45-degree angle, the missile drove through the towed array -- ignoring it completely. The IR-producing heat pods had failed, thus solving the mystery of the missed tones. RedEye continued directly into the drone's engine exhaust port and exploded.

It was at this point that control of the drone was lost as it rolled over on its back and veered sharply to the left. It was now heading directly over the right side of the grandstands. An emergency parachute deployed but was soon set on fire by the flames coming from burning fuel pouring from the badly damaged flying machine.

You know that scene in the movie "Animal House", when the horse has a heart attack in the Dean's office? Well, to quote the great John Adam Belushi: "Holy Shit!" All the color drained out of my instructor's face as the drone proceeded to crash about 200 yards behind the seating area.

"Well," I said, "at least we didn't kill anybody." I found out later that the drone cost about 400,000 dollars, so a quick calculation would show that the deduction from my Army salary would require me to remain in the service for the next 60 years.

Now, I know most of you have never had the opportunity to shoot down an airplane, but I have got to say if you ever get the chance, make sure it is affiliated with a communist government. What a rush!

I figured the instructor would run from the firing station toward the grandstands, yelling, "I told him not to fire, I told him not to fire," but he didn't. Instead, when we were both summoned to the General Dynamics VIP pavilion, he told me to let him do the talking. I wasn't sure, but this might have been my first glance of leadership.

The General Dynamics representative was talking to a group of civilian reporters when we entered the tent.

"Blowing up heat pods is boring at best," we heard him say, "but shooting down a jet airplane demonstrates the real capability of the RedEye weapons system." The Sergeant and I turned to look at each other as the conversation continued.

"I'll bet none of you will forget today anytime soon," the representative said to group gathered around him.

"I know I won't," I said to my Sergeant instructor. "That would be the understatement of the year if the *out of control*, flaming jet aircraft had crashed into the grandstands where they were sitting," I added.

"Keep your comments to yourself until I find out how much trouble we're in, Fontain. We clear?"

"Clear, Sergeant," I responded.

The representative's name was Barry Flax. He was the Vice President in charge of the RedEye research and development project. He was 38 years old, five feet seven inches tall, held a graduate degree from MIT and appeared to have had way too much coffee that morning. After a few more questions, the reporters left the tent. Barry then turned his attention to us.

"Great job, guys," he greeted us and shook our hands. "Hell, we should sacrifice one drone during every live fire demo. I'll bet if there were any doubters in the audience today they certainly have changed their minds after seeing that direct hit on the drone!" He then turned his attention to a young woman who had walked up to us and handed him a piece of paper.

"Excuse me for one minute."

"He seems almost happy with us," I whispered, "And, he's assuming he'll be able to find anyone who went running off into the desert."

"Quiet," my instructor said. The young lady turned and left the tent as Barry Flax returned to us.

"Sir, the last two of the IR pods must have failed," said my instructor.

"Sergeant, you can't buy this kind of publicity," said Barry Flax.

He was right, of course, but the Sergeant and I both suspected we would still wind up inventorying mess kits in the Aleutian Islands.

When we walked out of the pavilion I was amazed to see that the grandstands seemed to have even more spectators than before.

64

Most were standing and watching the Air Force Fire/Rescue services surrounding the wreckage of the downed drone.

Barry Flax had followed us from the tent and stood looking up into the grandstands. "Sergeant, could you gather the other RedEye shooters and bring them over to the stage so we can conduct the awards ceremony in front of the grandstands?"

"Yes, Sir, Mr. Flax," said my instructor.

The awards procedure was short and sweet. Barry addressed the crowd for several minutes before inviting an Army officer from the audience to come forward and present the awards. General Dynamics must have had a relationship with the French government because a few minutes later I was being kissed on both cheeks by a French Army General. I keep the pin on top of my dresser to this day.

Figure 5
Redeye Pin

VI

THE LONELIEST NUMBER

6TH CAV
FORT GEORGE G. MEADE
MARYLAND
1700 HOURS THURSDAY 5 SEPTEMBER 1968

Now, before you try and sell the RedEye technical data listed in the last chapter to the Russian Embassy, I assure you that besides being over 45 years old and obsolete, all of it is easily sourced via your local library. Of course, now that you know how to operate a ground-to-air missile system you may want to register with the Department of Defense as soon as possible.

Remember Jake the Magnificent, the Ft. Dix company clerk from the New Jersey Turnpike Exit 7? Well, when he was helping me select Redeye as a school, he also was able to select the best military unit, at least on paper, that would be a good fit for the RedEye anti-aircraft technology.

The unit we chose was the 6th Armored Cavalry, located on the campus of Fort George G. Meade[37]. However, the 6th CAV was never

---

[37]   Fort Meade became an active Army installation in 1917. Authorized by an Act

notified about the many splendid capabilities of the U.S. Army's first shoulder-fired guided missile system nor did they want anything to do with anyone trained in that particular expertise.

On December 20, 1948, the former 6th Cavalry Regiment was reorganized and re-designated the 6th Armored Cavalry. The regiment returned to the United States from Germany in 1957 during *Operation Gyroscope*[38]. How appropriate[39]!

FIRST SENSE OF DUTY
FORT MEADE—6TH CAV
HEADQUARTER'S COMPANY
ORDERLY ROOM
0600 FRIDAY 6 SEPTEMBER 1968

It was September 1968 that I arrived at my *semi-permanen*t

---

of Congress, it was one of 16 facilities built for troops drafted for the war with the Central Powers in Europe. The Maryland site was selected June 23, 1917 because of its close proximity to the railroad, the port of Baltimore, and Washington, D.C. The cost for construction was 18 million dollars, and the land was purchased for 37 dollars per acre. The Post was originally named Camp Meade for Maj. Gen. George Gordon Meade, whose victory at the Battle of Gettysburg proved a major factor in turning the tide of the Civil War. An important development occurred on January 1, 1966, when the Second U.S. Army merged with the First U.S. Army. The consolidated headquarters moved from Fort Jay, New York to Fort Meade to administer activities of Army installations in a 15-state area.

[38] The 6th Armored Cavalry was then stationed at Fort Knox, Kentucky. Inactivated in 1963, the regiment reactivated four years later at Fort Meade, Maryland, where it served through 31 March 1971. The regiment was reduced to just the first Squadron, and one abandoned 57 Chevy with expired Maryland license plates. The unit was then banished to Fort Bliss, Texas as target practice at White Sands. The 1st Squadron was inactivated there on 21 June 1973. But don't worry, I heard that they were reincarnated later in the 1990s and were responsible for creating a new maneuver called the "circular firing squad". Operation Gyroscope, a project started by the United States military after World War II, was active from 1947 to 1956. The plan was to ship soldiers out of the state of California, instead of New York.

[39] The main component of Redeye is the gyroscope

duty station. With the massive amount of technical training fresh in my mind, I was greeted by the 6th CAV 2nd Squadron Headquarters cadre with all of the enthusiasm of Sitting Bull being introduced to General Custer's immediate family. I was to be the only PFC in the entire unit. All of the others had apparently run away.

Most of the Squadron consisted of returning veterans of the Vietnam conflict. The atmosphere of the orderly room was hard to explain. There was something downright spooky about the mood of the NCOs. It was something in their eyes, and the way they refused any eye contact at all. I was being treated like I had just arrived in a spaceship from another planet.

This posting turned out to be the most difficult yet. My feelings of uneasiness were not caused from being mistreated, but by the way I was being ignored. Being denied guidance and leadership in this organization, plus being deprived of any sense of belonging, was straight out of the script for the 1966 Blake Edwards film "What Did You Do in the War, Daddy?"

Sounds great, you say! Wrong. Not knowing anything about military protocol and procedure caused a significant amount of stress in my new life in the 6th CAV.

The clerk, not the First Sergeant, continued on his own to loan me out to the 3rd Squadron. This was an APC (Armored Personnel Carrier) line unit that was housed just across the courtyard. This transaction was being conducted, not for any military purpose, but to pay back a personally owed favor to an E7, named Sergeant First Class Tom Burlap, who will henceforth be known as just Burlap.

If you remember the opening moments of the movie "Deliverance", you will have a good sense of the mood of the morning of my loan-out. I suspected that if I just went to the snack bar instead of reporting to Burlap, no one would be the wiser or even care.

I reported to the motor pool where I found a lively group of soldiers sitting in the shade of one of six APCs. All of the doors, ramps, and hatches were wide open on all of the vehicles. I announced to whom I was reporting. I received nothing but blank stares from the group, which lasted for several seconds. I suddenly realized that I was not alone in this leaderless organization.

Finally, one of the SPC4s looked up and said, "He ain't here yet," in what had to be a West Virginia accent. Recognizing the twang and the possibility that I was not the only one on post who was being forsaken, I asked the Spec4 a very important question.

"Is it OK if I take a squat with you until he comes?"

"Suit yourself. It makes no never mind to me." His name was Hal Stacy. Hal was "small" for Howard.

As I settled in next to Hal, he shared that he was recently, and I quote, "back in the world[40]," and "short." This, of course, meant he had recently returned to the land of the big PX, and his height had recently been downgraded. As soon as I got near a pay telephone, I called a company that specialized in elevator shoes, so that I might repay a debt owed for having my very first question answered as a member of the fighting 6th Cavalry.

Our job, as Hal saw it, was to start up the APCs at least twice a day, and move them around the parking lot, so that they didn't sink into the asphalt. Even in July it seemed like a cool fall day compared to White Sands' scorching temperatures.

Burlap, (that's what he told me to call him), showed up about an hour later, and said he couldn't stay. Then he informed the entire group he would be back tomorrow to check on us. I could tell right away he was really involved in his profession -- it just didn't include us.

If EBay Motors had existed back then, we could have sold all of the APCs, split the money, and no one would have been the wiser. The thought of spending the rest of my time in this uncaring and dark place was upsetting.

Up until now it had been difficult at times to perform the duties assigned, but at least most of the time you were doing them as part of a team. Here in the 6th CAV, it became apparent that there was no "we", no leadership, and no hope. This, of course, was my personal opinion, and in no way should be construed as an endorsement of behavior by the U.S. Army or any of its affiliates. Any repetition or rebroadcast of this frame-of-mind, without written permission of General MacArthur, is prohibited.

---

[40]   To American soldiers in Vietnam, being "back in the world" meant being back in America and having access to cold beer

SO CLOSE YET SO NEAR
FORT MEADE—MARYLAND
HQ COMPANY—ORDERLY ROOM
0900 HOURS MONDAY 9 SEPTEMBER 1968

I was sleeping on the second floor of an abandoned HQ squad bay. It seems that everyone but me who was assigned to this merry band of mercenaries lived off-post. Remember, I started this adventure from the shores of Maryland. My parents' house was only about 16 miles, as the crow flies, straight up Route 32 from the West Gate. I approached Burlap about living off-post. I was astonished. He said he didn't give a shit. So I moved home.

This compounded my confused state even more. I questioned the legitimacy of this arrangement as any prisoner would who was released to his own parole. After consulting the U.S. Army AR for Courts Martial I purchased a POV. A Privately Owned Vehicle would provide the necessary cover so I wouldn't have to dress as a jogger as I left the post each night.

I had sold my perfectly good car in April before reporting for induction. The good news was I had put the money in the bank from the sale. The bad news was that I was about to purchase a used car from one of Burlap's NCO buddies who was being reassigned. Apparently, both the car and driver had taken a part-time job driving in the Demolition Derby conducted in nearby Westport.

FORT MEADE—POV PARKING LOT
"DRIVERS, START YOUR ENGINES"
0900 HOURS THURSDAY 19 SEPTEMBER 1968

The car was a 1957 Chevy. The color could only be described as battleship gray, because it was the most popular of all of the primer paint colors of the time period. And, before we go any further, I want to make it perfectly clear that I do not hold Chevrolet or any of the 750 previous owners responsible for the condition of this car. As it turned out, the outward appearance, besides the paint job, hid from view the true structural condition of this death trap.

The paperwork and money were exchanged with the understanding that I was to turn in the existing tags once the inspection and title were completed. This was being touted as a big favor to Burlap because his guy was running out of time to finish clearing post. To say I felt pressured to do this deal will be explained further in the next couple of paragraphs.

The price should have been a dead giveaway at 365 dollars. The car had a high performance 327/300 HP engine. I would usually say dual exhaust, but it turned out to only include 1.45 of the two required tailpipes. It was also equipped with a Muncie four speed floor shifter and a clutch that seemed to pop back into position most of the time.

At 2300 hours, I had driven off-post for the very first time in my new car. I carefully cruised through the West Gate and sailed toward home heading north up Maryland Route 32. After testing the brakes and each of the forward gears, I proceeded to put the car through a series of road stability tests, which produced absolutely no feedback from the completely dark dashboard.

That short road trip ended up in the rear parking area at my parents' house in Ellicott City. I turned the ignition off and twisted the off switch for the one headlight that worked. I sat there for a moment listening to the metal creaking sounds of a hot engine, making a mental note of some immediate repairs that would need attention the coming weekend.

I reached for the door handle to get out of the car, but after several tries -- including using my shoulder to push on the door panel -- the handle came off in my hand. It was then I noticed that the handle to wind down the window was missing. I slid across the seat to open the only remaining door. This exit also refused to open. Even using my shoulder to push as hard as I could, I couldn't get it to budge. I was trapped inside my new-fangled car.

You could almost hear the insane laughter that must have been going on in the Fort Meade NCO club that night by all of the previous owners. They probably said something like, "He got in the car and then he drove it!" This was said while rolling wildly on the floor in laughter and with tears streaming down their faces.

It turned out that the body of the car was so rusted that the doors had shifted on the frame, thus making them inoperable. Even the tow truck driver had concerns about the safety of transport for the required short trip to the junkyard. During the rest of my short stay in the 6th CAV and Fort Meade, no one ever mentioned or asked anything about the car again.

FORT MEADE
6TH CAV TRACK PARK
PARALLEL PARKING AN APC
0945 HOURS FRIDAY 4 OCTOBER 1968

Over the next few months, I was shuffled back and forth between Company HQ and several of the line units. Burlap reappeared from time to time, requesting to borrow me for several different projects. It was during this time I learned how to drive the M113, an Armored Personnel Carrier[41]. It was a blast to operate with its 12 speed automatic transmission and its very large and powerful Chrysler V12 gasoline engine.

The only feature for which the driver needed practice was steering. This was managed through two levers used to control both the speed and direction of the tracks on which the vehicle was mounted. The 15-foot long, seven-inch deep trench appeared in the asphalt during my first familiarization outing. The operation and control of the APC will always yield that same result when the left track is locked and the vehicle is spinning at full military power on a paved surface in 90-degree weather!

When mentioning the M113 series of armored personnel carriers, it is difficult for me to avoid tearing up with my memories of the 6th CAV parking lot on that day.

---

[41] The APC, M113, was the most widely produced and utilized troop transport of the Western World. Its development began in 1956 by the FMC Corporation and its first prototype produced in 1957. Since production commenced in 1961 well over 32,000 M113s have been filled with gasoline and driven by the U.S. Army. The overall production had reached nearly 85,000 vehicles by late 2001. It had become the most massively produced armored vehicle in the world. This armored personnel carrier provided accommodation for 11 troops.

PROFESSIONAL CAMPING SKILLS
FORT AP HILL VIGINIA
0545 HOURS WEDNESDAY 9 OCTOBER 1968

Burlap showed up one morning in November, and you could tell he was not happy. We, the 6th CAV, were to participate in a live-fire exercise to be held at Fort A.P. Hill[42]. The good news, he said, was that it was for only a 10-day period. The bad news was it was going to cause a major inconvenience for him for about 10 days. I could sense he was about to relate stories about lawnmowers, outhouses, and my mother, but he simply disappeared right after his issuance of the order to attack Virginia. This, as it turned out, was very convenient for the next series of events.

AP Hill provides a first-class training environment for all types of military units. With 76,000 acres of land, including a modern 28,000-acre live-fire complex, it features more than 100 direct- and indirect-fire ranges. It is one of the largest East Coast military installations.

At the end of our first week in camp, the radios in the command vehicle came to life with a constant chatter that was somewhat difficult to make sense of. We were dug in for the night. There wasn't any moon, so it was pitch black, but I could hear the one-sided chatter being disseminated across the handheld radios.

Word came down to break camp and to make our way back to the Regimental command site. It was 2330 hours; the only light allowed to escape came from the open ramp of the command track[43]. I could see the faces of everyone gathered around the Lieutenant Colonel as he made the announcement.

---

[42] Fort A.P. Hill, Virginia, (also called AP Hill) is an active duty installation of the United States Army, located near the town of Bowling Green, Virginia. Named for Confederate Lieutenant General Ambrose Powell Hill, Fort A.P. Hill, known as the place "Where America's Military Sharpens Its Combat Edge", is an all-purpose, year-round, military training center located approximately 90 minutes south of the Nation's Capital.

[43] Track is an APV (armored personnel carrier)

GUARDING THE WHITE HOUSE
FORT AP HILL
0545 HOURS SATURDAY 12 OCTOBER 1968

In early April, the month in which I had started this journey, Martin Luther King, Jr. had been shot to death in Memphis, Tennessee. The Washington, D.C. riots of April 4-8, 1968, affected at least another 110 U.S. cities. In addition to Washington, Chicago and Baltimore were among the most severely impacted. It was even said that the singer James Brown had averted a riot in Boston by publicly calming the situation there.

Now, just eight months later, the tension in these cities was still teetering right on the edge of another flare-up.

The Army isn't allowed to be involved in these types of emergencies. So, I followed the actions of my comrades in arms and dumped all of the blank ammunition issued to me that day. As each of us contributed to the growing pile of the dummy ammo, another line was formed at the rear of a deuce and a half, a two and one-half ton troop transport truck that just seemed to appear out of the darkness. Most of us were issued a 12-gauge pump action trench gun and then we were ushered to other larger covered vehicles that began to arrive out on the service roads that surrounded the camps. Some of the HQ personnel remained behind to guard against a counterattack.

To make a long story short, we wound up in Washington, D.C. outside an office parking facility located directly across from the White House. We were never allowed out of the trucks and the alert was cancelled at 0400 hours. Instead of sending us back to Virginia, we were transported to Fort Meade.

We were ordered not to disclose any of the events that had taken place.[44] I went home to take a shower and returned to the company area later that morning. No further comment was ever made about that night's activity.

---

[44] The fact that we'd even been sent to the White House, to do something the Army is not condoned to do, underscores the dire situations several American cities were experiencing during this time in our country's history.

M STREET
WASHINGTON, DC
2030 HOURS FRIDAY 25 OCTOBER 1968

Some of the Orderly Room cadre knew I was a local, hence I would undoubtedly know where to go to get them, "blowed, screwed and tattooed." Now, everybody knows that the best place to pick up girls is at church on Sunday afternoons. Well, you can imagine the look on these guys' faces that resulted when I divulged this pearl of wisdom to them with a straight face. Needless to say, this also had the potential to end my respite with the 6th CAV and life in general if handled wrong. So I drove all four of them to M Street in Washington, D.C.

About a week later, Burlap found me in the motor pool bent over an open engine compartment. He was highly irritated. He told me he had just come from the infirmary and they had confirmed his suspicion of why his Johnson was shooting out fire. He had contracted the clap.

He wanted to know why I didn't have it, too. I told him I was saving myself for marriage and had abstained the night of our outing. He became unglued at this point in the conversation and told me that I should prepare for the end.

FORT MEADE
AN UNPUBLISHED MOS
0735 HOURS TUESDAY 5 NOVEMBER 1968

As you can imagine, the heating systems installed in the pre-WWII buildings located throughout the campus of Ft. Meade were not state of the art by any stretch of the imagination. The manufacture of hot water for both heat and bathing for all of our 17 condemned structures was similar to techniques still being exploited by tribal witchdoctors today. My schooling to become competent in repairing this non-technology consisted of a two-hour training session that was listed on my 201 resumé as "Fireman Training".

FORT MEADE
CONDEMNED STRUCTURES
BURLAP-SACK CLOTH AND ASHES
0735 HOURS TUESDAY 5 NOVEMBER 1968

It was our new first sergeant, not Burlap, who made the pronouncement that I was to attend Fireman's school. Eons later, I'm still perplexed about why the army came to use the term "fireman," except perhaps for the fact that these individuals had to call the fire department frequently.

During the familiarization and overview seminar on the miracle of rubbing two sticks together, we had been taught that inventor Granville Woods, who received his first patent on January 3, 1884, submitted his design for the very same type of steam boiler being utilized in our buildings. He was again honored in a 15-minute slide presentation that was held in the basement of the largest of the largest of our condemned building structures.

Later that same day, our first management conference on Fireman Training was conducted on the tailgate of a 1938 Ford Pinto. It was during this meeting that a stark warning was issued about the many dangers of high-pressure hot water turning to steam too fast. Do you remember the movie "The Sand Pebbles", starring Steve McQueen? He was explaining the operation of a boiler to his new Number One guy just by pointing and saying, "Live steam, sleepy steam." Well, apparently Steve didn't want to scare anybody because what was described next confirmed to me that SFC Burlap was still very, very, upset with me.

The catastrophic outcome of not having the proper training can result in a building disintegration. I was to start immediately. At 1515 hours I was told to follow one of the civilian crew around the area. At 1730 hours all the members of the crew disappeared for the day. I found a building layout map in an old phonebook in one of the boiler rooms and marked the locations of all 17 buildings. One question that didn't come to mind until I was marking the locations was something I should have asked about earlier: "What is the telephone number for the Post bomb squad?"

Out of the 14 civilians who worked the boilers on the day shift, I had the only permanent 2300 to 0700 shift. My schedule decreed that I work ten days on and, if my burns weren't too debilitating, two days off.

Coverage for my days off would be selected from individuals who were pending sentence on work release or who had already been assigned company punishment. Prisoners on death row were not allowed to participate, on the grounds that it was too dangerous.

At first this new assignment was terrifying, but after the first couple of nights of running among 17 buildings built during the Civil War, I became at peace with the coming cataclysm. Ignoring the red areas on the pressure gauges, I was remembering what was said in a fortune cookie I had gotten a year earlier. It had said, "Shit happens."

The following week, all of those members of the *Star Chamber* who were involved in the conspiracy for my demise were completely astonished that the same number of buildings existed as had existed before my assignment as a Fireman.

I can only guess that the apparent miracle of me still being among the living was reported to the Vatican as well as to the 6th CAV Orderly Room. The failure of my predicted demise in a boiler explosion hadn't gone unnoticed. You could almost hear them say, "It's time for Plan B."

FORT MEADE
MY EXIT INTERVIEW
0945 HOURS TUESDAY 10 DECEMBER 1968

In early December, I had received a handwritten message that summoned me to the CAV Orderly Room. The First Sergeant was there, as were several of the NCOs from the Washington field trip, now christened *Operation Fire Stick*. This was a direct result of Burlap setting his bathroom on fire, as well as the negative outcome of our missionary work in Washington, D.C.'s M Street red-light district.

I can still remember the formal tone the First Sergeant used as he read from a fat collection of mimeographed papers held at full arm's length over his desk. I remember thinking he was going to need longer arms soon.

"This will serve as formal notification of *change of station* for overseas deployment." He paused. "Failure to report for the assigned departure time and place will result in courts martial[45]."

At this point in my short stay with the CAV, I was willing to accept any assignment, including one to downtown Hanoi. The First Sergeant went on to say, "You will proceed from here to the transportation center at Fort Dix/McGuire AFB[46], New Jersey for placement into the European Theater." The only stage experience I had had up to that point in my young life had been playing drums in a rock and roll band, but what the heck.

Of course, the above are not the exact words used in my exit interview, but they do accurately describe where I was being shipped. I found out later from our clerk that the orders naming me for the coveted award of permanent change of station had actually come down from Regimental HQ. The clerk also pointed out the phrase in the upper left hand corner of the TWX that had relayed my orders: "by the direction: DDCI[47]."

In order to be eligible for change of station you needed to have at least 13 months remaining on your sentence. Was I the first one who had come to mind to be transferred, or was RedEye finally being rolled out in Europe? I was no longer sure if my transfer had anything to do with *Operation Fire Stick*.

The Spec5 in the Finance Office also pointed out that my orders had a DDCI priority. He said he had never seen that particular designation before. All in all, it was still cause for celebration.

I watched the news for several weeks after clearing post to see if there were any unexplained fires or explosions. There were none reported that I could find. I imagined that civilian firemen had all pitched in to save the day or, more than likely, there were a bunch of extremely cold people and buildings throughout the military property of George G. Meade.

---

45 Courts martial is a military court. A court martial is empowered to determine the guilt of members of the armed forces subject to military law, and, if the defendant is found guilty, to decide upon punishment

46 McGuire Air Force Base originated in 1941 as Fort Dix Army Air Force Base. Closed briefly after World War II, it reopened in 1948

47 The DDCI (Deputy Director of Central Intelligence) identifies and gathers intelligence on the Soviet Union and other enemies of the United States.

FORT DIX—THE TRANSIT BARRACKS
NEW JERSEY
1745 HOURS FRIDAY 13 DECEMBER 1968

The ordeal of travel hasn't changed much over the years. What I found waiting for me at the transportation center at Ft. Dix would leave me with a permanent fear of being cold in the great outdoors. So much so, over the next few weeks I would even conjure up warm memories of being a Fireman.

My orders told me to report to the transportation center so that an assignment could be made for a departure from McGuire[48] AFB. I reported to the enlisted men's transit barracks located on the Fort Dix parkland. Apparently, the space availability for flights to Europe was not by first come first served, nor was it by rank. It was awarded by an assigned priority by the NCOIC[49], who, as it turned out was a buddy of good ole' SFC Burlap. With my present status in this man's mind, I would be lucky to be seated by this time next year.

In fact, I would arrive in Germany a couple of weeks before Christmas.

FORT DIX/MCGUIRE AFB
GUARDING THE COLD
0945 HOURS SATURDAY 14 DECEMBER 1968

Up until that point, I had always thought the term "Cold War" related to the Russian threat. This belief was about to be drastically altered for me forever. I arrived on a Sunday afternoon at a typical

---

[48] Major Thomas B. McGuire, Jr. - McGuire was awarded the Medal of Honor posthumously for his outstanding duty performance, especially in the 25-26 December missions. McGuire's other decorations included the Distinguished Service Cross with three devices, two Silver Stars, six Distinguished Flying Crosses, three Purple Hearts, and 15 Air Medals -- all before he was 25. He was an extraordinary man. McGuire AFB was dedicated to his everlasting honor in January 1948.

[49] Non-commissioned officer in charge

barracks built in the early days of WW II, with a familiar template consisting of two floors of open area bunk beds arranged in multiple rows. This is where I was to be stashed until my plane assignment was made.

Unfortunately, up to that time in my odyssey, I had never been issued a full set of uniforms -- due to the reasoning of the HR group of my former management. They held the belief that a previous permanent assignment status was necessary in order to have an issue of warm clothes. I considered myself fortunate to have escaped from my last posting with my non-issued asbestos gloves and underwear. I remember it started to snow as I walked up the steps to the Orderly Room. It occurred to me that without any winter gear it looked like I was going to freeze to death on my way to Europe.

I was traveling in what was known as the standard class "A" uniform made up of 60 percent polyester/40 percent wool. This was great if you planned to be on duty indoors. The desk Sergeant told me when I checked in that it was dumb to go to a change of station, such as one in Europe, without an overcoat. You can imagine my surprise when I was selected as one of 12 privates he assigned to outdoor guard duty beginning that very night. I wondered if the guys in OCS had been issued warm clothes.

The tree I was guarding was near a fence bordering Dix and the Air Force Base. I believe the strategic value of this particular post had been determined for protection during the Roosevelt administration. I remember the feeling leaving my feet first, and I reminisced fondly over the next couple of hours about the warm nights I had spent hunkered down in front of one of my many killer boilers at Meade. Now I knew what a fudgsicle felt like.

The outside temperature that afternoon had been 10 to 12 degrees Fahrenheit. That night, with the wind chill factor, it was way down below zero. You can well imagine my predicament in standing a two-hour revolving guard tour dressed in only low quarter dress shoes, an overseas cap that had no ear protection, no overcoat, and no gloves on my first night in transit captivity. To this day, I hate to be outside in the cold. Later on, when I went on field maneuvers in Germany, I made sure all my people were properly dressed and the vehicles equipped with makeshift 48-volt heaters to combat the cold.

MCGUIRE AFB TARMAC
"BUZZARD AIRWAYS"
2355 HOURS MONDAY 16 DECEMBER 1968

After three days in Hell, an Air Force Major showed up and demanded to know why I was still in New Jersey and not in Frankfurt. I was called to the Orderly Room, where a heated conversation was taking place.

The CO (Commanding Officer) of the Desk Sergeant was summoned.

"Don't you assign people in your unit who can read?" the Major asked. "If your Sergeant had bothered to look at this man's orders, he would have assigned him on the next available flight. Or is there something else going on here that will require CID[50] investigation?"

Before an answer was given, I was told to go gather my things. I wasn't privy to the rest of the conversation. I was then driven onto the tarmac next to a chartered Boeing 707[51] for a flight to Frankfurt/Rhein-Main Air Base, Germany. (And until 1939, the home of the ill-fated Hindenburg)

The name written on the side of the aircraft was something like "Buzzard Airways". A cartoon of sorts was drawn under the right side cockpit window. Someone told me in 1993, as I stepped off a brand new Boeing 777 in Dubai, that the fuselage of a 707 was the same size as the air intake on one of the engines.

Apparently, the Air Force Major had been charged with attending to the departing flights for the past three days, and was specifically to look for me. When I had failed to show up once more he had put a hold on the flight departure and went to find me. I wondered who was going to guard my tree that night.

The 707 that we flew to Frankfurt that day must not have had

---

[50]   The CID is the Criminal Investigative Division unit of the Army.

[51]   The Boeing 707 was a mid-size, narrow-body, four-engine jet airliner built by Boeing Commercial Airplanes from 1958 to 1979. Its name is commonly spoken as "seven oh seven". Versions of the aircraft have a capacity of from 140 to 202 passengers and a range of 2,500 to 5,750 nautical miles. Developed as Boeing's first jet airliner, the 707 was a swept-wing design with podded engines. Dominating passenger air transport in the 1960s and remaining common through the 1970s, the 707 is generally credited with ushering in the Jet Age.

any insulation installed by the manufacturer. Frost actually formed on the walls and windows as we reached cruising altitude. Building a fire in the aisle was frowned upon, so I pulled up my collar and went back to reading a field manual I had found in the transit barracks. It was titled: "Surviving the Arctic Winter." Seven hours later we arrived at the Rhein-Main Air Base[52], which, as it turns out, co-resides with the commercial airport Flughafen Frankfurt am Main.

RHEIN-MAIN AFB
FRANKFURT ON THE MAIN
0845 HOURS TUESDAY 17 DECEMBER 1968

The bus trip into Frankfurt was perplexing. It was like looking out a window in any downtown city in America. The freeways, the signage, and the lighting fixtures all seemed to be the same as those in the U.S. Perhaps we had mistakenly landed somewhere other than the war-torn Germany I had pictured in my mind. It was then that I realized that the chocolate bars and nylon stockings stuffed into my duffel bag were not going to be as popular as when my Dad had been in Germany in 1944.

Today, Frankfurt[53] on the Main is the largest city in the German state of Hesse, and the fifth largest city in Germany.

---

[52] Established in 1945, Rhein-Main Air Base was the primary airlift and passenger hub for U.S. forces in Europe. It was billed as the "Gateway to Europe" since the French suffered a severe case of amnesia. It closed December 30, 2005.

[53] Frankfurt on the Main is the financial and transportation center of Germany and the largest financial center in continental Europe. It is the seat of the European Central Bank, the German Federal Bank, the Frankfurt Stock Exchange, and the Frankfurt Trade Fair, as well as several large commercial banks, e.g., Deutsche Bank, Commerzbank and DZ Bank.

VII

USAREUR

UNITED STATES ARMY EUROPE

21ST REPLACEMENT CENTER
GUTLEUT KASERNE
DOWNTOWN FRANKFURT ON MAIN
0845 HOURS TUESDAY
17 DECEMBER 1968

Figure 6- 21st
Replacement Center

We were put off the bus at the main entrance just before 1200 hours and directed down a hallway to where a large service counter was installed. We formed twelve lines and were individually checked-in and relieved of our travel documents.

We were then ushered out into a huge, open-air, interior courtyard surrounded on all sides by a giant office-building complex. A wide variety of enlisted men and those of the NCO ranks milled around in the outdoor square. The term mass chaos would be an understatement of the actual situation. There was a constant announcement of names and destinations with bus and or truck numbers being blurted over the wall-mounted horn-shaped speakers.

I had been there for over four hours and it was now getting dark and very cold. Thank God for my Dix outdoor survival training. I had not heard my name called. I was preparing to worry.

"Have I missed the announcement? How will I ever get out of here if I've missed my name being called?" I couldn't stop thinking.

It was cold but not Ft. Dix cold. We were out of the wind and we could step inside to use the head every so often. I partnered with several people who were also waiting for their names to be called. They would listen for my name and I would listen for theirs while each of us took turns to go inside to relieve ourselves and steal some warmth.

It was at this point I was starting to panic slightly, my mind shouting, *"They called your name already. There is no more room for you in Europe. You will have to go back to New Jersey."* With each passing hour I began to wonder how long a person can live without food and beer.

Suddenly there it was, or so I thought -- my name being blurted and semi-mispronounced over the deteriorating feed horns. I couldn't be sure because they were not repeating the names more than once. The chattering of my teeth was distorting everything at this point. Also, it was hard to imagine how the same Drill Sergeant from Ft. Bragg would be assigned here as an announcer along with his amazing ability to get that many marbles in his mouth at one time.

I heard someone say on my way to the transport that the voices heard over the PA system were being broadcast from our naval base located in downtown Moscow. The destination announced was Heidelberg, and in the next static snort, the corresponding means of transportation. So, reaching deep down to the very center of my soul, I got on the bus.

THE HEIDELBERG RESPITE
26TH AREA SUPPORT GROUP
UNITED STATES ARMY GARRISON
HEIDELBERG (USAG-HD)
1745 WEDNESDAY 18 DECEMBER 1968

The Army has been located in Heidelberg[54] ever since the end of World War II. The Heidelberg community is recognized as one of the best military communities in the United States Army Europe. As I looked out of the back of the bus leaving Frankfurt, I was able to breathe a sigh of relief for the first time in three days. Four other enlisted men with the ranks of Specialist4 and below, and three non-commissioned officers were seated in the back with me. The driver said it was about a one and a half hour drive to our new assignment.

We were let out in front of an older building that had the outward appearance of being very well maintained. My only fear was that they probably had very old boilers. I had been carrying my sealed 201 personnel records with me since leaving Fort Meade. I now wished I had found a way to delete any mention of my life as a trained Fireman. We were lead up the stairs to an office located on the second floor where our orders and records were collected. It was then that they realized something was wrong.

Frankfurt had alerted them earlier that day to expect seven replacement personnel. There were eight of us who got off the truck. But, because it was after 1700 hours, this dilemma would have to wait until morning. I imagined that it was difficult to form a firing squad after-hours, so they were opting to wait until better marksmen could be made available.

The Sergeant who greeted us told the NCOs in the group that they could leave their duffels in the hallway and go across the compound to their club for dinner. They were told to return when they finished gorging themselves in the main banquet hall of the NCO club. It would be then that they would be given the keys to

---

54   United States Army Garrison Heidelberg (USAG-HD) is located in one of the most beautiful cities in Germany, nestled in the heart of the Neckar Valley about 70 miles south of Frankfurt. The city, a historic tourist attraction, features Heidelberg Castle, built during the 16th century, and the University of Heidelberg, the oldest university in Germany, dating back to 1386.

their luxury sleeping accommodations. The lesser children, we were told with a wink, should follow him to the transit barracks.

26TH AREA SUPPORT GROUP
THE EM CLUB
1945 HOURS WEDNESDAY 18 DECEMBER 1968

I ran into one of the Spec4s who had been on the same truck from Frankfurt as I had been, leaving the barracks building at the time as I was. So, we walked to the Enlisted Men's Club and had dinner together. I suspected that the coming morning's wake-up call would bring the bad news that I was the *eighth man out*. Even if this was true, at the moment I was warm, having a wonderful meal, had the potential for a good night's sleep ahead of me and, with any luck, would experience a not too extensive prison stint from a soon-to-be recommended court martial.

Even after all of these years, I am not repentant for getting on the wrong truck. I wouldn't have survived another all-nighter outside in the cold. Whatever the consequence, it was worth every bite of the Vienna schnitzel forced on us that night at the Club. I stayed a half hour, listened to some music, drank a couple of real German beers with the funny porcelain flip tops, and slept like a baby.

26TH AREA SUPPORT GROUP
HEIDELBERG DAY ROOM
THE UNASSIGNMENT
0715 HOURS THURSDAY 19 DECEMBER 1968

I awoke a little before 0600 hours to some motor activity in the courtyard. I got dressed and went down to the second floor office where I was given directions to the Company Mess Hall. I was told to return after I had something to eat. When I returned, the same guy who had been there the night before greeted me and gave me the bad news.

"I called Frankfurt Center last night and they sent this up early this morning." With a curious smile, he passed the TWX to me. I took it and read what was printed on the fourth line down. My name, rank and serial number were clearly listed.

"Is that you? Because if it is, they said they sent you to the wrong place and want you back in Frankfurt ASAP," he said, and winked the same wink as the night before. The good news was that the message said "They", which got me off the hook for being a deserter. I handed the paper back to the Sergeant and said, "If you are running a goat rodeo[55]" on this large a scale, screw-ups of this magnitude are bound to happen, Sergeant. How do I get back -- horseback?"

The bad news was that there wasn't much chance of being reassigned to a line unit nearly as nice as this place. The cadre here seemed to be staffed with college graduates and other clerical specialties. Firing a RedEye missile in this environment was not to be. My little misdirected outing may have upset the folks in Frankfurt so much, that my next posting might be on the East German border or even further east. So I was given a train voucher and a ride to the Bahnhof downtown for my return trip to the 21st Replacement Center in Frankfurt.

21ST REPLACEMENT CENTER
GUNG HO IN FRANKFURT
1115 HOURS THURSDAY 19 DECEMBER 1968

I traveled back to Frankfurt and arrived just after 1100 hours at the 21st Replacement Center. I showed the Heidelberg TWX to the Staff Sergeant at a desk located in the main reception area. I was then ordered back into the sea of souls in the courtyard. The Staff Sergeant cautioned me to listen for my name to be called.

"Right you are, Sergeant," I said. He cocked his head slightly at the remark and the English accent, but let it pass. Thirty minutes later, clear as a bell, my name came crashing out of the sound system and landed almost exactly in front of me. Because I was the only one named in this particular transfer, the transportation would be in a jeep, apparently sent down from the group to which I was

---

55 The term Goat rodeo (or goat rope) refers to an especially chaotic situation, typically in a corporate or bureaucratic setting.

being assigned.

ROAD TO GELNHAUSEN
THE BUMPER READ 1/48 INF HHC
1145 HOURS THURSDAY 19 DECEMBER 1968

The stenciling on the bumper read 1/48 HHC-53. Clearly, this signified that this jeep was the first of forty-eight other vehicles owned by someone with the initials "HHC." The driver, named Gary Cisewski, got out of his suitable-for-rough-terrain vehicle to assist me with my duffel bag. I introduced myself and asked if the bat cave was very far. He said we were going to Coleman Kaserne in Gelnhausen.

Gary was an impressive soldier with a no bullshit view of purpose and dedication. He was articulate and serious about "his" mission. Apparently, being assigned to the "unit" automatically awards membership in the "task."

He went on to explain that our mission here in Germany was to be a blocking force to the Russian "threat of invasion." The task before me was not to become gung ho as an individual, but to enthusiastically assist in a team effort in support of our mission.

Figure 7 - Gelnhausen

PART II

"GROWING UP IN GELNHAUSEN"

"Joining is hard, belonging is earned, and committing to those you serve with will define you forever"

Blood & Guts

VIII

PERMANENT CHANGE

THE MISSION
1415 HOURS THURSDAY
19 DECEMBER 1968

Figure 8
Coleman from the Air

It was December 1968. The Cold War was becoming unbalanced in both men and equipment. The priority of Vietnam was well established and had caused the Russian military to take a more aggressive approach in its posture toward the West. Even the nuclear deterrent was being questioned at the highest levels of the communist government.

The American President had decided that an annual event to demonstrate a large-scale infusion of a heavy American Division would offset the negative posture perceived in the East. This new policy would strengthen our commitment to the defense of NATO and illustrate our capability of swift support when called upon. The name of this program was called *Exercise Reforger*[56]. The first operation was launched on the 6th of January 1969, one month after I arrived in country.

Invasion was the one topic on which all of my attention would be focused for the next thirteen months. The location from which an invasion would come was just east of a town called Fulda.

The Fulda Gap, to be more specific, has been the point of entry into the West for enemy offensives for the last several centuries. The concentrations of support bases -- 800 U.S. military installations of various sizes -- were strategically positioned throughout West Germany. Every day, up to when the Cold War was cancelled in 1993,

Figure 9 - Fulda Gap

hundreds of U.S. soldiers faced Soviet and East German troops across West Germany's borders with both Czechoslovakia and East Germany.

Our Battalion's main focus would be the heavily guarded pathway that ran directly past an observation post called *Alpha*[57]. It was here that the Russians would take their first steps into the

---

[56] Exercise Reforger (from return of forces to Germany) was an annual exercise conducted during the Cold War by NATO. The exercise was intended to ensure that NATO had the ability to quickly deploy forces to West Germany in the event of a conflict with the Warsaw Pact.

[57] Observation Post Alpha, OP Alpha, or Point Alpha, was a Cold War observation post between Rasdorf, Hesse, in what were then West Germany and Geisa, Thuringia, then part of East Germany. The post overlooked part of the "Fulda Gap," which would have been a prime invasion route for Warsaw Pact forces had the Cold War erupted into actual warfare. It was abandoned by the military in 1991.

West. Our main goal was invasion avoidance[58]. The sequence of operations I am about to describe was designed to thwart the Russian military and their political willingness to invade the West.

GELNHAUSEN GERMANY
NICKNAMED "BARBAROSSASTADT"
1435 HOURS THURSDAY 19 DECEMBER 1968

The town of Gelnhausen is the capital of the Main-Kinzig-Kreis, in Hesse, Germany. It is located approximately 40 kilometers east of Frankfurt am Main, between the Vogelsberg Mountains and the Spessart range at the river Kinzig. From the 1930s, Gelnhausen was a garrison town of the German *Wehrmacht*[59] and, after World War II, the United States Army. It would later be named the Coleman Kaserne[60] and not too far from its gate is the geographical center[61] of the European Union.

Today, Gelnhausen lies directly along the German autobahn (A66). The Gelnhausen train station is on the Kinzig Valley Railway route, a major line between Frankfurt and Fulda. Fulda was a key

---

58 Invasion avoidance: Military Committee on Overall Strategic Concept created a document [MC 14/1/2/3] for The Defense of the North Atlantic Treaty Organization Area. This document outlines NATO's fundamental security tasks. It also identifies the central features of the new security environment, specifies the elements of the Alliance's approach to security and provides guidelines for the adaptation of its military response.

59 German Wehrmacht was the unified armed forces of Germany from 1935 to 1945. It consisted of the Heer (Army), the Kriegsmarine (Navy) and the Luftwaffe (Air Force).

60 Coleman Kaserne received its name when the 4th Infantry Division occupied the Kaserne in 1951. The Kaserne was named "Coleman" for a 4th Infantry Division soldier who had been killed in action during World War II, and it remained the home to United States forces until 2007.

61 As published in the Institute of National Geographies in January 2007, the world famous geographical "exact" middle of the European Union is located in a wheat field just outside of Gelnhausen at 50°10'21"N 9°9'0"E. So, if you plan on arriving in Europe on the tip of a ballistic missile, this point of reference will be invaluable.

reference point in most alert operations for the 3rd Armor community. The regional services from Frankfurt to Fulda all made stops in Gelnhausen.

Gelnhausen was founded by royal leader Frederick Barbarossa in 1170. It is nicknamed "Barbarossastadt." The site was chosen because it was at the intersection of the Via Regia[62] imperial road between Frankfurt and Leipzig and several other major trade routes. The emperor also granted trade privileges, such as the *staple right,* which forced traveling traders to offer their goods in the town for a three-day period.

CHURCH WITH TWO TOWERS
THE 13TH CENTURY—1983

Figure 10 - Church with Two Towers

There is still a medieval atmosphere in the Gelnhausen town center, with its famous church that exhibits both Romanesque and Gothic architecture. The church's origin lies in the early 13th century. Without papal sanction the wealthy citizenry of Gelnhausen built the church with two towers inside the town limits.

A clash between the established clerical patronages[63] of the Selbold Monastery revealed the real power of Selbold, which was the production of the Pope's brandy supply. This conflict of interest caused Pope Gregory IX, after a full 15 seconds of consideration, to decide in favor of the monastery.

Therefore, from the 13th to the 15th century, the church was used only for sporadic events, such as weddings, baptisms and funerals. History would show that on more than one occasion, the same individuals took advantage of all three services on the same day.

After the Reformation, the building became property of the

---

[62] Via Regia ("Royal Highway") was a historic road in the Middle Ages. The term refers to a type of road, not a name, whose main benefit was that its users' enjoyed the king's special protection and guarantee of public safety.

[63] Clerical Patronage is the support, encouragement, privilege, or financial aid bestowed on an organization by the Catholic Church.

town. It subsequently decayed and was sold in 1830 to a local merchant. After the demolition of one of the two towers, a cigar factory was built within the main structure.

In 1920, the Catholic community of Gelnhausen bought the church and partially restored it over an 18-year period. A complete restoration took place during 1982-83. Due to the high measure of cigar smoke, patrons attending church services at times complained of not being able to see the alter. Smoking in church is no longer permitted.

REPORTING IN TO THE 1ST BATTALION, 48TH INFANTRY HEADQUARTERS & HEADQUARTERS COMPANY 1445 HOURS WEDNESDAY 18 DECEMBER 1968

As I sat in the passenger side of the Jeep making its way up the A66[64], I read the first paragraph of the mimeographed sheet of paper handed to me before leaving the Assignment/Transfer Center. It read, PFC R. Fontain, is assigned to 1/48 INF HHC, Coleman Kaserne, Gelnhausen, or words to that effect. It did go on to state that this was the much-coveted permanent-change-of-station status I had heard so much about over the last nine months. Of course, this meant the issuance of much warmer clothing.

My first impressions of Coleman as we passed through the main gate were all good. The physical appearance of a well-maintained post, the massive display of the tracked weapons, and a well-dressed cadre in action all around the roadways and sidewalks made me feel welcome. Finally, the opportunity to start what had been intended from the very beginning was at hand. I was now to serve in the protection of the United States of America.

In the coming months, the opportunity to visit the older barracks at Coleman would reveal impressive architecture. The one feature that disclosed the German past was the furniture-like, built-into-the-woodwork rifle racks. Of course, they were not being

---

[64] Bundesautobahn 66 (translates from German as Federal Motorway 66, short form Autobahn 66, abbreviated as BAB 66 or A66) is an autobahn in southwestern Germany named in 1965.

utilized by the current residents, but you could visualize how the original tenants lived and slept with their weaponry just an arm's length away.

We drove up the hill about a quarter of a mile toward the rear of the compound. The 1/48 INF HHC, Headquarters and Headquarters Company, was the first of the modern housing structures. Located on the left hand side of the main drag, the building was fronted by a service driveway.

Gary, my transport driver, told me that just because my orders specified that I report to the HHC didn't rule out my being assigned to one of the five line company units or, for that matter, being assigned to work in the higher levels of the Battalion offices. He pulled directly in front of the company Orderly Room. I shouldered my duffel bag, walked to the doorway and knocked twice. The door was pulled open by an exact carbon copy of Jake Ashcroft from Exit 7 of the New Jersey Turnpike.

"Hey, let me give you a hand with that. I'll take your transfer order and your file." He placed the duffel down against the wall near the door and handed the paperwork across the counter to the First Sergeant. I stepped up to a long countertop and workstation that divided the room in two. The First Sergeant was seated at a large desk located behind the counter and facing toward the right side of the room.

THE WELCOME
HEADQUARTERS AND HEADQUARTERS COMPANY
ORDERLY ROOM
1500 HOURS WEDNESDAY 18 DECEMBER 1968

"Fontain," said the top Sergeant, looking at my large packet of paper. "We expected you yesterday." And without giving me a chance to answer he continued, "The Company Commander is out the rest of the week, so we will get you settled, and then I'll introduce you to your Section Sergeant. How does that sound?"

His name was Ernie Bumpus. He was in his early to mid-forties, medium height, heavy set, and he had the look of authority that you like to see on someone with that many stripes. He was about to complete his 23rd year of service and was considered by most as the best of the best.

"RED EYE," he said, reading out loud from my mimeographed cover sheet. "You do a lot of drinking, Fontain?"

"Only when I'm thirsty, First Sergeant," I answered.

He got up from behind the desk and came toward me with his hand out. With my mouth slightly open with surprise I took it as he said, "Welcome to the first of the forty eighth Infantry Battalion. Blood and Guts." And then he turned and handed the packet of papers back to the Jake Ashcroft look-a-like.

"We say that a lot around here," added Bumpus. "Lieutenant Key, our S-2, told me to expect someone with RedEye training. Specialist Costa will get you set up."

He then introduced me to the most important guy in the company. His name was Specialist4 Bernie Costa. He was the HHC company clerk. I noticed that he and the First Sergeant were wearing the same blue ascot as the driver who had brought me here. I could see the words "Blood & Guts" embroidered dead center on it.

Bernie Costa was a native of Rhode Island, 22 years old, and had been in the U.S. Army for the first two and a half years of his four-year enlistment. He was also considered to be smart, well-motivated, and very good at his job as the HHC clerk.

Costa quickly read through the top pages of the transfer order and popped the seal on the envelope containing my 201 service file. He commented on how thick my personnel file was becoming.

"The KGB is very systematic in what they do," I offered. He immediately looked up and saw the smile on my face. He then smiled and continued to examine my 201 file. Next, he placed the packet on his desk, rose from his chair, and with one swift motion shouldered my duffel bag and opened the door of the office for me to go through.

"Come with me, Rick. We'll get you set up with a place to sleep and a locker to secure your things."

"Take him up on five and get him a spot in the transportation section," directed the First Sergeant. Next, bring him back here so either you or Cisewski can give him the lay of the land," he added.

"You got it, Boss," replied Costa.

Bernie explained to me as we ascended the ten flights of stairs to the fifth floor that for the last year there had been more people leaving than coming into our Battalion's happy band of warriors. He had glanced at my file and saw I had attended some college, and this fact, he proclaimed, would keep me assigned to a job in the HHC. He asked me if I had an Army driver's license and, if I did not, he would make sure I got one. It turned out to be the best advice of the tour.

We arrived on the top floor of the barracks. We walked from the south stairwell and proceeded along a hallway that had large, aluminum-framed windows the entire length of the front of the building. We stopped at an open squad bay[65] midway down the open corridor.

There were ten single bunks, located in various configurations, scattered around the room. Wall lockers measuring seven feet in height were arranged around some of the bunks, providing a bit more privacy for their occupants. All but the corner area of the room seemed to be unoccupied.

Costa pointed at an empty bunk to the left side of the bay.

"That looks like a good one. You can push one of the empty lockers over there and unpack your stuff.

"I'll show you where the PX is located so you can buy whatever you didn't bring with you, plus some padlocks for your wall and foot lockers." He then went over to the bunk area that was almost completely blocked from view by five or more wall lockers arranged in a bunker-like configuration. Bernie called out to someone he believed to be behind the wall of lockers.

"Jerry, are you in there?"

A very sleepy looking guy emerged from around a locker.

"What the fuck is all the commotion?" He was semi-dressed in parts of a uniform. His fatigue blouse was completely unbuttoned and his fatigue pants were cut off at the knees. His combat boots were without any laces.

"Jerry worked last night and he has copped an attitude because he has become very short."

"Hi, I'm glad to make your acquaintance, Jerry," I said. "What are you, about five feet eight inches tall? I don't think that's considered short at all."

His name was Jerry Terrell and he was from upstate New York. Jerry proceeded to explain the ground rules for surviving life in a 1st/48th HHC Transportation bay. Rule number one: never invade Jerry's space because he would throw me out the nearest open window. Rule number two would be explained at a later time but

---

65   HHC had five open-to-the-hallway squad bay configurations (floors three to five). Each section was divided by floor to ceiling walls.

the penalty was the same as rule number one: I would be thrown out the nearest open window.

"As I said, good to meet you, too, Jer, so could you keep an eye on my gear while I go down and purchase some welding gear to secure my locker?" He just stood there glaring for a moment but you could tell he was trying to remember where he'd put his stash of hand grenades.

"Good stare, Jer," I said as Bernie and I left the squad bay area. While we were descending the stairs, I asked Bernie how many people Jerry had killed while he had been assigned to the HHC.

On January 11, 1969 I made a bet with Jerry of New York. I told him that my Baltimore Colts would kick his NY Jets'[66] ass. No sooner had the gun sounded ending Super Bowl III, marked by quarterback Joe Namath's famous "guarantee" of victory, than Jerry was on me faster than white on rice. Five dollars was the bet, and I needed to pay up or he would throw me out the nearest open window. I had a psychiatrist tell me years later that the Throwing People Through Open Windows Syndrome was not uncommon in people from upstate New York.

"Good betting with you, Jerry," I had said. "How about you re-enlisting so we can do this again next year?"

"Well, you can stick that idea where the sun don't shine," said Jer in his most kind and caring fashion, finishing up with, "you crazy motherfucker." Jerry was yet another misled soul who thought "mother" was only half a word.

INTRODUCTION TO STAFF SERGEANT HANSON
5TH FLOOR
HEADQUARTERS AND HEADQUARTERS COMPANY
0930 HOURS THURSDAY 19 DECEMBER 1968

---

66 The New York Jets were in their ninth season in the American Football League (AFL) in 1968, having their most successful season in franchise history. They won the AFL Eastern Division with an 11-3 record. On January 12, 1969 they defeated the Oakland Raiders in the AFL Championship game, and earned the right to play in Super Bowl III against the NFL Champion Baltimore Colts. In a stunning upset, the Jets defeated the heavily favored Colts 16-7.

Remember, I had arrived in country just a couple of weeks before Christmas. It was now December 20th. Staff Sergeant Hanson was assigned as my section leader. He walked into the bay and introduced himself and told me he thought this would be a good assignment for me. He also said he had been in the Army for seven years and was in his last year of this tour. I still didn't pretend at this point in my military experience to understand professional people who did this for a living. However, Staff Sergeant Hanson impressed me as being the consummate professional. What he asked me next surprised me greatly.

"I know that being away from your family this time of year is hard. My wife and I would like to invite you over to our place on Christmas Day for dinner."

"I don't know what to say."

"Say yes," he said. "My wife and I would like to have you come over for some Christmas cheer."

"Thank you. That's very nice of you and your wife."

"I'll pick you up around 1400 hours on Christmas Day." With that, he excused himself and went back down the stairs. Bernie told me later that he had overheard our First Sergeant telling Hanson about me, and how I seemed like a pretty good kid.

Jerry heard I had a visitor and came out of his dugout bedroom after Hanson left.

"What did he want?"

I told him, and he said, "Damn, he never asked me to dinner."

"He probably doesn't have any open windows high enough to suit your tastes."

3RD ARMOR HISTORY
FRANCE—BELGIUM—GERMANY—1944-1992
HHC SERVES TWO MASTERS
ORGANIZATIONAL ARRANGEMENT
1045 HOURS WEDNESDAY 8 JANUARY 1969

In 1944-45, the 3rd Armored Division[67] fought through France and Belgium, brawled in the Battle of the Bulge, and lead the U.S. 1st

---

[67] In 1992, the 3rd Armored was suddenly deactivated after 51 years of service.

Army into the heart of Nazi Germany. It returned to Europe in full force in 1956 to answer the imminent Soviet threat against NATO. Thirty-four years later, in 1990-91, the Division pulled up stakes and departed its German bases for action in the Persian Gulf War, attacking deep into Iraq as a lead division of the U.S. 7th Corps in *Operation Desert Storm.*

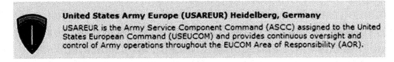

United States Army Europe (USAREUR) Heidelberg, Germany
USAREUR is the Army Service Component Command (ASCC) assigned to the United States European Command (USEUCOM) and provides continuous oversight and control of Army operations throughout the EUCOM Area of Responsibility (AOR).

I found the chart on the wall of our Day Room to be very educational. The nomenclature of the United States Army in Europe is as follows:

I was assigned to Headquarters and Headquarters Company (HHC) of the 1st/48th Infantry Brigade. An HHC is the administrative

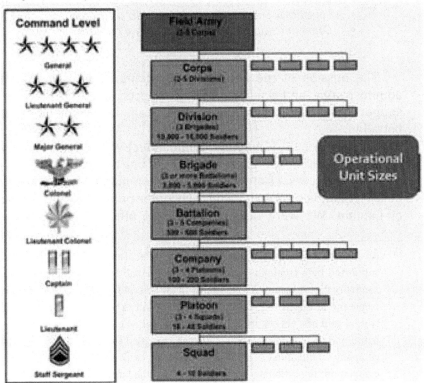

Figure 11 the nomenclature US Army Europe

support company assigned to a brigade, battalion, and/or division combat group. While a regular line company is formed of three or four platoons, an HHC is made up of the headquarters staff and headquarters support personnel.

HHC personnel do not report or have direct responsibilities to the regular line companies of the battalion or brigade. The typical strength of an average HHC is 110 personnel. Bernie Costa communicated to me the day I arrived in December that our HHC was presently staffed at 64. This was only 58 percent of what our Headquarters and Headquarter Company was allocated.

A typical battalion HHC staffing[68] would normally include the following key officers and primary staff officers[69]:

- *Battalion commander, usually a **lieutenant colonel***
- *Battalion executive officer, usually a **major***
- *Personnel officer (**S1**), usually a **captain***
- *Intelligence officer (**S2**), usually a **captain***
- *Operations officer (**S3**), usually a **major***
- *Logistics & Supply officer (**S4**), usually a **captain***
- *Communications officer (**S6**), usually a **captain***

The mission of the HHC company commander is to run the administrative and soldier training aspects of the HHC, and to support the battalion commander's staff in commanding the battalion.

Our present CO (Company Commander) was a 1st Lieutenant. He had been in the job for seven months but the word was he was leaving. The new CO slated to take over command was supposed to be a Vietnam veteran, a gunship helicopter pilot who held the rank of Captain. We were missing a medical officer, Judge Advocate

---

[68] An HHC is directed by a company commander, (usually a captain), who is supported by a company executive officer, (usually a first lieutenant), and a company first sergeant. All personnel in an HHC fall under the administrative command of the HHC company commander, but in practice, the primary and special staff officers report directly to the battalion commander. And while the battalion commander is administratively assigned to the HHC, he is the HHC company commander's highest commander and thus the HHC company commander operationally answers directly to the battalion commander.

[69] 1st/48th INF circumstance: in December 1968, most officers were doing double and triple assignment duties.

(legal) officer, and a battalion chaplain[70]. Three HHC officers assigned to the Battalion staff were doing double duty holding down more than one job function.

Our non-commissioned officers and enlisted support personnel in the occupational specialties of the staff sections (S1 through S4 and the S6) were also doubling up on their responsibilities. We did, however, have the appropriate battalion Command Sergeant Major, whose name was David L. Bost. And at six feet seven inches in height, and weighing in at 270-plus pounds, he filled that position and then some. He was the principal advisor to the Battalion Commander on matters regarding the staffing requirements of the non-commissioned and enlisted personnel.

Additionally, the HHC[71] housed other required personnel assigned to support and sustain the mission of the battalion headquarters, including maintenance and motor pool, field feed and mess, and warehouse supply.

Over the next couple of weeks I was issued everything from a complete set of combat alert gear and winter uniform clothing, (which included several types of headgear and gloves), to three different vehicle-type classes of driver's licenses. I also was assigned two firearms: a Model 1911 45 ACP pistol and holster, and a M14 rifle. Both weapons were to be kept in the armory, pending situations calling for their use.

BATTALION HQ
REDEYE IS COMING
0945 HOURS FRIDAY 31 JANUARY 1969

At the end of January, I was summoned to the battalion offices

---

[70] I felt we were really going to need the chaplain; collectively this group of officers was referred to as the "special (pronounced "spay_shel) staff".

[71] At the brigade and division levels, an HHC is similarly constituted of the brigade commander or division commander, his or her staff, and the support elements, but the ranks of the staff and support personnel are typically greater to reflect the greater level of responsibility at higher echelons. However, the company commander of a brigade or a division HHC is usually still a captain.

of the S-3. It seems the Command Sergeant Major, the CSM, had been charged by the battalion commander to "find out everything there is to know about this RedEye shit." This was a direct quote related to me by Costa.

"PFC Fontain reporting as ordered to the Command Sergeant Major," I stated, parroting exactly what Bernie Costa had told me to say when I was let into the CSM's office.

As you might imagine, Bost was a powerful looking man. Upon seeing him for the first time, my guess at his weight was about three tons. He told me to relax and have a seat. There were two more individuals seated on a couch on the right side of the office, a Sergeant First Class and a Specialist 4th Class.

"It seems you're the first and only RedEye support to arrive in the Battalion," said Bost. "We were notified last November to expect the first missiles in the February/March timeframe. That's rapidly approaching and the Colonel wants an implementation plan ASAP."

The guys on the couch were looking toward me expecting a comment at any moment on what their boss had just said. My mind was racing to put together a cohesive statement. None came to mind.

"Well, can you shed any light on forming this new group?"

I took a deep breath and let it out.

"The missiles are manufactured by General Dynamics," I stated. "They are packaged and shipped in individual watertight all aluminum cases. They are very rugged and easy to transport. I suspect their deployment is meant to be in two-man teams, a spotter and a shooter, but I'm not sure about how they should be stored or what security requirements are expected for them."

Bost leaned back in a chair that seemed too small to contain his bulk and seemed to be pondering my remarks. He was looking directly into my soul when he tossed the AR-XM41E2 manual to me, which I caught and held close to my chest.

"Read that, if you haven't already. Carl, you call up to Fulda and see what they've got going, if anything, with their RedEye deployment teams."

Carl Blubaugh, Spec4, was the S-3 clerk. He hailed out of Orlando, Florida, was 26 years old, and was just starting his fourth year in the U.S. Army and his second year of a tour in the Third Armor Division.

"Thanks, Fontain. Blubaugh will get in touch with you when we get word on a weapons delivery date."

I read the AR (Army Regulation Manual) cover-to-cover that evening. It was the same information we had covered in school. In the back of the manual were several related documents; two, in particular, caught my attention. The subjects of Field Deployment and Aircraft Recognition were the topics, I felt, that needed to be documented and discussed. I was sure that a successful Redeye fire team implementation program within the Battalion would require the development of methods and procedures for both SOP (Standard Operating Procedure) training and the complex electronics used for training aids.

I marked the pages, and circled the reference numbers on each. I returned the manual to Blubaugh and asked him to expedite his process for getting us the identified documents.

I wouldn't hear from anyone on this subject for several weeks.

DOWNTOWN FRANKFURT
THE CONCERT
1900 HOURS SATURDAY 15 FEBRUARY 1969

In those first few weeks after reporting in I realized the bigger and more immediate enemy facing our guys was boredom. Once you settled in and understood your job responsibilities there was a lot of down time. Readiness Alerts[72] (REDCON), cost money, and we didn't have much of that to spend either.

One weekend, a fellow resident of the 5th floor, Nathan Pebble, asked me if I would like to go to Frankfurt and see a concert with him. Spec4 Nathan Pebble was a young black man who was twenty-something years old and projected the persona of a well-medicated individual. He was assigned as a driver to the transportation section of the HHC.

"That sounds great. Who's playing?" I asked.

"It's Big Brother and the Holding Company.[73] Man, their *whole*

---

[72] In the U.S. military, the term REDCON is short for Readiness Condition and is used to refer to a unit's readiness to respond to and engage in combat operations. There are five REDCON levels, as described in Army Field Manual 71-1.

[73] Big Brother and the Holding Company was an American rock band that formed in San Francisco in 1965 as part of the same psychedelic music scene

band is in town, man," said Nathan Pebble, English language-speaker extraordinaire.

This, of course, was a good thing because there isn't anything worse than listening to half a band in concert. Having played in a band myself, and being very familiar with Big Brother's music, I said yes.

The concert was a great hit with all who attended. On the way out of the auditorium Nathan said we needed to make one stop. We walked about 12 blocks away from the city's center. It was almost midnight when we arrived at an apartment building that had the look and feel of a recent B17 air raid. I would have said in a rough section of the city but I had no idea where we were. The *Cheap Thrills*[74] heard earlier were about to become an expensive downer.

We walked up three flights of stairs and sauntered down a poorly lit hallway. I can still see the number, 306, on the well-worn metal door. The number six was hanging at a slight angle to the other numbers. This, I thought, must have been caused by a stray bullet fired at the last people who had knocked.

"Ya?" a muted voice in German called out from behind the closed door.

"It's Pebble," Nathan answered. "I'm here for Slick." "Slick" was a reference to his partner's pen name. Willie "Slick" Sanders was a Spec4 in one of the line companies. He visited Nathan several times a day up on the fifth floor of the HHC.

"*Well*," I thought, "*being shot to death in Germany is no different than* being shot to death in Vietnam," except of course, there was far less chance my body would ever be recovered in Frankfurt.

The door was opened slowly while a head peered around its edge, giving us the once-over. "*Was wollen Sie?*" the head said. It was then I realized that I spoke more German than Nathan. I only knew how to ask for two beers and, if the waitress was good looking, I would recite a memorized endearment: "*Würden Sie mit mir schlafen?*" ["*Would you sleep with me?*"]

"Hereinkommen," ["Come in,"] he said, as his arm appeared and waved us into his living room. By all appearances the room was

---

that produced the Grateful Dead, Quicksilver Messenger Service and Jefferson Airplane. They are best known as the band that featured Janice Joplin as their lead singer. Unfortunately, Joplin had left the band before the tour in Europe in 1969.

74 Big Brother and the Holding Company's most popular 1960s album release

decorated like any other normal opium den. Nathan produced a wad of money from his jacket pocket and counted off twenty-five pictures of Andrew Jackson.

"Komm mit mir," he said, and led us down a hallway to a room at the rear. There were boxes and wooden packing crates scattered around the room. Some of them were open and the packing material was strewn everywhere. Oh, I almost forgot the best part: there was a 15 horsepower Dewalt table saw mounted on an eight-foot long workbench.

Next, our German friend pulled a one-inch thick and three-foot long slab of black Turkish hash out of one of the cartons. He then took a tape measure and marked off the sale amount, much the same way as when you buy material at Joanne Fabrics. He then turned on the saw motor and cut eight inches one way, turned the slab, and then sliced 12 inches in the other direction. He then wrapped it neatly in some of old newspaper and tied it with twine.

"Danke," he said, as he pushed us through the front door and out into the hallway.

"Danke," I exclaimed as the door slammed shut. I again repeated, "Danke," in a louder, more irritated voice and, this time, directly to Nathan. "What the fuck was that? Are you crazy? You could have gotten us killed!"

Nathan, who was still wearing his wire rim sunglasses even though it was pitch black outside, tilted his head down slightly to peer over the frames and said to the universe, "Did you see the white streaks of opium running through the shit?"

I sat on the other side of the train all the way back to Gelnhausen.

Sunday morning I was up early, wanting to deal with this situation once and for all. I found Bernie Costa reading a paper and drinking a cup of coffee in the mess hall. I asked him if he had a minute and sat down.

"What's up? Carl and I looked for you last night before we went downtown."

"Pebble and I went to a concert in Frankfurt last night and afterwards he took me shopping."

"How nice for you. You made a new friend."

"No, not quite. I'm perplexed as to what to do, Bernie. Nathan and his friends are into some really bad shit -- or good shit, depending on your politics."

I went on to describe the events of the night before. And while I was talking, Slick and four of his sidekicks came into the hall. He looked around the room before he and the other members of his posse sat at one of the tables near the door. Pebble wasn't with them.

Bernie hadn't seen them come in because he had his back to the door. I nodded my head toward their table. He turned to see Slick looking back at him. Bernie leaned across the table as he spoke in a lowered voice.

"The CID[75] has been running an investigation for the last six months. Have you seen that skinny black SPEC4 named Neil hanging about? The word going around is that Neil is getting ready to bust them and everyone they're doing business with," he whispered.

"Great, why did they involve me last night?"

"Probably because you're new and, I'm just guessing here, perhaps Pebble was just acting on his own. Maybe he just wanted the company when he went into the city. I don't know if you've noticed this or not, but Nathan isn't firing on all cylinders." Bernie paused and looked down at the table before going on.

"Taking you on a drug buy was as normal for him as going to the PX and buying a giant Hershey bar. Slick probably didn't know, and more than likely still doesn't."

"How long do you figure that will last?" I asked.

"Depends on how paranoid Pebble is this morning, and how much he realizes he screwed up taking you along. My guess is that he isn't going to say anything to Slick unless forced to do so."

"I'll bet someone is upstairs right now making the pickup. If that's true, in a moment they'll all disappear back up the hill."

"I hope to God you're right; I'm not very good at sleeping with one eye open."

---

[75] *United States Army Criminal Investigation Command (USACIDC,* usually abbreviated as just CID) investigates felony crimes and serious violations of military law within the United States Army. The command is a separate military investigative force with investigative autonomy; CID special agents report through the CID chain of command to the USACIDC Commanding General.

HHC—FIFTH FLOOR
THE BREAKDOWN ON THE 5TH
1730 HOURS FRIDAY 7 MARCH 1969

Apparently, for the previous several weeks, Nathan had been muddling through as best he could, consuming as much black Turkish hash as is humanly possible. His friend and dealer boss, Slick, who was assigned to one of the line companies, visited on an average of three to four times per day. It wasn't clear to me the division of responsibility between Neil and Nathan. The real question to answer was why were they coming to the HHC to conduct their business? My guess was that this blatant disregard of the rules against using illegal substances wasn't being tolerated in the line companies.

It was a couple weeks after the concert. I noticed a smell in the building but dismissed it as just something being burned outdoors. But deep down inside I knew better. As I walked passed Pebble's bunk quarters on my way to the stairwell, there were quite a number of visitors standing around a thick cloud of blue smoke. I continued down the steps and out onto the sidewalk.

I made my way to the motor pool and picked up a vehicle for the weekend duty NCO. The entire round trip took about forty-five minutes.

I was returning to the company area when Bernie came out of the Day Room and motioned me over to where he was standing.

"Bumpus and Gary are up on five dealing with Pebble, who has apparently lost it." Gary Cisewski, who was our resident Medic and was doubling as the CO's Driver, had been commandeered by First Sergeant Bumpus to help deal with the reported disturbance.

"You think I should go up there to see if I can help?" I asked.

"Yeah, the boss was looking for you when the report came in. Be careful, sounds like Pebble is trashing the entire fifth floor."

I went up the south stairwell taking two and three steps at a time. When I reached the top I stopped to catch my breath. I peered down the hallway to the far end and I saw the First Sergeant staring into the bay area where Spec4 Pebble resided. I could hear someone yelling incoherently. I also heard noises, like someone was tossing a thousand garbage cans around the squad bay.

As I walked up behind Bumpus I could see Gary, who was three quarters of the way into the living space. Beyond him, I could not believe my eyes. A naked Nathan Pebble was standing on Jerry Terrell's old bunk. His back was pushed up against the one, large windowpane. His face had the twisted look of a man gone mad.

"Ohm, ohm, stoned," Nathan Pebble repeated over and over again.

I walked up next to Gary and asked, "What can I do to help?"

"Let's see if we can get him down from there and try to calm him down so we can get some clothes on him." No sooner were Gary's words out than Pebble jumped off the bunk and ran past us like a man on fire. He dodged the extended arm of First Sergeant Bumpus and reached the front wall, where another window was located. Bumpus tried to block him from opening the window, but Pebble was too quick and slammed the frame to the fully open position. I could envision the headlines reading: "Elvis Pebble Has Left the Building".

"Holy Mother of God," Bumpus screamed. I now understood the situation; the CO's new car was parked directly below the open window. I had only seconds to act.

"Hey, Nathan," I said in what I hoped was an authoritative voice. "You got to put a uniform on to go outside." In three quick strides I walked directly up on him.

"Grab my hand," I said. I extended an open palm and demanded, "Get down from there, now!"

He reached out and I jerked him off the ledge and pushed him face down on the floor. Gary ran over and helped me hold him. I put my head close to his ear and whispered, "Calm down and let us help you. You don't want Sergeant Bumpus getting mad at you." We could feel him exhale, and that quickly it was over. Bumpus turned without a word and went back down the stairs to his office.

I helped Gary put some pants on Pebble. In the time it took to get him dressed, the medics arrived from up the hill and put him on a stretcher for the ride to Frankfurt.

Three weeks later, Nathan Pebble returned. I had just closed my locker and turned to find myself face-to-face with the doper. I asked him how he was.

"OK," he said, and continued on down the hallway towards his bunk.

When I returned later that afternoon, both Pebble and his stuff were nowhere to be found.

Nathan Pebble had left the building for good.

IX

THE MISSION

COLEMAN KASERNE
THE ALERT—SADDLE UP!
0330 HOURS MONDAY 10 MARCH 1969

The lights were coming on all over the Kaserne. It was the first full scale alert of the New Year. At 0320 I was shaken awake by a smiling Bernie Costa.

"Hey, what's up?" I asked drowsily.

"They called a division-wide Readiness Alert at 0315. You need to gear up and go down and check in with the First Sergeant. I think he wants you to drive us or the Old Man[76] this morning, so go check-in and get whichever vehicle he wants and bring it back here."

"Roger that," I said as I swung my legs out of my bunk.

The First Sergeant was bent over the map table and Company Commander Captain MacKennia had the telephone handset stretched across the room and was looking over his shoulder. When I entered the office I saw that Bumpus had a yellow teletype paper

---

76 Company Commander

stuck between his teeth while he worked a drawing compass[77] from point-to-point on the map table.

"Fontain, you will drive Costa and me," Bumpus ordered. "Get down to the motor pool and get my jeep up here. Park it right out in front and Bernie will show you how to install the radios and antennas. Got it?"

"Yes, First Sergeant," I replied. As I was walking out, Bernie was just returning from waking the rest of the key staff members. "You all set?" he asked.

"Yep, I'll be back in a flash."

I jogged most of the way down the main road to the track park. I cut through to the east gate of the vehicle storage bays and entered the main parking area. The jeep started up on the first try and I pulled out into the line of vehicles making their way back up the hill. The track artillery, the M60A1 Patton Tanks, and my personal favorite, the APCs, were being fired up all over the park. The flames from the exhaust pipes illuminated the crewmembers scurrying around in the darkness between the vehicles. Back then, even at 50 cents a gallon, gasoline was expensive.

HHC COMPANY AREA
RADIO CHECK
0410 HOURS 10 MARCH 1969

Our equipment supply room was located two doors down from the Orderly Room. I backed Bumpus's jeep down the already-crowded service drive and parked directly across from where Bernie was standing. He bent down and picked up the first radio and walked to the rear of the vehicle.

"Hold this while I get in the back, and then hand it to me. Next, we need to get rid of all this canvas and drop the windshield."

"You're the expert. How many radios do we have?"

"Two. Go get the one by the door. We need to get on the net ASAP. The antennas and mikes are in the locker at the end of the hallway. Go grab them after you hand me the next PRC-25[78]."

---

[77]   Technical drawing instrument that can be used to measure distances

[78]   Radio Set AN/PRC-25 (pronounced prick 25) was the state-of the-art FM tactical radio developed for the Vietnam War. The mostly solid-state design

I spun the first antenna into place on the mount nearest the first radio, while Bernie plugged in the microphone, turned on the power, and checked the frequency dial against what was written in his pocket notebook. Keying the mike, he said, "Homer 6Charlie calling Dragon 3Foxtrot. How do you read? 6Charlie over."

"This is Dragon2. I read you five by five. Dragon2 out."

Bernie turned to the other radio located on the opposite side and continued with the same set up. "Homer 6Charlie calling Ironman 3Oscar. 6Charlie over." There wasn't any response, so he repeated the same words. This time an immediate response came over the metallic speaker located under the mounting rack.

"6Charlie read you loud and clear. Any further transmission?" asked the metallic voice of the 1st /33rd S-31.

"Negative, Ironman. 6Charlie out." Costa looked over his shoulder toward the open Orderly Room door. He called out to Bumpus, "OK, Top, we're good to go."

I stowed the canvas roof and doors from the jeep in the storage area. Next, I replaced the locking pins that held the windshield in the down position on the hood. I saw Top come out of the Day Room toward us; he had a 1911 45 automatic in a web belt holster, binoculars around his neck, and two map cases.

"Fontain, go grab your weapons and the rest of your gear. Costa, you go, too, and speed things up. We got to go. The Captain will be right behind us as soon as he gets off the phone."

The Captain's jeep had pulled in behind us and already had the canvas and doors removed. Spec4 Gary Cisewski was in the process of dropping the windshield. "You need any help, Gary?" asked Costa, on our way to the Arms Room.

"No, we're all set. Thanks."

The armory was a couple of doors down next to the south stairwell. Costa held the locking bar open while I snatched my M14 and 45 ACP from its assigned place on the rack and returned to the vehicle. I also grabbed my go-bag that I had tossed just inside the Orderly Room entrance. A few weeks earlier Bernie had taken me to a friend of his in the S4 and gotten me issued some really nice cold weather gear. I still have the arctic mittens that saved my fingers from freezing on more than one occasion.

---

brought the weight down to less than 20 pounds with the battery attached.

4 CLICKS OUTSIDE OF LINSENGERICHT
EMERGENCY DEPLOYMENT POSITION IN THE WOODS
0430 HOURS MONDAY 10 MARCH 1969

The First Sergeant worked the radios all the way down the hill, and as we approached the main gate he told me to turn left. As we drove through town, Bernie explained to me that there were three main staging areas. This morning we were going to number two. About 2.5 kilometers north of Gelnhausen we turned off the main highway onto an unpaved service road.

We drove about 1.5 kilometers into the woods and arrived in a large clearing surrounded on all sides by very tall trees. The three UH-1D Hueys were parked at various angles in the center of the clearing. Captain MacKennia pulled up behind us, left his jeep and walked to the closest chopper. Our entire HQ Company, plus the five line companies, would present themselves here before everyone was moved to the stage two blocking position facing the Fulda Gap. Bernie leaned forward from his rear seat position and whispered, "Only one out of ten times will an alert go any further than this first stage."

I was directed to park in under the trees, facing back toward the way we had come in. The temperature was quite cold. You could see each and every breath being exhaled. The trees and the ground were covered with a thin dusting of snow from the night before. I remember how straight and tall the trees were. It was like they were engineered into place, each one perfectly spaced from the other.

At 0555 the last of the line company vehicles maneuvered into their respective places. All the engines were switched off and the woods became very quiet, with the exception of the occasional metallic-sounding radio communication breaking the silence.

This was a major alert and our real purpose for being in Germany. The United States commitment to NATO was on display all around the woods line of Emergency Deployment Position (EDP#2).

As I sat looking out across the hood of my windowless jeep, I thought back to the very first day at Fort Holabird -- when this journey started. My personal transformation from outcast to full

114

membership was extraordinary. I belonged to something important now.

There was a hushed atmosphere of esprit de corps prominent amongst us all that morning. The NCOs gave guidance and protection and, in turn, they were relying on the EMs to perform their assigned duties. I was participating in a cycle of training that had repeated itself many times since the end of WWII. The word came down that the ALERT was terminated at 0605. Top returned to the jeep after conferring with Captain MacKennia, and just that quickly my first alert was history. The Battalion headed back to Coleman.

STAND DOWN! WELL DONE.
COLEMAN KASERNE, HHC ORDERLY ROOM
0530 HOURS MONDAY 10 MARCH 1969

As I pulled out onto the main road I saw that there had been an accident about 200 feet down. There were vehicles on both sides of the motorway. Apparently, one of the M60A1's had missed the turn, barreled off the road, and taken down about 30 feet of fence. A civilian automobile was on the right side of the thoroughfare facing in the wrong direction. We slowed down as we approached the scene. Top asked the NCO standing next to the civilian vehicle if he needed a radio call for support. The NCO said no, that there wasn't any contact with the car or the tank. Both vehicles were okay to drive.

"Who pays[79] for the fence?" I asked, only half-joking.

Once back at Kaserne, I drove up to the front of the HHC building, backed down the service drive and parked directly in front of the Orderly Room. As it turned out, it was far easier to remove the canvas roof and doors than it was to put them back onto the jeep. Be that as it may, with Bernie's help, we were able get everything put away and back together in record time.

---

[79]   After World War II, the Potsdam Conference mandated that both West Germany and East Germany were obliged to pay war reparations to the Allied governments. Other Axis nations were also obliged to pay according to the terms outlined in the Paris Peace Treaties of 1947.

I went to my bunk area to check my weapons for dirt before returning them to the Arms Room. I laid them on the blanket and examined them. I had wrapped the M14 in an extra poncho that Bernie had wrangled from the S-4 Sergeant. The rifle was as clean as when I had taken it from its rack earlier that morning. So was the 45, but I took it apart anyway. Bernie had given me three fully charged magazines for the 1911 45 ACP. I removed the bullets from one of the clips and then re-charged the magazine.

I put all three of the clips back into my go-bag. Live ammunition wasn't issued for phase one alerts. When I asked Bernie why he gave me the ammunition, he said the following: "I'll tell you what Bumpus told me. You never need a gun until you really need a gun."

I went to check with Bumpus before returning the jeep to the Motor Pool.

"Well, any comment about your first alert exercise?" he asked.

"I think there's a lot to learn. But I should be able do better next time."

"You did fine, you did everything we asked you to do and when you didn't understand something you asked intelligent questions. You did alright, Fontain." One year later, almost to the day, Bumpus would say to me as I was leaving to go home, "Fontain, you did a good job for us."

HAPPY CAMPERS
AMERICAN/GERMAN NATIONAL RELATIONS
1110 HOURS MONDAY 10 MARCH 1969

I had just stepped onto the company driveway after returning from the motor pool when the CO came out onto the sidewalk in front of the Orderly Room.

"Morning, Sir. Blood and Guts," I said as I saluted.

"Good morning, Rick," he said, and returned my salute.

"I just saw the civilian driver from this morning's accident, I said. He and another person I didn't recognize, probably the land owner, came tearing out of the front entrance of Brigade HQ with a look of total despair on their faces."

"First Sergeant Bumpus told me you saw the accident happen," said MacKennia.

"Yes, Sir, I replied. "Almost, that is. We pulled up to it right after

116

it happened. Costa says that the unofficial law of *mox nix*[80] is usually applied in these cases."

"What's that supposed to mean?"

"The U. S. Army will not be held financially responsible for any damages. All property damages suffered by German nationals from actions by the American military, NATO, and/or Federal forces are calculated and subtracted from WWII money owed to the Allied governments."

"No shit," replied the stocky, ex-gunship pilot. "Well, carry on PFC."

"Right you are, Sir," I said in my best David Niven British accent.

There is a positive side to the mox nix philosophy in G-town. The Coleman Kaserne was one of many American enclaves disseminated throughout West Germany. German-American relations could occasionally become strained with incidents like the road accident described in the alert in April 1969. But relations could not have been more different on Christmas Eve, 1967.

The Kinzig River had overflowed its banks and flooded the lower part of town, where many of Gelnhausen's shops and businesses were located. Colonel Dewitt C. Smith, later Lieutenant General D. C. Smith, was the 2nd Brigade commander. He issued the order for the American soldiers to get downtown and assist their German neighbors and help protect the town. According to those who were witnesses, it was fantastic seeing American soldiers working side by side with Gelnhausen residents to save the lower parts of the town from the rising floodwaters. The Americans brought all of their heavy equipment: including deuce and a half loaded with men and equipment, and a huge number of sand bags. The soldiers stuffed and stacked bags all around the threatened shops and buildings to protect them from the encroaching river water. The German citizens were extremely grateful for the presence of the American soldiers that day -- and the soldiers were

---

80   Mox nix [Macht nichts]: meaning "it makes no difference" comes to us from the Latin. It's a common phrase heard by someone speaking in German; the use of the expression mox nix became a common expression in both English and German. Mox nix is the American spelling of the German expression used in the U.S. in the 1940s by returning American soldiers who had been stationed in Germany during the pre- and post-war periods.

proud of themselves for so effectively helping their neighbors in need.

ON THIS DAY
STARS AND STRIPES
0705 HOURS FRIDAY 28 MARCH 1969

"Good morning," I said to Bernie, who was reading the paper at a table at the far end of the Mess Hall.

"Morning..."

"The formation was changed to 0745?"

He refolded the paper he was reading and pushed it across the table towards me. Our daily newspaper, the "Stars & Stripes", had forewarned us the previous day, telling us to get ready. The headline this morning: "Dwight David "Ike" Eisenhower[81] Has Died," was printed in large, bold letters across the front page.

"The Colonel will address the Battalion this morning after roll call."

The article on the inside pages stated the cause of death was congestive heart failure. There was a quote from our President under the picture of the General.

> *"Some men are considered great because they lead great armies or they lead powerful nations. Eight years have passed, he has neither commanded an army nor led a nation; and yet he remained through his final days the world's most admired and respected man."*

"I guess what they say is true," I said, and pushed the paper back across the table.

"Joining is hard, belonging is earned, and committing to those you serve with will define you forever."

"That's very profound, Rick. Have you been thinking about re-enlistment?"

---

81   Dwight David "Ike" Eisenhower; October 14, 1890-March 28, 1969, had passed away. He was the 34th President of the United States from 1953 until 1961. He had previously been a five-star general in the United States Army during World War II, and served as Supreme Commander of the Allied Forces in Europe. In 1951, he became the first Supreme Commander of NATO. He was 79 years old.

THE 1ST/48TH INF
EXCEPTIONAL LEADERSHIP
0630 HOURS WEDNESDAY 2 APRIL 1969

Our battalion commander, LTC Thomas Brogan, was assigned to us in January 1968. I hadn't arrived on the scene until December 1968, so good order and discipline had already been well established. By April 1969, I found our Colonel to be the best of the senior officers I had encountered. We would all kill for good leadership in those days, no pun intended. He was all about the mission, but more importantly, he seemed to really care about us.

Our Colonel's specific mission views were disseminated down through the ranks by the NCOs, who guided us through each day, never letting us forget why we were there. This, of course, kept us focused and allowed us to feel confident in all of our training.

When we met in a group, the theme of the Colonel's message was always the same: "If the balloon goes up," he would say, "they will come over the line to try to kill us." And they would be coming through the infamous Fulda Gap.

He would always finish the conversation by saying, "We will hold until relieved. Blood and Guts." This, of course, was a necessary attitude and our motto in April 1969.

I had asked Bernie how the "Blood and Guts" motto had come into practice. He told me that the idea was the Colonel's but it may have had its start from the days when General George Patton had made quite a few flamboyant speeches during his rise to stardom.

Figure 12 - 1st/48th Coat of Arms

The movie "Patton", made in 1970, and starring George C. Scott as Patton, had a scene in which two GIs were watching Patton drive by on a crowded road full of tanks and trucks on their way to the front lines. One soldier said to the other, "There goes old Blood and Guts himself." The other guy said, "Yeah. Our blood and his guts." We said, "Blood and Guts" to each other to remind us why we were here and what would be required to block an invasion.

"You are quite the historian," I said to Bernie. "Where is all of this information coming from?"

"Last year I met this guy in Bravo Company named Martin

Milco. He rotated out last month but he showed me what he had written down about the events during his tour. It was a pretty interesting read. Basically, Milco said that most members of the 6th Artillery and the 33rd Armor Battalions laughed at our open display of the Brigade crest, and our "Blood & Guts" motto displayed on our infantry blue ascots. But since the 1st/48th INF was better than pretty much anyone else at everything during this time period, especially in sports and combat training, we didn't care if they laughed at us.

Milco also said that the regimental crest with the "Blood and Guts" tab was instituted during his tenure. They were told that there would be plenty of blood and guts in the "Gap". So, to instill maximum unit cohesion, the Colonel directed that all salutes be exchanged with a verbal address of "Blood and Guts". Wolfgang Fischer's tailor shop stocked the logo word patches, and they were sewn beneath the regimental crest on our infantry blue ascots."

I later learned that the 48th Infantry Coat of Arms[82] consists of a shield and crest. A lion rampant in gold represents the organization's actions in the Ardennes and at St. Vith, for which it was cited twice in the Order of the Day of the Belgian Army[83].

After this last alert, because we did move the tracks out of the vehicle park, we would be spared a long walk around the Kinzig River Valley. On several occasions, when the alert would be terminated without any vehicles leaving the Kaserne, and while the other units went to breakfast, our Colonel would take us, on foot, to

---

[82]   The unit crest of the 48th Infantry designated the unit as Dragoons. National Guard units serving in the First World War and Armored Infantry Battalions of the U.S. 7th Armored Division served in World War II. The 48th Armored Infantry Battalion, the 1st Battalion 40th Armor, fought a tough battle in Vielsalm, Belgium, holding off the German V Panzer Corps for three days at the crossing of the Salm River, during the German Ardennes Offensive (also known as Battle of the Bulge).

[83]   The wavy chevron in the top left is the recognition of the former

members of the 519th Port Battalion. Belgian Army's 1946 Order of the Day was an official thank you for the Americans who served in Belgium during WWII.

the various points of interest outside the city limits of Gelnhausen.

"If a flight of Soviet MiG aircraft came in unannounced and destroyed some or most of our vehicles in a surprise attack we would have to beat feet to the EDP[84]," the Colonel informed us. This was one of the reasons why he wanted to get RedEye deployed as soon as possible. It was also why I would later recommend moving four of the RedEye missiles to the HHC Arms Room from the base ammo bunker. To modify a recent quote: "You never need a missile until you really need a missile."

STAFFING FOR SUCCESS—MOVING ON UP
1325 HOURS TUESDAY 8 APRIL 1969

Bernie told me at dinner that Bumpus was going to surprise me with a promotion to SPC4. Most everyone driving the management around was being paid at the E4 level. This was indeed good news because it meant a $69.30 a month raise in pay.

As a PFC, I was making $155.10 per month plus a personal living expense of sixty bucks for a grand total of $225.10. As an SPC4, base pay would increase to $224.20 with a personal living expense just over seventy bucks. It was time to buy a car. I made a mental note to write to SFC Burlap back at the 6th CAV to see if he had any friends in Germany who had a car for sale.

The German family who ran the laundry and tailor services on post would sell the new rank insignias and sew them on our uniforms -- in my case, each of my Class A[85] and fatigue uniforms. By this time, I had acquired several sets of work clothes, most inherited from the guys rotating back to the "US of A." Tailoring made everything look and feel better. I was really starting to enjoy being a soldier.

---

84   Emergency Deployment Position

85   The U.S. Army service uniform is the military uniform worn by personnel in situations where formal dress is called for. It is worn in most workday situations in which business dress would be called for, while the Army Combat Uniform is used in combat situations. It can be worn at most public and official functions.

REDEYE: NEVER LEAVE BASE WITHOUT IT!
1045 HOURS WEDNESDAY 9 APRIL 1969

I was in the motor pool getting a wheel bearing packed on the left rear side of the First Sergeant's ride when a Sergeant Burgraff called my name from the office door located at the rear of the lift bay.

"First Sergeant Bumpus called. Said you need to report to the Battalion S-3, Spec5 Blubaugh, at 1100 hours. Don't be late is the important part." He had yelled out this entire war plan over the multiple engine noises being created in this rather small workspace.

"OK, Tom. Thanks." I decided to leave the jeep in the bay with the wheel off and finish it up later.

I made my way across the tarmac, continued through the track park and headed around the pond to the Battalion HQ building. I entered the lobby and took the stairs up to the second level. Newly promoted Spec5 Carl Blubaugh, the S3 Clerk, was seated behind his desk in the outer area of the S-3 section.

"Hey Carl, Bumpus sent word for me to meet you here at 1100 hours."

Carl looked up with his ever-present smile and whispered. "Yeah, Captain Beck received word that the RedEye is being delivered today and they want you on hand at the AD[86] when they arrive. Give me a minute and I'll get you in to see Beck so he can tell you how he wants to handle the delivery. Grab a cup of joe and a seat, and I'll be right back."

My ass had barely hit the chair when CSM Bost came out of Captain Beck's office and told me to follow him down the hallway. Turns out most of the offices on this side of the building had connecting doorways.

On my way out Carl shrugged his shoulders as if to say, "*I don't have a clue.*" CSM Bost walked briskly down the hall and turned left into a large meeting area, which doubled as a map room. There was a large conference table with over a dozen chairs arranged around it. I was told to take a seat.

Bost left for a few minutes and returned with his arms full of folders, manuals, and our Battalion CO, LTC Brogan, following immediately behind. I started to jump up when I saw him come in

---

[86] Ammo Dump

the room, but was quickly told, "As you were," which meant to remain seated.

"We're pretty informal in here. Blubaugh told me that you're our resident RedEye expert," said Brogan. The situation required a moment before I found my voice.

"Sir, I've had the General Dynamics hands-on course taught at Fort Bliss, and I have studied the AR on deployment and staffing, but I'm no expert, Colonel."

"Well, you damn sure know more about this weapon than anyone here, so what I want you to do is head up the reception committee this afternoon when the missiles arrive. You OK with that?"

"Yes, Sir... how can I help?"

"Staff Sergeant Kirtwin from the HHC Arms Room will meet you at the entrance to the ammunition dump at 1530 hours today. Do you know where it is?"

"Yes, Colonel, First Sergeant Bumpus took me there last week after the alert."

"Good. Staff Sergeant Summering, the S-4, will also be on hand. You need to make the point that we need a secure storage location with immediate access capability. The closer to the main access gate the better and the bunker selected should be cool and dry. Is that clear?"

"Yes, Sir. Clear."

"Also, the type of transport to be used during operations hasn't been decided yet, but the loading and unloading of the weapons should be considered with the types of vehicles available. You have anything to add to that, David?"

"Fontain, you need to sketch out for me what you and Sergeant Summering come up with. Tomorrow, at 1300, report back to Captain Beck's office."

"Yes, Command Sergeant Major."

Bost continued, "I've read through some of the AR and this other crap but it led to more questions than before I started. For example, should there be two- or three-man teams? How many teams are required? Are the teams deployed inside or outside a convoy and/or formation? Those are just a few that came to mind."

"Command Sergeant Major, we always trained in two-man teams, one to spot and track a target, and one shooter. But in a combat situation it will be necessary to move from the firing position as quickly as possible after launch. Therefore, depending on the type of transport assigned, a third team member may be required to drive.

"The ARs I've seen don't offer any suggestions on vehicle types nor do they contain any field deployment logistics in any detail," I said with a certain air of confidence.

"Do you have any recommendation for the type of vehicle in which RedEye should be deployed?"

"Yes, Sergeant Major. Actually, a combination of two types of vehicles would work best. APCs could be deployed as outriders in static situations, and jeeps with trailers could protect inside a moving convoy."

Colonel Brogan spoke to Bost next. "It appears Blubaugh was right. He will be able to find his ass with both hands." He then turned to address me. "You're dismissed, son. Thanks for helping out with this project."

"Yes, Sir. Thank you, Sir," I said with some enthusiasm as I stood, saluted, did an about face and left the room.

BATTALION HQ 2ND FLOOR CONFERENCE AREA
1300 HOURS WEDNESDAY 9 APRIL 1969

I had cornered Carl at the EM club the night before. "What in the hell have you got me into? Bost indicated that if things did not work smoothly, there would be a human sacrifice in my immediate future."

Carl laughed and said, "Look at the bright side. If a MiG lights up the Colonel's command track and you're able to frighten it away with your little missile, you'll be considered a real hero."

"Really, what do you know that you're not telling me?"

"After you left yesterday to go to the Ammo Dump, I overheard Bost tell Beck, 'Fontain will be the go-to guy to get this RedEye shit off the dime. Our friends from Virginia are due in any time and the Colonel wants this project to go off without a hitch.'"

"What friends from Virginia?"

"Lieutenant Wirth, our S-2 and S-6, says that there's a CIA project request being channeled through Division that includes RedEye expertise."

"Fantastic," I said.

"I'm supposed to tell you to be in Battalion HQ tomorrow at

1300 to answer some logistics questions."

"Great...."

"It is great. You produce, and you get promoted."

"I just got promoted."

"Look, all I'm saying is that if you contribute to a plan for this RedEye weapon, and it goes smoothly, you'll get rewarded. Bost can promote whoever he wants, whenever he wants."

"Fantastic, and if our track park gets lit up by a Russian Kamikaze I can expect castration followed by execution by firing squad, yes?"

"Relax. You're too low on the food chain to catch any blowback. If something big goes wrong, it'll be an officer who gets blamed."

"Right, see you at the office."

At 1255 I popped out of the stairwell on the second floor as Carl was coming out of the S-3 section.

"You're going to this meeting?" I asked.

"Noooo....It's by invitation only," he replied. I forced a smile and continued down the hallway to the conference area. The room was empty. I checked my watch. It was 1259 hours.

"Fontain, down this way," a voice boomed from the stairway door at the opposite end of the building. I recognized Bost's voice even before I turned to look. As I got near the stairway entrance the CSM said, "We're meeting upstairs." Bost, in spite of his gargantuan size, started climbing the stairs taking two and three at a time. I was puffing a bit by the time I reached the third floor landing. I followed him into a conference room.

Colonel Brogan was seated at the far end of the table, with maps, charts and manuals scattered at various angles in front of him. There were three other officers located around the table: Captain Beck, the S-3; Lieutenant Bob Wirth, the S-2; and... I'll be damned!

It was the mysterious Mister Dobbins from London! His Class-A uniform displayed a rank of major and a name tag bearing the name "Carlstrum".

Brogan looked up as we entered the room and said, "Fontain, how did you make out yesterday with the delivery?"

"Sir, S-4 got us a good spot near the front. But I need to inform you, Sir, before we discuss anything further, that I have met this officer before," I said, pointing at the Major. He told me his name was Dobbins -- not Carlstrum." All the heads in the room turned toward Carlstrum, or whoever he was.

"I told you he was smart," Carlstrum said with a smile. "I tried my best in London to get him to tell me all about his training and where he was stationed. He told me he was not trainable and that he was stationed in Europe."

At that comment, Bost laughed out loud. He leaned back in his chair and said, "Fontain, meet Major Bill Carlstrum, who is here to get our help gathering INTEL[87] on certain Russian aircraft. The Major, in his other life, works for another company of concerned citizens -- if you take my meaning."

"Yes, Sir. No disrespect, Sir, but I wanted to get that fact out upfront." I turned to "Mr. D" and continued. "I gather this meeting was all prearranged?" I asked the question and went on without waiting for an answer. "I reported our London encounter to my Company CO, who I believe is a friend of yours."

"As well you should have," said the Major. "And yes, Captain MacKennia and I served together."

"What did you do, follow me to London, Sir?" I asked the Major.

"No, but I was notified by 3rd Armor that you were going to London. The reason we hooked up was your potential assignment to this project." He waved his arm over the material scattered around the room. "What I'm about to share with you is Top Secret/Sparrow Signature[88]. The Russians have a wide variety of their military aircraft converted for commercial applications."

"We think there is a unique opportunity to update our aircraft recognition database while providing some insight into why some of the Russian engine signatures have changed," added the Major.

"This will provide a good opportunity for a hands-on, up close and personal experience for your new RedEye teams," said the Sergeant Major.

"Sir," I said, looking directly at Colonel Brogan, "this project sounds like it's well suited for RedEye. How would you like us to proceed?"

"Fontain, RedEye has been presented to me as the best available ground to air defense. The keyword here is *available*. The M48

---

[87]   INTEL = Intelligence

[88]   Air Craft Recognition Project program called "Sparrow Signature". Developed jointly by General Dynamics, Lockheed, and Bell Laboratories designed to catalogue infrared (IR) signatures for foreign military aircraft.

Chaparral and the M61 Vulcan systems both can use the M113 APC as a platform, and both provide excellent protection from an air attack. At present we have neither available to us. What we do have is RedEye. For the next several weeks what we are going to do is set up the necessary protocols to integrate RedEye into the Battalion air defense. Clear?"

"Yes, Sir."

"First things first," interjected Sergeant Major Bost. "The CSM asked you for a location sketch of the RedEye Ammo Dump deployment."

"Roger that, Sir," I said as I passed my clipboard sketch that I had drawn up the night before.

"Sir, depending on the type of vehicle used to transport the Redeye, as well as access, loading/unloading and exiting, the AD deployment can be accomplished with a minimal time delay," I added.

Brogan looked down at the sketch and passed it over to Captain Beck, and then to CSM Bost.

"The vehicles that will be used by the RedEye section will be jeeps with trailers. I understand there are five unassigned trailers parked outside HHC and there are five jeeps held in reserve in our motor pool?" asked Brogan.

"Yes, Colonel, that is correct," replied Captain Beck.

"Fontain, go down to the motor pool this afternoon and get the status of these five vehicles and the trailers parked at the HHC. Get their vehicle IDs and get the info to Blubaugh today."

"Yes, Sir."

"Captain MacKennia has been briefed on your equipment requirements. Your First Sergeant will arrange alert room and storage space in the HHC Readiness Alert locker area. Tomorrow, you and Lieutenant Wirth will meet to work out the logistics for this space and how to store your new commo[89] gear," instructed Brogan.

"Yes, Sir," I said again.

Bost held up the clipboard with my sketch. "This will work. In the next couple of weeks you'll get three additional RedEye people from Bliss. The four of you will get the vehicles and equipment ready for deployment."

---

[89] Communication radio equipment

"Yes, Sergeant Major."

Major Carlstrum, aka "Mr. D", spoke next.

"There's a fifth member being assigned to RedEye. His name is Clark. Interesting fellow. Grad student, chemical engineering background, plus expertise in photography. He's due in next Monday, 14 April. He's coming directly from Bliss."

"Is he in the band also, or is he totally in the dark as to what is going on here, Sir?"

The Major ignored my "band" question. "He was drafted out of graduate school, run through basic and AIT, same as you, and assigned to the RedEye program. He's a PFC, born in Illinois, and has a superior IQ."

"So, you have a specific job in mind for him?"

"I suggest you and I get together over this weekend to discuss the potential threat posed by Russian aircraft being utilized in Europe. You should check out the new photo lab recently relocated and made available here from a government group in Heidelberg. I believe it's been installed on the second floor of the base Service Club[90]. Our Mr. Clark will find it a truly fascinating place to practice his hobby," explained Major Carlstrum.

"Yes, Sir, I'll make myself available for that conversation."

"You can take off, Fontain," said Carlstrum. "Get that vehicle information to the S-3 clerk as soon as possible and he'll set up a time and place to meet tomorrow afternoon. Any questions?"

"Several come to mind, Sir, but I'll organize them first."

"Good. You are dismissed."

"Yes, Sir. Thank you, Sir." I stood up and saluted as I said "Blood and Guts." Bost handed me my clipboard and winked at me as I passed by his chair on my way out.

COLEMAN SERVICE CLUB
1630 HOURS WEDNESDAY 9 APRIL 1969

After I had pried the vehicle information away from the

---

[90] In 1974, "Service Clubs" were officially re-designated "Recreation Centers", and the familiar blue uniforms, mandatory hats, heels, and gloves worn by the civilians who staffed the clubs were history.

guardians of the motor pool, the Sergeant in charge told me "good luck" with getting any of them started, much less making them roadworthy. I informed him that he'd need the luck more than I would.

"What do you mean by that?"

"The Colonel told Bost, who told me, to get these five jeeps set up to deploy our new Battalion Air Defense Teams as soon as possible. I suspect anyone who has borrowed any parts and/or caused any damage to these vehicles, making them unable to defend our country, will be executed by firing squad.

"Look, work with me to get a couple of these guys running," I said in my most persuasive voice. "I'll report that the others are down waiting on parts. That will give us a two or three week window to get another one up and running. If not, I guarantee Bost will be down here before you can say 'mess kit repair, Aleutian Islands'."

"Ok, ok...we'll get two up and running by next week, but you're gonna need some way to tackle the paint and the stenciling. I don't have any of that crap down here anymore."

"Thanks, we'll figure that part out ourselves."

When I left the motor pool I walked across the track park, crossed the road at the main gate, and entered the Post Service Club. It was located right inside the main gate, facing Highway 40.

I had noticed the list of Service Club activities posted in our Day Room when I first got here. A Photography Lab was not listed as a service or as an activity. I picked up a new pamphlet from the rack located just inside the main entrance as I entered the building. There was still no mention of a photo lab.

I went up the stairwell to the second floor. I found an older German gentleman coming out of the unmarked door at the end of the hallway.

"Wenn es einen auf diesem Fußboden gelegten Foto-Labor-Raum gibt?" I asked in German. In English I inquired, "Is there a photo lab located on this floor?"

"I'm supposed to ask for your favorite eye color."

"That would be red."

"Yes, yes, Sehr Gut. Please come in." He inserted his key in the lock, pushed the door open and waved me inside.

It turns out that in January there had been an anonymous donation made to Coleman's Service Club, with specific instructions to establish a state-of-the-art photography lab. My tour with the older German man lasted twenty minutes, and it left no doubt in my mind that whatever photo needs were required by RedEye and PFC Clark would be easily satisfied within those walls.

My tour guide went on to relate the story of how he was hired, as well as how all of the equipment was provided by a government group in Heidelberg.

"A German government group," I thought. *"Small world."* What was it that "Mr. D" had said about PFC Clark? *"A chemical engineering background, plus an expertise in photography?"*

When I was walking through the parking lot after leaving the Service Club I saw Captain MacKennia talking to the driver of a 1968 Porsche 912. The driver of the car was Major Carlstrum.

It was the Captain who had made it known to me that "Mr. Dobbins" was not the mystery man's real name. The Major obviously didn't want attention brought to their prior relationship. It was pretty clear that Major Carlstrum didn't want anyone to know his real name was Bill Douglas.

I continued on up the hill to the Battalion S-3 to comply with my orders to provide the vehicle IDs, respective statuses and locations for the new RedEye section's transportation needs.

1ST 48TH HHC
GROUND LEVEL LOCKER & STORAGE AREA
0800 HOURS THURSDAY 10 APRIL 1969

I entered the hallway equipment storage area located just three doors to the right of the Orderly Room. The space being allocated to RedEye was a small 8 X 8 foot storage closet. There were 56 cases of C-rations[91] stacked up on the rear wall from the previous leaseholder. They were all dated March 1943 through June 1946. There were three empty wall lockers, four empty wooden footlockers, two shovels and a push broom.

---

[91]   The C-Ration, or Type C ration, was a canned, pre-cooked, and prepared wet ration. It was intended to be issued to U.S. military land forces when fresh food (A-ration) or packaged, unprepared food (B-Ration) to be prepared in mess halls or field kitchens were impractical or not available.

There was a one-bulb light fixture hanging from the ceiling that was controlled by a pull-chain. Bernie had given me an envelope with four keys inside. He said I could get more if I needed them.

The room assignment turned out to be a blessing from the get-go. Of the five jeeps being assigned to us, only one was drivable and that one would not pass a simple inspection. This lockable secure storage area was just what the doctor ordered. All of the removable jeep parts for all five vehicles could be kept here until the mechanical systems, engines, brakes, and wheel bearings could be put right.

All five vehicles appeared to have been manufactured in the early 1900s. Three of the jeeps had a list of shortcomings as long as my arm; none of them would start. The fifth jeep must have been cannibalized for parts by carnivorous mechanics because the entire passenger seat and its frame were missing. The steering wheel was also missing. And because it was not removed by conventional means, (it had been cut off with a hack saw), other major parts were now required. I promised the maintenance Sergeant that I wouldn't tell the CSM until he had had a chance to research a fix.

Carl Key (2LT S-2/6), who wore several different hats, had not been part of Wednesday's meeting. He had gone to Frankfurt to procure our special radios. There was a knock at the door to the storage area. "Guten Tag, Fontain. I'm Lieutenant Key, Communications. I've got five special radios for you."

PRC-25

"Blood and Guts, Sir. I'm pleased to meet you. You said special radios, Sir?"

"You will have the regular PRC-25's for each jeep, plus a second AN/PRC-77[92] which will provide a ground-to-air link."

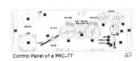

Control Panel of a PRC-77

PRC-77

"Yes, Sir. **T**hank you, Sir. You will forgive me, Sir, but all of this," as I waved my arm around the half-empty room, "is all new to me and a bit confusing."

---

[92]   AN/PRC 77 entered service in 1968 during the Vietnam War as an upgrade to the earlier AN/PRC 25. It differs from its predecessor mainly in that its final power amplifier stage is made up of solid-state components and does not use vacuum tubes.

[93]   77's is a reference to the AN/PRC-77

"Don't worry Fontain," he responded. "In a couple of weeks all of it will become second nature. Bost thinks you'll do well putting this group together, and he's usually right. Anyway, this room will be a good place to secure the radios. Come out to the truck and give us a hand with the 77s[93]."

FLIEGERHORST AIRFIELD KASERNE, HANAU
0700 HOURS SATURDAY 12 APRIL 1969

I got a telephone message via the Orderly Room from Major Carlstrum Friday evening. He was returning to England the next day. He would pick me up at 0630 in front of the HHC.

On Saturday morning I was drinking a cup of coffee in the Orderly Room and talking to Bernie Costa when we heard the double tap of a car horn. I peered through the blinds to see "Mr. D" wave from the driver's side window of the same green Porsche 912 that he'd been driving on Thursday. "There he is, right on time. I'll catch you later," I said as I pulled the door open to leave.

"Play nice."

Neither of us was in uniform. I went around to the passenger side and got in. "Guten Morgen." Major Carlstrum shifted the car into reverse and backed down the entire length of the service drive and out into the main drag facing downhill toward the main gate.

"And how is my favorite Spec4 this beautiful morning? Have you had breakfast yet?"

"No, I usually don't eat before my 5K run on weekends."

"You're kidding?"

"Of course I am. I haven't been able to run very far since I caught a slight cold in basic training."

"You call double pneumonia a slight cold?"

"Sir, who are you really?"

The Major ignored the question. "We're going over to Fliegerhorst Airfield. There's a snack bar there, so we can grab something to eat while we talk."

"Nice ride," I said, admiring the exquisite interior of the 912 sports car.

---

[93] 77's is a reference to the AN/PRC-77

"It belongs to a friend of mine who's here for a conference. Did you know they're using these as police cars in Holland?"

"No shit."

"I want you to drive it back here after we talk. Park it in front of the Service Club, lock it, and put the keys on top of the left front tire."

"Yes, Sir, yes, Sir, three bags full[94]." The comment got me a funny look.

We took a table by the window, which allowed an unobstructed view of the main runway. The waitress came over. "Guten Morgen. What can I get you?"

"Just coffee for me," replied Carlstrum.

"Make that two please, just black." The server went back behind the counter to get our coffee.

"I'm catching a ride on a Huey that should be leaving in the next half hour," Carlstrum said, pointing out the window towards a cluster of gunships parked in the distance.

"Where are you off to -- or is that a secret?"

"The chopper is going to Rhein-Main, and from there I'm going on to London."

"Are you still living with Paul?" I asked, smiling at my wit.

"Paul who?"

"You know -- Abbey Road, Paul McCartney. Did you forget our London excursion?"

Laughing and shaking his head, he said, "I'd forgotten about that. We need to cover some issues before I get called to the flight line. I was assured by your Colonel that we will have carte blanche in setting up your team."

"My team," I repeated, trying not to let the surprise show on my face or in my voice.

"Be on the lookout this week for three PFCs coming in from the Transportation Assignment Center in Frankfurt. Clark should have graduated this past week and will be sent here directly. They're all college graduates and they all, like you, decided not to go the OCS route."

"How did you know I opted out of OCS? Oh, I get it now: it was

---

94   I was repeating words from an 1870 nursery rhyme that starts "Baa, baa, black sheep"

the secret agent and the test scores in Zero Week, right?"

"Not entirely. There were other factors, such as certain personality traits that flagged our interest."

"My homicidal tendencies, or was it just my strong craving for coffee? So, what is it that you want me to do?"

"We need to update the information on certain Russian aircraft being flown into German airspace. There are several types and models of military jets that have been reconfigured for commercial use. They're using them to fly passengers into Western Europe from Russia. In particular, FRA, the Frankfurt Am Main International airport, which is directly across from our very own Rhein-Main. Did you get that pocket notebook I suggested?"

"Yes, Sir, I got four of them. They were 20 cents each at the PX. I'll give one to each of the new guys. I assumed Clark would come armed with his own."

"Why would you assume that?"

"No reason other than I should have bought five notebooks instead of only four."

"Hey, relax. You're very well suited for this type of assignment. You have the exact skill set we need to conduct this operation. I won't be in country when this goes down. You OK with that?" asked the Major.

"I'm good," I answered.

"OK. Write these details down. In three weeks' time your Battalion S-3 will schedule a training mission at Rhein-Main. Your contact will be a guy named Bob Ketter. He's the base Flight Communications Chief. He'll get you onto and off the base. He'll hand deliver a sealed envelope with specific target timetables."

I laughed.

"What's so funny?" asked the Major.

"I was trying to imagine Mr. Ketter without any arms."

Carlstrum ignored the comment. "Ask your Company Clerk to call the Frankfurt switchboard and connect you with Ketter. Call him tomorrow. He expects your call. Three weeks will be Monday, May the 5th. You'll need at least two vehicles ready by then. Any questions?" he asked.

"No, everything is as clear as mud, Sir."

"Look, just concentrate on getting your equipment up to speed. Make sure the new people arrive and get settled in. If there's a problem, see Lieutenant Key. The Lieutenant will also be the one who will release the RedEye trainers for you to take to Rhein-Main.

"The people you are meeting are coming from New Jersey. There will be representatives from Bell Labs, General Dynamics, and the Lockheed Skunk Works."

"That's an impressive technical support group."

"Their service techs will retrofit your RedEye trainers to record infrared and temperature data. But, the trainers will continue to function in the same way as the ones you used in school."

"Ketter will make the introductions and coordinate the set-up. It will be up to you figure out how to get close enough to use them." Carlstrum saw someone waving his arm over his head by one of the choppers parked on the flight line.

"I gotta go. I'll try and check in with you later on next week."

"Is there someone here I can go to if necessary? You know, just in case something goes askew?"

"First, go to Lt. Key. If he isn't available go to your CO, Captain MacKennia. We took a long walk together in Nam."

"Yeah, he mentioned that to me when I was reporting our time together in London. He also told me your real name isn't Dobbins."

"That is not for public consumption. I really don't want George involved in this, so don't go to him unless the Russians are bombing Gelnhausen. Understood?"

"Aye, aye, Sir," I answered.

I watched "Mr. D" run across the tarmac and get in what appeared to be a fairly new gunship. Within seconds it went light on the skids[95] and rose about ten feet off the tarmac. It then followed the main runway until it launched itself into the morning sky, banked to the left and was gone from sight.

I looked down at my opened notebook. I had only the one entry: three weeks, Monday May 5th." I ordered another cup of coffee and spent the next 30 minutes outlining our conversation with as much detail as I could recall.

---

95   Lifted off the runway

X

OPERATION

SPARROW SIGNATURE

THE NEW GUYS
1st/48th INF HHC—COMPANY ORDERLY ROOM
1450 HOURS MONDAY 14 APRIL 1969

Gary Cisewski drove up to the front of the Orderly Room. He was driving a M35 2.5 ton "Deuce and a half" with a canvas top which enclosed the rear cargo area. The front passenger seat was occupied by a slick, blonde-haired kid wearing black-rimmed glasses. His name was Jack Swanson. He was 25 years old, single, and had worked as a radio broadcaster for CBS News out of Chicago before being drafted.

"Jack Swanson," he said, offering an extended hand to me as he stepped down from the truck cab.

"You have a good trip over?"

"Well, the plane didn't crash. Where exactly are we anyway?" We walked together to the rear tailgate.

"You're in the Coleman Kaserne just outside of Gelnhausen, Germany," I replied.

"No shit," said Jack.

"No shit -- we say that a lot around here. We say 'Blood and Guts' a great deal more when we salute."

Gary was already unfastening the safety chains to drop the metal tailgate.

"I'm Rick Fontain, RedEye Tour Guide," I said loud enough for the two passengers riding in the back to look up and hear what I had said.

Their names were Larry Stockert and Von Boyd.

Larry was an athletic looking individual who moved easily from the rear of the truck to the ground. At six feet two inches and 255 pounds, the former college star and All American guard fit every bit of the description detailed in the advanced copy of his 201 file that had arrived a few days ago.

Von Boyd, on the other hand, was of a similar body structure, but appeared to be more of the academic type. His file indicated a set of well-developed management skills. In his former life he had been in management for J.C. Penney, based in Kansas City.

Both Larry and Von were married, and were looking forward to bringing their wives to Gelnhausen as soon as the situation permitted.

Von grabbed one of the three duffel bags and handed it down to Gary and Jack. He snatched the other two and slid them out over the dropped tailgate. I left the bags sitting on the edge of the tailgate until Von had jumped down. We shook hands all around and I ushered them toward the Orderly Room, and an electrifying career on the 1st/48th RedEye team.

THE LAY OF THE LAND
1st/48th INF HHC—5TH FLOOR REDEYE LIVING QUARTERS
1750 HOURS MONDAY 14 APRIL 1969

Bernie excused himself after dinner to check the message center before going off duty. My new team and I finished our meals and took the north stairwell to the fifth floor. Everyone seemed to be in good spirits. First Sergeant Bumpus had issued instructions to rearrange the transportation section, and assigned the entire center bay to our RedEye team. The S-4 organization had been their usual model of efficiency assigning everyone lockers and issuing bedding just one hour after their arrival.

I explained that while there was an extra effort involved in getting up this high in the building, it actually translated to more privacy and less chicken shit. I further emphasized that once they received their Army driver's licenses they would be even further removed from harm's way. The trials and tribulations of being a PFC in today's modern HHC would present enough of a challenge.

"Tomorrow, Bernie has agreed to personally walk you through the S-4 shop and get you issued your alert paraphernalia. The S-4 warehouse is located just off the main road that runs in front of this building. The web gear and some of the all-weather clothing can be stored on the first floor RedEye team room."

I handed each one of them a key. "Bring the whole kit and caboodle back here and I'll show you the best way to clip everything together. In the next couple of weeks we have been charged with an assignment to make ready five vehicles and trailers for use in the deployment of RedEye.

"Last week we received twenty-eight missiles which I personally helped carry into an underground containment shelter in our Ammo Dump. That bunker isn't located miles from here. It's only 300 yards up the road that runs past this building.

"You will figure this out for yourselves as time goes by, but don't become complacent just because you didn't wind up in Vietnam. There are people 65 miles from here who are trained to come and kill you. Our job will be to protect this Battalion from being strafed by that enemy."

I let that announcement sink in for a moment before continuing. "There are two training simulators that came with the RedEye shipment. We will move those trainers to our team room downstairs as soon as we accomplish our more immediate transportation assignment," I said. "We'll spend a lot of time practicing with them."

"Once our vehicles are certified roadworthy we will then begin training to protect this base and any convoy we are assigned. As you already know, RedEye is a great weapons system. All we need to do is figure out who to shoot and when to pull the trigger."

I paused and looked around the room. "Do you have any questions or comments? No, well if you think of anything, I'll be in the room at the end of this hallway. Last door on the right. I'm bunking in the same room with Costa."

I didn't think any additional information was warranted at this time. Major Carlstrum had said not to discuss the special mission with anyone. I started to leave the area but turned back to face the group.

"After we have breakfast tomorrow we'll walk the Coleman campus and get you acclimated to where everything is. After you get back from the S-4 I'll take you down to the motor pool and introduce you around. They seem to be a pretty competent bunch of mechanics, but I suspect there will be some difficulty in acquiring the material we need and negotiating their time to get the vehicles drivable."

"These assigned vehicles. Are they in really bad shape?" asked Jack.

"Yes, they are. There isn't a whole lot we can do about the parts availability, but establishing relationships with the people who perform the maintenance function will determine our success in the completion of this first project.

"I'm really glad you guys are assigned here. I know it's too early for you to have formed an opinion of this assignment, but take it from me -- this is an exceptional place to work. There are truly some really shitty places you could have been sent." I paused and looked at each face looking back at me before I said, "Good night." I turned and walked down the hall, but paused in the shadows when I heard Jack Swanson's voice.

"I was talking to the driver on the way out here and he told me that our new fearless leader, Fontain, is a standup guy who's well connected. He said the word going around is that he has a *rabbi*, whatever that means," Jack said.

"What do you think he was doing before we got here?" Von asked of the others.

"I don't know, but I think we can count on a fair deal from that one," Larry said. "He seems pretty capable."

"Yes he certainly does. That one's a front-runner, I think," said Von. "I'm going to grab a shower."

I quickly and quietly continued down the hall.

139

THE MYSTERIOUS MR. CLARK
1st/48th INF HHC—COMPANY ORDERLY ROOM
1430 HOURS MONDAY 22 APRIL 1969

Jack Swanson and I were leaning over a topo[96] map spread out on the hood of Redeye "Jeep One" on which the freshly stenciled bumper lettering **1/48 RE-1** was still drying. The map was a detailed elevation graphic depicting the runway system at Rhein-Main Air Force Base.

A double tap of its horn announced the arrival of a military police vehicle. Jack and I turned to look as the jeep pulled into the company area and stopped directly in front of the HHC Orderly Room.

The staff sergeant in the passenger seat stepped out onto the concrete as soon as the vehicle came to a stop. He grabbed the top edge of the seat and pulled it forward to allow the traveler seated in the back to get out. A PFC in a Class "A" uniform, displaying a slender build and wearing thick, black-rimmed glasses, emerged from the jeep.

"This must be the renowned Mr. Clark," I supposed.

"Jack, excuse me for a minute," I said, and pointed to each end of the drawing. "Check the map scale with the distances here, and here, and make a notation in the corner of the map here," I placed my finger on the upper right margin.

"You going to tell me why we're looking at an air force runway layout?" asked Jack.

"Not right now," I said, and walked to where the military police vehicle was parked.

Clark, Kenneth's mini 201 file described a man with an IQ of 162. He had worked as a PhD research assistant at Dartmouth College until he'd been drafted three months previously. His training consisted of basic and AIT training at Fort Dix, New Jersey, and he had received his Redeye electronics overview at Fort Bliss, Texas and the White Sands testing facility. He had not been allowed

---

[96]   A topographic map is a type of chart characterized by large-scale detail, depicting surface areas with contour lines. A topographic diagram shows both natural and man-made features.

any leave since being inducted.

His special skills included chemistry and high-speed photo electronics -- which meant he was expert at taking pictures and processing the film. I walked briskly toward the Orderly Room so I could get a better look at his name tag. Sure enough, the name "CLARK" was etched in white lettering on the black plate that was pinned atop his uniform pocket.

I offered my hand as I introduced myself, and guided him through the open door of the Orderly Room. I then went back and helped the SPEC4 driver get Clark's duffel bag out of the back seat. I thanked the Staff Sergeant for bringing Clark all the way up from Frankfurt. I hefted the duffel bag onto my shoulder and returned to the office.

He was almost standing at attention in front of Costa's countertop workstation when I re-entered with his bag.

"Kenneth, relax and stand easy," said Costa. "I just want to do a quick check of your orders and the seal on the 201 file label."

"Rick, this is PFC Clark, whom I understand you were expecting."

"Yes, we were," I said as Clark turned to see who had come into the room. "We just met out front. I'll put your bag right here against the wall."

"Thanks," said PFC Clark.

"Did you have to wait long at the Replacement Company in Frankfurt?" I asked.

"No, I didn't. They met my plane when it landed, got my bag out of the baggage compartment, then brought me straight here."

"Oh, how was Rhein-Main this time of day? Jam-packed, I bet."

"I don't know, I came in on a commercial flight to Frankfurt International," he replied.

"No shit. Well for now, we'll just keep that piece of travel information between us, if that's okay with you?"

"Sure. I was told to report to a Spec4 Fontain, to keep my mouth shut and he would take care of the rest," said Clark, and then blurted out, "When do we get to shoot the Russians?"

Bernie's head popped up at that moment. He had undoubtedly heard the remark. I made immediate eye contact with him and shook my head slightly from side to side, signaling for him to ignore the comment. Bernie acknowledged with a nod. He went back to examining the documents.

"I don't think I have ever seen a DDCI[97] authority on assignment orders before," he then exclaimed.

"Yes, you have Bernie. DDCI was prominently displayed at the top of my PCS[98] order that sent me to the 3AD. Mr. Clark has brought to us several talents that will ensure the final victory." I then asked if the First Sergeant was around.

"Yeah, he's in with the CO. Is that other bunch of paper for me, Private?" asked Bernie, pointing at the manila envelope tucked under Clark's arm.

"No, Sir," replied Clark.

"I'm Specialist Costa, or just plain Bernie. Don't "Sir" me -- I work for a living."

The door to the CO's office opened and the First Sergeant and Captain MacKennia walked out. Both welcomed Clark into an exciting career in the 1st/48th Headquarter and Headquarters Company. Captain MacKennia told Clark he was a welcome addition and was very glad to have him onboard.

First Sergeant Bumpus told me to take Clark up to where the RedEye section was housed. Bernie came around the counter and offered to help him with his duffel bag.

"Thanks, Bernie, but I'll take him up," I offered.

On the way up the stairs, Clark handed me the envelope. "An MP pulled up to the boarding stairs and made me sign for that before I got on the aircraft to come here. It's addressed to you."

I showed Ken where he would be living and where to get his sheets, blankets, and pillowcases. Next, I walked him back downstairs to the RedEye team room.

"Take this key and put it on your dog tag chain. There's a lot of expensive equipment and some sensitive documents kept in here, so always lock up when you leave the room."

"Yes, S__." He stopped himself from saying "Sir". "OK," replied PFC Clark.

While we were still alone, I cautioned him about only discussing assignment information and our handler, Major Carlstrum, with me.

"Yes S__. Right," he responded. "Handler?"

"What would you call him?"

---

[97] The Deputy Director of Central Intelligence (DDCI) is the United States government office of the Central Intelligence Agency. The DDNI reports only to the DDCI and the President of the United States.

[98] Permanent Change of Station

"Spooky, I guess," replied Clark.

"Yeah, you're right. And from now on we refer to the Major as *Spooky I Guess.*"

The manila envelope Clark had carried with him from the States had my name neatly typed on the label. I pulled the tape off the flap and opened it. Inside were two typewritten sheets of paper.

The first was a memo from someone named Joe Wilson, and the second was a copy of a travel authorization order with a list of names, a date and time of arrival, and a tentative departure schedule.

4/18/1969
To: Spec4 Rick Fontain
                    From: Joe Wilson
Re: Operation Sparrow View

Attached is a copy of EXORD# 69-771455, which authorizes civilian travel on government aircraft and the participation in OP Sparrow View on 5 May 1969. No alternate date will be considered.

Your Rhein Main AB contact: CWO Bob Ketter, Chief FLT OP Supervisor PFC K. Clark will inspect photo lab & all camera equipment upon arrival.

Any equipment or logistics problems will be reported to your S-3 for referral to this DESK.—Joe Wilson, DHIC - Europe

---

Figure 13 - Joe Wilson Memo

Jack Swanson came into the room.

"Meet Ken Clark, RedEye gunner extraordinaire," I said. They shook hands. Jack went to the wall locker and replaced the map case back with the others.

"Clark is coming in from Bliss and has been assigned to our merry band of warriors."

"Cool. You married Ken?"

"No. Why do you ask?'

"I was just thinking. Make sure you get protection before you go downtown."

"What's that supposed to mean? Protection? Protection from what?" Ken asked in a slightly concerned tone.

"Do you smoke cigarettes and drink hard liquor, Ken?"

"No. Why are you asking me all of these questions?"

"Well, first let me say I do smoke and drink, and my roommates upstairs are moving out soon. I thought we could share a hobby."

"Smoking and drinking is a hobby?"

"How long you been in the Army, Mr. Clark?"

"Five months, three days, thirteen hours and," he looked at his watch, "12 minutes."

"On second thought, I think I will prefer you as a sober companion."

"Jesus, Jack, give Ken a few days to get settled before you reveal the fact that you're insane," I suggested.

"What did you decide about the jeep?" asked Jack.

"Leave the jeep parked right where it is. Top -- that's Bumpus, Ken -- said the duty NCO will need it to run the updated code books up the hill. It also has become common knowledge that we are in possession of one of the few vehicles with a legitimate trip ticket[99]. If he needs to go off the post later this evening he'll be all set."

"How about you walk Mr. Clark. . ." I started to say.

"Call me Ken."

"How about you walk Ken down the hill and give him the lay of the land and stop by the motor pool to see if Larry and Von have made any progress on RE-2. I'm going over to S-3 and report Ken's arrival. We'll meet back here at 1600. That's 4PM Jack. OK?"

"Very funny," replied Jack.

"Hey, I just didn't want you to have to take your shoes off again to figure it out."

THE PLOT THICKENS
1st/48th INF S-3 SECTION—2ND FLOOR BATTALION HQ
1450 HOURS MONDAY 28 APRIL 1969

---

[99] This regulation describes Department of the Army (DA) policy, responsibilities, and procedures to safeguard and preserve Army safety in the operations of vehicle transportation.

"Hey, Carl," I said as I entered the S-3 office located on the second floor of the Battalion HQ. "Is Captain Beck in his office?"

"No, he and Colonel Brogan are both away."

"Please tell him when he returns that the man we were expecting has arrived. His name is Clark."

"Will do," replied Carl. "Beck said you requested this from the safe," he said as he handed me a sealed eight and a half-inch by eleven-inch envelope marked *Project: Sparrow View*.

"Can I keep this or should I read it and leave it here?"

"I guess it's yours to keep. He didn't say one way or another."

"Can I use the conference room for a few minutes?"

16 April 1969

Rick,

I can't be there on the 5th. You are meeting with our guy, Bob Ketter, at Rhein-Main AB. If you haven't made contact, do so immediately. Most of the special guests you haven't met, but one you have.

This project is important, so get it right on the first go-round. The folder included with this will detail contacts, dates and times. The people attending request that the date not be changed.

Get Clark to check out the new photo lab and camera equipment. Go to Lt. Key if you have any problem. I know you can pull this off. Good luck.

BD

Figure 14 - Note from Bill Douglas

"Sure, there's nobody in there."

I took the seat nearest the door and pulled the sticky tape off the flap and unwound the string around the fastener. There were six sheets of paper stapled together. The top sheet was a hand written note from Major Carlstrum, aka *Spooky I Guess*. It was dated two weeks prior to the one that Clark had hand carried.

"B and D" were the initials at the bottom of the handwritten note. Captain MacKennia had told me Carlstrum's real name was Bill Douglas.

"*Interesting,*" I muttered to myself as I read the note.

I left the Battalion HQ and headed over to the company area. Von and Larry were in the parking lot with our latest jeep resurrection. They were adding the ID markings to the front bumper.

"Hey, guys," I said as I walked up to the rear of the vehicle.

"We finally got the wheel bearings installed this afternoon," said Larry.

"After we do these stencils we'll be able to get the trip ticket authorized," Von said with a bit of pride in his voice.

"Good job," I said. "Where's Jack hiding? I sent him and the new guy down your way."

"Jack and the S-4 Sergeant are on the phone with the Division maintenance guy trying to requisition a seat and a steering wheel," replied Larry. "The new guy walked over to the Service Club. He said something about a photo lab."

Von added, "We also found out that to stay warm in these damn things you need heater hoses, a 48-voltS motor attached to an enclosed radiator with a squirrel cage fan box mounted between the seats, and several non-standard engine block fittings."

"I'll vote for staying warm."

"Good, because the cost for each jeep will be 38 U.S. dollars," replied Von.

"Well, let's have a meeting with everyone to see what they think."

"Already did," said Larry. "Everybody is willing. Even the new guy Clark said he was in."

"Great. Count me in, too. Where do we get the parts?"

"You don't want to know," replied Von.

"What prompted all this research?"

"Larry hates the cold, and one of the line company grunts was regaling him with stories of jeep drivers freezing to death with a dreaded disease called *blueballs.*"

"When Jack gets back we need to have a quick meeting with everyone, either before or right after dinner."

Von reiterated, "Everyone is onboard with this."

"We need to meet about the off-post exercise scheduled for the fifth. The heaters are fine with me. Do it."

"I'll ride down after we finish this and get the latest status on jeeps 3 and 4. I'll stop at the S-4 on the way back and let Jack know about the meeting."

"Thanks, Von."

THE GANG'S ALL HERE
BASE EM CLUB
1950 HOURS MONDAY 28 APRIL 1969

It wasn't as nice as the club in Heidelberg, but the décor was modern and it was stylishly furnished. I hadn't been in our EM Club since it had been renovated the previous month. The beer had always been a plus. It was locally brewed and was shamelessly offered at 15 cents a glass or 75 cents per pitcher.

There was a bar that extended down the entire left side of the room. A raised stage was centered at the rear of the hall. There were both rectangular and round tables evenly spaced throughout. All had been set up with black and red tabletops containing a well-stocked condiment caddy.

The entire room was done in a ceramic tile that encircled the full outer edges, as well as several access paths to the center of the room. We chose one of the round tables in the center. I told everyone to grab a seat and I went up to the bar and asked for a pitcher and five mugs.

When I returned with the drinks everyone but Clark was engaged in conversation. He seemed to be preoccupied with something. I poured the first round. Jack sprang for the second.

I tried to keep the conversation upbeat and casual. Most of it centered on what had been accomplished since they had arrived. I told them about the exercise to take place at Rhein-Main on the fifth of May.

I told Von and Larry that First Sergeant Bumpus (Top) had given his blessing about them being allowed to live off-post. They told me they were counting the days until their wives would be able to join them. Unfortunately, the entire financial responsibility for this to happen would fall completely on them.

We left the club after the second round and headed back up the hill. Von, Larry, and Jack were walking three abreast in front, and Ken and I hung back slightly.

"You seem kind of quiet tonight, Ken. Is everything OK?"

"I left the States is a real hurry. I didn't have much time to put things in order before leaving. I haven't been home since I was inducted. It's my Mom. Her letter today said she was having some medical issues. I'm more than a little worried."

147

"Ken, in the future when you have a problem please come to me as soon as possible. I'll see what can be done about getting a call set up so you can talk with her. Just hang in there until I talk to the CO. If your Mom needs help, we have people stateside who work for the Major who we can contact. Hell, I can even call my Mom and ask her to help if needed."

"Thanks. That's very kind of you," replied Ken.

"I'll check with Top to find the fastest way to set up a call as soon as I get back to my bunk. OK?"

"Yeah, talking to her would at least let me understand the health issues she's facing."

"I'll come by the Redeye bay and tell you what he suggests about the best way to set up a call."

Bernie wasn't in his room. Sometimes he stayed out overnight, so I scribbled a note on his pad and told him to find me in the morning. I went and told Ken, took a quick shower and turned in for the night.

THE DEUTSCHE BUNDESPOST
DOWNTOWN GELNHAUSEN
0950 HOURS (1550 CHICAGO TIME)
WEDNESDAY 30 APRIL 1969

The post office, it turned out, was the only venue available to quickly place an international call.

I was waiting outside in our newly resurrected RE-3 as Clark exited the building.

"How did the call go?"

"Great. She sounded good. She said the doctor has her on new medicine, so she's feeling much better. I gave her the emergency contact number that Captain MacKennia got from the States. Thanks so much for setting this up. You don't know how relieved I am."

"Ken we all care for each other here. Let's go get ready to stalk some airplanes."

MOTOR POOL, TRACK PARK
COLEMAN KASERNE
1045 HOURS WEDNESDAY 30 APRIL 1969

Clark and I drove directly back to Coleman. We passed through the main gate and made a slight right turn onto the track tarmacadam[100]. I drove RE-3 slowly into the motor pool area at the far end of the Track Park.

"Oh, this doesn't look good. It appears Jeep Number One has a problem." Larry was lying on the ground with his head looking up in the right front fender area of the engine compartment.

"Hey, Larry, how's it going? Do we have a problem with RE-1?"

"She's leaking like a sieve. Sergeant Carson says the head is probably warped," Larry replied. "There's more bad news, RE-4 is still waiting on parts; probably another two to three weeks. And the really bad news is that RE-5 may have to be completely scrapped. Carson said the S-4 lieutenant has referred it to Division procurement for a verdict."

"That does indeed sound bad. Where are Jack and Von?"

"They took RE-2 up to the Company area to re-stencil the IDs on the bumpers. It seems our cardboard stencils didn't have the correct spacing. They also said that the First Sergeant Bumpus wanted our trailers rearranged and parked at the far end of the driveway. Are we going to need any trailers for our trip to Rhein-Main?"

"Yes we are. We're taking both training trackers. If we only have two jeeps then I guess we'll only be pulling two of the trailers."

"Rick, I'm going to walk across to the photo lab and see how Herr Schmidt is doing with the packaging of the bulk film," interrupted Ken.

"Okay. I'll stay here and give Larry a lift back to the Company. Let me know if you run into any problems over there."

After Ken walked away, Larry asked, "What's with the bulk film?"

"We're going to take lots of pictures on our field trip to Rhein-Main on the fifth."

---

[100] Pavement constructed by spraying or pouring a tar binder over layers of crushed stone and then rolling

"Is Ken's Mom doing OK?"

"Affirmative. She's doing much better according to Ken. He seemed really relieved after speaking with her."

We drove out of the motor pool and ran into Clark, who was on his way back up to the Company area. We parked at the far end of the HHC driveway in front of the newly painted and stenciled RE-2.

I noticed the door to the RedEye team room was open as we drove past the alert locker and team room hallway. When we walked in, Jack and Von were seated at a small table recently liberated from a storage shed in the Ammo Dump. Bernie had found us the six folding chairs rescued from the recent EM Service Club renovation, five of which were arranged at various angles around the small room. It was crowded, but it was all ours.

"Gentleman," I said, and slid sideways into one of the chairs, "the moment you have been waiting for has arrived."

"The war is over. We're being discharged," said Jack in his best imitation of David Brinkley[101].

"No, not exactly, Jack. Will you pull the Rhein-Main AFB map out of the locker please? This operation will be right up our alley."

---

[101] David McClure Brinkley was an American newscaster for NBC and ABC in a career lasting from 1943 to 1997. From 1956 through 1970, he co-anchored NBC's top-rated nightly news program, The Huntley–Brinkley Report".

XI

PHOTO OP

RHEIN-MAIN AIR BASE

435TH TACTICAL AIRLIFT WING
BUILDING 692—THE OLD BASE HOTEL NEAR THE FRONT GATE
0645 HOURS MONDAY 5 MAY 1969

We had left Coleman at 0515. Traffic had been light, and the directions given to us by the newly promoted First Lieutenant Carl Key had been right on the money. As we pulled into the main gate of Rhine Main a military policeman emerged from his lair to greet us. As I handed him our clipboard with our trip tick paper work he greeted us in a very friendly manner.

"Welcome to Rhine Main Gentleman. Is that vehicle part of your team?" he asked and nodded towards our other jeep.

"Yes Sergeant it is. Can you point us to base coffee shop?"

"Go three blocks down turn left. It will be on your right just this side of the movie theater."

"Thanks. Take off Jack," I ordered and extended my arm out the passenger side to signal for RE-3 to follow us. The coffee shop was where Bob Ketter had suggested we meet. He was the base communications officer and the chief of operations for the 435th Tactical Airlift Wing.

I spotted an empty table near the rear of the shop as we came in. I told everyone to grab a seat. I used the courtesy phone on the wall to dial an extension number that was included in the briefing document generated by Bill Douglas. Larry and Von went to the counter to get coffee for everybody.

I had just taken my first sip when in walked a guy in his early to mid-thirties wearing a baseball cap, flight jacket and sun glasses. It was still dark outside. Even though the room was fairly crowded with pilots and crewman, he walked directly over to us.

"Hi," he said. "Which of you is Fontain?"

I raised my index finger on my right hand, which was wrapped around my coffee cup. "Guilty….," I replied.

"Any trouble getting on base?"

"No, I just showed him our trip ticket and our stash of guided missiles and the nice man waved us right in."

"You're kidding, right?" queried our unintroduced contact.

"No, he seemed like a very nice man," I replied.

"Humm….well good, when you finish your coffee we'll drive over to Building 549. Your friends arrived about 20 minutes ago."

"And you are?" I inquired.

"Ketter, Bob. I've been assigned as your tour guide and get out of jail free card should things get exciting as the day progresses."

All the heads at the table, as if on cue, turned at the same time to look at me.

RHEIN-MAIN AIR BASE
BUILDING 549—HANGAR COMPLEX
0710 HOURS MONDAY 5 MAY 1969

We had brought the only two working vehicles with us that morning. The trailers contained the two RedEye teaching trackers that were stored snuggly in their all-aluminum, watertight carrying cases. These were, of course, the exact same type of cases used for

152

the actual Redeye weapon system.

There was something not quite right about this operation. Being granted access to an airport with two ground-to-air missile simulators in our possession was causing me to be suspicious of our host. We followed Ketter in his own POV[102] to building 549. He sounded his horn and the left side hangar door was rolled back so we could drive right in.

Once the doors were shut, the overhead lights came on. We were inside what appeared to be a hangar maintenance area. Ketter told everyone to remain where they were for the moment and for me to follow him upstairs to the mezzanine level.

"Can we set up and test our trainers in here while I'm upstairs with you?"

"Sure thing, but everyone must stay in this part of the hangar. There are armed guards at all of the exits and there are certain areas in here that you aren't cleared for."

"You heard the man. Hang tight," I said to the team at full-volume. I then went over to RE-3 and leaned in the passenger side. I spoke in a soft voice so I wouldn't be heard outside the vehicle.

"Jack, get the trackers out of the trailers. Use those tables." I pointed to four tables set up directly across from where we were parked. "Watch them closely. Don't let them out of your sight."

"You are going to tell me why, yes? Or would that just scare the shit out of me?" asked Jack.

"Just don't take your eyes off of them, OK?"

I followed Ketter up the stairs to the mezzanine floor. We entered what appeared to be an electronics workshop with workbenches, meters, and soldering irons scattered throughout. We walked to the back of the room and into a small conference area. A civilian, a man in a leather flight jacket, burst out, "Well, look who it is. It's been some time since we met. Do you remember me?"

He looked familiar, and then I remembered him and, more importantly, where I had met him.

"Yes, Sir. It has been awhile. Have you come to collect for the aircraft?"

Ketter turned his head to hear the response to that comment.

"Hell, no," he exclaimed, and extended his hand. "I suggested we start shooting down one drone every class but they said it was too

---

102   Privately owned vehicle

dangerous." He was the General Dynamics manufacturing representative in charge on the day I shot down his very expensive drone jet aircraft at Fort Bliss.

Introductions were exchanged all around the table. Bob Ketter did not offer his name to anyone in the room. My guess: he was probably in the band[103] and didn't have a name to offer.

There were three other civilians: Don Coover and Les Baxter, both with Bell Labs, and Roger "Kelly" Johnston, Chief Engineer at Lockheed's Skunk Works. LTC Milision, USAF, turned out to be the pilot in command of the giant aircraft that was parked out front.

I was feeling a little better about this operation. These civilian personnel apparently had enough pull for an assigned airplane and a LTC to fly them from New Jersey to Frankfurt. I would have remained in a guarded condition had I not met the General Dynamics guy previously. I took a seat on the far side of the table facing the door. The 1911 45 ACP stashed in the small of my back was decidedly uncomfortable.

The man from General Dynamics, Barry Flax, was the VP and R and D section lead for RedEye. Barry continued, "This young man scored a perfect hit on one of our aircraft during a live fire exercise last year."

Ketter took a seat next to me at the table. "You're not in jail; I'm impressed," he whispered.

"The day is young," I shot back.

"We came in this morning from New Jersey," said Barry, waving his hand across the table to the other civilians. Introductions were made all around.

Barry went on, "Major Carlstrum has arranged this meeting in order for us to be able to gather certain aircraft identification statistics."

"This data is critical for our combat identification and guidance systems software," said Kelly Johnston.

"The statistics we're after can only be obtained by getting up close and personal with the engine types we believe the Russian military has installed and/or converted on several of their commercial aircraft," continued Les Baxter.

"An IR signature locking problem was encountered last year. Our F-4 and the German F-104 pilots have reported a significant

---

[103]   Central Intelligence Agency (CIA)

decrease in the ability to paint[104] certain types of Russian jet aircraft. Certain engine types have apparently been modified to dampen the IR output signature," said Kelly Johnston.

"Or, they've found an electronic method to mask the signature," added Les Baxter. "A physical damper coupled to an after-burner device may have been installed."

"Infra-Red engine signatures are unique for each engine type," said Don Coover, who spoke for the first time. "The Russians have recently converted several military aircraft for civilian transport, and several other civilian passenger planes now are equipped with military designed jet engines."

"The good news, and the reason we're all here today, is that for the last six months Ivan[105] has been flying these types of aircraft into Western Europe. Frankfurt International is the only airport that shares its main runway with the U.S. Military," said Barry Flax.

"This operation has been designed to identify these specific military engine characteristics. The Russian commercial flights into Flughafen Frankfurt Airport lend us an opportunity to get up close and observe the engine configurations and outputs on many of these aircraft," said Kelly Johnston.

"Our people have been over on the commercial side where these planes are parked. Physically there is no indication on the outside of the engine of what has changed," said Coover. "That's why we requested a RedEye team."

"I trust you brought your trainers," inquired Flax.

"Yes. I had my team put them on the tables next to where we parked."

"Excellent," said Johnston. "The conversion kit only takes about ten minutes to install."

"Conversion? Sounds like we're getting the latest in high tech?" I asked.

"New electronics and mainboard software, plus three types of EE-prom recording registers[106]," replied Coover.

---

[104] Technique using a laser that is kept pointed at a target. The laser radiation bounces off the target and is scattered in all directions. This is known as "painting the target".

[105] Ivan - a slang term meaning the Russians

[106] EEPROM (also written E2PROM, and pronounced e-e-prom, double-e prom, e-squared, or simply e-prom) stands for Electrically Erasable Programmable Read-Only Memory and is a type of non-volatile memory used in computers

"Outstanding, how do we proceed?"

RHEIN-MAIN AIR BASE/FLUGHAFEN FRANKFURT AIRPORT
EAST END OF COMMON RUNWAY THREE SIX
0935 HOURS MONDAY 5 MAY 1969

The conversion of each RedEye trainer only took about 15 minutes. Von, Larry and Jack seemed fascinated with the civilians pulling off the X41A3 tracking arm and replacing it with the new electronics. Sensor devices -- encased in a round, tube-shaped shell -- fit snugly into the empty missile compartment of the tracker. The new sensor array would not only perform the original ID and locking function, but would also time-stamp and record sixteen other data characteristics.

Clark didn't seem interested in the activities surrounding the RedEye equipment modification. He and Kelly Johnston were off in a corner fully engaged in conversation. Clark was changing the lenses and loading film into both cameras. Kelly was testing the light and distance meters that would be used to document the approximate time and frame numbers against the data being time-stamped in the trackers. Kelly was also interested in the color and shape of exhaust coming from each engine type. To document these images we had brought with us 36 rolls of ASA 200 bulk film prepared by Herr Schmidt who managed our new photo lab.

"Ken, here is a silhouette profile of today's five scheduled aircraft that we hope to photograph and scan," I said as I handed him the folder containing the prints. "You guys come take a look at these," I said as I motioned for everyone to gather around. Ken took the shadow prints out and laid them on the hood of RE-3.

"The new sensor array in our trackers will require us to get within 150 to 200 feet of the aircraft to record properly."

"How in the hell are we going to be able to do that?"

"We're RedEye. The difficult will take a few minutes; the impossible takes slightly longer. Relax, Jack. If you get too close and your clothes catch fire there's an extinguisher in the jeep. Look

---

and other electronic devices to store small amounts of data, e.g., calibration tables or device configuration that must be saved when power is removed.

here," I said as I unfolded a sketch of Rhein-Main provided to us by Ketter. "As you can see from this diagram, Rhein-Main shares the main runway with the civilian traffic of Frankfurt International. Each end of the main runway has a berm that dips down into wooded areas here, and here," I said, and pointed to each end of the runway.

"Ketter says the berms slope down at a 15 degree angle. The same configuration exists at each end. Today, all traffic is taking off toward the west, so we'll set up here." I pointed to the east end of the main runway layout. "Planes make their final turn from the service lane that runs parallel to the main runway, right here," I said, and pointed to where the service ramp entered the main runway.

"Chief Ketter has some people stationed on the commercial side. When one of the Russian planes pushes back to depart they will signal Bob and he'll call us on the radio."

"According to the scale on this map, this wooded area will provide good cover, but the distance looks to be well over 500 feet," said Larry.

"Yeah, I saw that. So what I think we should do is remain out of sight on the back side of the berm until the aircraft makes a complete turn onto the runway facing to the North."

"Even from the top edge of the berm it's still at least 350 feet to the aircraft," said Jack.

"Well, I guess we'll just have to hustle. If the pilot doesn't give us enough time after making the turn, we'll have to regroup and figure out something else to get close enough. Being as unnoticeable as possible will be a priority. We should assume most of these pilots are armed."

"I must have missed that tidbit of information in the briefing," replied Jack.

RHEIN-MAIN AIR BASE/FLUGHAFEN FRANKFURT AIRPORT
EAST END OF COMMON RUNWAY THREE SIX
1045 HOURS MONDAY 5 MAY 1969

"Sparrow6, this is Tour Guide. Bird One has left the nest. Acknowledge."

"Tour Guide, Sparrow6. Roger that. Tour Guide out," I said as I placed the mike on the seat and walked to where the two teams were waiting. Larry and Von would be up first, Ken would take the pictures, and Jack would work the second camera from the top of the berm.

We heard the sound of the engines increase as the aircraft started to make a U-turn onto the main runway. As the plane completed its turn I could clearly see the name of the airline

Figure 15 - Russian Military Commercial Application - Rhein Main AFB - 1969

stenciled on the fuselage: *CESKUSLOVENSKE AEROLINIE.* According to our briefing documents, the silhouette shape was the Ilyushin Il-62, a Soviet long-range jet airliner[107] conceived in 1960 by Ilyushin.

The Russian military was now utilizing similar equipment configurations to the Il-62. This aircraft was one of the airframes and engine configurations we were here to record. I yelled out over the hood of RE-2, "We're good to go. She's on the list."

Ken had rigged one of the cameras with the largest of the telephoto lenses and was standing on the hood of RE-3, which was parked just out of sight on the slope of the berm. I could hear the auto winder of the camera advance every time he snapped a picture.

Von and Larry had advanced out of the wooded area and waited at the top of the berm until the aircraft was facing away. They started their advance toward the airplane. The pilot did not stop the

---

107   The Ilyushin Il-62 (for whom the NATO ID was "Classic") was a successor to the popular turbo-prop Il-18 and, with capacity for almost 200 passengers; the IL-62 was the largest jet airliner when it first flew in 1963. It entered Aeroflot service on 15 September 1967 with an inaugural passenger flight from Moscow to Montreal. One of four pioneering designs (the others being Boeing 707, DC-8, and VC10), the Il-62 was the first such type to be operated by the Soviet Union and a number of other nations, becoming the standard long-range airliner for several decades. It was the first Russian pressurized aircraft with non-circular cross-section fuselage and ergonomic passenger doors, and the first Russian jet with six-abreast seating. [Photo by Ken Clark, 1969]

aircraft after the turn. The engines went to full throttle and the jet started its advance down the runway. They were still about 250 feet away when Larry got down on one knee and started the tracking recorder. The tone lock was very, very strong, but the recorder signal strength indicator was pulsing way too fast.

"Damn," I said to myself, and lowered my binoculars. *"We need to get a lot closer than that the next time."*

I went over to Jeep Three and grabbed the microphone. "Tour Guide, this is Sparrow6. The Bird left in a hurry -- not enough time for proper introduction. Do you have any suggestions for a longer honeymoon? Over," I said and un-keyed the mike.

"Sparrow6, this is Tour Guide. Wait one." Five minutes went by.

"Sparrow6, Tour Guide. No friends are present in bird's eye. Try and position for a longer introduction. Tour Guide, Out."

"No friends present in bird's eye? What does he mean by that?" asked Clark.

"Bird's Eye is the control tower. He doesn't have anyone up there to help delay a takeoff."

Larry and Von jogged back to the vehicle and laid the tracker on the hood.

"What kind of tracking tone were you able to get before it started down the runway?"

"The infrared signal volume was normal, but once the plane moved further away the strength of the recorder beeps got crazy."

"Yeah, Mr. Flax told me that a fast beeping signal indicates no lock-up for the recording registers. A two and a half to three second pause between beeps will indicate a good sample is being taken."

"The more time between beeps the stronger the signal?"

"That's what the man said. We need to get a lot closer for the next one. And, we need to do it without being seen by the cockpit crew. Are there any ideas, people?" I asked.

Jack was the first to speak. "Why don't we just go out there and be standing at the edge of the turn-around when the next one takes off?"

"For one thing, we can't draw any attention to what we're doing, and for another, there wouldn't be any way to hide our trackers while standing in plain sight," I reminded him.

"Well, it has to be at least 300 feet from the edge of the apron to where the plane positions for takeoff," replied Jack.

"I've got an idea. Jack, help me take the canvas off of this jeep. The rest of you uncouple the trailer and push it back down the hill and out of sight."

RHEIN-MAIN AIR BASE/FLUGHAFEN FRANKFURT AIRPORT
EAST END OF COMMON RUNWAY THREE SIX
1225 HOURS MONDAY 5 MAY 1969

"Sparrow6, this is Tour Guide. Bird Two has left the nest. Acknowledge."

"Roger that, Tour Guide. Sparrow6. Out," I responded. Ken had installed his camera on a tripod, concealed just below the rise of the berm. He would have a direct view of the approaching aircraft and would move up onto the concrete area once the aircraft completed its turn.

Jeep Three, minus its canvas, was parked on the backside of the berm just out of sight facing up toward the aircraft turn-a-round. The concept was simple. Once the plane made the turn, I would signal for the Jeep to proceed up the hill out onto the tarmac to within 100 feet of the aircraft. Jack was in the passenger seat and would work the RedEye tracker. Von would drive and Larry would work the second camera from the back seat.

Once the readings were taken, the jeep would reverse back down the hill out of sight. The strategy would work as long as another aircraft wasn't following the Russian too closely from the Runway 36 service access.

It worked! We did this four more times before returning to the hangar for the mission de-brief.

RHEIN-MAIN AIR BASE
BUILDING 549—HANGAR COMPLEX
1735 HOURS MONDAY 5 MAY 1969

As we approached the front of the hangar we saw the same C-141 Starlifter being prepped for the return trip to McGuire. The left side door of the hangar was rolled open and we parked in the same place as before.

I jumped out as soon as the jeep came to a stop and held the seat forward so Ken could get out. I signaled Jack to kill the motor and remain behind the wheel. I walked toward Von and Larry, made the kill sign across the throat and indicated for them to stay seated. Bob Ketter, Don Coover and Les Baxter were behind the two tables that were set up to the left of where we parked.

Barry Flax, Kelly Johnston and LTC Milision, who was now dressed in a USAF flight suit, were leaning over the railing up on the mezzanine level looking down on the activities.

"Is it OK to get the trainers out and onto these tables?" Ketter asked.

"Sure, both units are under the tarp in this trailer," I said, and pointed to the trailer attached to RE-2.

"Sergeant, would you please get the trackers out and put one on each of these tables?" Ketter directed his request to one of the four air crewmen who were standing to the rear of the tables. Each table had one of the original flip-up tracking units that had been removed that morning.

"We're going to leave the units modified with the new sensors," said Flax, walking from the staircase onto the hangar floor. "But the EE-proms will be removed and fresh ones will be installed. I gave Mr. Clark a box of 24 proms which can be utilized for future projects."

The removal process took only a few minutes. Our trainers were repacked and put back into our trailer, and the Bell Labs guys put their stuff in similar General Dynamics RedEye containers, and ordered that they be taken out to the waiting aircraft.

Ken and Mr. Coover were off to one side and were speaking in undertones. Ken handed him the used film canisters. A detailed description of each aircraft recording was listed on his clipboard. Ken took the top seven pages from the clipboard and handed them to Coover. Coover leaned in and said something I couldn't hear. Ken smiled and shook the offered hand.

Kelly Johnston walked up to our group and placed his left hand on Ken's shoulder as he said to everyone in the group, "Thanks for doing this. It will make a big difference to all our combat airplane drivers. See you at our next get-together." He turned to follow the others leaving the hangar.

Two boxes, each containing twelve, RedEye charging batteries, were placed in the trailer of RE-3 by Barry Flax.

"Thanks for helping out today. The data you gathered will benefit all of the people who use our weapon systems. You and your team did a great job. Thank you," he said, shook my hand, and walked out of the hangar.

Bob Ketter informed me that "Mr. D" would be in touch.

"You call him that, too?" I asked. Ketter laughed but made no response.

"Blood and Guts, Bob," I said, and got into the passenger side of RE-2. We left the base and returned to Coleman Kaserne.

Operation Sparrow Signature was complete.

XII

JUNKYARD FRIENDSHIP

It had been over three weeks since our outing at Rhein-Main. Von and Larry's wives had just arrived. The First Sergeant had given his permission for the RedEye married guys to live off-post. Linda Boyd and Nancy Stockert had linked up, bought tickets and traveled together to Frankfurt.

An apartment would be a large out-of-pocket expense for married enlisted men. Meals and transportation expenses would add to that burden. The good news was that the current exchange rate was 3.92 DM[108] to a dollar. The PX in Hanau would be a good, inexpensive source for food and clothing.

The Germans with apartments to rent near and around Gelnhausen welcomed our married enlisted men with open arms. In each situation both landlords were very gracious to Von and Larry, and both offered very nice accommodations.

The rumor was started, by whom we didn't know that Larry was so taken with the German custom of using beermen instead of milkmen that he was considering staying in Germany after his tour was over.

---

[108] The German Deutsche Mark was the official currency of West Germany (1948-1990)

"Not true," said Larry. He was adamant that the fact that the Germans didn't believe in milkmen had no influence on his interest in a possible re-enlistment. He did, however, admit, "The use of the beerman service industry is a must for those living out in the German empire."

Beermen, like the tooth fairy, would come to the house in the wee hours of the morning just to replace the empty bottles from the night before. Of course, Jack went immediately to First Sergeant Bumpus to solicit his backing for the beerman service for the barracks.

POST JUNKYARD (NEAR THE AMMO DUMP)
1100 HOURS SUNDAY 25 MAY 1969

When I arrived at Coleman Kaserne in December, there was a goofy, good-natured guy named Joe Benson, an E-6, who was just back from a tour in Vietnam and had recently purchased a brand new Triumph TR-6 sports car from a dealer in Frankfurt. He had taken delivery in the morning and by mid-afternoon the car was totaled. He had wrapped it around a tree on one of the nearby country roads. It is said that God takes care of both fools and drunks. Joe told me that God probably just didn't like sports cars. He was not injured but had been reduced in rank to a PFC-in-waiting.

There was a vehicle storage and/or junk car area next to the Ammo Dump at the rear of Coleman. A friend of Bernie's had recently gone home and had left his 1956 VW parked there. The car had failed inspection and needed a lot of work. The VW was parked next to the wrecked TR-6. The body of the vehicle was black, but the hood and trunk, as well as both doors, were all different colors. I looked around the parking lot and I could see that the three other junked VWs were the major contributors to the multi-colored appearance of this particular car.

"Hey, RedEye. How's the war going?" The voice came from the rear of the wrecked TR-6.

"Hi, Joe. What brings you to 3rd Armor's used car lot?"

"I'm just cleaning out some personal things. The insurance company finally sent me word that this is a total write-off. No collision insurance. The good news is that I used my re-enlistment bonus to buy it and don't owe anybody anything. The bad news is that this car cost me 468 dollars for each of the six hours it was alive.

"Well, at least you weren't hurt."

"Amen," replied Joe. "Would you like to have my very expensive tools? I'm clearing post in two weeks and I don't want to be carting them with me."

I walked around to the rear of the Triumph and looked into the trunk. This part of the car appeared to be completely unaffected by the accident. There were three trays containing wrenches, a metric socket set, and one with various screwdrivers, pliers and a hammer.

"Well, I certainly will need tools to work on the Bug. That is, if I can get it started. But I don't have any way of locking them up."

Joe tossed me the keys to the TR-6. "Leave them here until you get locks on the VW."

"How much do you want for them?"

"Nothing. I'll let you buy me a beer before I go."

Joe walked back to the driver's side of the VW. "This thing looks like the 1950's color chart for VW."

"Yeah, it definitely doesn't lack variety."

"Give me the ignition key." Joe got in and pumped the accelerator and tried the ignition. It was dead. "The battery for this thing is under the back seat. If the battery in the TR is still good, we'll see if we can get this Bug[109] to start."

A half hour later we had the engine running on the VW.

"Where's your next assignment?" I asked.

"London. We have a mutual friend there: a Major Carlstrum. Bost is giving me back my stripes before I go. It's supposed to be a secret, but the Major called me last week to give me a heads-up."

"You know, Carlstrum seems to be very well connected."

"Yep, that's true. I met him at a data encryption course at Fort Meade. He was dressed as an English businessman."

"I'll be damned. Small world," I said, and added, "He must have a limited budget for disguises."

---

[109] Nickname for the Volkswagen model formally called the Beetle

1ST 48TH HHQ
REDEYE EQUIPMENT ROOM
0930 HOURS MONDAY 26 MAY 1969

I was seated alone at the table in the RedEye Equipment Room, facing the open doorway. I was halfway through the latest AR bulletin on RedEye battery storage and replacement procedures when a voice said, "You got a minute?" It was "Mr. D" in his Major suit, and he was smiling and leaning against the door jamb.

"Yes, Sir. I was getting worried that you may have been lost behind enemy lines. It's been quite a while, Sir."

"Who told you I was in 'Nam?"

"No one. I was just kidding. You were in 'Nam?"

"Let's start over. Rick, you got a minute?"

"Yes, Sir, yes, Sir, three bags full," I sang. "Mr. D" laughed and said, "Let's take a walk."

On the way past the Orderly Room I stuck my head in the door and told Bernie that I was going down the hill. Carlstrum and I walked out to the main road and started walking toward the main gate.

"Congratulations on making the promotion list for Sergeant."

"No shit!" I answered.

"You guys did a good job at Rhein-Main. Kelly Johnston told me to tell you that the readings you took were first rate. They were used to enhance the Lockheed tracking software."

"How do I get all of my guys bumped to the next level?"

"That shouldn't be a problem," replied Carlstrum. Then he added, "Flax said the Bell Labs guys are assisting in some minor changes to the RedEye guidance system EE-prom software. All in all, everyone is pleased."

"So, you came all the way over here to congratulate us?"

"No, not exactly," he said, and then continued. "Not quite." We walked on without talking for a while. I could tell he was organizing his thoughts.

Finally, I said, "That just leaves the real reason why you're here. Your Ray Charles[110] approach to project feasibility is always exciting for us." Carlstrum laughed out loud and continued on down

---

[110] Ray Charles Robinson (September 23, 1930 - June 10, 2004) was a blind American musician known as Ray Charles.

the hill.

"How is everyone working out?" he asked.

"Everyone is pulling their weight. They all get along well, the married guys have their wives here now, and we have most of our equipment functioning."

"Most...?"

"Jeep Number Five either needs an engine and a way to steer it or it needs to go to its just reward."

"Which is?" asked Carlstrum.

"The great junkyard in the sky," I replied.

"Steer, you said."

"Yeah that is what I said. Someone cut the steering wheel off with a hacksaw. Go figure..."

"You heard of a place called Grafenwohr[111]?"

"Yeah, it's always used in the same sentence with roughing it, nightmare, and dangerous. We're scheduled to go there for battalion maneuvers in the June/July timeframe. Why do you ask, Sir?"

"There's a large, experimental helicopter gunship reportedly being field tested just across the border near Grafenwohr. Our East German Desk says that the Soviet pilots are calling it the 'flying tank'."

"Sounds lethal. It backs up what I said about what I know about Grafenwohr. And you're telling me this fascinating story because...?"

Carlstrum ignored the question and continued. "Eyewitness reports confirm that this aircraft is heavily armored and will require a thorough analysis to determine its silhouette profile and engine configurations."

"I don't suppose they'll be flying that great big son of a bitch into Frankfurt International any time soon?"

"Mr. D" snickered. "You know, Sergeant, you are not seeing the big picture. This is a real opportunity to enhance your resume with this type of field research."

"Like I said, Sir," I stopped walking and turned to face Mr. Douglas and continued, "three bags full, Sir."

---

[111] Grafenwöhr is a town in the district Neustadt, in eastern Bavaria, Germany. It is widely known for the United States Army military installation and training area, called Grafenwöhr Training Area, located directly south and west of the town.

1ST 48TH NCO CLUB
AA SPONSORED PROMOTION PARTY
1830 HOURS TUESDAY 27 MAY 1969

The Tuesday before we were to go to Grafenwohr, CSM Bost had the six of us who were being promoted down to the NCO club after business hours. We were ushered into a small, private dining room located in the back of the club. There were several NCOs from Battalion and HHC standing around the walls of the room. They all had huge smiles on their faces. We were told to take seats at the table in the center of the room.

CSM Bost was seated at the far end of the table. There were three, half-gallon, unopened, Jim Beam[112] bottles on display. In front of each of us was a brand new, 20 ounce, German beer stein, complete with pewter, thumb flip-top lid. I still have the stein on a shelf in my office.

Being the only SPC4 from HHC, I was totally unfamiliar with what was to be revealed as a pagan ritual designed as the first step to a membership in Alcoholics Anonymous. The rest of the guys, who were from the various line companies, seemed perfectly fine with what was about to take place.

"Gentleman, we are here today to wet down your recently approved promotion to Sergeant E5." There was an outburst of "Hear, Hear" from the very thirsty-looking cadre holding up the walls of the dining room. Bost got up from his seat, grabbed two of the bottles, and turned to two of the NCOs leaning on the wall and ordered them to open the bottles, post-haste. He then took the remaining bottle and, with one twisting motion, decapitated Jim Beam and proceeded around the table pouring 10.3 ounces of liquid into each of the colorfully decorated beer steins. The leftovers in the second jug were used to fill the somewhat smaller glasses being held by each member of the taunting crowd.

With a snap of his fingers, the third bottle was delivered and the remaining glasses were topped off. Each stein remained at attention, filled to half capacity. Glasses were produced for all of those without one, and these were also filled.

---

[112] Jim Beam is a brand of bourbon whiskey produced in Clermont, Kentucky.

"Blubaugh, let's have the stripes," Bost commanded. He then went around the table dropping the three-stripe pin rank of Sergeant E5 into the giant beer mug sitting in front of each of us.

There was loud laughter and the yelling of words of encouragement and congratulations from the peanut gallery[113]. Bost now stood back at the head of the table, raised his glass and said, "You wanted them. Go get them!"

I looked from side to side to see how the others were going to handle the situation. I knew full well that if I attempted to drink that much whiskey in one sitting it would probably kill me.

So I unsnapped the button of my right cuff and proceeded to push my sleeve up so I could reach into the stein and complete the promotion process.

I had just started to put my hand in when I heard a booming slap on the table and a voice shout out, "Hey, Fontain! No cheating." Bost was already in the process of refilling his own glass.

So, without further ado, I picked up the stein, popped the lid with my thumb and proceeded to down the whiskey.

It was at this point that I wished I had been born with a longer tongue. I could see the little plastic E-5 insignia resting at the bottom of this fish-tank size beer stein.

"Why couldn't Blubaugh purchase the ones that float," I thought.

Jim Beam was overflowing out of both sides of my mouth, but the little pin wasn't moving at all until I increased my head tilt to 86.9 degrees. At that same moment, my promotion suddenly arrived at a place on the center of my tongue.

I slammed the cauldron down on the table and spit the stripes into my left hand and held them up for everyone to see. I had clearly won, but the others seemed content to finish their provided refreshment.

I had only consumed about a quarter of what was in the mug. Now all I needed to do was figure a way to get back to the barracks without being arrested. The fumes alone coming from my thoroughly saturated shirt would be enough to intoxicate anyone who came within six feet of my person. If I had only worn my rain gear!

---

[113] A peanut gallery was, in the days of vaudeville, a nickname for the cheapest (and ostensibly rowdiest) seats in the theater, the occupants of which were all too willing (in the view of the performer) to heckle

I knew I should get some fresh air and something to eat -- immediately, if not sooner.

GRAFENWOHR: COME OUT, COME OUT, WHEREVER YOU ARE!
1630 HOURS
WEDNESDAY 28 MAY 1969

Figure 16 Grafenwohr

We left Gelnhausen and took A3 south to Nuremburg, then headed northeast on A9. It had taken us about four hours. The training complex was exactly as I had pictured it: a major U.S. Army training installation, spread over a 234 square kilometer area, and located just a stone's throw from the civilian town of Grafenwohr.

We arrived just in time for dinner. Our HHC field mess unit had arrived the day before. It was the first time I had used mess kit utensils since Basic Training. As part of the Advance Party, we were assigned a group barracks tent-building. The construction consisted of wooden sides with a canvas stretched over a wood roof. It had a potbelly stove in the center of the room for heat. It was set up with twelve cots.

I had everyone help unload the trailers and pull the radios and weapons out of the vehicles for the night. I didn't know what to expect, so I decided to err on the side of caution. We secured the steering wheels and trailer hitches with lengths of chain and padlocks. First Sergeant Bumpus had recommended this to us.

The real Advance Party, including the Battalion S-3 staff, wouldn't be arriving until this weekend. My orders were to find and report to the camp training and range officer and say to him "Sparrow6".

"*So far, so good,*" I said to myself as I drifted off to sleep in my warm and comfy sleeping bag, which rested on top of a sure-fire prescription for emphysema: the M-439468A air mattress.

We were up and moving at 0600. We reloaded all equipment back into the vehicles. We drove down to the far end of the tent city to where our HHC field mess had taken up residence. Jack and I stayed with the vehicles while the others went in for breakfast.

"Larry, can you get us a couple cups of coffee out here? We'll watch the equipment and orient ourselves with this post area map."

Larry was back in a couple of minutes with two canteen cups

with steaming hot coffee. "The mess Sergeant says the mugs are not unpacked yet, but they do have food trays and utensils this morning. Give me your canteen cups. I used Von's and mine to bring you these."

GRAFENWOHR TRAINING CENTER, BASE HQ
0630 HOURS THURSDAY 29 MAY 1969

Base operations, housed in multiple buildings, were located one half click[114] from the 1st/48th Tent City. As we pulled into the parking lot, I observed that all of the buildings in the complex were old but well maintained. I found the sign marked *Plans and Training* and went in the main entrance and walked to the nearest occupied desk.

"Good morning, 1st 48th RedEye. I'm looking for Captain Jamison."

"Does he expect you?" asked the Spec4.

"Yes. Can you tell him I'm here, please?"

The Spec4 walked to the back, and almost immediately an officer and a gentleman, thirty-something, came out of his office and approached me "I'm Captain Jamison. And you are?"

"Sergeant Fontain, Sir. Sparrow6."

"Excellent. Wait here while I get your project package from the safe."

He returned in a few minutes with his arms full. "This package was hand-delivered via an Air Force Officer Courier on Monday. The cover sheet on this folder directed me to place the project package in the safe and put together a complete map kit for the Germany/Czechoslovakia border areas. Package two is not to be opened until you reach objective One Tango. Understood?"

"Yes, Sir. One Tango."

"Whatever the hell that is," I mumbled to myself.

"These two folders are to go to your S-3 when you're finished with the project. The map case is to be returned to me. Is that clear?"

---

[114] A click is slang for one kilometer - a pseudo-condensed pronunciation of kilometer or onomatopoetic word for the sound of a military odometer.

"Yes, Sir, it is."

"Come with me. I'll get you oriented on the big board so you'll know what you'll be dealing with. My orders are to make known these two map points. Here," he said, and picked up a pointer, swinging it to a point north, and well outside, the boundaries of the training center, "and our present location, here." He pointed to a small blue star marked HQ.

I thanked the Captain and assured him that his map cases would be returned. I left the building and returned to the parking lot.

"Let's drive back to the mess kitchen. I need another cup of coffee while I read the contents of this folder. We might as well be comfortable while I do it," I said to Ken.

The RedEye team walked together from the Mess Hall to the parking lot. Four jeeps with trailers were parked side by side. I walked to the vehicle with the bumper marking RE-4 and unfolded the largest of the area maps on the hood.

"Gather around and take a look at this," I said as I opened the thicker of the two folders. "This exercise is called *Operation Sparrow View*." There is an old castle ruin here," I indicated on the map. The location was northeast about 50 kilometers, and was well outside of the boundaries of this training area, as well as very close to the Czechoslovakian border.

"Jack and I will lead in RE-1," I said, and handed him the local road map that Lieutenant Key had given me before we'd left Gelnhausen. "Von, you will bring up the rear in RE-2, Ken you follow Jack and me, and Larry fall in behind Ken. OK, do you have any questions before we take off?"

"Are we coming back here tonight?" asked Von.

"Probably not. We've been directed to set up an observation post in a place called Tillyschanze," I said, pointing at that name on the map. "I'll be able to tell you more about this assignment once we're there."

We left the Training Center through the main gate. We headed north for about 35 kilometers before turning east toward the town of Barnau, which was just 15 kilometers west of our objective.

TILLYSCHANZE, NEAR THE CZECHOSLOVAKIA BORDER
1330 HOURS THURSDAY 29 MAY 1969

We missed the turnoff on our first attempt to locate the access road. The pathway described in the briefing document wasn't shown on our map. Jack measured the distance we had traveled from Barnau as exactly 15 kilometers on the odometer. We drove slowly east on the shoulder for approximately 500 meters. No sign of the access road was found.

We turned the vehicles around and went back a half kilometer from the 15 kilometer point of reference. I got out and walked the shoulder. We found a driveway of sorts at the 14.8-kilometer measurement. The entrance was completely overgrown and not visible from the road. It did not show any sign of recent use. We tiptoed the vehicles up the drive for a quarter of a kilometer and emerged from the undergrowth directly alongside a large stone wall in various stages of decay.

As we drove on a little further we could see that parts of the wall were no longer standing. I told everyone to remain seated as I took my binoculars from my bag and walked through an opening in the wall. I found myself in a large, open space that appeared to be the courtyard for the deteriorating complex in front of me.

The only part of this old ruin with any height was a turret structure built into the wall in the southeast corner of the courtyard. The tower was about three stories tall. The open doorway on the side of the tower revealed a stone stairway that looked to be in good condition.

I proceeded through the opening and started the climb upward. The stairway wound its way through the second level and continued on to the top floor. It was a circular room with a stone floor, but it was missing its roof. A window facing east provided an excellent view of what appeared to be a small municipal airport.

I put my binoculars up to my eyes and the term airport instantly changed to airbase. There were several hundred Russian military personnel milling around the property. The majority of the soldiers were concentrated around the largest of the hangars.

These facts were not detailed in the first briefing document. However, assigning us to use this old castle ruin as an observation post made perfect sense. Someone, somewhere, had figured out that the Russians would most likely be forced to utilize existing airfield facilities for both housing and testing of new aircraft. Accommodations to hide and test an experimental aircraft were few and far between in Eastern Europe. This particular airbase was the only one that could be observed from the western side of the border. I walked back down to where the team was waiting.

"What did you see up there?" asked Jack.

"What I saw was the country of Czechoslovakia and what appears to be a military air base."

"You're kidding," replied Von.

"The task we have been assigned is the surveillance of an experimental helicopter. The particulars on how to accomplish this are not specified in the briefing documents. At least they weren't explained in stage one. I haven't opened the second one, but I doubt it will detail for us how to conduct the surveillance. It will be up to us to figure out the best way to do it. The tower over there has a direct line of sight into the airbase and should be a good platform to observe from. Clark, are you privy to any additional information about this project?"

"No, absolutely not," said Clark.

"Then it appears the methods and procedures we use to gather this intelligence are up to us."

"Another Rhein-Main in other words," said Larry.

"It appears so," I replied.

"OK, let's make camp while we still have plenty of daylight. I strongly suggest for as long as we are here that we conduct all of our activities as quietly and inconspicuously as possible.

"Von, you and Larry scout out the basement room that is supposed to be under the courtyard on the other side of this wall. The entrance is in the southwest corner. That's over in that direction." I pointed down the wall to the right. "Check it out and see if you think it will be a good place to set up shop."

"Aye, aye, Sir," said Von in his best naval accent.

"Jack, you think we can get these vehicles through there?" I pointed to a place in the wall from which most of the stones had been removed -- most likely by the local farmers.

"Yeah, they should fit. What's on the other side?"

"It opens into a courtyard. It should be good cover for us while we're here."

TILLYSCHANZE, NEAR THE CZECHOSLOVAKIA BORDER
BASEMENT AREA
1830 HOURS THURSDAY 29 MAY 1969

"GrafTrain6, this is Sparrow6. GrafTrain6, this is Sparrow6."

"Sparrow6, this is GrafTrain Six-Alpha. Read you five by five. Over."

"GrafTrain, Sparrow6. We have arrived at destination One Tango.[115] Please notify BG3 of status. 6 Over."

"Roger. Sparrow6 at One Tango. GrafTrain relays to BG3. Out," said GrafTrain6. I put the mike down on the rear seat of RE-1.

"If the basement looks good, pull the radios out of the other vehicles and move them downstairs. Leave these radios running for our scheduled radio checks," I said, pointing to RE-1.

Getting all of our equipment down the narrow stone stairs wasn't easy, especially since the staircase made a 90-degree turn halfway down. The room was large and surprisingly dry. We found several lanterns that when lit exposed what must have been the area where the previous tenants made and kept their wine.

The basement cavern was at least one-third the size of the large courtyard above, and included a ceiling that was at least 20 feet high. There was a boarded over panel in the ceiling that appeared to have been used for access to the courtyard at one time. Three huge and two smaller wine casks in various stages of disrepair stood against the opposite wall from the stairs. Bits and pieces of old wooden furniture were scattered around the room. It appeared that we were not the first to use this basement for shelter, but we were certainly the first to use it in a very long time.

"Everybody," I called out, "gather round. Over here please." I gestured toward a table Clark had found and set up in the middle of the room. I waited until everyone had gotten settled before continuing.

"I just finished reviewing the second project package."

The instruction printed on the front of the envelope in bold red lettering read, "*Do not open until arrival* at *One Tango*." I unfolded

---

[115] Old castle ruins called Tillyschanze, near the Czechoslovakia border

the area map and dumped the printed material from the package labeled with a large number two onto the tabletop.

With everyone seated on two benches and an old chair, I moved to the open end of the table.

"The Russians are field testing a new prototype, designated the Mil Mi-25[116]. It's a helicopter gunship -- a great big son-of-a-bitch, and the powers that be think it might be going through a series of field tests right across the street from where we are sitting. Since we did such a bang-up job at Rhein-Main, we've been charged with observing, photographing, and running our trackers on this aircraft should the opportunity present itself."

"Will we use the same data collection procedures we used at Rhein-Main?" asked Von.

"Yes, except that after we cut the whole in the fence, Jack will be on his own in the mine field," I said in my most official voice.

"Great," said Jack. "However, Plan B stipulates that Von and Larry crash the border fence in RE-3 with trackers blazing. Clark and I will be up in the tower photographing the entire heroic effort." Everyone laughed and then just sat there in silence staring at the map and the material that had come out of the second project package.

"The fence won't be as difficult as the mine field, Jack," I said. "I suggest you sit on that extra case of C rations during your test drive.

"Clark, these were in the second package," I said as I tossed a small box of parts onto the table. "The instruction sheet included with the parts says to replace the existing installed EE-proms with these. Distance sensitivity is increased to over 2700 feet." Clark took the lid off the box and examined the new EE-proms.

He said, "These have the same socket type, and they're color coded the same way as the ones already installed. Ten minutes tops to change each tracker. I'll get started right after the meeting."

"OK. Jack, belay the order to clear the mine field," I said and everyone laughed.

---

[116] The Mil Mi-25 (NATO nickname: Hind) is a large helicopter gunship and attack helicopter and low-capacity troop transport with room for eight passengers. It is produced by Mil Moscow Helicopter Plant. Other unofficial names for it are "Crocodile" -- derived from the helicopter's camouflage scheme, and "the Glass" -- which describes the flat glass plates that surround the cockpit.

TILLYSCHANZE, CZECHOSLOVAKIA BORDER
BASE CAMP 1A, BASEMENT AREA
TEAM MEETING
2200 HOURS THURSDAY 29 MAY 1969

After re-reading the last project requirement contained in package two, I called the group together.

"On Sunday, June 1, we will conclude this exercise with F-4s out of Mildenhal AFB doing a down-on-the-deck fly-by at this location. There will be three flyovers: two from north to south and one from south to north. The thinking behind this exercise is the belief that this will stir the pot across the way. That is, if there hasn't been any sighting of the test subject before Sunday's date.

"My guess, worst case scenario, we get some tracking practice in at the end of this exercise. Because at this point we don't know if the Mil Mi-25 is even here," I finished the presentation.

"Comments? Questions?"

The silence was deafening and, as a final point, Larry said, "Is what we have been asked to do legal?"

I considered the question and said, "Let me address that issue this way. Clark and I went up in the turret to take a look after dinner and there was no sign of the Gunship Mi-25. However, one of the hangars -- the largest -- on the far side of the field had a heavy guard around it. If the gunship is here then it is more than likely in that hangar."

"Is this legal?" Von re-asked Larry's question.

"What you are really asking is, is this training or is this considered to be spying?" I said. "Before I answer that let me say this. Clark was sent here specifically for the Rhein-Main operation. The data we gathered was worth its weight in gold. The pictures alone will be incorporated into our aircraft recognition program worldwide, but the real benefit was in the enhancements of the Lockheed and General Dynamics software and to the EE-proms. I don't know about you guys, but up to this point in my military experience this assignment has been my only opportunity to contribute.

"Having said that, if any one of you wants to return to Graf," I paused and then continued, "I'll see to it that there is absolutely no blow back for any of you who decide on that course of action. Because up until we arrived here and opened package number two, neither Clark nor I had any idea of what we are being asked to do. And, one more thing, now that I think of it: our people stand all along this entire border, and so do their people -- each side watching what the other side is doing. So, to answer your question, not only is it legal, it's our duty to gather this information."

Jack was the first to speak. "Let me understand. What we are being asked to do is observe the operation of the Russian testing of a chopper called the Mil Mi-25, if indeed it is here, take photos of its activities on the airfield directly across from us, and run the RedEye trackers if it flies close enough to get a lock on it."

"Exactly," I said, and took a sip from a flippie[117] that Larry had brought from home in a makeshift cooler. "And, we accomplish all of that while standing in the confines of West Germany. However, there is one very important caveat," I said. "The strafing maneuvers of the F-4 Phantoms scheduled for Sunday morning will allow us to track and shoot the type of aircraft we are expected to knock down in protection of our Battalion. And, of course, possibly panic our Russian friends across the way into exposing what's in that hangar if they haven't done so by Sunday morning."

"In either case it's a win-win for us as I see it. The last part of this exercise is what our Battalion S-3 is paying us for."

"Paying us," Jack parroted. "I was following right along with your logic sequence up until that wild-ass exaggeration." Everyone laughed and fell silent again.

"I discussed with Clark whether or not it was wise to light up an enemy aircraft from across the border and we both think that the chances that they would be running surveillance detection on takeoff is unlikely. And if they did see the hit they probably would assume that it was one of their own systems doing it.

"Our radio SOP[118] for the ground-to-air traffic has a contact listed call sign Sultan6. Their main responsibility is listening in on Russian radio communications. I don't see any problem in contacting them if and when we engage the Mi-25. That way they can call us if radio chatter is detected concerning our trackers. If we're discovered and reported by the Russian pilots we can quickly disengage.

"I'll say this again, if any one of you feels this is not something

---

[117] Nickname for a German style beer bottle with a porcelain stopper flip top, sometimes called swing top, used for resealing purposes.

[118] Standard Operating Procedure

you want to participate in, you can go back to base camp and wait for the main BG[119] force to arrive on Saturday. No questions asked."

I let that sink in for a moment and continued. "There is an archway located across the courtyard which is connected to the left side of the tower. This opening in the wall was probably the main entrance at one time. There is a slight depression located under the covered ceiling area, probably created by the locals removing the stones from the floor and adjoining wall structures.

"We can use this position to set up the trackers, and no one will be able to see us unless they are standing on top of the border fence. As I see it, not only will we be out of the weather, but also this position will provide a clear view of the sky over the airbase.

"Clark, you haven't said much. Do you have anything to add?"

"No, except now I know why Herr Schmidt from our photo lab lent us a three thousand dollar set of telephoto lenses for the Pentax cameras. We should have no trouble seeing if our friends across the wire are in need of a shave or not."

"So, you think we can pull this off?" I asked him.

"Oh yeah! We have a clear line of sight into those buildings across the way, and as far as the trackers go, you remember the cigarette demo at Bliss[120]? We shouldn't have any problem getting a read on the Mil Mi gunship if it goes flying," said Ken.

"I remember that demo," said Larry. "He's right. The trackers should be good for the distance to the area in front of the hangar buildings."

"Jack, Von, what do you think?" I turned to the two of them.

Von spoke first. "The only problem I have is what happens if we're spotted over here. These guys don't play nice most of the time. They shoot first and deny all knowledge of it later." He paused for a second before continuing. "What the hell, you can count me in."

"In for a penny, in for a pound," said Jack.

"I'm in," said Larry.

"Thanks, guys. I think what we're doing is important. Von, I agree we should strive for absolute minimum exposure. The only point of detection is at the top of the tower. So, don't scurry around up there when conducting surveillance on the airport, and watch

---

119   BG is the abbreviation for "Blood and Guts" the motto of the 1st/48th Infantry

120   A RedEye demonstration conducted at Fort Bliss, Texas that tracked a lit cigarette at a range of one thousand feet.

the reflection in sunlight on the binocular and camera lenses."

"That shouldn't be a problem," said Jack. "The sun hasn't been out since we pulled in here."

"Ken, the SOP calls for a radio check with Graf every four hours. I'll do the one at 2300. Von, if you can take the watch at midnight to 0100, and Jack from 0100 to 0200, I'll do the radio and the watch from 0200 till 0300. Ken will take it until 0400, and Larry will take it to 0500 and then wake me at five.

"Check your gear and secure the vehicles before you turn in. Lock and load your 14's[121] with the clips Bernie got for us and keep them close while we're here. I'm going to do a quick walk-around before the radio check. Are there any questions, comments?" There were none. "Thanks everyone. Let's call it a night."

I was walking to the stairwell and I turned back to the table area. "Hey, Jack. Can you blow my air mattress up?"

I was answered with silence, followed by a universal hand gesture.

TILLYSCHANZE, CZECHOSLOVAKIA BORDER
BASE CAMP 1A, COURTYARD
EQUIPMENT CHECK
0630 HOURS FRIDAY 30 MAY 1969

We had just finished running the engine to charge the batteries in RE-1 when we heard the noise, faint at first, but rapidly growing into the high pitch sound of a turbine engine being brought to full power.

"Well, it sounds like our friends are up early. Ken, go grab your gear and get up in the tower. Jack would you go get the spotter scope, and Larry and Von, go on down and put a battery in one of the trackers and be prepared in case we get a shot at this guy."

When I got to the window opening at the top of the turret I used my newly issued Zeiss binoculars to look out across the fence line. Clark already was running the Pentax. You could hear the auto-winder advancing the film as Clark kept snapping picture after

---

[121] M14 rifle, officially the United States Rifle, 7.62 mm, is an American selective fire automatic rifle that fires 7.62×51mm NATO (.308 Winchester) ammunition. It was the standard issue U.S. rifle from 1959 to 1970.

picture -- 36 to 40 pictures in less than three minutes.

It turned out it wasn't the Mi-25 but a fighter aircraft taxiing to the northern end of the runway. None of us could recognize the model designation.

"Larry, light up the tracker and come see if you can lock on to this dude."

"Coming up Boss. Make way the gyro is spinning up."

The jet started its takeoff roll toward the south and away from us. Von and Jack moved to the stairwell to make room for the shooter. The signal was not very strong at first and got even weaker as the plane got farther down the runway. As the MiG rose up 100 feet or so, the tracking signal came on steady and loud. "Got ya!" exclaimed Larry.

TILLYSCHANZE, CZECHOSLOVAKIA BORDER
BASE CAMP 1A, ARCHWAY, ATTACHED TO TURRET
STRUCTURE
1145 HOURS FRIDAY 30 MAY 1969

It had been raining hard for over an hour, so I had everyone except Von move out of the turret and into position under the archway. Jack and Ken took a couple of shelter halves up in the tower and made a makeshift roof to keep the rain off Von and the equipment.

The rain had just about stopped when Von called down from the turret, "I hear an engine off in the distance; it's faint but it seems to be getting louder."

I'll be right up," I called out. "Larry put a battery in one of the trackers. Stay put until I call you. There isn't much room up there under the tarp."

I used my field glasses to search the horizon for where the engine sound seemed to be coming from. Finally, way off toward the Northwest, Von announced he could see, using the spotter scope, a black dot of an aircraft making its way toward us.

As the aircraft got closer I said, "My, my, that is a big bastard isn't it?"

I could hear Clark start to shoot some pictures. "I think the Mi-25 has just arrived, fellows. OK, Larry," I yelled down the steps. "Come up and see if you can get a lock on to this big boy. The rest of you can come for a look see, too, but squeeze in tight so you don't interfere with the camera or the tracker."

The gunship came in low and dropped down on the north end of the runway and hover-taxied to a point just to the left of the largest of the hangar buildings located on the far side of the airport. The tracking signal was good, but was definitely stronger when the aircraft was facing away from us. We watched for about fifteen minutes while the Russian crews pushed the gunship into the hangar and slid the doors closed.

"GrafTrain, Sparrow6. GrafTrain, Sparrow6. Over." I un-keyed the mike and turned to Von. "Go up and relieve Ken for a while. Tell him to come get some coffee and get warm."

"Sure. This part of the country really gets cold when the sun isn't out," said Von.

"Ain't that the truth? I'll order up some hot chocolate when I get them on the horn," I said and re-keyed the mike.

"GrafTrain, Sparrow6. GrafTrain, Sparrow6. Over." I repeated.

"Sparrow6, this is GrafTrain. Over."

"GrafTrain, Sparrow6. The bird is in the nest. I repeat. The bird is in the nest. Please notify BG3. Over."

"Roger, Sparrow6. Bird is in the nest. Passing info to BG3. Out."

It started to rain again, this time even harder than before.

TILLYSCHANZE, CZECHOSLOVAKIA BORDER
BASE CAMP 1A, TOWER ROOM
1450 HOURS SATURDAY 31 MAY 1969

"Here we go. They're rolling the doors open," Ken shouted down from his position up in the turret. The sun had finally made an appearance, warming up the afternoon by at least ten degrees from what it had been the day before. For the end of May it was still too damn cold.

The Mil Mi-25 had been pushed from its hangar by the time I reached the top of the steps. It was resting in all of its glory not far from the hangar entrance. A fuel truck had pulled up and proceeded to attach hoses to the fuselage, presumably to top off the tanks.

"You think she's going to go flying?" asked Ken as I came out of the stairwell to take a look at our target.

"I don't know if *she* will," I said in a correcting tone. "The

Ruskies[122] tend to name everything with *big boy* male names, such as, 'General Asshole' or 'Admiral Dickhead'."

"I think the briefing documents indicated the Mi-25 had several different nicknames. If memory serves, there were several published quotes from a press release that labeled it 'The Tank' and 'The Crocodile'." Take your pick. Both seem to be appropriate," I said, looking out across the fence separating Germany from communist-held Czechoslovakia.

By now, Von had taken his position on the spotter's scope.

"Fuel truck is leaving and the ground crew is turning the Mil Mi-25 around to face us."

Clark was taking pictures in rapid succession. When he finished a complete roll of film in one camera he would drop it down on his chest, where it hung suspended by a wide leather strap. He would then bring up the other Pentax with the slightly smaller telephoto lens.

"Ken, you want me to reload that one for you?"

"No, I'll get it. This bulk film is tricky to get out sometimes."

As he finished the second roll, he removed both cameras from around his neck. He bent down and retrieved a couple of new rolls of film from his ditty[123] bag, and with amazing dexterity swapped the old with the new for both cameras.

"Where would you like me to store the exposed rolls?" he asked.

"You hang onto them. Keep them on your person at all times. I'll ask BG3 on our next call if they want them run down there or if we should keep them here until we're done."

"Looks like they started the engine," said Von. "The rotors are moving."

Ken peered through his camera lens. "Yep, *General Asshole* is getting ready to fly."

I yelled down into the courtyard, "Jack, put a battery in the other tracker. Take it under the arch. Snag a shot if they come at us with any height."

"Roger that," replied Jack.

The Mi-25 went light on its landing gear and rose to a height of

---

122 Communist Russia

123 Ditty bag was originally called "ditto bag" because it contained at least two of everything: two needles, two spools of thread, two buttons, etc. With the passing of years, the "ditto" was dropped in favor of "ditty".

about twenty feet. The giant chopper then proceeded from where it was parked and came toward us to within six hundred feet of the border fence and hovered.

We could all hear the engine sound and prop wash quite clearly now. What happened next was truly amazing. The only maneuver that could have been more photogenic would have been if the Mil had flown across the fence and landed in the courtyard behind us.

The pilot brought the chopper to a complete stop facing us. It then turned in place, 360 degrees in slow motion. I was so mesmerized that I forgot to give the order to start the tracker. Larry, however, did not hesitate to power up. I heard the gyro spinning up and then the speaker pressed next to Larry's ear started emitting a steady tone that only varied slightly when the engines were turned away from us during the presentation. The recording beeps were chirping steady at three-second intervals.

Then, as if on cue, it moved first to the left and then moved another fifty feet back toward the main runway. The demonstration had lasted a full eight minutes. PFC Clark had taken six complete rolls of film.

I was confident that the EE-proms in this tracker had recorded a substantial amount of data on this brand new enemy war machine. Finally, the Mil Mi-25 made a sharp turn to the southeast and continued to gain both speed and height. The gunship was out of sight in less than 30 seconds.

Our mission, it would seem, would have a good outcome. I called down to Jack to ask if he had had any luck. "You get anything, Jack?"

"No, I saw it at the very end as it was climbing to the southeast but it was too far away for a tone lock."

"Ken, tell me you got some good shots?"

"We couldn't have asked for a better photo op," he replied in a very excited voice. "Yes, hell yes, we got some great shots. Oh, man did we ever! Wow, I think "Mr. D" will be really pleased."

Von came up the steps after helping Larry put the tracker back in its case. "Do you think they'll be back today?" he asked.

"They weren't here when we arrived on Thursday," I said. "They came in from the northwest on Friday and left today toward the southeast, so probably not.

"They're probably running some sort of circular point-to-point test for a thousand hours. The briefing document said they run certification procedures similar to our own. However, just to be on the safe side, we need to keep watch until it gets dark. Great job everyone."

"*What a rush,*" I whispered to myself.

TILLYSCHANZE, CZECHOSLOVAKIA BORDER
BASE CAMP 1A, ARCHWAY, ATTACHED TO TURRET
STRUCTURE
1650 HOURS SATURDAY 31 MAY 1969

"GrafTrain, this is Sparrow6. GrafTrain, this is Sparrow6. Over."

"Sparrow6, GrafTrain. Read you five by five. Wait one." Then almost immediately the speaker came back to life.

"Sparrow6, GrafTrain. Be advised that BG is now present at Bravo1. Over."

"Roger, GrafTrain. BG present Bravo1. Break-break," I replied and re-keyed the mike.

"BG6, this is Sparrow6. BG6, this is Sparrow6. Over."

"Sparrow6, BG61. Go," said the voice that sounded very much like my favorite company clerk. The fact that he responded with a "1" after the "BG6" confirmed it was, indeed.

"Sparrow6, BG61. Move to Bravo1 is complete. Use BG location and call signs effective immediately. Over," said Spec5 Bernie Costa.

"Roger, BG61. Message follows to BG3: chicken has flown the coop. We have updated family album. Do you require scrapbook your location now or later? Over."

"Sparrow6, BG61. Hold one for BG31," was the reply. There was a thirty-second wait.

"Sparrow6, BG36. Sparrow6, BG36. Response is hold until completion. I repeat, hold until completion. Scheduled meeting with the Angels is still a go. Acknowledge."

"Roger, BG36. Understand hold to completion. Meeting with Angels still a go. Over."

"BG36, out," replied the Battalion S-3.

"Sparrow6, BG61. Any further traffic?"

"Negative, BG61. See you soon. Over."

"Roger, Sparrow6. Be safe. BG61. Out." And Bernie was gone.

GRAFENWOHR, TRAINING AREA
BATTALION HQ, S3 SECTION
2200 HOURS SATURDAY 31 MAY 1969

A green Porsche 912 pulled up in front of the Grafenwohr field HQ of the 1st 48th Infantry Battalion. A First Lieutenant got out and strolled through the main entrance and asked the Sergeant on duty for Lieutenant Key.

Key wasn't there but CSM Bost was just about to leave the CQ when the First Lieutenant came in.

"Can I help you, Sir?" asked Bost.

"I'm Dutch2; you were told I was coming?"

"We got the TWX yesterday before we left Gelnhausen. It said Major Carlstrum was delayed and that you would be available for the debriefing on Sunday."

"I'll be conducting the debrief, Command Sergeant Major."

"Yes, Sir," said the CSM. "Do you have a place to bunk tonight, Sir?"

"Yes, thanks. I came up with my team. We found a place in town."

That wasn't entirely true. Most of his team wasn't even on the western side of the border that evening. The CIA safehouse he was staying in was not even in Nuremberg, nor was it an actual house, but an entire floor of a hotel located about 46 kilometers to the northwest.

TILLYSCHANZE, CZECHOSLOVAKIA BORDER
BASE CAMP 1A, ARCHWAY
1650 HOURS SATURDAY 31 MAY 1969

"Sparrow6, this is BG6. Over. Sparrow6, this is BG6."

"BG6, this is Sparrow6. Over."

"Sparrow6, stand by for Dutch2" Carl Blubaugh said, about to hand me over to Lt. Pezlola. "Wait one, Sparrow6."

"This is Dutch2. Over."

"Go ahead, Dutch2," I replied.

"Fast birdies arriving your location at zero seven one five hours. Be advised, severe weather expected by morning. Halt all further operations after visit and return this location. Over."

"Roger. Return after visit. Sparrow6. Over."

"Sparrow6, Dutch2. Radio check at zero six three zero hours for weather update and arrival status. Over."

"Roger that, Dutch2. How's the Porsche running? Sparrow6. Over."

"Running just fine, Sparrow6," said First Lieutenant Jim Pezlola. "And, by the way, I'll be conducting the debriefing on Sunday. Dutch2. Out." Pezlola un-keyed his mic and I followed suit.

"Sparrow6 out."

"Who's Dutch2?" asked Ken.

"He's a buddy of Mr. D's. His name is First Lieutenant Jim Pezlola," I answered. "When Mr. D came to visit a while back he borrowed Pezlola's car, according to the papers in the glove compartment. The parking pass and registration indicated the First Lieutenant lives and works in Hilversum."

"Hilversum -- where's that?" asked Von.

"The Netherlands."

"Why is the Lieutenant going to conduct the debriefing on this project and not the Major? What do you think is going on?"

"I guess the Major is out of town on business, Ken. The good news is we can pull up stakes after the F-4s fly by tomorrow morning. We've been here long enough and it's time to go."

"Amen to that," Von and Larry offered up together.

TILLYSCHANZE, CZECHOSLOVAKIA BORDER
BASE CAMP 1A, ARCHWAY, ATTACHED TO TURRET
STRUCTURE
0640 HOURS SUNDAY 1 JUNE 1969

"Oh, man, it's really coming down," I said as I dashed in under the archway enclosure. Jack was standing there looking out through the front of the archway. The wind and rain had rolled in just before daybreak.

"I can't see diddly-squat in this shit. I know Pezlola said that the F-4s[124] were still on track, but do you think they really are still

---

[124] F-4 Phantom Combat Jet Aircraft

going to come?" asked Jack.

"Your guess is as good as mine," I said. "We need to be ready in either case. Larry and Von are loading the last of the gear from downstairs into the vehicles. We can leave as soon as we get to shoot or this exercise gets cancelled."

"Good," said Jack. "Ken went up in the tower to check the tarp."

"Stay dry. I'll be back after I check on him. Von and Larry will be over when they finish loading. It's dry enough in here to store the tracker until it's time to shoot. Tell them to sit one of the trackers in the center of the floor. Here," I pointed.

I stepped out into the rain and saw Von come out of the basement stairwell. I yelled across the courtyard, "Leave one tracker in the trailer. If it clears up we can shoot the second tracker from where the vehicles are parked. But it's not looking good."

THUNDER AND LIGHTNING
TILLYSCHANZE, CZECHOSLOVAKIA BORDER
F-4 ANGEL FLIGHT
BASE CAMP 1A, ARCHWAY ATTACHED TO TURRET STRUCTURE
0706:48 HOURS SUNDAY 1 JUNE 1969

Now I know what you are going to say: "How can someone remember the exact time of an event, especially after forty-three years?" *Truth be told, I still have the stainless steel Seiko timepiece that is frozen at the very moment it took its last breath. But I'm getting ahead of myself.*

"Jesus, did you see that flash across the way?" asked Jack, who was kneeling on the forward edge of the archway just across from where I had sat down. This was followed in two seconds with a very loud clap of thunder.

"Von, pull the tracker out and get it ready. If the F-4s are still coming they should be about five minutes out."

Larry had just run in with a fresh battery he had retrieved from the RE-2 trailer. I stuck my head out and yelled up the tower steps, "Ken, you still okay up there?"

"Yeah, but the visibility is still not good."

I sat down next to the trainer case and watched Von unsnap the clamps as Larry produced a fresh battery from under his poncho and prepared to install it. Both men focused on preparing the tracker in case the storm quieted. The PRC77[125] that was leaning against the side wall was running on its battery pack adapter. The handset skipped to life and a static charged voice called out. "Sparrow6, this is Angel1. Sparrow6, this is Angel1. Over."

I reached for the mike and pulled the spring cord to its full length. I pushed the mike key and said "Angel. . . ." That was as far as I got.

"Sparrow6, Angel1. Sparrow6, Angel1. Sparrow6, Angel1," said the F-4 flight leader for the third time. He received no answer.

Later he would tell me that he had immediately changed frequencies and contacted the guys monitoring the Russian radio surveillance system and reported not being able to contact us. After several unsuccessful tries at reaching us, they had notified Jim Pezlola -- who had been monitoring the transmissions all along.

I remember the complete absence of sound and color. My body arched backward for an eternity it seemed. The heels of my boots touched the back of my head. I remained in this position and lost consciousness. I awoke sometime later, not sure how long I'd been out, to see a gaping hole in the archway ceiling with rain pouring through directly into my eyes. I passed out again.

When I awoke for the third time my body was completely without feeling. One of my legs and my left arm seemed to be missing. I found out later from Clark that both were pinned under the weight of my torso. My head was frozen to the right at a 45-degree outlook. I could see Larry and Von lying on their backs about five feet away. Their bodies were motionless. I couldn't see where Jack was.

It was hard to tell how much time had passed. I couldn't even blink my eyes at this point. There was no sound or color. Everything was being presented in black and white.

The RedEye tracker case lay open between Larry and me. Pieces of the ceiling were scattered everywhere. Rainwater was splashing on the dirt next to my face. There was an enormous volume of liquid pouring down from a large hole that had appeared above us.

The depressed floor was filling with water at an amazing rate. The rainwater was already up on my cheek just below my nose. All I

---

[125] Ground to air radio communications unit

could do was watch.

What had happened? Had the Phantoms dropped some ordinance on us, or was it the Russians who had fired on our position?

No, it was neither, I had realized. We had been struck by lightning.

"It couldn't have been a direct hit; I'd be dead. Maybe I am dead," I thought. In a few more minutes it wouldn't matter either way. The river of water was almost up to my left nostril. My eyes started to be able to blink and I could now hear the wind and rain splashing all around me. However, I was still frozen in the same position. *"What a way to die,"* I thought, *"hit by lightning and drowned in a hole on a hilltop near Grafenwohr."*

I could see the back of Larry's head. A hand came into view and was reaching down to grab his collar. It pulled him up the slight incline at the rear of the archway a few inches at a time, keeping his head above the rising water.

Next, I saw two boots slide into view and the same hand tug at Von's fatigue jacket and moved him up to where Larry was positioned. Then, something caused my head to flop from side to side. My right cheek was sliding through the mud and the water a couple of inches at a time. The jerking movements continued until my head was directly in line with Larry's and Von's.

I could see the sky above us through the hole in the ceiling. The rain was still hitting me directly in the face. I couldn't feel it much, but it was splashing in my eyes affecting my vision. A face appeared. It was Ken Clark, minus his cape.[126] He was yelling something that sounded like, "Take a breath, God damn it."

His head was turning from side to side in a rapid motion. He shouted again that he would be back. He yelled Jack's name and stepped toward the front of the archway. I could tell as he walked away that Ken was also injured. He was dragging his right leg, and his left arm hung slack at his side. He held it in place with his right hand.

He came back into view after a few minutes and yelled into my face for a third time, "Everybody's breathing, but the lightning strike has zapped the four of you good."

"So my diagnosis was correct," I said to myself.

"This radio is fried," said the excited Mr. Clark. "I'll go to the jeep

---

[126]   Reference to Superman

and call for help."

"Good job, Ken," I said to myself, as I was still unable to speak. "Check *the guys again before you do that."*

XIII

AIM OF THE SPARROW

TILLYSCHANZE CASTLE
BASE CAMP 1A
1255 HOURS SUNDAY 1 JUNE 1969

"BG6, Sparrow25. BG6, Sparrow25. Over," called PFC Kenneth Clark in the calmest voice he could muster. His entire team was down. A lightning strike, on the top of the east wall of RedEye Base Camp *One Tango*, had occurred directly over the archway where the team had been waiting out the storm.

"Sparrow25, this is BG61. Come back," said Spec4 Bernie Costa, who had just finished a call from Sultan64.

"Bernie, our whole team is down. We've been hit by a lightning strike. Get us some help up here as soon as possible. Over."

"Roger, Sparrow25. Understand. Request for medical assistance received. Over."

"Yeah, and the sooner the better, Bernie. It's really bad, man. Stand by to copy basecamp coordinates. Wait one."

Ken pulled out a map that indicated our coordinates. "BG61, Sparrow25. Copy coordinates. Over."

"Roger, 25. Go," said Bernie.

"BG61, Whiskey X-ray 150.230 and Victor X-ray 121.032. Over," relayed Ken.

"Roger, Sparrow25. Whiskey X-ray 150.230 Victor X-ray 121.032. Help is on the way."

"Roger, BG. Please come quickly. Out." Ken let go of the mike and turned his attention back to us.

He got the shelter-halves down from the tower and made a makeshift lean-to stretching the canvas off the side of RE-3 and utilizing pieces of wood found in the courtyard to prop it up.

He then returned to the toppled archway and pulled each one of us completely out into the courtyard and under the canvas. It wasn't much shelter, but it got us out of the rain.

Ken told me he was going back inside to secure the RedEye tracker and put it back in its carrying case. He completed the task by pulling the case outside and getting it back in the trailer.

We had all regained consciousness by that time, but none of us could move very well. "How are the others?" I whispered.

"Everybody is breathing," replied Ken. "Help is coming right away," he continued. "Pezlola called back right after I talked to Bernie and they can't get a chopper up in this shit. So they're coming by convoy."

"Good. Make sure the film is secure. Ken, don't let it out of your sight." I fell unconscious for the fourth time.

It took one hour and twelve minutes for the first responders from Grafenwohr to arrive. There were five vehicles in all: two jeeps, one six by six, one deuce and a half containing a rifle squad from Bravo Company, and a green Porsche 912 belonging to Dutch2. The military ambulance was dispatched from Nuremberg and arrived 25 minutes later.

NUREMBERG, ARMY HOSPITAL
EMERGENCY ROOM TRIAGE
1545 HOURS SUNDAY 1 JUNE 1969

Figure 17
Nuremberg Hospital

I awoke to a bone-jarring bounce that lifted the stretcher off the rack supports jutting from the wall of the ambulance. There was a dim ceiling light that revealed two stretchers on the opposite wall.

The vehicle was hitting every pothole and fallen tree available on our journey to the graveyard. My head was being thrown from side to side. The suspension system on this vehicle had obviously been omitted by the manufacturer. There was another stretcher directly above me.

Every part of my body was aching now. The skin on my face felt like I had severe sunburn. I saw Clark seated on a bench in the aisle between the stretchers.

"Is everybody in here? Where are they taking us?"

Before Ken could reply, a voice from above called out. "Fontain, the next camping trip you schedule, you can leave me at home," said Jack, in his usual, best radio announcer's voice.

There was chuckling coming from the other two racks across the aisle. "Thank God we all came through," said Larry.

I wondered what the horrible smell might be.

We arrived at the Nuremberg Hospital[127], which had been personally dedicated by Adolf Hitler in 1937. During World War II, the hospital was expanded to serve 1500 patients. That morning the hospital was a mere shadow of itself with only a 175-bed capacity.

There is something erotic about a woman in uniform. Her name was Captain Janice Prasonio. She had attended the University of Maryland's School of Medicine. She was 27 years old, five feet eight inches tall, and had the most delicious, silky, auburn hair. She was built to the exact specifications that most young men desire.

The first time I saw her I knew she was someone very special. She was standing in the ambulance bay as the doors to the cattle mover were swung open.

The Emergency Room crew unloaded the stretchers, transferred us onto gurneys and rolled us one at a time into a larger

---

[127] The U.S. Army Hospital, Nuremberg, was the first German Army Hospital to be built after the renouncement of the Treaty of Versailles. Construction was begun in 1934 and completed in 1937. In the closing months of WWII, the six story central section was bombed causing severe damage which was not completely repaired until March 1947. The U.S. Army, in June 1945, took control. The 116th General Hospital group set up operations in the Main Building. Since 1945, the Hospital has been occupied by multiple U.S. Army Hospital units.

examining area. There was an oval-shaped administration island in the center of the room. The entire perimeter was partitioned into individual treatment cubicles each equipped with a privacy curtain.

Dr. Prasonio asked for the medics' clipboard containing our vital signs. She quickly reviewed each and proceeded to issue orders to the staff assigning each of us to an exam room.

I had never felt so stiff and sore in all of my life and was beginning to wonder if I would ever walk again.

I was the last one to be pushed out of the ambulance bay. Doctor Prasonio walked to the head of the gurney and said. "Do you know where you are, Sergeant?" She had cupped her hand on my right cheek.

I had heard accounts of the magical occurrence termed *love at first sight* but had dismissed them until this very moment. Some say the condition is produced by touch and a chemical reaction between the male and female. Others suggest that it is Nature's way of promoting the strongest of the warrior class with the most able of the feminine species. I didn't consider myself to be in the warrior category, but when she touched me, and I looked up into her eyes, my heart almost leapt out of my chest. She pulled her hand back as if she had been burned. She continued to study my face, and repeated her question.

"I'm Doctor Prasonio. You're going to be OK. Do you know where you are, Sergeant?"

"This is heaven, right? And you said you were Italian?" I was wheeled deeper into the ER by the worker bees. Doc Prasonio stood there for a few seconds holding the clipboard at her side, and watched the gurney disappear through the double glass doors.

The orderly whipped the curtain closed and helped me sit up and remove my field jacket and fatigue shirt. The smell became more pronounced. As he hauled my shirt tail out of my pants, my 1911 45 ACP, which I had tucked in the small of my back, came out and flopped behind me on the exam table. No one seemed to notice.

As I sat upright on the exam table the orderly unlaced my boots. He pulled both off but held the left one up for me to examine. The back of the boot was melted in places and the entire heel was missing.

More of my clothes were removed. The smell became even more pungent. There was a burn mark on my field jacket and also on both the fatigue and tee shirts. It actually turned out to be a hole burned through three layers of clothing on my left shoulder. He held the shirt up for me to examine. The hole was about the size of a quarter.

With great difficulty I tried to pull my undershirt up, but we ended up just cutting it off. It seemed to be stuck to the skin in places. When I was naked from the waist up I heard the orderly say, "Oh, sweet Jesus." I looked down to see what he was talking about.

Clark pushed the curtain back and came into the exam room. He was sitting outside and heard the comment made by the orderly. He walked over to me to get a better look. I noticed he had my binocular case draped around his neck.

"Why did you bring my binoculars in here, Ken?" He reached down and flipped open the case and pulled out a half melted pair of field glasses.

"You were wearing these when you got hit. I took them off of you and put them back in the case before anyone arrived." I tilted my head down to look at my chest.

There was a red line about an inch and a half wide extending from my left shoulder and spreading down under my armpit to the center of

Figure 18 - Lightning Strike

my chest. The area where my field glasses would have been hanging was an unaffected area exactly the same shape as one side of the metal lens tube of the binoculars.

The angry red line extended from the bottom of the unaffected area on the chest down the abdomen where it veered to the left and continued down my leg. I found out later the metallic case and glass lenses had acted as a makeshift fuse and probably saved my life.

I extended my arms and looked at my chest. Every capillary on both sides of the burn line seemed to have exploded. My face, hands and feet showed similar redness. I was also missing a great deal of body hair. This, I assumed, explained the smell.

Doctor Prasonio came in and asked the others to wait outside, and within seconds we were alone. She walked toward the exam table and stood directly in front of me. She took the stethoscope from around her neck, connected it to her ears and placed the transmitter on my chest.

"Are you having any trouble breathing?" she asked.

"Just now," I said, "when you came in." She looked up and smiled. She walked to the other side of the exam table and listened again to my breathing. It was then that she saw the gun butt sticking out from the remnants of my cut up tee shirt.

She picked up my pistol and slipped it into the pocket of her lab coat without saying a word as the orderly returned with the sponge bath paraphernalia. He hadn't caught what she had done.

"I'm sure you're going to explain to me, Doc, why I'm still alive. And while you're conducting your tests perhaps we need to do a sperm count to see how many of the little guys are still with us." I could hardly believe my own words. The realization of my near-death experience washed over me and my hands started to shake, and I got really, really cold.

The doctor pressed the stethoscope in another spot against my upper back and placed her left hand on my left bicep. Her face only a few inches away from my ear, she whispered. "It's the adrenaline that is causing the tremors."

"I'm sorry. I shouldn't have said that. I'm not myself today," I apologized. She smiled and laughed as another doctor came into the room. This one was full Colonel, complete with the silver chickens attached to each of his collar points. He must have heard what I said because he had whipped the curtain aside and stopped dead in his tracks. He was glaring intently at both of us.

"Uh-oh, you're in for a real treat," Dr. Prasonio leaned in and whispered in my ear as she stepped to my front again and held her stethoscope on another part of my chest.

"Who is he?" I asked, trying not to move my lips.

"That's Dr. James D. Lattermire. He runs this place. As I said, you're in for a real treat."

"Wonderful. Again, I'm sorry for what I said. Don't bother testing. I'm sure all the little bastards are dead."

She smiled and turned to greet Doctor Lattermire.

Dr. James D. Lattermire was 54 years old and the commanding officer of the Nuremburg Hospital Center. He was also the CIA's chief forensic psychologist in Europe.

"Captain Prasonio, is this man giving you any trouble?"

"Why no, Sir" she replied. "He was just expressing concern about the extent and seriousness of his injury," she replied.

"I see. And what is your recommended treatment for these men?"

Before she could answer I said to the chicken Colonel.

"I apologize for my outburst, Sir. I haven't been my usual cheerful self this morning."

Dr. Prasonio was still facing me when I said what I said. She made a cringing expression.

"I may need my gun back," I whispered.

"Not now. Later," she replied in a low voice, not understanding at first why I might need it. She laughed as she finally understood the request and announced on her way out of the room that she would return in a few minutes.

I could see a slight smile appear on the Colonel's face as he looked down at the clipboard attached to the end of the gurney.

What the hell," I said to myself. *"It's his hospital."*

"What do you recommend for this type of injury, Colonel?" I said in a voice that was wrapped with great religious conviction.

Dr. Lattermire put the clipboard back onto a hook at the end of the exam table and walked over and stood directly in front of me. He ran his finger down the red line from the top of my shoulder to the area at the center of my chest. "Aspirin" he stated without delay.

"Aspirin, you say? Why aspirin, Doctor?"

"For the muscle and joint pain, aspirin will do the most good. With light duty you should be back to normal activities in a couple of weeks."

"Aspirin," I said again, "All you have is aspirin?"

"Look here, is it Sergeant?" he asked.

I nodded my head in the affirmative. Being naked to the waist, I said, "Yes, Sir. I haven't had time to get to the tattoo parlor."

"That so?" said the Doc. "I was told that you express yourself slightly differently than most NCOs in similar grades," he said without waiting for a reply. "We've had several people brought to us over the years who were hit by lightning, but...."

I cut him off, "But...?"

"But your people, and of course you are included, are the only ones who were alive on arrival to our ER. To date, that is." He let that sink in before continuing.

"These aren't burns you see," he pointed to the reddened area under my armpit. "This redness is a disruption of the capillaries under the skin."

"So, what does that mean?"

"It means that the best treatment for this type of occurrence is aspirin. The only burned areas are this one small area here," he pointed to the top of my shoulder, "and here," he said as he slowly lifted my left leg and bent down to examine the bottom of my heel. "I stand corrected. The electrical discharge traveled mainly on the surface area of your skin. You are one lucky young man."

"What is the smell?"

Doc Lattermire ran his fingertips across my chest around where my binoculars had been.

"Your body hair has disintegrated along the path of the electrical charge. It'll grow back."

"Marvelous..."

"I received a phone call from your Major Carlstrum. He sends his regards and is delighted to hear that you survived to fight another day."

"Great," I said again. "Is he still vacationing in the south of France?"

Doc Lattermire ignored the comment like he already had the 411[128] on me, and said, "I served with his father in the OSS."

"Then you know his name isn't Carlstrum?" He smiled and winked and said, "Neither was his father's," and without any further comment he turned and left.

"Well, you seem to have friends in high places," said Captain Prasonio, who had come back in as the Colonel was leaving.

"Oh, did fat Charlie from the Mess Hall call?"

"You are all going to be released to Lieutenant Pezlola".

"Is that good? The word on the street is that he is even crazier than Bill Douglas." Her surprise was quickly replaced with a professional look that melted into a complete smile as she turned her head quickly away to examine something on the table by the door.

Jack stuck his head through the curtain and said, "Larry and Von are asking how you're doing."

"I'm doing great. I'll be even better once I get some aspirin. How are you doing?" Doc Janice rolled her eyes at the aspirin comment.

"We're all good. Nobody got burned like you did," said Jack.

"Oh, contraire, Private, I have been disintegrated, not burned," I replied. Doc Janice just shook her head from side to side and laughed. What a nice laugh it was.

"Clark said CSM Bost is in the waiting room," said Jack.

"Wunderbar..."

"Put these on," said the gorgeous doctor as she handed me a set of hospital scrubs. She paused before leaving, "You'll be OK; you understand that, don't you?"

I put my hand on her arm for her to pause.

"I seem to be making an ass of myself since arriving, but I want

---

[128] Information

to thank you for taking care of us."

"You're very welcome, Sergeant," she replied. She turned to leave but stopped and said again, "It's the adrenalin that's making your hands shake."

"I will of course defer to your professional expertise, but I'm sure we both know that it is you that is making me shake, Ma'am."

"You'll be fine in a few hours."

"I doubt that, Captain," I replied.

"I'll be back in a minute to get you all discharged," she said and walked from the cubicle, pulling the curtain closed as she left

"That is one fine looking Doctor," said Jack Swanson as he stuck his head inside my cubicle curtain again.

"Yep, we need to do this again next weekend," I grinned.

"Sorry, I have other plans. Seriously, how are you doing?"

"My back is still stiff, but the quicker we can get out of here the better."

"That's quite a red mark you have there. Will it scar?" asked Jack.

"Nah, I just took some aspirin. Better go tell the others we'll be leaving soon," I said and lifted the scrub top slowly and painfully over my head.

He started to leave and I asked, "Jack, where's Ken?"

"He went out front to see Bost and hasn't come back yet," replied Jack.

"They probably shot the messenger. I'll bet this is going to cause a shitload of paperwork for somebody." Jack laughed and left the room.

HOTEL BERGHOF
OCHSENKOPFSTRASSE 40
BISCHOFSGRUN, GERMANY
2200 HOURS SUNDAY 1 JUNE 1969

We exited the ER into the hospital's main lobby. Larry, Von, and Jack were walking out under their own power. I, on the other hand, was being wheeled out in style. CSM Bost and Lt. Pezlola were there to greet us.

"Good evening, Sir," I nodded to Pezlola. "Command Sergeant Major, sorry to have kept you waiting," I addressed Bost.

"No problem, Fontain. The Colonel wanted to be here but he was called away at the last minute. Do you know Lt. Pezlola?"

I extended my hand to his and said, "No, but I think I drove your car a few weeks ago."

"Major Carlstrum said you were good at filling in the blanks."

"Lieutenant Pezlola has graciously offered to put your team up for the night at his hotel," said CSM Bost.

I nodded to the Lieutenant and said, "Yes, Sir. Thank you, Sir."

"I borrowed a six by six from Bravo Company," said Bost. "It's parked out front and the trip ticket is in the glove box. Check in tomorrow with Blubaugh."

"Yes, Sergeant Major," I replied. Doctors Prasonio and Lattermire had walked out into the lobby and were watching the exchange.

"The Colonel and I were relieved to hear that Redeye will live to fight another day," offered the CSM.

"Thank you, Sergeant Major, for coming to get us."

"Lieutenant Pezlola and Command Sergeant Major Bost, may I present our saviors, Doctors Prasonio and Lattermire."

"Thanks for taking care of them," said the CSM, who went over and shook hands with both of them. The Lieutenant remained where he was and nodded his head, saying, "We've already met."

"I've got to get back. Doctors, Gentlemen," said Bost, who turned and walked out to a waiting jeep.

"You can follow me to the hotel," said Pezlola. Fontain, you can ride with me if you can bend your torso at the required angle to access the Porsche. How about you guys? You about ready to go?" he asked the standing members, no pun intended, of the Redeye Team Leaders.

"We're all ready," I spoke on everyone's behalf. I struggled to get out of the wheelchair. Clark and Captain Janice came to each side of the chair and helped me to my feet.

"Well, I guess this is goodbye, Doctor. You don't make house calls by any chance?"

"You never know, Sergeant. Take it easy until you get your sea legs back."

"Aye, aye, Sir, Ma'am," I replied. She smiled and laughed.

When we reached the sidewalk out in front, I said, "Ken you drive, I'm going to ride with the LT. Flash your lights if you need anything. See you at the hotel," I said and carefully lowered myself into the passenger side of the sports car. Von and Larry climbed stiffly into the back of the truck. Jack rode shotgun up front with Clark. The distance from Nuremberg to the sleepy little town of Bischofsgrün would take just 52 minutes by car.

"You going to be alright, Sergeant?" asked Pezlola.

"I'm definitely a lot taller than I was this morning, but to answer your question, Sir: I'm not so sure. If you had asked me that earlier I would have said no problem."

"And why not now?" he asked.

"I really can't explain it, Sir. Doctor Prasonio takes my breath away." We rode on for a while in silence.

"The Major will be here sometime tomorrow. Until then you will be our guests in a very nice hotel in a town called Bischofsgrun. How does that sound?"

"What is the story on Doctor Prasonio?" I asked, ignoring the information about the hotel. "I noticed you seemed to have had a prior encounter with the good doctors."

"Nothing on the social level," replied the LT. "But I do have a friend who can get you a great deal on some oxygen tanks." It took me a moment to cross-reference his meaning.

"That's funny, Sir. And they say officers don't have a sense of humor."

"A word to the wise, Sergeant, is that you should be careful of what you wish for."

We arrived at the Hotel Berghof just before 2200 hours. Built in 1962, it was a low profile, modern, two-story structure and appeared to be well maintained. We parked, and I painfully got out and directed Clark to park the truck next to the Porsche.

Everybody piled out and followed the LT into the lobby. I looked around hoping that a.) The bar would be still open, and b.) Some type of food would be made available. Before I could ask about the hotel's topless bar and restaurant the Lieutenant marshaled us into the elevator and inserted a key into the panel.

On the ride up we were told we were going to the second floor in the west wing. The elevator opened to a well-lit hallway that was carpeted and elegantly decorated. The Lieutenant told us that there were a total of five first class suites on the floor and that we were the only tenants. We followed him halfway down the hallway. He stopped and said each suite had three bedrooms with a bath. "My guys have the two suites on the right side of the hall. I suggest you divide yourselves up between these two suites, numbers 27 and 29," Pezlola said, pointing to the left side of the hallway.

"I took the liberty of having the Bravo Company guys put your duffel bags on the truck before your vehicles went back to Graf. I had one of my people come to the hospital and bring your gear back here.

"I believe everything has been placed in this suite," he continued as he pointed to the door marked 27. Let's meet in an hour at the end of the hallway -- Suite 30."

"Thanks, Lieutenant, I really appreciate the hospitality," I said, and everyone else parroted their thanks. Everyone else filed through the doorway of Suite 27.

I remained in the hallway with the Lieutenant.

He said, "Sergeant, in here you can call me Jim."

"Thanks again, Jim. Please call me Rick."

"Go grab a shower, Rick. I've got a surprise for you later," he said and turned and walked to Suite 30, knocked twice, and then once more. After the single knock, the door was opened.

Clark came out in the hallway carrying both of our duffel bags. "Looks like you and I will have to rough it in 29," said a very tired looking PFC Kenneth Clark.

"Grab a quick shower and a change of clothes," I said as we walked into Suite 29. The entrance of the suite opened into a large living room area with two of the bedrooms located on the left wall and one on the back wall at the far end of the living room.

"I'll go straight and you go left," I said, and added, "That didn't come out right, but you know what I meant."

"OK, see ya after I shower," Ken said.

"Ken," I said, and he turned to face me, "thanks for taking care of all of us today. You saved our lives. We owe you a great deal."

"All of today's events seem almost dream-like, so I'm not really clear on what transpired earlier. I'm just glad everybody made it through," he said and hefted his bag and walked toward that wonderful vision of unlimited hot water.

HOTEL BERGHOF
SUITE 30
BISCHOFSGRUN, GERMANY
2355 HOURS SUNDAY 1 JUNE 1969

After the longest shower that I have had since high school, we gathered in the large living room of the even more impressive accommodations of Suite 30. Jim Pezlola told me later that this hotel was specifically designed and built to accommodate in-country ski enthusiasts.

Jim's influence had generated a phone call from the hotel owner, Max Gresonine, to the night manager. He in turn had arranged for the preparation of a complete breakfast buffet. This was delivered and waiting for us when we arrived. Scrambled eggs, hot cakes, home fried potatoes, bacon, sausage and large pitchers of milk and orange juice. There was also an enormous container of coffee.

Jim pointed out a fully stocked bar on the opposite side of the room. We were told to help ourselves. *"The spy business must pay well,"* I thought to myself.

The sunken living room in this suite was larger and a little deeper than the one in Suite 29. There were two steps down into an area containing three sofas and a large glass-top coffee table in the center. The furniture looked and felt expensive. There was a spiral staircase to the right side of the bar that coiled its way to a second level loft area.

I had just settled back in my seat when the door chime sounded and was followed by the same knocking sequence that Jim had used before. Jack, who was seated on one of the bar stools, slid stiffly off with the great caution that was usually exacted by an eighty year old man. That accomplished he started toward the door. Jack called out as he shuffled along, "I'll get it."

"Check and ask who it is before you open it, Jack," Jim called from across the room.

"Right." He looked through the peephole and announced, "It's the doctors from the hospital." I looked over to Lieutenant Jim who was seated across the room. He was grinning from ear to ear.

Doctors Prasonio and Lattermire walked in and proceeded to hang their jackets up in the hallway closet with a certain familiarity that suggested that this was not their first visit to suite number thirty.

They were both dressed in civilian attire. Dr. Lattermire, who I guessed was at least in his early fifties, was wearing a tan, camel hair sports coat and blue slacks, and Janice Prasonio was dressed in a white turtleneck sweater and hounds tooth pleated skirt with a single strand of black pearls around her neck. She was by far the prettier of the two.

"All right, guys. Line up. The aspirin is here," I announced. This earned me a very dirty look from Janice but it got a good solid laugh from Doc Lattermire.

"Heads up," he called and tossed a large bottle of aspirin to me from across the room. I snagged the thirty-foot shot with my left hand right at ear level.

Janice walked down into the living room and took a seat next to me on the couch.

"I could have sworn you were right handed. How are you feeling?" asked Janice. She then whispered, "You really don't want to get on his bad side."

"You keep saying that, and he keeps giving me aspirin," I said, and shook the bottle. "I think he loves me. Speaking of love, to what do we owe this wonderful surprise?"

Doc Janice didn't respond to that comment and turned her attention across the room to where Larry and Von were sitting.

"How are you feeling? Has the muscle soreness subsided any?" she asked.

"Much, much, better Doctor. Thanks for asking," said Von and Larry at almost the same time.

"I am four point two inches taller thanks to God's free electricity," said Jack. "I will need to call my tailor when we get back to Gelnhausen."

Janice chuckled and asked, "Where's PFC Clark?"

"He's up in the loft studying the secret code books," I said. "Let me guess why you're here: the results of my sperm test are back. Go ahead. Tell me. I can take it."

"You're crazy."

"Is that your professional opinion?"

"No, it's just a personal observation."

"Too bad," I said and continued. "I've been reading about this type of diagnosis. It almost always leads to a miniscule but well-known Army policy termed Section 8[129]."

"You really are crazy."

---

[129] The term Section 8 refers to a category of discharge from the United States military when a soldier is judged mentally unfit for service. It also came to mean any serviceperson given such a discharge or behaving as if deserving such a discharge, as in the expression, "He's a Section 8". The term comes from Section VIII of the World War I-era United States Army Regulation 615-360, which provided for the discharge of those deemed unfit for military service.

"Now we're getting somewhere. Can *you* help me fill out the necessary application forms?"

"No," she said, laughing. "How about we change the subject and you buy me a drink?" She got up and started toward the bar.

"OK, but I think everything in here is either free or classified."

"Hmmm," was the sound she made as she continued across the room.

When she returned from checking on everyone and saying hello to Jim, she returned to sit back down next to me.

"Everyone seems to be doing well."

We talked for almost two hours nonstop. We discussed everything from high school to our favorite music. It turned out she grew up in Maryland not far from where I did. She even had heard of the band I had played with. If there was such a thing as a soul mate, she was mine.

The attraction I had experienced at the hospital was now in double triple overdrive. She seemed to be having similar feelings. She would reach over and touch the back of my hand in recounting a point she was describing. This would send shivers up and down my back.

I would rest my arm along the top of the sofa so that I could touch her hair every so often with the tips of my fingers. And she would respond by shifting her head into my open hand. Each time it would result in a slight pause in the as to why we were acting and feeling this way.

HOTEL BERGHOF
SUITE 29
BISCHOFSGRUN, GERMANY
1155 HOURS SUNDAY 1 JUNE 1969

I announced that I was having a hard time keeping my eyes open -- which was a lie -- and was going to turn in. Janice said it was getting late and she was going to call it a night.

"I'll walk you out."

Von had left earlier to make a phone call. Jack and Larry were at the bar. Clark had climbed the stairs to the loft again and was deep in conversation with one of Pezlola's crypto people. Dr. Lattermire and Lieutenant Pezlola were seated at a small table on the far side of the room having a private conversation. We called out to everyone and said good night.

As I was helping Janice into her jacket she turned to me and said, "I have something of yours that I need to return."

"Oh, what might that be?"

"I have your pistol."

"I had forgotten about it to tell the truth. Since I met you today I haven't been able to think of much else." We walked down the corridor toward my room. She opened her shoulder bag and retrieved the 45 and handed it to me.

"Can you come in for a moment? I want to ask you something." I turned the handle and pushed open the door. I put the 45 on the table near the door and led the way to the edge of the living room.

"Nightcap?" I asked as I stepped down and took a seat on the closest sofa. Janice followed and took a seat next to me. She saw that I was still moving like a very old man.

"All my muscles wish they were back to the same length that they were enjoying yesterday," I said.

Janice smiled and said, "Do you want something for the pain?"

"No, I'm okay."

"Well if the aspirin doesn't do the job, let me know and I'll get you something stronger."

"How about that night cap then?"

"No thanks, I have a long drive ahead of me. What did you want to ask me?"

"Did you clean the pistol?"

"No, but I removed this from the chamber before I put it in my purse." She tossed the 45 caliber round to me. "That's not what you wanted to ask me, is it?"

"No, it's not." And I reached over and put my hand on her cheek and moved my head to within an inch of her face, paused for a second, and kissed her lightly on the lips. I moved back to look at her face. Her eyes were still closed and she seemed to be very okay with the kiss. So I kissed her again, but this time I pressed a little harder and let it last a lot longer.

When our lips finally parted she had wrapped her arms around my neck and pulled me very close. We stayed that way for a good long while. Finally, I whispered in her ear, "If I left unsaid what I'm feeling tonight I know I would regret it for the rest of my life."

"I'm glad you kissed me. I've been thinking of you ever since you left the hospital. I can't explain it, but I've never felt this way about anyone before," she confessed.

"I had almost convinced myself it was the trauma making me feel this way," replied Rick.

"Until Doctor Lattermire said that Jim Pezlola had called and asked if we could come up tonight, after shift, I didn't realize how much I wanted to see you again."

"Remind me to thank Jim."

She stood and reached down and took my hand in hers and pulled me to my feet to face her. She looked up into my eyes. I started to speak but she put her finger to my lips. She then placed both of her hands on both sides of my head and pulled me toward her. The kiss started ever so softly intensifying with every second that passed. Finally, our lips parted and we looked at each other.

She asked, "Which room is yours?"

HOTEL BERGHOF
SUITE 29
BISCHOFSGRUN, GERMANY
0610 HOURS MONDAY 2 JUNE 1969

The rain had finally stopped during the night, and the sun was trying to work its way around the edges of the curtains. Janice was lying on her stomach with her arm draped across my chest.

"God, she is beautiful. It's hard to believe that just a few hours ago she was trying her best to give me a heart attack."

I had awakened at 0500. I put one foot on the floor and, with great effort, got up to pee, stretch my muscles, and took some more aspirin. I got back in bed and had been lying there ever since, just watching her sleep.

Finally, with her eyes still shut, she smiled and said, "Good morning Sergeant. Did you sleep OK?"

"Not much sleep but the 2000 push-ups really did help realign my spine to its original length ," I said with a laugh. "You never answered my question last night."

"Which was?"

"Are you attracted to me?"

"Well, I guess it's too late to take the Fifth, but yes, I feel a certain something towards you."

"Great. You want to get a beer later?" I said in an off-hand tone.

This was followed by her getting into a kneeling position and hitting me repeatedly with one of the pillows. There is nothing like a pillow fight to get the old juices flowing.

She lifted her leg up and over to straddle me. I reached up and pulled her close nuzzling my face between her breasts. I felt her hips rise up slightly and with her left hand she reached down and gently caressed my penis. And without any hesitation she guided it to place that seemed to perfect to comprehend.

We made love one more time before getting dressed.

HOTEL BERGHOF
LOBBY COFFEE SHOP
0830 HOURS MONDAY 2 JUNE 1969

Janice decided to skip breakfast. What she said next was in a most serious tone.

"We need to be discreet."

"You're right, of course. We should never leave this room."

She told me she had to go on duty at 1300. I told her I thought she was pure love. She followed that up with the Army regulation about touting a relationship between a NCO and an officer in public. I told her I thought I could get her promoted to Sergeant. She reaffirmed her original premise that I was truly insane.

Finally, she sat on the edge of the bed and said, "I feel like I could love you forever, Rick. I've never felt like this before, never. How can we do this?"

"I'm no expert on this subject, but I think you have a natural aptitude for the activity." It took just a moment for her to take my implied meaning.

"You idiot," she said affectionately.

"You can get the paperwork for applying for a Section 8, yes?"

"While I'm at work, think about a plan of action that will allow us to serpentine through the rest of your Army career and deliver us safely together at the other end."

"No problem. The difficult takes minutes and the impossible takes slightly longer," I intoned.

"The important word to concentrate on is *together.* Your file indicates that you are very creative when it comes to thinking outside the box. Let's see how you do thinking up a project we'll call: *Operation I Don't Want to Be Court Martialed.*

"Look, you're the one who stands to really get annihilated in this situation. If you think we should not continue..." I said softly.

"Oh, my God, what am I doing? You're having second thoughts...," This last statement she said to herself more than to me.

"Excuse me; I am not having second thoughts. As a matter of fact I have never been so sure of what I want to do. I love you and I will do whatever is necessary to keep you safe in all of this. With that said he put his arms around her and they stayed that way for a good long time.

"Did you say *my* file," I asked. "How did you see my file?" She ignored the question but was smiling.

We walked out to the front of the hotel. She hadn't parked near Dr. Lattermire's car the night before so she thought our secret was safe for the time being. I asked again about her having seen my file and she told me that she shouldn't have mentioned anything about it, and she wasn't free to discuss it.

"Are you in the Band[130], Janice?" She ignored that question, too.

"Here," she handed me a card. "This is my number at the hospital and this is my home number written on the back. I work evenings the rest of this week. Call me and let me know what they decide to do with your team."

"Will do... You want me to come down your way tonight?"

"No, I'll come out to get you. We can decide where to go then. And by the way, Major Carlstrum is the only one who can answer your questions or offer any insight on his operation here in Bischofsgrun[131]."

"Did you know you have a habit of changing topics in midstream?"

"Only really smart people could know that," she said and smiled. She got in her car, started the engine and rolled the window down.

"I had a very nice time with you, Sergeant Fontain."

"Oh, shucks, Janice. Call me Rick." I bent down and kissed her a

---

[130] CIA

[131] Bischofsgrün (English translation: "Bishops green") is a municipality in the district of Bayreuth in Bavaria in Germany. Bischofsgrün is situated within the Fichtelgebirge mountain range between the range's two largest mountains; Schneeberg (1051 m) and the Ochsenkopf (1025 m).

long goodbye through the open window. "Why don't we do this until you run out of gas?"

"Are you kidding? Have you seen the price of gas here?"

MEETING: MAJOR B. D. CARLSTRUM AND LTC THOMAS BROGAN
GRAFENWOHR TRAINING AREA
BATTALION HQ 1/48 INF
1030 HOURS MONDAY 2 JUNE 1969

"Sir, thank you for seeing me," said Major Carlstrum as he saluted Lt. Col. Brogan, who was seated at one of the folding tables inside the HHC field tent.

"At ease. Have a seat, Major," Brogan said casually, returning the salute. "Our RedEye guys were almost disintegrated on Sunday morning. CSM Bost tells me that your Lt. Pezlola is nursing them back to health as we speak."

"I spoke to Dr. Lattermire this morning, Sir. They're all recovering with no long-term effects expected. Sergeant Fontain was the only one burned, and that was limited to the small area on his shoulder and the bottom of his left foot. All five of them experienced severe electric shock. Apparently PFC Clark was not as close to the strike point as the others and was able to keep the others from drowning."

"Drowning?" asked the LTC, his voiced filled with disbelief. "How in the hell can you drown in a castle ruin?"

"It's pretty incredible, really. Clark was up in the third level of the tower. He was standing on some sort of wooden crate to get a better view of the Russian air base. His left elbow was the only part of his body that was touching the stone wall when the lightning strike occurred. He was thrown across the room. He got up and limped down the stairs. His left arm and leg were partially paralyzed.

"When he reached the archway, all four of his team mates were down. They all appeared to be unconscious and trapped under the rubble of the collapsed ceiling. He pulled all four of the men, a couple inches at a time, out of the low spot in the floor which was rapidly filling with rain water."

"What you're describing is right out of a Hollywood film script."

"Yes, Sir. May I continue?"

"Please. Go ahead," said Brogan.

"There's not much more to tell except that Clark got on the horn

and notified BG of the emergency. He secured the camp and the equipment, and he kept everybody safe until the EVAC convoy came and got them."

"I see," said Brogan. "Why wasn't any of this told to us yesterday?"

"Lt. Pezlola ran a de-brief last night after the team was released from Nuremburg Hospital. Sir, this entire operation has to remain Top Secret/Sparrow View. My boss asked me to personally come and thank you for your support and to brief you on the results of the operation thus far."

"How did we do on the data gathering?" asked the LTC.

"The film was received in Langley on Sunday evening. Clark will come here tomorrow and remove the e-prom recorders from the trackers. Lieutenant Pezlola will send them on for processing. I'm waiting to hear how the pictures turned out, but from what I was told, this operation was a complete success."

"I'm glad to hear that, Major."

"Sir, we have a facility about 50 clicks from here. Your RedEye team is there now. They're welcome to stay there until released from light duty. That is, of course, with your approval, Sir."

"I have no problem with that arrangement. Tell CSM Bost or SPC5 Blubaugh what you're doing on your way out. And let them know how to contact you in case the need arises."

"Yes, Sir," said Carlstrum.

"So, when can I expect my RedEye team to be back protecting my Battalion from the communist air forces?"

"Sir, I've been told that the light duty restrictions should last no more than ten days."

"Good, I'll look forward to getting them back."

"We have nothing in the hopper that will involve them in the immediate future, Sir. If a situation should occur, an effort would be made to incorporate that into their normal training activities. Thanks again for all of your support," said Major Carlstrum, alias Bill Douglas. He leaned forward and extended his hand to LTC Brogan. Carlstrum stood, saluted and left the HQ.

After the Major was safely out of earshot Brogan called out to his S-3 clerk. "Carl, come in here and bring your pad. It seems we have a hero amongst us."

Bill Douglas went to a black Mercedes sedan parked across from the HHC area and got in the driver's side. He reached down under the seat and pulled out the mike cord to its full length. He keyed the microphone and called.

"Sultan62, this is Paradine6. Over." The comeback was immediate. *"Paradine26, this is Sultan 25. 22 is on route. Go."*

"BG7 updated with Redeye/Sparrow project details. Seeds planted. Returning your location. Out."

HOTEL BERGHOF
SUITE 30
BISCHOFSGRUN, GERMANY
1615 HOURS MONDAY 2 JUNE 1969

I was just stepping into the hallway from my room when, lo and behold, walking up the hallway towards Suite 30 was the mysterious "Mr. D".

"Good afternoon, Sir. Three bags full."

"Someday, not today, you'll have to explain to what you're alluding with that phrase. How are you, Rick? From what I've been told, you all had an electrifying experience, no pun intended."

"Yes Sir, the phrase has to do with wool gathering and cruelty to sheep, no pun intended, but it originally comes from a nursery rhyme. If you can spare it, Sir, I'd like a couple minutes of your time."

"Sure. Come with me while I check in with Lt. Pezlola. We can chat after that."

"Yes, Sir," I said and followed him into the suite. We walked around the edge of the living room to the circular staircase. I followed him up the steps into the loft.

There were a half dozen teletype machines located back-to-back in the center of the room. Two of the guys I recognized from this morning in the coffee shop. They were seated by a row of rack-mounted radio equipment.

On the far wall was an array of electronics labeled INTELSAT and on the wall closest to me was a set of bookcases containing at least 25 very sophisticated looking handbooks and binders. *Rockwell Collins, Cedar Rapids, Idaho* was displayed prominently on most of them.

"Nice stereo," I commented. My attempt at humor with Bill Douglas, as usual, went unnoticed. Or, so I thought. Never discouraged, I continued. "Are you involved in the upcoming Apollo moon launch?"

Something on one of the teletypes had caught Douglas's attention and he wasn't hearing anything I said. Lt. Pezlola was on the phone with his back to us, seated in front of one of the other machines.

Douglas turned to me and said, "Forget you saw any of this, please?"

"Yes, Sir, I'm erasing it now."

"Let me check in with Jim and I'll meet you down by the bar."

I went back downstairs and poured myself some of the Haig & Haig Scotch that I had tasted the night before.

"OK, that's taken care of," said "Mr. D", winding his way down the stairs. "I'm all ears. That looks good -- what are you drinking?"

"Scotch," I replied.

Bill Douglas went behind the bar and fixed himself a drink and while he had his back to me said, "So, you first. You wanted to talk?"

"Jim told me that the doctors want us on light duty for the next couple of weeks. I would like to figure a way to get my married guys back to Gelnhausen. The problem is we don't have wheels."

"That shouldn't be a problem. You can borrow one of the cars from here. How many of your guys are married?"

"Two: Von Boyd and Larry Stockert are the only ones."

"Tell them they can take off tonight but to be back up here on Friday afternoon. We should know where Bost wants you by this weekend. When the Doctor releases you, and you're more nimble, you may be ordered to take your vehicles back to Coleman. At least that's what your S-3 Clerk suspects. What's his name? Blueballs?"

"Blubaugh, Sir," I said, laughing.

"See Pezlola about which car you can use."

"Thanks. And there is one more question. Who do we reimburse for the rooms and the food? This has been a real treat."

"We keep this floor year round. You're welcome to stay here any time you're up this way. Just call before you come."

"Are you saying we will be working up this way in the near term, Sir?"

Ignoring my question, he said, "I have a deal with the owner who is a friend of a friend of the family."

"Are you talking about yours or Uncle Sam's?"

"Everything is taken care of, so enjoy."

MEETING: CIA HEADQUARTERS RUSSIAN DESK
COMBAT SYSTEMS ANALYSIS
LANGLEY, VIRGINIA
2035 HOURS MONDAY 2 JUNE 1969

"Who took these pictures? These are better than the ones provided from our people inside Mil Moscow[132]. Look, the air intakes are just below the rotor assembly on this one. This is the prototype with two engines. These rear shot photos confirm what we thought. They're using the same baffle configuration as the Backfire[133] engines, said an excited Brent Cummings.

Daryl Russell, who was in the process of pouring a cup of coffee, had come to collect the material he had lent out the previous evening. The meeting was taking place on the third floor in the Combat Systems Analysis section. There were over a hundred photographs spread on the tabletop.

"Daryl, did these pictures come from the same guys who did the Rhein-Main project for us?" asked Cummings, who ran the East German INTEL Desk. Those were great, and these are even better."

"Glad you like them. Yep, same guys, and the EE-prom data will be available by the end of the week," added Russell.

"That's really good news because it looks like we can shoot this big son-of-a-bitch from all sides," said Cummings.

"Yeah, the reports submitted with the photos say 'RedEye tone solid' at 625 meters, which means no software adjustments are necessary at this time," added Russell.

"Outstanding, outstanding," said Cummings.

"I'm presenting the findings at tomorrow's department update."

"Thanks for letting us preview the results before the announcement tomorrow.

"Hey, we all have to share our good fortune don't we?" said Russell. He had just come from a briefing on the sixth floor. Sultan6 had reported large amounts of activity of Russian military armor in

---

132 Mil Moscow is the Russian manufacturing facility located outside of Moscow

133 The Tupolev Tu-22M (Russian: Туполев Ту-22M; NATO reporting name: Backfire) is a supersonic, swing-wing, long-range strategic and maritime strike bomber

the rail yards 50 kilometers east of Geisa[134], which was a town in the Wartburgkreis district in East Germany. "Alert or Invasion" was the issue of concern.

COLEMAN KASERNE
GELNHAUSEN GERMANY
1ST 48TH INF PARADE GROUNDS
0830 HOURS WEDNESDAY 2 JULY 1969

"Attention to orders," LTC Thomas Brogan boomed into the microphone. Present on the parade grounds was the entire battalion minus Charlie Company, which had just left for Grafenwohr to receive training on the M72 LAWS[135] Light Anti-Armor Weapons System.

Everybody was dressed in his summer Sunday best. The Army khaki cotton uniform, composed of khaki shade-1 cotton twill shirt and trousers, was the traditional mainstay of summer garrison duty attire.

My guys described it as "a drab color that looked warm on a hot summer day."

"Today, we get to recognize some of our own for a job well done," said Colonel Brogan. "While the nature of the act is still classified, I can tell you that through their efforts this nation is a lot safer today because of it. Would PFCs Boyd, Stockert, and Swanson step forward and be recognized?"

Bernie and I had rehearsed what they were supposed to do the evening before. The only difference that morning was that the Colonel didn't call PFC Ken Clark's name with the rest of the team. Larry, Von and Jack made a left face from where they were standing and proceeded in a single file to a place directly in front of our Commanding Officer.

"Would PFC Kenneth Clark also please come forward?" Ken did

---

[134] Geisa is a town in the Wartburgkreis district, in Thuringia, Germany. It is situated in the Rhön Mountains, 26 kilometers northeast of Fulda.

[135] The M72 LAW (Light Anti-Tank Weapon, also referred to as the Light Anti-Armor Weapon or LAW as well as LAWS Light Anti-Armor Weapons System) is a portable, one-shot, 66-millimeter, unguided anti-tank weapon.

a left face and took his position next to his teammates.

"You men have earned the honor and respect of the entire 3rd Armor Division. Through your actions you have honored this Battalion, this Division, and the United States of America. Attention to orders," the Colonel boomed again into the microphone.

"PFC Clark, it is with great pride that I have the honor of presenting you with the Army Commendation Medal.[136] This award is presented for sustained acts of heroism in protecting and saving the lives of your team members while conducting field operations near Grafenwohr, Germany. Your actions reflect well on yourself, the 1st/48th Infantry, and the United States Army." Colonel Brogan walked to where Clark was standing at attention.

"Congratulations," said the LTC as he pinned the ACM to Ken's blouse.

Colonel Brogan returned to the podium. "It is also my distinct honor in announcing the following individual promotions to the rank of Specialist-4, Pay Grade E-4, with an effective promotion date of One June Nineteen Hundred and Sixty-Nine."

Colonel Brogan returned to where all four RedEye shooters remained at attention. He then proceeded down the line, handing each man his new rank insignia, shaking their hands and congratulating each by name. But when he got to Clark he rested his hand on his shoulder. Leaning in slightly, the Colonel whispered something in Ken's ear.

I could see Ken blush and then break out into a big smile. This was noticeable all the way back to where I was standing. Ken never told any of us what was said, but knowing the Colonel it fit Spec4 Kenneth Clark like a glove.

The Colonel returned to his former position and said, "Company commanders, dismiss your men."

---

[136] The Commendation Medal is a mid-level United States military decoration that is presented for sustained acts of heroism or meritorious service. The medal is a bronze hexagon, and depicts the American bald eagle with spread wings on the face. The eagle has the U.S. shield on its breast and is grasping three crossed arrows in its talons. On the reverse of the medal are inscriptions "FOR MILITARY" and "MERIT" with a plaque for engraving the recipient's name between the two inscriptions. A spray of laurel, representing achievement is at the bottom. The ribbon is a field of myrtle green with five white stripes in the center and white edges.

A short time after the award ceremony, First Sergeant Bumpus, Captain MacKennia, Major Carlstrum, and I were standing on the sidewalk outside of the HHC Arms Room.

"Clark looked embarrassed," said our CO, Captain MacKennia.

"That guy saved my life. He deserves that promotion and more," I said.

"Thanks for inviting me down today, George, Top," said Carlstrum to MacKennia and Bumpus. "Rick, I need a word with you before I go.

We walked back toward the Orderly Room where he had parked Jim Pezlola's Porsche.

"Jim said you called and said you were going to be up in Nuremberg again this weekend."

"Yes, Sir, I did."

"Well?"

"Well what, Sir?"

"You wanna tell me why you're going to Nuremberg?"

"I'm not sure you want to know that I know that you know, Sir."

"Come again?" responded Douglas.

"Are you sure you want to know?"

"We both know it's too late for that." He went on without waiting for me to answer. "First of all, let me say that Dr. Prasonio is one of the finest doctors, and nicest people, I've ever met. She also happens to be my boss's boss's granddaughter."

"Oh, Jesus, this is not going to end well, Rick," I said to myself.

"She called me and told me that she was seeing you, and was that going to cause any problems," said Douglas.

"Sir, we have been getting together several times a week and every weekend for the last month."

"So I understand. I told her that I had no problem with it but the Army would not think it was a great idea for her to be dating a sergeant," said Douglas.

"We discussed the same thing, but we decided to take the risk."

"She made it clear that it was something she would deal with when it became necessary," said Douglas. He paused and let that sink in before continuing.

"So, I asked if Lattermire knew about the two of you and she said she had already had that conversation with him. She told me that he already had figured it out. He'd seen her car on the parking lot the night you two left together. He also told her that he would have to be blind not to notice the way the two of you were looking at each other."

"Lattermire is pretty sharp. What's his role in all of this?"

Douglas didn't answer directly. "He also said he was glad that she had found someone, and that it was a real blessing that it was you."

"Jesus," I said again, this time aloud. "What am I supposed to say to that? Do you want us to stop seeing one another?"

"You're not listening. Lattermire is a big fan of both of you. You two do what you need to do. Just be damned careful from here on out."

"We have been very careful for the last month. Our short term plan is to remain invisible until I rotate out of here in April."

"And then?" Douglas asked.

"If she will have me, I'm going to ask her to marry me," I said and paused. "I love her very much. Tell me something, Major. Does what Doc Lattermire do for the company have anything to do with his statement about Janice being blessed?"

"Doctor Lattermire is wearing several different hats at the moment. The one I think you're interested in is his expertise in developing and evaluating psych profiles for all our people in Europe. So, to make a long story short, et cetera, et cetera," said Douglas.

"Has he read-in on me?"

"If you're asking has he seen your file, yes, he's read it and he maintains it. It turns out, Rick, that you are one of those rare individuals who comes along once in a great while. It was one of the reasons I had you sent here. Your profile shows you to be a person who will always, no matter what, protect those you work for, those who work for you, and more importantly, those you love. For you Rick, there is no difference among the three," said Bill Douglas with a look I hadn't seen before.

"You people got all of this wisdom from a hundred-plus questionnaire administered at Fort Bragg?"

"Yes. We find them to be extremely accurate. Combine that with your uncanny ability to walk and chew gum at the same time, it's no wonder old Doc Lattermire has become one of your strongest admirers."

"Marvelous. Are you going to be around this weekend?"

"No, I have to go to London. It seems our friends across the border are getting restless. I'll check in with you when I get back.

See you later, Rick."

Major Carlstrum aka Bill Douglas stepped off the curb and walked toward the Porsche. He turned around at the halfway point and walked back.

"Rick, you're doing a great job for us. I don't think I told you that lately. Thanks for all you do. I'm very happy for you and Janice," he said and turned to leave. He opened the car door, slid into the driver's seat and drove out of the Company area.

TWO MONTHS TWENTY-THREE DAYS AFTER
NUREMBERG, ARMY HOSPITAL
OFFICE OF THE COMMANDING OFFICER
0045 HOURS SUNDAY 25 AUGUST 1969

The call came at 1930 hours on Saturday. Bernie came up to my room with a message to call Lt. Pezlola in Hilversum, ASAP. I called back. Pezlola wasn't in his office, but he'd left a message for me to call Dr. Lattermire as soon as possible.

I called Doc Lattermire at the hospital, but got his assistant. The message was to come and see him as soon as possible. I called Larry and borrowed his car. I had just about killed the VW of many different colors with the frequent trips to Nuremburg over the previous two and a half months.

I had arrived at the Nuremburg Army Hospital at 2315. Doc Lattermire's office assistant met me in the lobby and said he was helping the wife of a soldier who was having difficulty giving birth.

Over an hour and a half ago had passed since then. At 2400 I was told that Doctor Lattermire had moved the patient from the ER to surgery and would not be available for several hours.

I had tried to call Janice three or four times: once, before leaving Gelnhausen, and several times since arriving at the hospital. There was still no answer.

We had spent every minute we could together over the last eleven weeks. She had duty this weekend so we had decided wait and get together mid-week. Since the day we'd met, I knew this was someone I hoped to spend the rest of my life with. Sitting here now, I was thinking about our first morning together. Her smile, her laugh, the way her arm felt draped across my chest.

Finally, Lattermire appeared in front of me. "Sorry I wasn't here when you arrived," he said, and nothing else. He looked tired and distraught. He was standing there acting like he didn't know what to say. He was dressed in surgical scrubs, his head covered with a cap, and with a mask hanging down on his chest. There was blood on his scrubs. He must have come directly from surgery.

"I didn't see you walk up," I said. "I was told you were in surgery. Is your patient doing all right?"

"The patient is fine," said Lattermire. "Let's take a walk." We walked across the lobby without saying anything. One of the ER nurses who took care of us the day the team was brought in was coming out of a side corridor. She looked at us with little recognition. She was highly distressed and she'd obviously been crying.

"Hi... are you OK?"

Without any acknowledgement of what I had asked, she raised both hands to her face, started to cry again and ran down the hallway.

"I wonder what's wrong. She seems to be in a bad way," I said. Lattermire had no comment.

We continued through the lobby and walked out into the front of the building. Doc Lattermire guided me over to the fountain. We took a seat on the wall. It was 0120.

"Rick, I want you to get hold of yourself," said the head Doc. A chill went down my back. A feeling I had never experienced before or since swept over me. I was filled with absolute terror. I couldn't catch my breath.

"How?" I finally whispered. I stood and turned toward the sound of the falling water. "Can I see her?"

"No, you do not want to do that," replied Doc Lattermire in a tone that left me in a very dark place.

She had died instantly. Her car was struck broadside about four blocks from the hospital. A truck traveling at a high rate of speed had driven directly through a stop sign. Janice was on her way home after her shift. She was pronounced dead at the scene.

A German man, the truck driver, was being charged with driving under the influence and vehicular manslaughter. It was pretty senseless, really.

XIV

ONWARD AND UPWARD

TECHNISCHE HOGESCHOOL EINDHOVEN (THE)
UNIVERSITY GROUNDS
POST BUS NO 2—56 MB EINDHOVEN
THE NETHERLANDS
1145 HOURS SUNDAY 7 SEPTEMBER 1969

Things, some things, had been fairly quiet for the previous month. One of the S-3 staff handed me a TWX on a Saturday morning in the HHC Mess requiring my presence for a meeting in Holland. The purpose, the location, and the method of transport were not stated.

Bernie called me to the Orderly Room on Saturday evening. SFC Gary Lawson, the COMM (Communications) Center Supervisor in Bischofsgrun, had telephoned to say he would pick me up the next morning at 0700, Sunday the 7th of September. "Wear civilian clothing," he had said.

It turns out Gary didn't have any more information about this trip than I did, or he was under orders not to say. I guess I expressed some reluctance about this junket when he picked me up on Sunday morning, because he asked, "Is there a problem?"

"Yeah. RedEye needs an officer. An E-5 NCO doesn't move very well inside this giant chess game that 'Mr. D' is running. We've been put on permanent guard tour until further notice. Two of our vehicles are in need of major parts. We haven't trained in weeks."

"Roger that," replied Gary. "I'll pass it to the Lieutenant when I get back."

"Where is the notorious Bill Douglas these days?"

"Not sure. Jim seems to think he's in 'Nam doing a job for David James."

"Who's David James?" I asked.

"He's Douglas's boss," replied Gary. We rode on in silence for a while.

"You wouldn't happen to know who Mr. James works for would you?" I asked.

"No, but David James is the CIA Station Chief, London Desk."

"Hmm..."

All we had was an address on the University campus called "THE," (Technische Hogeschool Eindhoven), which as it turned out, had ties to Philips Research, Bell Laboratories, NATO, and select members of the international intelligence community. I was never told, and I never asked, what was going on in Hilversum. But, I had the feeling that whatever it was, it was about to change -- or not.

Gary had picked me up in his personal car -- a white 1968 BMW 2000cs. He said we had about a three and a half hour drive. So I sat back, closed my eyes, and relaxed. My short time in and around Nuremberg operations had taught me not to ask questions.

For the previous month, sleep hadn't come easily. I would catch a catnap here and there whenever the opportunity presented itself. Every time that I fell asleep my mind would immediately run the same ol' movie highlights. I miss her so much.

I had been allowed leave[137] to travel to Janice's funeral. Bill Douglas arranged for a seat on a flight into Andrews AFB. I met Janice's parents, Daniel and Mary Prasonio at the services at St. Mary's in Annapolis. The Catholic Mass and eulogy revealed to me that I was not the only one who thought their daughter was so perfect. She would be buried with full military honors, as she

---

[137] Excused absence

deserved.

I said my goodbyes to Daniel and Mary -- extremely nice people even in their grief -- at the rear of the church. I turned from my last view of the center aisle and pushed open the door leading out to the courtyard. I did not attend the burial.

I called Ken's Mom and asked how she was doing and if she needed anything. I explained I worked with Ken in Germany and that he was doing well. She said she knew who I was and that she was a lot stronger these days. Ken's letters were keeping him close she said.

"Call us if you need anything. You do still have the contact number just in case -- yes?"

"Oh, yes I do," she had said. "Not to worry. Tell Kenny I'm fine and that I miss him."

"Yes, Ma'am, I will."

My thoughts went back to Janice and I was reaching to touch her face....

"You awake, Rick?" Gary asked. "We're about five minutes out according to the signs. I've never been here before so we might have to stop and ask for some direction."

We found No. 2—56 MB Eindhoven. The sign in front was marked Philips University Research Center. We entered the lobby and walked to the information desk.

"We are here to see Dr. Kevel Natton," Gary said, and asked for the meeting location.

"Yes, the others are already here," said the receptionist. Her name tag identified her as Mary.

"Are you usually open on Sundays, Mary?"

"Please sign the visitors log and take one of these badges."

"Thank you."

"Erik," she called out to a security officer seated behind the information desk. "Could you please escort these gentlemen to STW 3.39 on the third level?"

Returning her attention to us, Mary said, "No, we are not usually open on the weekend."

"I see. Thank you, Mary. Enjoy the rest of your weekend," said Gary.

TECHNISCHE HOGESCHOOL EINDHOVEN (THE)
STW 3.39—THE PLAN
POST BUS NO 2—56 MB EINDHOVEN
THE NETHERLANDS
1145 HOURS SUNDAY 7 SEPTEMBER 1969

Bill Douglas was standing beside an overhead projector at the head of a large oval conference table. The lights were dimmed.

"Good, you're here." Douglas pointed and said, "Grab those seats on the left. Let me finish this and then I'll introduce everyone." It took a full minute for my eyes to adjust.

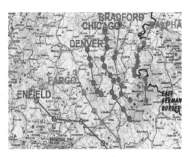

Figure 19
Planning Operation Sparrow Hawk

I leaned over and whispered to Gary, "It appears 'Mr. D' has changed out of his jungle fatigues."

The overhead being discussed was a map of the NATO lines of defense. An arrow pointing toward the east had the letters FULDA at its base with multiple arrows pointing toward the west. Douglas went on for five more minutes and then the lights were turned up.

I wondered if this was the meeting where I would learn the secret handshake or just be fitted with the hush-hush cyanide tooth capsule.

The previous slide had also depicted the six main blocking points that would be formed when the Russians came across the border. This known invasion route was called the *Fulda Gap*.

The six main blocking points were named Alpha, Bradford, Chicago, Denver, Fargo, and Enfield.

In September 1968, during a speech at the Fifth Congress of the Polish United Workers' Party, (one month after the invasion of Czechoslovakia), Brezhnev outlined the Brezhnev Doctrine[138], in

---

138 This doctrine found its origins in the failures of Marxism-Leninism in states like Poland, Hungary and East Germany, which were facing a declining standard of living contrasting with the prosperity of West Germany and the

which he claimed the right to violate the sovereignty of any country attempting to replace Marxism-Leninism with capitalism. During the speech, Brezhnev stated:

> *"When forces that are hostile to socialism try to turn the development of some socialist country toward capitalism, it becomes not only a problem of the country concerned, but a common problem and concern of all socialist countries."*

For the previous two weeks, apparently, there had been increased activity all along the border. These activities included Soviet troop and armor units pulling out of the line in several established bases in the extreme northern and southern points and repositioning about 150 kilometers across the border from Fulda.

Bill Douglas started off the introductions. "The two gentlemen who just came in are Sergeant First Class Gary Lawson, who is with my group in Bischofsgrun, and Sergeant Rick Fontain, our resident RedEye expert.

"Uh oh, this isn't good. I'm being touted as an expert; that means it will be the cyanide capsule, not the secret handshake."

"Sergeant Fontain and SFC Lawson, that is Dr. Kevel Natton," said Douglas as he extended his arm and pointed to an older man with a beard and long, untamed hair. "Dr. Natton is a faculty member here at the University, and a member of the technical research division at Philips."

Douglas moved his arm and pointed to the man seated to the right of Natton. "That's David James, from our London office." James wore the same type of horn-rimmed glasses as Ken Clark. He was wearing a dark blue, three-piece suit, which, for someone at his level, would be as casual as it got.

Douglas then turned and pointed to Barry Flax and Roger "Kelly" Johnston, who were seated in the two chairs directly to my left. As you probably remember, Barry was the General Dynamics Vice President and General Manager for Research and Development, and Kelly was the heavy hitter from Lockheed. His expertise was in targeting software and the development of supporting hardware.

---

rest of Western Europe.

Bill Douglas had made it plain to me in the preceding meeting in Gelnhausen that he did not want it known that he (in any of his personas) and I had a prior relationship. There were several other people seated at the conference table who were not introduced. They offered little, if any, comment during the entire meeting.

On 6 May 1969 NATO's[139] Military Committee approved MC 48/3[140] as a Military Decision and forwarded it to the Secretary General of NATO. The cover of the briefing document that lay on the table in front of me is shown below. Apparently this had been a work in progress since 1949.

"Lord only knows how RedEye is involved," was my thought at the time.

North Atlantic Treaty Organization
THE EVOLUTION OF NATO STRATEGY, 1949-1969

The Strategic Concept for the Defense of the North Atlantic Area

Decisions of Defense Planning Committee in Ministerial Session [DPC/D (67)23 11.5.1967] Measures to Implement the Strategic Concept [MC 14/3(Final)] 16/1/1968]

Figure 20 - Strategic Concept MC 14/3 "C"

---

139 The North Atlantic Treaty Organization, also called the (North) Atlantic Alliance, is an intergovernmental military alliance based on the North Atlantic Treaty, which was signed on 4 April 1949. The organization constitutes a system of collective defense whereby its member states agree to mutual defense in response to an attack by any external party. NATO's headquarters are in Brussels, Belgium, one of the 28 member states across North America and Europe.

140 The Defense Planning Committee in Ministerial Session by DPC/D(69)62 of 4 December 1969 adopted MC 48/3 as guidance for measures to implement the strategic concept for the defense of the North Atlantic Treaty Organization Area.

TECHNISCHE HOGESCHOOL EINDHOVEN [THE]
CONFERENCE ROOM STW 3.39
THE ULTIMATE MILITARY RESPONSE
1515 HOURS SUNDAY 7 SEPTEMBER 1969

> **Briefing Document: Strategic Concept, MC 14/3: 311/413**
>
> *The deterrent concept of the Alliance is based on a flexibility which will prevent the potential aggressor from predicting with confidence NATO's specific response to aggression and which will lead him to conclude that an unacceptable degree of risk would be involved regardless of the nature of his attack. MC 14/3 spelled out the types of military responses to aggression against NATO.*

Figure 21
NATO Strategy Document

Dinner was brought in about an hour after Gary and I had arrived. When I went out to use the rest room I noticed there were security men at each end of the hallway. I wasn't sure if it was the meeting in its entirety that was being guarded or if it was simply one or more of the attendees who were under observation and/or protection.

The discussion so far had revealed only an old laundry list of battlefield proposed responses. There were several comments that suggested that most of the existing policy deterrents to an invasion were no longer effective or believed.

The list was new to me but not for most of the others, I surmised as I panned the faces surrounding me at the conference table. Why was I there? How would RedEye fit into the implementation of MC 14/3? What was all of this leading up to?

Apparently, the upper crust of the Russian military believed that NATO no longer subscribed to the idea of MAD[141].

---

[141] Mutual Assured Destruction (MAD) is a doctrine of military strategy and national security policy in which a full-scale use of high-yield of mass destruction by two opposing sides would effectively result in the complete,

The cover sheet on the brief placed on the table in front of me was labeled MC 14/3—Addendum C. Page two of the briefing document was actually marked 305 of 413. What I read on page six caused me to hold my breath until I had finished reading the entire page.

The first examples listed mandated that other conventional responses to thwart unsolicited aggression be implemented. For example, the opening of another front by initiating a naval action in response to low intensity aggression was just one of twenty described.

I wondered where they were going to get all of the water.

The second approach made use of NATO Strategy documents 1949-1969 *XXV,* a nuclear weapons directive that called for selective nuclear strikes on targets outside the invasion areas.

The third, and the main focus of today's meeting, was the hatching of an elaborate scheme to convince the Russians of *this* new NATO strategy, laid out in the briefing document. The ultimate military response had been approved by council and would now be put to a vote.

"The U. S. President has been asked to sign off on MC 14/3 C and the German Chancellor is meeting with his cabinet next month for final approval of this NATO policy change," announced David James, who had spoken for the first time in this meeting. There was a long pause during which no one said anything.

Finally, Bill Douglas continued. "Our teams returned last night from a six point border insertion that verifies our latest satellite recon[142] data. He placed another map drawing on the projector.

"These troop movements are much more than the usual readiness exercises run in the previous years," added Douglas. "They may be coming across this time. Gary, do you have anything to add to that?"

"Yes, Sir. LT Pezlola told me to emphasize the fact that these armor units are moving their entire infrastructure with the relocation," said SFC Lawson. "This is a procedure that has not occurred in past exercises."

"What does that mean?" I inquired -- and quickly regretted it.

"It means that they're not planning to return to their initial positions. And, this may be the precursor to test our resolve," said

utter and irrevocable annihilation of both the attacker and the defender.

142   Reconnaissance—a military term for gathering information

Dr. Natton.

David James stood and walked to the end of the conference table.

"The CIA will begin immediately to implement project *Synchronized Sparrow.* Utilizing the latest in air-to-ground and ground-to-air missile technology, we plan on running an extensive demonstration of our RedEye and TOW[143] capabilities. The exercise will be conducted on the border at a location known as *OP Alpha.*"

I leaned in on Gary Lawson's right side and asked in a low voice, "Did you know about this"? He shook his head slightly from side to side.

"Mr. Flax, would you give us a run-down on what support we can expect from General Dynamics?"

"Sure thing," said Barry. "The idea for *Synchronized Sparrow* actually was created by Sergeant Fontain. Last year he shot down a target drone using a RedEye shoulder-fired guided missile. The resulting impact of the missile was a spectacular show of force with a very expensive technology."

"Excuse me, Mr. Flax, but you're not suggesting that we shoot down a drone to make the Russians rethink an invasion attempt?" said Dr. Natton.

"Yes, Sir, I am," said Barry. "Let me elaborate on our plan if I may?"

There was a slight nod of the head from Dr. Natton, indicating Barry should proceed.

"OK, then," began Barry. "We have named our operation *Synchronized Sparrow.* The entire event will be conducted in full view of the East German border. The optimal location recommended is *OP Alpha*, which sits at the tip of the Fulda Gap. We expect this show of force to make known our commitment to defending against invasion."

"You can't be serious in thinking that shooting off a few shoulder-fired missiles will have any effect on the Russian mindset," said one of the un-introduced gentlemen sitting directly across from me.

"What Mr. Flax is proposing to us is a great deal more than merely shooting a few missiles," said Bill Douglas. "Thirty-two RedEye weapons and ten pilotless jet aircraft will be made available

---

143   TOW (Tube-launched, Optically-tracked, Wire-guided) is an anti-tank missile

to demonstrate a state-of-the-art technology that will inject a new variable into the Russian decision making process. It will show the Russians that attacking our ground forces by air will come at a high price for them."

"Thanks, Bill," said David James. "Mr. Johnston, do you have anything to add?"

"Yes. In conjunction with the RedEye deployment, we will present the new aerial TOW platform integrated into the Bell HD1D helicopter gunship. We expect this show of force technology and its observable lavish price tag will give pause to the Russian generals and the Politburo decision makers who have designs on an invasion of the West," replied Kelly Johnston of Lockheed.

"So, our message, Mr. Johnston, will be one of Capitalism and technology versus Communism and brute force. That is an interesting game you propose," said Unidentified Participant Number Two, who was seated directly across the table from me.

"I like it; I think this approach has merit," said Johnston.

"Believe me when I tell you this," said David James. Our options here are severely limited. This is not a game; this operation will be designed only to buy us more time. Once MC 14/3 C is approved, phase two, *Operation Sparrow Hawk* will already be in progress."

The nameless person seated across the table from me nodded his head, but didn't comment further. The meeting broke up about 1600. "Mr. D" told us that we were to follow him back to the house in Hilversum[144].

"Don't discuss anything on your way out of the building and leave all material handouts on the table," we were told.

As we were leaving, the security guys swooped in and were putting everything in paper Burn Bags[145], each one stenciled on both sides with bold, red lettering.

Barry and Kelly exchanged goodbyes with us in the lobby and headed off to Amsterdam's International Airport. Dr. Natton came into the lobby and thanked everyone for coming. I heard David

---

[144] Hilversum lies 30km (19 mi) southeast of Amsterdam and 20 kilometers (12 miles) north of Utrecht.

[145] A burn bag is the informal name given to a container (usually a paper bag or some other waste receptacle) that holds sensitive or classified documents which are to be destroyed by fire or pulping after a certain period of time. The most common usage of burn bags is by government institutions, in the destruction of classified materials.

James ask him when they were going to leave for Brussels[146]. He said in the morning.

"Mr. D", Gary and I left them in the lobby after exchanging handshakes. David James held my hand in his grip and moved slightly closer so as not to be overheard by the others. "I'm glad I finally got to meet you, Rick. Bill Douglas was spot-on to bring RedEye in on this."

"Yes, Sir," I said, because that was the only thing I could think to say. And, I was still pondering the British expression *spot-on*. Obviously, I had the textbook look of someone who didn't mind being dropped behind enemy lines.

MANSION HOUSE
LEEUWENLANN 24
POSTBUS 9936, 201 GM HILVERSUM
1930 HOURS SUNDAY 7 SEPTEMBER 1969

The drive took about 50 minutes. We saw the city lights off in the distance as we approached Hilversum. However, we never went into the city proper. We took several side roads and wound up on the other side of town in a heavily wooded section of what appeared to be an upper-class neighborhood.

The country estate had a high stone wall that completely surrounded the complex. It contained several outbuildings and what appeared to be a large mansion in the center. All structures were constructed out of the same material as the walled enclosure.

A massive wrought iron gate was opened by one of the security guards and his dog. There was a circular drive that wound its way through a courtyard allowing vehicles to drive directly up to the front entrance.

A five bay garage was situated just off the right side of the manor house. From the pitch of the roof and the position of the window gables it appeared that living quarters were located on the upper levels of the house.

"You have a nice place here, Mr. D."

"Thanks, but it's not mine. It belongs to Jim Pezlola. His parents

---

146 NATO Headquarters

willed it to him. His mother was Dutch and Jim's father was an American officer.

"Was he in the OSS?"

"As a matter of fact they both, Jim's mother and father, were involved in the community[147] up until the end of WWII. The OSS was dissolved and Jim's Dad went back to work for the Army CIC at Fort Meade in Maryland."

"No kidding, small world. I've got some friends there."

"Well, we'll get some dinner and afterwards I need to talk to you about what will be required of you and of your team."

"Yes, Sir. That should be exciting, I'm sure." The voice in my head added, *"Three bags full, Sir."*

CIA HEADQUARTERS
LANGLEY VA
OFFICE OF THE DHIC, EUROPE
0930 HOURS TUESDAY 9 SEPTEMBER 1969

On March 6, 1969, Lt. Gen. Gerald Bushman, USMC, while serving in Vietnam, was nominated by President Richard M. Nixon to be the Deputy Director of the CIA. This morning he was visiting the fourth floor of the main complex at Langley, specifically the East German Desk.

A memo sent by David James, London Station Chief, requesting the latest INTEL on the projected intentions of recent Russian Troop movements, had been sent for the third time because it had never received a response.

The prior evening, after a complete re-read of MC 14/3 and the recently added 130 page analysis of section C, Bushman had come to the same conclusion as David James. They needed to buy some time. And the first step to accomplishing that would be the successful completion of NATO's phase one operation designated Top Secret/Synchronized Sparrow.

The General needed the DHCI for the East German desk to assign a full time analyst. The INTEL being supplied via satellite and by the

---

147 The community—slang term referring to the Organization of Strategic Services and, later, the Central Intelligence Agency

border recon teams needed to be constantly evaluated and harmonized. The successful completion of Plan A, Synchronized Sparrow, would depend on it. It was to be an extravagant show of some very expensive technologies.

Plan B, however, would be more elaborate and would unfold in two parts. The first would be an operation called Sparrow Hawk. It would be a complete reconfiguration of the NATO blocking forces.

Part two would address the actual NATO response strategy to invasion. With the demise of the MAD inhibitor in the minds of the Russian military, new protocols had been formulated. This was described in specific detail in MC 14/3 C. David James and his people would leak this lethal new policy across the wire[148] in a way that would not jeopardize the actual intent of Sparrow Hawk.

To accomplish all of this NATO needed to buy some time.

In 1941, then Capt. Bushman was aboard the USS Pennsylvania at Pearl Harbor when the Japanese attacked the ship and other naval installations on December 7. He joined the 9th Marine Regiment as a Major and battalion executive officer in May 1942.

Major Bushman was promoted to Lieutenant Colonel and appointed Commanding Officer of the 1st Battalion, 9th Marines in June 1943.

During the two years Bushman held that post, he earned the Silver Star and the Navy Cross during the Iwo Jima program in March of 1945.

He was also Janice's grandfather.

"Good morning, Joe," DDCI[149] Bushman announced as he entered the office of Joe Wilson, DHIC,[150] Europe.

---

148 The Iron Curtain

149 Deputy Director of the Central Intelligence Agency (DDCI) is a senior United States government official in the U.S. Central Intelligence Agency. The DDCI assists the Director of the Central Intelligence Agency (DCIA) and is authorized to exercise the powers of the DCIA when the Director's position is vacant or in the Director's absence or disability.

150 Deputy Director of Intelligence (DHIC) is responsible for the evaluation of sometimes incomplete and contradictory information, transforming it into unique insights that inform U.S. policy decisions. Members of the DI help provide timely, accurate, and objective all-source intelligence analysis on the full range

"Good morning, Director. What brings you down to our humble abode?"

"David James is getting pushback on MC 14/3 from your East German desk. I know the investment of the Shah[151] has taken top priority of your resources for AP and the Middle East, but unless we successfully implement Plan A of MC 14/3 a WWIII scenario will supersede all of your activities down here. Am I clear?"

"Yes, Sir. May I ask your guidance on how you want this handled?"

"Who's running the RUSS/EG[152] desk?" asked the DDCI.

"Brent Cummings and Daryl Russell are running INTEL for both. Four of their people have been reassigned to work the Mid-East situation."

"Pick one, Cummings or Russell, to go and brief the 1st/48th in Gelnhausen. Tell him to see me before he goes. This is important, Joe. Let's not screw it up."

US EMBASSY
25 GROSVENOR SQUARE, LONDON W1A 2LQ
UNITED KINGDOM
1830 HOURS TUESDAY 9 SEPTEMBER 1969

"Mr. James, you have a call on the secure line. It's Director Bushman." This was announced through the intercom on James's desk. "Thanks, Carrie." He then pushed the flashing button on his TSEC[153] desktop unit.

---

of national security and foreign policy issues to the President, Cabinet, and senior policymakers in the U.S. government.

151 Mohammad Reza Shah in April 1969, he abrogated the 1937 Iranian-Iraqi treaty over control of the Shatt al-Arab. Iran ceased paying tolls to Iraq when its ships used the Shatt al-Arab. Iran claimed as its own territory Bahrain (which the British had controlled since the 19th century) and three small Persian Gulf islands. The Shah negotiated an agreement with the British, which ultimately led to the independence of Bahrain (against the wishes of Iranian nationalists). In return, Iran took full control of Greater and Lesser Tunbs, as well as Abu Musa in the Strait of Hormuz -- three strategically sensitive islands which were claimed by the United Arab Emirates.

152 Russian/East German Desk

153 The KY-3 (TSEC/KY-3) is a secure telephone system developed by the U.S.

"This is David James, Director. How may I be of service?" he said
into the handset of the KY-3.

*"David, Joe Wilson has assigned Daryl Russell to assist with the
operation in Fulda. Wilson has freed up the necessary resources and
gotten you the support you requested. I'm sending Russell to
Gelnhausen to brief Tom Brogan."*

*"Yes, Sir. Thank you for getting involved, Sir. I didn't know what
else to do."*

"This is important *David. We need to do everything we can to
convince the Russians not to come -- at least not right away. Tell
Douglas we need this one done right."*

"Yes, Sir, I will."

"Call me when you have the briefing set up."

"Yes, Sir." The line went silent. The General had hung up.

CIA LISTENING POST
HOTEL BERGHOF - SUITE 30
BISCHOFSGRUN, GERMANY
2430 HOURS TUESDAY 9 SEPTEMBER 1969

*SFC Gary Lawson was leaning over a table pushed up against a
bank of Teletype Corporation ASR 33s. These babies ran at the
amazing speed of 110 bps, with an 8-level ASCII encoding scheme.
Today, of course, this would rank right up there with the invention of
papyrus paper.*

*Lawson was in the process of reading an analysis of the pictures
taken over the weekend by the Lockheed U-2, nicknamed "Dragon
Lady", a single-engine, high-altitude, reconnaissance
aircraft operated by the Central Intelligence Agency.*

*Russian armor and mechanized infantry units were redeploying
in large numbers from both northern and southern emplacements.
The recon also was indicating that these same forces were*

National Security Agency in the early 1960s. The "TSEC" prefix to the model
number indicates NSA's Telecommunications Security nomenclature system.
These were replaced by the STU/STE ISDN (Integrated Services Digital
Network) in the 1980s. The KY technology was sold to a lubricant company in
1971.

reorganizing within 50 to 175 kilometers east of the German border at Fulda.

The 1st Guards Tank Army was the largest part of the Soviet occupation force in Germany, known as "Group of Soviet Forces in Germany", with its headquarters in Dresden.

In 1968, the 11th Guards Tank and 20th Guards Motor Rifle Divisions took part in the Soviet invasion of Czechoslovakia. The Dragon Lady had confirmed their departure from their bases and was watching them head to the Northeast. The 2nd Guards Tank Army (HQ Fürstenberg), the Soviet 1st Mechanized Corps, the 9th Tank Corps, the 12th Guard Tank Corps, and the 4th Guards Tank Army (HQ Eberswalde) were all reported to be on the move.

Gary had seen this type of activity in the past. He had reported to Lt. Pezlola that this could just be a typical response to NATO's "Reforger" reinforcement exercise. The U.S. heavy division redeployment into West Germany had been conducted in January of that year.

However, the Russian combat units being re-deployed were much larger and numbered more than three times those in previous occurrences.

After reading the briefing book over the weekend and knowing firsthand the INTEL discussed on implementing MC 14/3, it was looking more and more to Gary like Ivan[154] was getting ready to come across.

---

[154] The Russians

XV

THE RUSSIANS ARE COMING

US EMBASSY, LONDON
25 GROSVENOR SQUARE, LONDON W1A 2LQ
UNITED KINGDOM
1030 HOURS FRIDAY 12 SEPTEMBER 1969

David James had just come from his flat after grabbing a quick shower and a change of clothes. It had been a long week and it was working its way to becoming an even a longer month. His staff had just finished their third all-nighter that week.

Reports of the Russian mechanized troop and armor movements were coming in from several key listening posts. Photo reconnaissance teams crossed the Czechoslovakian and East German borders and confirmed the large-scale activity.

That was the bad news. The really bad news was what the satellite had confirmed. The Russians were massing at the railhead in Bezirk Halle[155] only 176 kilometers east of the West German town of Fulda, and even closer to the outpost called Alpha.

The East German desk at Langley was still insisting that the Russians would never be so bold as to pre-announce their intent to

---

[155] The Bezirk Halle was a district (Bezirk) of East Germany. The administrative seat and the main town was Halle.

invade. David James wasn't so sure about that analysis. People safely located 3900 miles away could guess all they wanted. MC 14/3 Plan A needed to be executed as soon as possible. Until then he would treat the situation as if there would be an invasion.

Plan A had been hatched in a NATO-sanctioned think tank in Hilversum. The concept was simple and was going to be very expensive. The decision to proceed had come out of Washington two days before. The U.S. President was watching this one closely.

Addendum B, or Plan B, had been recently approved and added to MC 14/3. The official project name was Sparrow Hawk. The folder would remain in the safe until such time as the results of Synchronized Sparrow were evaluated.

James looked down on his desk at the open folder marked OPLAN MC 14/3 PLAN C. It was well named he thought. Every time he read the title on the cover sheet it had the same chilling effect on him. FULDA COLD was the project name, and the weapons mandated for use hadn't been employed in earnest since the end of the War in the Pacific.

"Mr. James, Bill Douglas has just arrived," the voice on the intercom announced.

"Please send him in, Carrie, and send in some coffee, please." David got up and went around his desk just as the door opened and Douglas walked in. The two men shook hands and exchanged the usual greetings.

"Are we all set for next week in Fulda?" asked David.

"I've briefed Colonel Brogan. He's moving RedEye and Bravo Company tonight and the rest on Saturday.

"Let's hope Langley is right for a change and this is just another case of "Ruskie[156]" sabre rattling.

"Barry Flax flew into Rhein-Main this morning. He's on his way to Gelnhausen as we speak," said Douglas. "He and Sergeant Fontain will unpack and inspect all RedEyes before they're transported to Alpha."

"How many teams are you going to use?" asked David.

"Four gunships, four RedEye teams, Sir," replied Douglas. "May I use the map to show you?" Douglas went to the wall at the rear of the office and opened the cabinet doors concealing the map board and proceeded to outline how Plan A was to be executed.

---

[156] American slang name for a Russian

COLEMAN KASERNE
GELNHAUSEN GERMANY
3RD ARMOR AMMO DUMP
1630 HOURS FRIDAY 12 SEPTEMBER 1969

Operational order *Synchronized Sparrow* required the 1st/48th to access Coleman Kaserne's Ammo Dump. Trucks and APCs were coming and going almost nonstop all morning. Four of the five RedEye jeeps and trailers had already been combat loaded. Only RE-1 remained outside the open bunker doors.

We had pulled the existing stock of RedEyes out of hiding earlier in the day and stacked them neatly outside the front entrance. This was done to make room for 32 brand new missiles that had arrived that morning on two trucks from Rhein-Main.

Designated MA41A3s with a part number 10662373, the missiles were loaded onto the RedEye trailers. Seven units each were loaded onto RE-2 through RE-5, and four containers were placed into the trailer of RE-1.

Barry Flax had helped unpack and inspect all but the last two missiles we were to take on the mission. Barry had transported the recently manufactured RedEye from Rhein-Main to Coleman to replenish the missiles that would be expended in the upcoming operation. I had suggested we take sixteen MA41A3s from the battalion inventory and sixteen from the ones Barry had brought with him.

Barry agreed and said that this would provide us with additional data on missile performance for those missiles that had been stored for several months in a non-temperature controlled environment. We were always after good data. Besides, if RedEye storage procedures were found to cause accuracy problems, shooting at drones was the time to find this out, not with Mig-21's breathing down your neck.

"There's only the one bad battery so far, Barry. That's pretty impressive."

"I carried three cases of replacement batteries with me on the plane. They're in the back of Clark's jeep," Barry responded.

"Thanks," I said. "The extra batteries will provide a great deal of comfort for all of the shooters."

COLEMAN KASERNE
GELNHAUSEN GERMANY
1ST/48TH HHC—REDEYE TEAM ROOM
1720 HOURS FRIDAY 12 SEPTEMBER 1969

Clark, Barry and I rode down from the Ammo Dump in Jeep One. We pulled into the HHC service drive and parked behind RE-3. I could see the door to the RedEye team room was wide open as we went by. I called out, "Hey, Jack, you in there?"

"Yeah, I'm looking for a spare mike."

"See if Bernie is still here," I shouted back. "He had three of them in his desk drawer. Lock up everything when you're done. Meet us out on the main drag by the S-4. We're parked this side of the loading dock."

"Roger that. Be there in five," said Spec4 Jack Swanson.

"We're supposed to get a Bravo Company APC escort all the way up to Fulda this evening, so don't dillydally," I yelled.

I turned to Barry. "Well Barry, I guess this is farewell. I want to thank you for coming all this way to check out all of the children and increasing the size of the family."

"You're more than welcome, but you can belay all that farewell crap. I'm going with you."

"I don't think old Blood and Guts is going to think that's such a good idea," I replied.

"Oh, it's been blessed by the higher authorities," said Barry. "The Air Force is landing at the field west of Fulda as we speak. They're staging the first five target drones I brought from California. And tomorrow, five more will be brought in as backup. This operation will leave nothing to chance," said Barry Flax, General Dynamics VP and Executive extraordinaire.

"That's the best news I've heard in a very long time. Make sure your dumb ass is out of the way when the drones start falling from the sky."

Barry ignored my request. "I told David James that I wasn't going to let these Air Force guys fly these brand new birds into the ground just because they claimed to have flown model airplanes with their daddies," said Barry.

"Well, I'm damn glad you're going with us."

Barry went on to say, "OPLAN[157] *Synchronized Sparrow* calls for the first five birds to be in precise locations for this to have the desired effect. If they had let me bring my own drivers[158] from Bliss, like I requested, I wouldn't have been as worried. But they didn't, so I'm going."

Just then a helicopter gunship came in low over the Parade grounds behind Brigade Headquarters. "That's my ride. See you up there. Good hunting."

"Thanks, Barry. Be safe."

ONE DAY EARLIER

OPLAN SYNCHRONIZED SPARROW
1ST/48TH BATTALION S-3 CONFERENCE ROOM
1320 HOURS THURSDAY 11 SEPTEMBER 1969

Figure 22
OP Alpha

The plan approval had come via TWX the previous afternoon. I had been called to our S-3, and we spent the next several hours using topo maps going over the entire landscape in and around *OP[159]Alpha*. We'd found three locations that looked promising for the deployment of the five RedEye fire teams. We wouldn't be able to tell which were usable until we drove up there and eyeballed the actual terrain.

I had picked up "Mr. D" in Hanau at the Fliegerhorst Airfield at 0445 Thursday morning. During a quick cup of coffee in the base Mess Hall I was given a preview of the latest data on Russian troop movements and their military classification.

A quick math calculation to total up the number of American military men and women standing in the proverbial doorway

---

157 An Operation Plan in Complete Format (OPLAN) is an operation plan for the conduct of joint operations that can be used as a basis for development of an OPERATIONS ORDER [OPORD].

158 Drone control experts

159 Pronounced "Oh Pee", an abbreviation for Observation Post

between Frankfurt and Fulda yielded an alarming statistic. We were outnumbered ten to one.

"Why are you telling me this?" I asked.

"Because the possibility exists that they may decide to come right in the middle of the execution of Plan A," answered Bill Douglas.

"And just when I thought it couldn't get any more exhilarating," was my response.

The ever-so cheerful Bill Douglas told me not to despair. Boots on the ground would always be an important factor in any conflict, and the technology they held in their hands would determine the outcome.

"That's truly comforting, Sir. Are you coming up on the line with us?"

"No. I wish I could, but I need to go to London and brief David James after tomorrow's meeting. I'll be back on the weekend."

"You don't know what you'll be missing, Sir. There is nothing quite comparable to inhaling rocket motor fumes right after your first cup of coffee."

Bill Douglas just stared for a moment before saying, "You're a very unusual young man, Sergeant Fontain."

"Yes, Sir. Thank you. Three bags full, Sir."

Daryl Russell, Bill Douglas (wearing his Major Carlstrum uniform), LTC Brogan, CSM Bost, and twelve other department heads of various ranks and responsibilities were all present that afternoon for what amounted to a pre-alert notification.

I stood as far back against the rear wall of the conference room as possible. My maneuver was short lived, however. Daryl Russell asked me to come forward and verify the present status of the weapons cache of RedEye missiles.

Russell gave us an update on the latest INTEL. The names and numeric designations of the Russian units that had deployed to the rail yards at Halle[160] were impressive. What wasn't discussed in any detail was what to do if we were attacked during the demonstration. Lt. Key had placed a case of thermite grenades in

---

160 Halle an der Saale is a city in the Southern part of the German state Saxony-Anhalt. Halle is a very important economy and education-center in East Germany.

my vehicle earlier that morning. I was told that no RedEye munitions were to fall into the hands of the enemy if we were overrun.

Operation *Synchronized Sparrow* was a go.

After Russell finished his presentation, Colonel Brogan addressed the group. He rattled off a complex listing of equipment requirements, the number of vehicles, and their respective positions in the convoy. He did this all from memory.

Brogan selected Bravo Company to provide an escort for the RedEye transport convoy, which would leave after 1730 hours the following day, the 12th of September. Bravo Company would also provide perimeter guard once a site was selected. HHC, Alpha and Charlie companies would follow on the morning of the 13th and position themselves around the small airport on the west side of Fulda. After the meeting, I went to the map board and again examined the terrain directly behind *OP Alpha*. The notation printed in the corner of the map stated in bold lettering, *NATO FULDA-GAP OPLAN 14-37.8.*

The five proposed blocking positions located to the rear of *OP Alpha* were named *Bradford, Chicago, Denver, Fargo and Enfield*. Each was constructed six to 12 kilometers apart with the exception of *Bradford*, which was only 3.6 kilometers from the back porch of *Alpha*. Each was described as a blocking and fallback point designed to slow an advancing invasion force.

One major concern, since the early 1960s, had been the bridge escape routes across the Rhine River being targeted by an invading force. The sole purpose of the five blocking points was to buy our guys time. There were several, battalion-

Figure 23
NATO's Lines of Defense

size, mechanized engineering groups charged with keeping the escape routes open. This would ensure that dependents and key military personnel had time to escape. This evacuation process would be greatly enhanced and entirely refocused under the next series of operations.

Before he had left to catch his plane, Bill Douglas had told me that the RedEye targeting demonstration, if done correctly, would give pause to the Russian military command. The whole point of this exercise was to buy us time to position and establish the platform for phase two: *Sparrow Hawk*.

"This is important, Rick," Douglas had said. "Get it done."

"Yes, Sir!"

The Cold War was getting hotter!

**OBSERVATION POST ALPHA
OPLAN SYNCHRONIZED
SPARROW
50°43'26.15"N 09°55'54.68"E
RASDORF, HESSE, WEST
GERMANY
0420 HOURS
SUNDAY 14 SEPTEMBER 1969**

Figure 24
OP Alpha Today

OP Alpha[161], or *Point Alpha,* was one of four Cold War observation posts spread across the border at Fulda. It was located between Rasdorf, Hesse, West Germany and Geisa, Thuringia, East Germany. The post's tower overlooked the most likely route through the Fulda Gap[162]. All of our INTEL indicated that this 2.7 kilometer open area would be the Russian choice for their primary invasion route. Due to its exposed position, this OP was often referred to as "the hottest spot of the cold war".

The position selected for Sparrow6, was number two on the favorites list. It was located 250 meters directly behind the *Alpha* tower, just inside the wood-line. We had come up from Gelnhausen on Friday night and spent the night west of town at the small civilian airport that had been quickly converted into an air base.

---

161 Observation Post Alpha was one of four U.S. Army observation posts along the Hessian part of the inner German border. *OP Alpha* was manned by the 1st Squadron 14th Armored Cavalry Regiment stationed in Fulda, and re-flagged as the 11th Armored Cavalry Regiment in 1972.

162 The Fulda Gap was one of two obvious routes for a Soviet tank attack upon West Germany from East Germany. The concept of a major tank battle along the Fulda Gap was a predominant element of NATO war planning during the Cold War.

Saturday morning we crept up an old firebreak that ran completely hidden from view all the way to the rear of *Alpha*. Bravo Company had set up camp at the base of the hill. They put out a perimeter guard on both sides of our position. They, too, were completely hidden from the prying eyes of the East German towers.

OP Alpha's position initially was chosen for its unimpeded view and its monitoring capability of military road and radio traffic. The use of the AN/PPS-5 ground surveillance radar had been added several years later.

Figure 26 AN/PPS-5 Ground Surveillance Radar

This radar feature allowed 24-hour checking of activity on the roads leading into the East German town of Geisa and several miles beyond. At the first sign of an invasion, the *OP Alpha* crew would withdraw to the first blocking point called Bradford. One of the NCOs in Bravo Company told me that these blocking points were commonly referred to as a series of traffic calming[163] devices that wouldn't slow down an ox-drawn cart with Stevie Wonder at the reins.

Figure 25 East German Tower at Fulda

OP Alpha was positioned between two very tall East German turret structures. The briefing document indicated that each tower had been observed to possess high-power spotter scopes and camera equipment. This was one of the main reasons we had selected *OP Alpha*. We wanted our *play of conciseness* to have an unobstructed view for as far as our friends across the border could see. We also wanted it photographed and the pictures published in that wild and crazy Russian magazine, "Invasion Weekly".

That night, after dark, the 1st Squadron, 14th Armored Cavalry Regiment, stationed in Fulda along with engineers and transportation units out of the Hohenfels Training Center[164], would

---

[163] Traffic calming consists of physical design and other measures, including narrowed roads and speed humps, put in place on roads for the intention of slowing down or reducing motor-vehicle traffic as well as improving safety for pedestrians and cyclists.

[164] U.S. Army Garrison Hohenfels provides premier installation management

deposit and stage twelve types of captured (from the Russians) military track equipment.

The stage props would include four T-34, three T-54 Russian main battle tanks[165]and several other captured truck vehicles. All of the vehicles were pulled from the gunnery range at Hohenfels. The targets would be evenly distributed across the flat .4km open area in full view of the East German towers.

OBSERVATION POST ALPHA
OPLAN SYNCHRONIZED SPARROW
800 METERS TO THE REAR OF OP ALPHA
1430 HOURS SUNDAY 14 SEPTEMBER 1969

I would say it's not rocket science to teach someone to shoot a ground-to-air missile, but I still would like to have taken more than a half hour to explain the nuances of the world's first handheld guided missile system to our volunteer spotters from the Bravo Company.

"Mr. D" was at the bird farm, located west of Fulda. He had flown in that afternoon with the Hughes Tech Reps. We had spoken briefly at 1100 hours that morning. After outlining the types of terrain and available cover choices, we both agreed the maximum number of RedEye teams would be required. I then outlined what arrangements I had made for Sunday morning.

We spent Saturday night at the base of the hill behind *OP Alpha,* inside the perimeter established by Bravo Company. I went to their CO, LT Grayson, for a minute of his time in the early morning hours

---

support and services that enhance the readiness of Joint and Multinational forces, and ensures the highest level of quality of life in a secure and sustainable environment.

165   The T-34 (pre-1940) and T-54 and 55 tanks were a series of main battle tanks originally conceived as medium tanks that were designed in the Soviet Union. The first T-54 prototype appeared in March 1945, just as the Second World War ended. The T-54 entered full production in 1947 and became the main tank for armored units of the Soviet Army, armies of the Warsaw Pact countries, and others. T-54s and T-55s were involved in many of the world's armed conflicts during the late 20th and early 21st centuries.

after we set up and bedded down for the night. I explained what my orders were and what was required to make ready the necessary shooters. He said Colonel Brogan had already had a word with him.

"First Sergeant Carstairs, may we have a moment of your time?" asked Grayson. "Sergeant Fontain would like our assistance with the upcoming exercise."

After looking at our team deployment requirements from an overlay I had marked up earlier, 1st Sergeant Jake Carstairs walked up the hill to see firsthand what we were facing. Five riflemen had been requested. Ten were assigned.

There were going to be four RedEye fire teams, plus one similarly armed central controller. The shooters would be the trained RedEye team members consisting of Jack, Larry, Von, and Ken. One Bravo rifleman would support each team, and an additional assignment of two M60 machine gun crews would be positioned just inside the woods at no extra charge.

Two RedEye teams would be deployed to the north and south sides of the *Alpha* tower. Each team would be spaced about 150 feet apart. The fifth RedEye team, the controller, would be set up directly center, and well out of view behind *OP Alpha*.

Two machine guns were located in the wood-line for complete coverage of the north-south fence line. Actual machine guns with real ammunition would provide the means to apply our battalion motto, Blood and Guts. Until that day it had always felt like we'd just been watching inside the peacetime army. That was all about to change.

TARGET AUDIENCE
REVERSE SLOPE
REDEYE FIRE TEAM BASE
OPLAN SYNCHRONIZED SPARROW
0855 HOURS MONDAY 15 SEPTEMBER 1969

We couldn't have asked for better weather. There wasn't a cloud in sight. The sun was climbing in the eastern sky and would be a slight irritation for each gunship pilot cruising in the Gap that morning. Conversely, the lighting would be close to perfect for the Russian photographers.

"Sparrow6, Bravo11."

"Bravo11. Go."

"Be advised that your Papa Bear is approaching your six.[166] Bravo11 Out." It was good to know that we had been accepted into Bravo Company as its little brother and that they were protecting us from all possible angles.

Two minutes later, Captain MacKennia, whom I considered especially supportive of the RedEye team, had pulled up beside where I was standing.

"Good morning, Sir. Blood and Guts," I said as he returned my salute.

"Morning. You all set up here?" he asked as he dismounted the vehicle the instant it came to a stop.

"Yes, Sir. The stage one target vehicles are being surveyed by our neighbors, and we have confirmation that Goldenwire[167] is set to engage," I replied.

"Bill Douglas said you should watch for any offside occurrences during, or directly after act one. He said you would know what that would entail. Just don't get overrun. You have instructed everyone how to use the thermites[168]?"

"Yes, Sir. The penalty is fifteen yards after the flag is flown[169], or in this case, the pin is pulled. Does the Captain know if prison time is served here or back in the States?" I questioned with as much solemnity as possible.

MacKennia at first just stared, and then laughed, shaking his head from side to side. "Prison time?"

"Yes, Sir. I expect anyone responsible for destroying over half a million dollars of government issued weaponry will be asked to pay the piper."

"If the Ruskies come across, you do what you need to do. I'll remain up here with Bravo Company until the show starts. If you

---

166 A clock position is the relative direction of an object described using the analogy of a 12-hour clock. One imagines a clock face lying either upright or flat in front of oneself, and identifies the twelve-hour markings with the directions in which they point.

167 Goldenwire was the call sign designation for the newly configured helicopter gunships equipped with the fresh-from-the-laboratory, top-secret, anti-tank missile systems

168 Thermite grenades

169 My poor attempt at a football analogy

need a hug, I'll be right down there," he said as he pointed down the hill.

"Yes, Sir, but if you see me run through One Bravo's base camp, and my clothes are on fire, you should try to keep up."

"Douglas doesn't want any equipment compromised by an enemy encroachment. Use your best judgment and make sure nobody up here fires into East Germany."

"Yes, Sir," I replied. "Would you like to see how the teams are positioned?"

"That's affirmative, Rick, but let me call in first. Show time is scheduled for 0910 hours."

"Roger that."

REVERSE SLOPE
OBSERVATION POST ALPHA
OPLAN SYNCHRONIZED SPARROW
RASDORF, HESSE, WEST GERMANY
0820 HOURS MONDAY 15 SEPTEMBER 1969

"Alpha36, this is Sparrow6. Alpha11, this is Sparrow6. Over," I said into the radio microphone. The PRC25 was mounted on RE-1's left rear fender well.

"Sparrow6, this is ACR6. Read you five by five. Over," replied the Squadron Commander, LTC Richard "Dicky" Stern, 14th Armored Cavalry.

"Holy shit," I said into the un-keyed mike. "The Squadron Commander is up there in Alpha1."

"ACR6, Sparrow6. We are set and waiting on target launch approval. Is there any activity in the peanut gallery? Over."

"Sparrow6, unusual activity. Much interest being generated over newly arrived lost children.[170] Wait one, Sparrow6." Then there was thirty seconds of silence.

"Sparrow6, there appears to be a sizable audience growing in both towers. The newly installed stage props are causing quite a commotion. Over," said ACR6.

"Roger that, ACR6. Out," I said and immediately re-keyed the mike. "BG31, this is Sparrow6. BG31, this is Sparrow6," I said,

---

[170]   Russian military track vehicles from Hohenfels that we had staged

hoping the S-3 would be available.

"Sparrow6, this BG61. Go," said the HHC Company Commander.

"BG61, we have a growing audience with heightened interest. Over."

"Roger, Sparrow6. I'll pass to bird-farm. Stand by for status. ETA[171] same, Out."

I put the microphone on the front seat of RE-1 as the rear speaker announced, "Goldenwire, this is GoldCharlie6. Goldenwire, this is GoldCharlie6. Over," said the CO of Charlie Company, Captain Steven Davies, calling out to the first TOW[172] fire teams as the acting FO[173] and ground support for today's operation.

Figure 27
Goldenwire TOW

"GoldCharlie 6, this is Goldenwire22. In position and cocked," was the first reply.

Then in rapid succession the rest of the teams checked in.

"Goldenwire23 positioned and cocked."

"Goldenwire24 locked and cocked."

"Goldenwire25 ready to rock."

TOW had been developed for use against armor and bunker-busting operations. Bill Douglas told me this fire system was chosen because of its impressive explosive characteristics -- it was a major attention getter.

This first phase of our fire demonstration would assure large audience participation by the Russian and East German military. The wire-guided accuracy would insure none of the projectiles would inadvertently cross the border to our welcomed spectators, who were just 785 meters across the fence.

Along with the placement of the enemy armor targets, platoon-size, full-body silhouettes positioned around each track vehicle would provide additional food for thought for the viewing audience.

---

171 Estimated time of arrival

172 TOW—[Tube-launched, Optically-tracked, Wire-guided] Missiles initially developed by Hughes Aircraft between 1963 and 1968, the XBGM-71A was designed for both ground-and helicopter-based applications.

173 Forward Observer

Not widely advertised within the Goldenwire repertoire were the M61 20mm Vulcan cannon[174]. They were bolted to the opposite side of the gunship fuselage. Their purpose would be self-explanatory during the upcoming demonstration.

Figure 28
20mm Cannon

The pricing of that day's menu was thirty-five hundred dollars for each TOW served. Each ignited RedEye listed out at seventeen thousand eight hundred dollars. And each fatally targeted drone jet aircraft would be sacrificed at around two hundred thousand. The captured Russian armor would be depreciated to zero.

Great care was taken for each angle of attack. The lanes of fire for each and every shot had been carefully calculated.

"Money is no object," I said to no one in particular. The point of this whole exercise and the real message was best summed up with a quote from our own LTC Brogan as he looked east from the open door of his command track: "You can come across the border, but we have the money and the technology to really hurt you if you do."

THE PRESENTATION
REDEYE FIRE TEAM BASE
OPLAN SYNCHRONIZED SPARROW
0915 HOURS MONDAY 15 SEPTEMBER 1969

The four gunships came in from the west splitting evenly in groups of two. Each pair of Huey's[175] split a second time, lining up

---

174 The M61 Vulcan is hydraulically driven and was configured with six-barrels. Each is air-cooled and electrically fired. It is a Gatling-style rotary cannon. The M61 fires 20 mm rounds at an extremely high rate of speed. The Vulcan has been the principal cannon armament of United States military fixed-wing aircraft for fifty years.

175 The Bell UH-1 Iroquois (unofficially, "Huey") is a military helicopter powered by a single, turbo shaft engine, with a two-bladed main rotor and tail rotor. The helicopter was developed by Bell Helicopter to meet the United States Army's requirement for a medical evacuation and utility helicopter in 1952, and first flew on 20 October 1956. Ordered into production in March 1960,

to prosecute their pre-assigned zoned targets of opportunity. They started their attack at a 35-degree angle to the northeast, first annihilating the silhouetted troops positioned around the tanks with Vulcan cannon fire. This was followed by a giant whooshing sound made by the ejection of multiple TOW missiles from the quad tube array.

The gunships walked their way down the line to the middle of the playing field. All targets were destroyed and on fire. The turret of one of the T-34s was blown at least 20 meters in the air by a well-placed strike by one of the first salvos. All gunships turned to the south and disappeared from sight. Total attack time only took six minutes.

I was sure by that point the Russian management was wondering what a hundred of these gunships would be capable of. What would come next would quash any notion of sending in their air support first.

During the next phase of operations, *Synchronized Sparrow* would map out hundreds of natural depressions found throughout the Gap that would be used to hide and shield a like number of aircraft and tanks.

"Sixteen touchdowns and one field goal, Goldenwire," I said into the PRC77 air-to-air. Sultan6 and the choppers were the only ones monitoring this channel. I let go of the binoculars and picked up the ground-to-air COMMs mike.

"Sparrow6 to Birdfarmer, Sparrow6 to Birdfarmer. Over."

"Sparrow6, BG63 standby for Birdfather11. Wait one."

"Sparrow6, this Londonbridge65. We are in position to your rear. All birdies are circling. Standby." Londonbridge was Bill Douglas, and the reference to London referred to his boss, David James.

"Break, Break, Sparrows 22, 23, 24, and 25. Five minutes, load and lock power. Out," I said, declaring the start of the entertainment.

"Sparrow6, Londonbridge. Birdfather says two birdies each side in four minutes. 45 second spread. Confirm."

"Roger, Londonbridge. Will confirm first view." The *bird farmers* were the drone drivers. *Birdfather* was the drone control leader,

---

the UH-1 was the first turbine-powered helicopter to enter production for the United States military, and more than 16,000 have been produced worldwide.

Barry Flax.

I raised my binoculars, scanned to the rear, and saw two aircraft racing up each side of the valley. "London, we have you in sight. Confirm two birdies inbound; two more way back. Break."

Clark, who was Sparrow25, team-4 leader, was positioned only 25 feet from RedEye central control. I said to him, "Let your guy shoulder the tube and make sure the battery is twisted tight." The "guy" to whom I was referring was Spec4 Bob Saur, on loan from Bravo Company.

"Don't power up yet," I called out to Clark, and then added, "Let's see if we can photograph the start of this historic occasion."

Clark went over to RE-2 and took the 35mm Pentax from the passenger seat and placed its strap around his neck. The camera had been fitted with the largest of the telephoto lenses from our kit.

"I should be able to cover all three teams from up here," said Ken.

"Good, get ready. The aircraft are coming into range," I said and keyed the mike.

"Sparrow 22, 23, and 24 power-up now. Un-cage gyros on turn to west. Wait for complete turn and solid tone before release. Sparrows observe tone lock only. All Sparrows shoot only on my command. Acknowledge."

Three sets of pre-arranged clicks were heard.

"OK, gentleman, we are inside the two-minute shoot sequence." I looked again through my field glasses and I could now hear the familiar engine noise of the pilotless target drones and make out the two aircraft that were circling a half a click out. Barry was doing a good job in directing his drivers.

I keyed the mike again. "All Sparrows, heads-up. Incoming. 22 and 24, POWER UP, spin your gyros, and wait for shoot authority," I threw the mike cord over my shoulder and picked up the 35-millimeter camera sitting on the back seat.

"Hey, M14 guy, did Clark show you how to work this?" I asked as I held up the spare 35mm camera. I was talking to a Spec4 who was watching over the rear area of the northern M-60 gun emplacement.

I grabbed the microphone again. "Londonbridge, all birdies appear to be running hot and true. Do you need me to count off for the turn? Over."

"Negative Sparrow. We have them in sight. All telemetry is in the green. Out."

I was facing the Spec4 when he walked over to RE-1. I said, "Well," as I thrust the camera into the Spec4's chest, "did he?" I repeated.

"Yes, Sergeant, he did."

"Good. Get over that way with Clark and take some additional shots as the drones approach, but concentrate on the missile strikes. Got it? And stay out of sight of the towers."

The aircraft were at 1000 feet and traveling at 350 miles per hour. The one to the north started its turn slightly south at first then turned a bit more toward the west, increasing its speed as it descended over the wrecked and burning tracks. The one drone to the south was positioned 40 seconds behind in its turn but followed the exact same flight path. These aircraft could really maneuver without the handicap of an attached tow array[176].

Barry put them in a slight downward pitch, increasing their speed as they passed over what was left of the burning tracks. The second flight of two was positioned 45 seconds behind.

The first two drones entered the arena and turned back toward the west and immediately started an upward journey at a very high rate of speed. Full afterburner performance was being applied in their climb for freedom.

"Spotters for 22 and 24 report," I said, just as the second turn maneuver was complete.

"Sparrow leader 22 has tone lock; 24 has tone lock," they replied respectively.

"This is Sparrow6. On my count: three, two, and one. SHOOT! SHOOT! SHOOT!"

UNEXPECTED GUESTS
REDEYE FIRE TEAM BASE
OPLAN SYNCHRONIZED SPARROW
0919 HOURS MONDAY 15 SEPTEMBER 1969

There was less than three seconds between the explosions.

---

176 An IR pod tow array was developed to train RedEye operators. A wire mesh containing eight to 16 IR pod generators was towed by cable by a pilotless drone aircraft during training.

What a spectacle as both drones completely disintegrated. Two huge orange fireballs filled the western sky in full view of the Russian towers.

I found out later that not only were the fuel tanks filled to capacity, 3.4 pounds of the high explosive C-4 were packed in the compartment behind the engine mounts. It was rigged with a failsafe control in case the control guidance signal was lost.

"Sparrows 23 and 25: refocus. Spin up your gyros and wait for shoot command. Sparrows 22 and 24: re-arm. Acknowledge," I said as the second set of drones started their first turn.

"Ken, take the weapon and give the camera to your spotter," I yelled. I could still here the cheers coming from One Bravo at the base of the hill.

"Camera guy, how are we doing on film?"

"I think there are more shots left."

"How many did you take? There are 35 to 38 on the roll."

"I took about twelve, maybe fifteen, so I've got about half a roll left, yes?" he inquired.

"Sounds right," I said. "Get ready to go again, camera guy."

"My name's Glen," he shot back. "Glen Towson."

"Glad to meet you, Glen," I said as I picked up the radio mike.

"Sparrows 23 and 25: start your tone sequence." The drones dropped even lower than their predecessors. Thirty seconds flying time separated the two.

"Ken, how's it going?"

"Gyros running, here we go," he replied with a touch of excitement in his voice.

"Sparrows 22 and 24: pull two arrows from your quiver. Power up and start your gyros. Do not -- repeat -- do not shoot unless ordered to do so."

Barry, the General Dynamics guru, had divulged to me while we were checking the weapons in Gelnhausen that we had been authorized to shoot up to ten missiles within this exercise. He said we could shoot more than one RedEye at the same target drone, if the situation allowed.

We were limited on drones and not so much on missiles. Enhancing the demonstration effect and snatching some invaluable OJT[177] at the same time was more than justified.

---

[177]   On-the-job-training

"Sparrows 22 and 24, switch positions with your spotters and provide tracking guidance." Jack Swanson on 22 un-shouldered the RedEye and pulled the power pack from the handle grip. Von on 24 passed the weapon to his spotter and unfastened and pocketed the battery.

Bravo Company was about to get some hands-on RedEye experience. Both drones made the last turn together. Barry had them climbing at a much steeper angle and at a higher rate of speed.

"Sparrows 23 and 25, un-cage gyros. Sparrows 22 and 24: power up and start tracking tone. Everyone stand by to fire."

Jack and Von re-inserted the power packs and gave the power-up command.

"Snap count, Sparrows 22 and 23 take first incoming. Sparrows 24 and 25 prosecute second incoming, All Sparrows un-cage gyros. Commence tone lock on the turn. Acknowledge." All Sparrows signaled with their prearranged handset clicks sent by the spotters.

I had emphasized to each team member the night before, "It is important to remain calm and focused during each shooting sequence. Listen for your call sign and concentrate on what information immediately follows. I'll guide each of your teams. All you need to do is concentrate on your call sign and do exactly what I tell you.

"We have used this routine in the past," I said, "and it works. I'll repeat the firing orders twice. Spotters are to repeat what you hear and repeat it to your shooter. If you don't understand the orders ask your partner for clarification.

"If for some reason both of you require additional explanation, get on the radio and call Sparrow61; state your call sign, and say, 'holding for repeat'. If you think you're out of time, hold your fire. Don't waste the shot. We'll regroup and get you set up for the next firing sequence."

Von told me later that night that my little talk had simplified the task at hand and the guys from Bravo had told him that they now felt confident they would be able to perform the duties assigned.

"Sparrows 22, 23, 24, 25, prepare to engage on my count: three, two, and one, STAND DOWN—STAND DOWN," I instructed as I caught David Russell waving frantically and making a cutting motion across his throat.

"Londonbridge, Sparrow request go around. Over," I requested. "All Sparrows refresh power packs on all ARROWS," I continued.

"Sparrow, this is Birdfather11. Birdies circling at safe distance. Suggest safe delay limited to hunger and uninvited response, over."

"Roger, Birdfather. Birdies circling. Out," I acknowledged. Flax was referring to the need to refuel as well as the increased need to be wary of encroachment by the Russians.

BIRDFATHER LOCATION
BASE OF HILL BELOW BRAVO COMPANY
OPLAN SYNCHRONIZED SPARROW
0929 HOURS MONDAY 15 SEPTEMBER 1969

Flax un-keyed his mike and looked over at Bill Douglas and shrugged his shoulders. "What do you think that was all about?" Flax asked.

Douglas, who was wearing a set of aviation style cans[178], flipped them off his head and let them rest around his neck. He turned to face Barry. "Apparently ACR6 is in contact with his boss in Frankfurt. I was just patched in with David James, who said Daryl Russell just told Sultan6[179] on the ground to air freak[180] that the LTC, ACR6, was asking for the delay. Russell is reporting that both of the East German towers are filling up with VIP faces not usually seen in this part of the world."

REDEYE FIRE TEAM BASE
OPLAN SYNCHRONIZED SPARROW
0931 HOURS MONDAY 15 SEPTEMBER 1969

I had been looking at the drone coming south through my binoculars. I dropped them and let them hang as I turned to check on the aircraft approaching from the other direction. I noticed Clark was looking east and pulling up his camera to record whatever it

---

178 Headphones
179 Sultan6 was Lt. Pezlola's border intercept and insertion group
180 Slang for frequency

was he saw. He was using his telephoto lens. I looked in the direction his camera was aimed. Ken was photographing a Russian soldier with a camera on a tripod, which was out on the roof of the northern tower.

"What kind of camera does that guy have, Ken?" I asked, looking through my binoculars.

"Looks like a 16 millimeter movie. It's probably a Scoopic 16[181]."

After I got Birdfather to park his flock for the moment, my radio woke up with three clicks.

"Sparrow6, meet me on the back porch," said Russell.

I put my binoculars back up on *Alpha* and I could see Daryl Russell standing next to ACR6 at the rear window. He had a microphone held up to his month. I responded with two clicks of my "push to talk" switch.

"Hey camera guy. Sorry. Glen, do you have a poncho in your kit?"

"Sure do, but it ain't gonna rain today, Sergeant."

"Can I borrow it for a few minutes? I need to take a walk." I re-keyed the mike. "Londonbridge, Sparrow6. I have been summoned by our favorite researcher. I'll be back in five. Over."

"Roger, Sparrow. Birdfarmer will pass to Londonbridge. Out."

Clark was taking pictures from the edge of the open area. He was using the largest of the telephoto lenses. He said it looked like standing room only over there. I was too far away to hear the clicking going on inside each of the East German watchtowers, but I bet it was deafening.

"Hey, Ken," I said. "Sweep both towers and the fence line with the telephoto. See if any of the un-friendlies are pointing any weapons over here," I said as I pulled the poncho over my head.

"There are a lot of people watching, but nobody looking hostile. You're clear," said Clark.

I had pulled up the hood over my baseball cap. I tugged the brim down as far I could, and proceeded out into the clearing at a fast pace toward the rear of *Alpha*. As I walked up the staircase of *Alpha*

---

[181] The Scoopic 16, launched in 1965 with its name derived from the word "scoop" in the jargon of news broadcasting, was developed by Canon as the world's first 16 millimeter movie camera with a built-in zoom lens that was not merely limited to news reportage but had many other wide applications, as well.

I was met by Russell.

"You think it's going to rain, Rick?" he asked.

"No, but Douglas told me to always travel incognito. Besides, I have no desire to have my picture in the KGB[182] version of "Terminate Weekly", especially this close to retirement. What's up? Why the delay request?"

I listened to his reasoning and made a suggestion that we bring back the Hueys and perform a more extensive demo on both Russian towers. Russell seemed to be thinking this over when he broke the silence and said, "No, I don't think we could sell that on such short notice."

"Jesus, Daryl, I was only kidding. Now I know why Douglas is the way he is. Lt. Pezlola told me that joking with you guys from Virginia could start WWIII."

"He's right," said Daryl laughing. "And WWIII would cause a total project rewrite. We'll give it a few more minutes but I think everybody who's important has already arrived over there. I thought the LTC, who had a background in intelligence, was going to wet himself looking through the spotter's scope at all of those Russian big shots."

"Would you say the majority of the people we're trying to impress are in the northern turret? If so, then I have a suggestion to make. We're getting some great pictures of people in the northern turrets that've been incognito for quite a while."

I went on and explained my idea and Russell said, "That'll work for me. Tell Douglas we can start up again in five minutes."

"OK," I said. "Answer me this: do you think I should serpentine on the way back to the woods or just low crawl?" I inquired with some immediate concern in my voice.

"Zigzag usually works, but for the really good snipers it shouldn't matter either way," replied the smiling Daryl Russell.

"You're a ray of sunshine on a cloudy day, Mr. Russell."

---

[182] The Committee for State Security, more commonly known by its transliteration "KGB," was the main security agency for the Soviet Union from 1954 until its collapse in 1991.

SENDING THE MESSAGE
REDEYE FIRE TEAM BASE
OPLAN SYNCHRONIZED SPARROW
0935 MONDAY 15 SEPTEMBER 1969

"Birdfather11, this is Sparrow6. Over."

"Sparrow6, Birdfather. Go." Barry's voice came back almost immediately.

"Birdfather, expect visitor with hall pass your location directly. Over."

"Roger, Sparrow. Just received. Back in one. Out." I had sent Glen the camera guy down to Douglas and Flax with a brief note outlining my suggested approach to the grand finale.

"Sparrow6, Londonbridge. Birdfather says plenty of bird food available. Repositioning now. *Show time* in suggested timeframe. Over." The fuel tanks on the drones each held 73.6 gallons of fuel.

Roger that, *show time* imminent. Out," I replied and re-keyed the mike. "Foggybottom6[183] watch the birdie. *Show time* 90 seconds. Over."

"Roger, Sparrow6. Out." replied Russell.

"This is Sparrow6. Sparrows 22, 23, 24, and 25, power-up. Show time is in 60 seconds."

I had pulled Sparrow 23 from their position looking south and repositioned them in line with Sparrows 22 and 24. I turned to Clark who was reloading both cameras.

"Ken, how would you like to become famous?" I asked just as Glen, who was slightly winded, returned from his errand.

"What do you have in mind?" asked Ken.

"Glen, will you lend your poncho to Specialist Clark?"

"This is Sparrow6. All Sparrows start gyro spin up now and proceed with tone locking sequence after turn. Be advised, multiple aircraft approaching your positions. Sparrows 23 and 24 will shoot first. Sparrow22 will track and shoot second incoming. All teams prep your spares. STANDBY."

Each team had started with seven RedEyes. Earlier that morning I had taken one RedEye container from RE-1 and laid it sideways across the trailer and flipped the lid open. I called out to Clark, who was just on the other side of the footpath facing north.

---

[183] Foggybottom6 was the call sign for CIA FO Bill Russell

"Ken, as soon as we shoot the second drone, give your camera to Glen and take this RedEye out to where we marked the path earlier this morning. Start your tracking as soon as you make eye contact with the target. I'll call out to you the firing sequence. You OK with that?"

"Just don't let anybody over there shoot me." Ken pulled the poncho over his head and walked to the edge of the opening between *Alpha* and the wood-line. He was trailed by Glen, who had shouldered the RedEye and with his left hand was putting a power pack into the handle grip of the launch tube.

"Glen, come back here a minute."

"Yes, Sergeant," he answered as he walked over to where I was working the radios.

"Your buddies over there on the M60," I pointed across the pathway to a position just inside the trees. "Are they good at what they do?"

"Yeah, they're on the 1st Sergeant's A list. Why do you ask?"

I explained what Clark was going to do, and Glen went over to the guys on the M60 and explained what I wanted done. As Glen was walking back to me, both of the M60 spotters stood up and trained their spotter scopes on each of the Russian towers.

I picked up the handset and pressed the talk switch, "All Sparrows, *show time* in 30. STANDBY."

"Birdfather, your table is ready. Out."

The two drones were advancing up the north side of the Fulda Gap. They were approaching at speeds of 350 MPH. Their present course would have put them crossing over the line of the recently destroyed vehicles in 20 seconds. They were flying side by side. There would be no time division. They would attack together in formation.

"Stand to, Sparrows. Wait for the turn before locking on. Sparrows 22 and 24 will take the target climbing on the extreme right," I said, holding the binoculars in my left hand. "Sparrow 23 will prosecute second aircraft on extreme left. Un-cage all gyros on turn. Wait for the turn."

"They're coming in Ken, get your camera ready," I instructed.

The first aircraft came in and turned south as expected. The second drone chickened out at the last moment and pulled almost straight up and turned off to the north and out of sight.

"Sparrows 23 and 24 will now prosecute first aircraft. Stand by."

"Sparrow22, no joy on second aircraft. Hold for target reacquisition."

The first drone made its turn back toward the west, gaining altitude from about 500 feet to 1000 feet in mere seconds. The jet's behavior turned wild. The aircraft dove at full power back toward the valley floor. Still at full power, the jet arched upwards at a 70-degree angle. It was as if the driver had suddenly awakened seconds before plowing into the grasslands of the meadow. The aircraft was well on its way to outer space.

"Sparrow 23, SHOOT, SHOOT, SHOOT!" I counted in my head 1001, 1002, 1003, and then shouted, "Sparrow 24, SHOOT, SHOOT, SHOOT!"

The missile hit the right rear stabilizer causing the aircraft to violently change direction to the north. It was spinning wildly and fuel was streaming out and immediately ignited by the fire shooting out of the badly damaged engine. The second RedEye struck moments later. The missile had radically changed direction right before impact to compensate for the jet's attempt to escape.

We heard it before we saw it. A third drone came screaming in from the southwest. It was now parallel with the border fence and flew at about 200 feet off the ground. It would pass directly over Clark, who was standing with his back to the East German towers at the edge of the woods.

The drone was approaching its max speed of 400 miles per hour as it headed out over the still-smoldering Russian tanks. With a sharp turn to the left and an almost violent turn upwards, it performed an even steeper climb than drone number one.

Without waiting for direction from me, Clark handed the camera to Glen and quickly trotted out into the open area surrounding *Alpha*. As he traveled, he pushed the power pack into the handle of the RedEye. He held his left hand up to signal he was ready.

"Sparrow25, acquire the target. SHOOT, SHOOT, SHOOT," I yelled. I saw Clark change his stance slightly as the missile came out of the launch tube. The second stage motor ignited and the RedEye traveled several hundred feet hugging close to the ground and then suddenly shooting straight up at a speed of Mach2.

A mental image of a Russian General smashing the ignited end of his cigar on the glass of enemy tower No. 1 popped into my mind. The shot would be considered textbook, and the smile on Ken's face said it all.

The RedEye had found the rear of the third drone and entered dead center to the drone's engine exhaust port. The resulting explosion echoed for miles around. The heat and the smell of jet fuel rained down on us from the enormous detonation and fireball. I looked over to where Clark was standing and yelled, "Hey, Ken, get back under cover. Now." He immediately started trotting back toward the wood-line, still smiling from ear to ear.

The M60 crew who had been covering him the entire time he was out in the open came over and was patting him on the back, telling him that it was a great shot. Mr. Ken would not have to buy any beer at the club for the rest of his tour.

The radio came to life again. "Sparrow6, this is Bravo5. You have an incoming bogy that will be directly over your location any moment. Acknowledge."

"Roger that. Out. Break-Break." I un-keyed the mike and called over to where Ken was being congratulated.

"Ken, go and get another weapon and cover the southern retreat path back to the west. You go with him, Glen."

I keyed the handset and quickly spoke, "Sparrows 22 and 23, weapons hot. Fast birdie arriving on your six[184]. Sparrow24, weapons hot. DO NOT shoot until command to shoot is given. WAIT, WAIT, WAIT. Sparrows 22 and 23, you will switch with your spotters. NOW. I repeat, switch with your spotters. Standby."

The aircraft came hurtling in directly overhead and turned sharply to the north. Birdfather had taken my advice and had orchestrated a true field test of a combat situation. Our Russian friends would be talking about today's events for a good long while, and so would my guys.

Instead of turning west, the drone continued north climbing at a very steep angle and disappeared over the horizon.

"Sparrow25, Sparrow6. Pick up, Glen." As I turned my head to the south I could see Sparrow25 standing next to RE-5.

"Sparrow6, Sparrow25. Over," said camera guy Glen.

"Sparrow25, watch southwest. Fast birdie may circle in on your

---

[184] The numbered positions on the face of a clock that are used to describe direction

side. Over."

"Roger that, Sparrow25. Out," replied Glen.

Forty-five seconds later the PRC25 came on. "Sparrow6, Sparrow25. Bogie incoming from the south at a high rate of speed. No joy. Over," said Clark as the drone passed overhead heading north, blocked by the taller trees behind *Alpha.* Ken had no choice but to pass the ball back to the northernmost teams.

"Roger, two five. No joy. Break. Sparrows 22 and 23, weapons hot. Fast birdie arriving on your three o'clock now. Sparrow24, power up. Same shooters. Hold fire until birdie flies west. Wait one."

This time the drone came in directly over us at treetop level on its way north. I re-keyed the mike. "All Sparrows weapons hot. Incoming, Incoming, Incoming. Wait for the turn," I said and released the mike button and pulled the binoculars up for a quick look.

"Sparrows 22 and 23 un-cage gyros now. Sparrow 24, spin up now. Hold."

As the drone reached the open space over the recently destroyed track vehicles it started a high-speed climb to the north. When it reached the top of its climb it continued in a loop maneuver (upside down) back toward the south.

At only 500 feet above the ground it flipped over to an upright position and continued its journey back to earth. At 300 feet it abruptly turned to the west. A long orange flame shot out of the tail as the afterburner went to full military power, and it started to climb almost straight up into the Fulda sky.

"Sparrows 22 and 23, un-cage gyros. Fire on tone lock. Spotters verify with a tap." The command would come from the spotter who rested his right hand on the left shoulder of the shooter -- confirming tone lock with a single tap.

"Sparrow 24, un-cage, and spotter verify tone lock. FIRE-FIRE-FIRE."

The first two missiles hit almost simultaneously, causing the drone to shed its left wing. The third missile hit the fuselage dead center. The resulting explosion disintegrated the aircraft. Tiny pieces of the plane were raining down all over the Gap.

BIRDFATHER LOCATION
BASE OF HILL BELOW BRAVO COMPANY
OPLAN SYNCHRONIZED SPARROW
0941 MONDAY 15 SEPTEMBER 1969

Bill Douglas, listening to the radio speaker located in the grill of the six by six assigned to him for the duration, whispered to no one in particular, "Sparrow6, you seem to be a natural at this shit."

Barry Flax, standing a short distance away, asked, "What did you say, Bill?"

"Mr. Flax, you are listening to a natural born Combat Commander direct this entire exercise like he has been doing it all his life. Our Sergeant Rick is a very capable guy."

"I've always said that, ever since the first time he destroyed one of my airplanes."

REDEYE FIRE TEAM BASE
OPLAN SYNCHRONIZED SPARROW
0942 HOURS MONDAY 15 SEPTEMBER 1969

I could hear the cheers coming from all the way down the hill. The troops in Bravo Company had been well entertained. All four of our teams just stood, not saying anything. This was as close to combat as most had ever been. Each man was watching the burning piles of rubble that peppered the floor of the Fulda Gap.

"All Sparrows stand down, stand down. Secure all weapons and prepare to move to One Bravo. All shooters, well done, well done. Break," I said and slowly took a deep breath. I placed the mike back onto the passenger seat. I started to walk over to RE-5 but stopped and picked up the mike and called, "Foggybottom6, Sparrow6. Over."

"Go Sparrow," came the almost immediate reply.

"Ask ACR6 if I may approach your position. Over."

"Roger that, Sparrow. Wait. . . affirmative. Over." was the reply.

"Be there in five. Out."

I yelled over to Glen who was helping Clark put the spent RedEye tubes back into their containers.

"Glen, I'm going to borrow your poncho again. Ken, before we pull out of here, go up to the top of the clearing and take a couple of rolls of each tower. Don't forget to switch out to our largest telephoto lens if you haven't already. See what you can get in the way of faces from each of the towers. I'll be back in a minute. Glen, tell all your guys to pack it up and get ready to boogie."

I kept my head down and the hood up as I approached the back of *OP Alpha.*

"Hell of a show, Rick," said Russell as he stepped down on the bottom step of the tower stairway.

"I wanted to say thanks for the support. I wasn't sure we would have any time later to chitchat." Before he could respond, the LTC of the 14th ACR, Richard *"Dicky"* Stern, came down the stairs and offered his hand to me.

"That was a very professional demonstration, Sergeant."

"Yes, Sir. Thank you. We train for this all the time," I said and crossed my fingers behind my back.

"We have RedEye munitions here but we don't have anyone trained."

"Sir, we could come up and run a training course for your people. I'm sure Colonel Brogan would allow us to do that."

"I accept, and I'll call Tom next week. Thanks for the support today."

"Who did you say, Sir?"

"I'll call Colonel Brogan next week to set it up."

"Yes, Sir. Blood and Guts," I said as he turned and re-entered the tower.

"I'm going to Frankfurt from here, or so I've been told, but that may change when Douglas IDs the faces on the photos we shot," said Russell.

"Well, you know where we live, keep in touch. Thanks again for the support," I said and zigzagged back to RE-1.

"Everybody packed?" I shouted as I reentered the wood-line. All of the jeeps and trailers were loaded and pointed at the trail to go down the hill.

"Bravo 61, Sparrow6," I said into the mike.

"Go Sparrow," was the comeback.

"Moving to your location. Sparrow6. Out," I said and put my hand into the air, making a wind-up-and-follow-me motion.

XVI

COLD WAR 2.0

"LINES IN THE SAND"

AFTER ACTION
FRANCOIS KASERNE, BLDG. 903
HANAU, WEST GERMANY
0915 HOURS WEDNESDAY 25 SEPTEMBER 1969

It had been two weeks since the operation at *OP Alpha*. This particular meeting was being held in Hanau at the Francois Kaserne. It was the first of many after-action briefings to be held on *Operation Synchronized Sparrow*.

In attendance were two silver chickens[185] from Division HQ, our LTC Brogan, LT Key, myself and 30 other personnel from a wide variety of local unit responsibilities. Both Bill Douglas and Jim Pezlola were noticeably absent. SFC Gary Lawson had been sent in

---

[185] Full Bird Colonels

their stead.

The briefing book on the table in front of me contained over twenty typed double-spaced pages, each stamped, "Top Secret". The document had obviously been derived from NATO 14/3, but all labeling had been scrubbed.

Some of the pictures projected opaquely were ones my team had taken.

A five-minute film clip highlighted the drone kills accomplished during Operation *Synchronized Sparrow*. There were several shots taken from a variety of angles, indicating multiple photographers.

Today's conference was the official *change order* notification to the NATO mission policy. Part A, paragraph 6, page 173 was labeled *MEASURES REQUIRING INTEGRATION*. Part B, paragraph 2, page 247 addressed the following:

- Intelligence Protocol
- Real-time Situation Reporting
- Early Warning Detection Technology
- Command Control Fallback Procedures
- Track and Shoot [DATALINK] Communications

We were about 45 minutes into the meeting when they finally got to the point. A Captain from the NATO staff in Brussels put up a slide showing the reconfiguration of key blocking components of the Fulda Gap. He told us of the newly formed ground-to-air missile and Vulcan squadrons that would be inserted into the recently vacated Fargo LOD[186].

He then introduced A.G. Galaiologopoulos, Lieutenant General, Hellenic Army Director of the International Military Staff located in Brussels.

"Good morning, Gentlemen," he opened in heavily accented English. "The recent armor and troop movements in East Germany and Czechoslovakia have shown the Russians' intentions to invade. Our existing policy, while vigorous in its methodology, has been mostly dependent on the MAD[187] factor."

He went on to say that recent intelligence had revealed a drastic change in the Russian military mindset. I leaned my head close to

---

[186]   Line of Defense
[187]   Mutually Assured Destruction

SFC Gary Lawson, who was seated to my left, and whispered, "No shit."

NATO ADOPTS FLEXIBLE RESPONSE DOCTRINE
FRANCOIS KASERNE NCO CLUB
1315 HOURS WEDNESDAY 25 SEPTEMBER 1969

The meeting had ended on a positive note. Operation *Sparrow Hawk* was announced. The results would be used to formulate a brand new resolve. The Greek General had charged on with his remarks for almost an entire hour. Most of his references to documents and paragraph numbers didn't make a whole lot of sense to me. NATO 14/3 was not mentioned by name.

Gary Lawson, however, had emerged from the briefing more excited than I had ever seen him. Apparently, most, if not all, of *their* recommendations, formulated by his boss, Bill Douglas, and his boss's boss, David James, were being adopted.

Sparrow Hawk, crafted in total by the Hilversum think-tank, had been approved by the U.S. President. A high level meeting was planned for final approval in December. The selective modifications to MC 14 and 48/3 three[188] had been submitted. The procedural plan known as *Fulda Cold* was not discussed.

"Gary," I said as we ascended the stairs to the Francois Kaserne NCO Club, "I'm surprised to see you. You were just in the neighborhood, I suppose?"

"Like you, it was a command performance," he answered as we walked through the dining room and into the bar.

"I was told to ask you for your first impressions of the meeting," he continued. We took a seat at the bar.

"I'm not sure what you're asking." Before Gary could respond, the bartender came over.

"What can I get you?"

"Do you have any fresh coffee made?"

"Yep... I just made a pot."

"I'll have a cup. Black, please."

"Sounds good," said Gary. "Make that two." The barkeep went

---

[188] NATO's military reaction strategies to invasion

off to fill the order. "Douglas told me he read you in on *Sparrow Hawk*. So I'll ask you again, how do you think the changes to MC 14/3 were perceived?"

"Is that what was being discussed?"

"Humor me," replied Gary.

"When the Russians investigate what we leak to them across the wire they will be forced to verify what they have heard. They will do this in a number of ways. The easiest and most reliable way will be to talk to people who are working the new NATO mission."

"How does that convince them not to invade?"

"It doesn't," I said. "The more they investigate the less will be explained. But, eventually, the repositioning of the nukes will be uncovered by Ivan. When that happens they'll be faced with whether or not to believe the original INTEL we leaked," I continued.

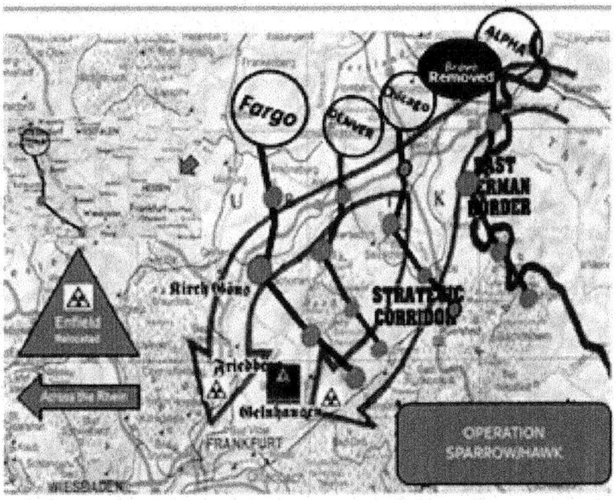

Figure 29

The Fulda Gap

"How so?" asked Gary.

"Sooner or later they'll realize that the NATO forces in the Fulda region are still outnumbered by a 10 to 1 ratio. Even with all of the neat new technology being applied, they'll be forced to examine the unspoken consequence of invading the West."

"Which is?" Gary asked in a tone that suggested that he didn't want to hear my best guess.

"Have you read MC 14/3 C[189]?"

"No. Have you?"

"Not in any detail, but it does have a catchy code name."

"Douglas said I shouldn't be surprised by your take on all this," Gary said with exasperation.

---

[189] The "C" version of MC 14/3: The CIA had submitted a comprehensive recommendation for the reconfiguration of the NATO and American Central Command Forces facing the potential invasion of armies of the Warsaw Pact. It was to be a complete reversal of tactic in dealing with the ongoing invasion threat.

"He said that with a straight face, did he?"

US EMBASSY, LONDON
CULTURAL AFFAIRS SECTION
25 GROSVENOR SQUARE, LONDON W1A 2LQ
UNITED KINGDOM
2315 HOURS THURSDAY 24 OCTOBER 1969

David James was assigned as the Cultural Attaché to the U.S. Embassy in London in March of 1964. He was 43 years old, married, and had two children. London was his third international assignment. His family had settled into a small township outside London called Bracknell, establishing many friendships since moving there in the summer of 1965. David James was a world-class master spy. He was the CIA's Station Chief in London with responsibilities on three landmasses.

Staff Sergeant Joe Benson, formerly of the 1st 48th INF, knocked once, entered the meeting room, and handed James a hand-written note on yellow message center carbon paper. James read the dispatch and excused himself to take a phone call.

The call originated from the 7th floor of Langley, Virginia. He walked out into the hallway and asked, "Joe, do you have the duty tonight?"

"Yes, Sir, I do. What do you need?"

"I need to send a TWX to Hilversum. Can you come down in about 10 minutes?"

"Yes, Sir, I'll be glad to."

"Hey, I saw the new Triumph in the courtyard. You'll have to take me for a ride."

"Any time, Sir." Joe started back to the COMM Center.

"Maybe Fontain will share some of his tools with you," the CIA station chief called out as he disappeared into his office.

"How in the hell did he know that I gave Rick Fontain my tools?" Joe wondered.

At that moment, David James was juggling a lot of balls in the air. He marched past where his administrative assistant would normally sit. Given the time, she and most other embassy staff had gone home hours earlier.

He went into his office and strode around his desk, picking up the handset of the KY-3 on the second ring. He dropped heavily into his leather executive chair.

"James," he announced into the phone. "Confirming secure line status green."

"David, Gerald Bushman here. A Huey with Bill Douglas on board has gone down near the Laotian border," said the Deputy Director Central Intelligence. "We can't get in there until first light. I know he was working on something important, so I wanted to let you know before you read about it in tomorrow's AAR[190].

"Thank you, Sir. I know the DDCI has more important issues to deal with than downed helicopters, so I really appreciate your contacting me."

"Nonsense, I know you two are close. I was also calling to tell you that the issue Douglas was returning to Germany to deal with next week may have resolved itself -- at least in the short term."

"That is good news, Sir. When will the analysis be complete?"

"Joe Wilson says the new SAT INTEL will be available tonight. The EGD[191] will have the information examined by early morning my time. It's been confirmed already that seven of the original re-deployed combat units from the western and southern military districts have returned to their respective bases. Two other armor units in Voronezh[192] look to be making plans to travel as we speak. It appears their exercise and/or invasion plan is in full decline," said the DDCI.

"Yes, Sir. Or they gathered the information they were after and have returned to await further orders," said James, pausing to wait for a response.

"David, all indications we've received from our sources in the East say that operation Synchronized Sparrow was the major factor for the de-escalation of the Russian buildup at Fulda."

"It was considered a long shot when it was conceived, Sir. That is good news about the result. Sir, how should we proceed with operation Sparrow Hawk?"

"NATO prime INTEL has decided that Bradford has been

---

190 After Action Report
191 East German Desk at Langley
192 Operating center of the Southeastern Railway (connecting European Russia with Ural and Siberia, as well as Caucasus and Ukraine), as well as the center of the Don Highway (Moscow)

compromised and should be dismantled," said Bushman. "It was installed too close to Alpha to have been effective."

"Has Sparrow Hawk been approved by the President? And, what is the decision on re-staging the bunker weapons?" asked James.

"We expect a decision to go, or no go, in the next couple of weeks," said the General. "However, the re-stage should be done regardless of the President's decision.

"We'll need to re-work Chicago, Denver, and Fargo at the same time," said James.

"The funding to prep Sparrow Hawk has been approved. Concentrate on the relocation of the Enfield facility and the removal of all nukes from Fargo. Phase-one for the new weapons systems being deployed from Ft. Bliss into Fargo is already underway," said Bushman.

"Hilversum has coordinated the reset of the view from Enfield. The new location will be fourteen clicks west of Mainz just across the Rhine," said James.

"That's my understanding also," said the DDIC. "The time constraints have changed back in our favor." Bushman was referring to the fact that the first stage, Synchronized Sparrow, had indeed given the Russians pause.

"The Hilversum information suggests that the re-evaluation of the corridor strategies passing through Chicago, Denver and Fargo will require that operation Sparrow Hawk be run as soon as it can be scheduled. The NATO battalion and the nukes at Fargo have been relocated to Enfield. An HHC company has remained in place to provide S-4 [supply and support] and guard security services for the incoming Hawk squadrons."

"The vacated bases at Fargo2, 3, and 4 will house the incoming Squadrons?" asked the General.

"Yes, Sir. That is my understanding," answered James.

"Once Sparrow Hawk is approved, 3rd Armor minus the 2nd/48th will act as the aggressor. They will attack from the rear of OP Alpha toward the vacated Bradford," said Bushman.

"The 14th ACR, 2nd /6th Artillery, and the 2nd/48th will be the defenders," he continued. "The Sparrow Hawk force, 2nd Cavalry Regiment, will provide an overwatch for the series of leapfrog maneuvers back through Fargo. This exercise will simulate a mini-invasion".

"That's how I understand it also, Sir," said David James. "The more traffic we can generate back toward the Rhine, through the

nodes of Chicago and Denver, the better the data we'll have to construct MC 14/3 C.

"With your permission, Sir, I'll alert Captain Pezlola to take the lead as soon as we hang up. He'll run Sparrow Hawk if Bill Douglas isn't available," said James, struggling to keep his voice devoid of emotion.

"Fine, David." I'll call you as soon as I hear anything on Douglas." The status light blinked amber. The DDCI had hung up.

UNITED STATES EMBASSY, SAIGON
2ND FLOOR COMM CENTER
NORODOM COMPOUND AT NO 4 THONG NHUT
SOUTH VIETNAM
1225 HOURS MONDAY 27 OCTOBER 1969

A smiling Bill Douglas walked across the lobby to the stairwell entrance and climbed to the second floor. He walked straight across the hallway and pushed open the door to the COMM Center. It had been four days since his chopper was forced down in the jungle in Laos.

"Afternoon Sergeant," he said as he held up his 'any level any area' white ID card with blue and yellow stripes. "I need to use your secure line." He went into the cubicle in the corner of the room and sat on the corner of the desk as he input the access code into the Embassy's PBX extension.

"Joe, Bill Douglas," he greeted Joe Wilson, of Langley's Russian/East German Desk. "You're working late these days."

"Christ, Bill. We were so relieved to hear that you survived the crash."

"That would make it unanimous. If it wasn't for MacKennia's old air group, I would be dining in the Hanoi Hilton." Then he added, "They came back three days in a row to find us. MacKennia trained them well. Listen, Joe. I need a favor."

"Name it," said Wilson.

"I spoke to David James this morning about the proposed start date for Sparrow Hawk. Do you know what it is?"

"The DDCI was up here this morning with the approved OP order," said Wilson. "Sparrow Hawk has been green-lighted with a one November start date."

"I'm booked on a Lufthansa flight into Frankfurt that leaves at 1800," said Douglas. "Pezlola is picking me up and taking me out to Fargo4. He's probably already left for Frankfurt, so, will you call over to Coleman and start the ball rolling?"

"Who should I talk to?" asked Wilson, the DHCI[193] for OREA.

"Alert the 1st/48th S-3, and tell him to pull the project package for Sparrow Hawk from their safe. Ask them to issue orders to Sergeant Fontain to have RedEye rendezvous at the coordinates specified on page seven. There's a project map in the package. Five November doesn't give them much time to get ready, so follow up your call with a TWX to the attention of LTC Brogan."

"You got it, Bill. Anything else?" asked Wilson.

"Let David know that you alerted Gelnhausen. I'll call you when I land. Thanks for the assist, Joe."

"I'll let David know. Take care, Bill," Wilson said.

SPARROW HAWK
RT40—14KM NE OF GELNHAUSEN
BAD ORB HESSE, NEAR THE NATURE PARK SPESSART
0950 HOURS WEDNESDAY 5 NOVEMBER 1969

As of Tuesday morning, November 4, RE-3 and RE-5 were still without their road-worthiness certification, which meant no trip ticket. Apparently, wheel bearings and a master cylinder for the brake system prohibit safe operation of a jeep. Go figure. The bad news was that the parts were not in inventory. The really bad news was that the time estimate for their availability was two and three weeks respectively.

"Von, you and Ken take RE-1 and drive up to the HHC and help Larry and Jack get our six trainers out of the arms room." Barry Flax had made us a gift of four additional modified trackers after the completion of *Synchronized Sparrow*. "Make sure we pack all of the spare batteries," I instructed.

"Roger that. What are you going to do about the repairs?" asked Von.

---

[193] Department Head Central Intelligence Office of Russian and European Analysis (OREA)

"When things get tough, I go and see the most powerful man in the Battalion."

"You're going to see the Colonel?" asked Clark.

"No, Carl Blubaugh."

All five of the RedEye vehicles and their respective trailers left Coleman Kaserne at 0915 on the following day, Wednesday the fifth. A six by six 1.25 ton truck with the bumper markings of the 3rd AD HQHHC had arrived in our maintenance facility at 1600 on Tuesday afternoon, bearing the necessary parts to correct the deficiencies. Spec4 Joe Gordon and two of his best mechanics had everything installed, tested, and certified by 1900.

Blubaugh had mentioned the RedEye vehicle dilemma to Joe Wilson in a TWX sent acknowledging the Phase One start date of *Sparrow Hawk*, and parts had suddenly become available.

We were ordered to map coordinates Alpha Charlie 504.964 and Bravo Echo 920.679, which directed us 8 kilometers east of the town of Bad Orb. The trip only took 45 minutes. We turned off Route 40 onto an old tree-lined firebreak. I pulled far enough into the forest so that we could not be seen from the highway.

I got out and walked back to the last jeep to make sure we were far enough into the forest. A detail from Bravo Company was scheduled to rendezvous with us within a few minutes.

"Jack, keep an eye out for the Bravo guys. They're due here by 1000." The same guys who had helped out at *OP Alpha* the month before had volunteered to the man to help out again. Word had spread through Bravo Company about the detail to RedEye, and 1st Sergeant Jake Carstairs had to turn away twice the number needed. So much for the unwritten rule that says never volunteer.

"Roger that," said Jack Swanson. "Are we going to be here a while or are we going somewhere else?"

"Don't have a clue," I said, "That mile marker we turned on was all that was referenced besides the map coordinates identified by the project document."

We heard the engines first and turned to look into the wooded area to our left. A tracked vehicle with missiles mounted on top emerged out of the forest. I recognized it immediately from the training center at White Sands in New Mexico.

Figure 30
Chaparral

Chaparral[194], the newly developed, self-propelled, surface-to-air missile system was designed for a much longer-range use than RedEye. The XMIM-72A missiles were poised on top of a M48 platform based on a M113 Armored Personnel Carrier.

Traveling directly behind Chaparral was the M163 Vulcan[195] mechanized fire-system. Specializing in short-range, short-time engagements, Vulcan would help keep the MIM-72A and each of the 80 thousand dollar missiles and the 1.5

Figure 31 - Vulcan

million dollar M48 fire podium safe from enemy aircraft that may have breached the outer limits. The Vulcan priced out at only pennies a day. RedEye would be utilized to keep both the Chaparral and the Vulcan safer.

The *Sparrow Hawk* fallback strategy had been recalculated. Three Squadrons of Chaparral /Vulcan were being integrated into Part B of MC 14/3[196].

Today would be a courtesy introduction of these new technologies to both our Battalion RedEye fire teams and our combat guardian angels from Bravo Company.

Coming down the road from the direction we were facing was an unusual

Figure 32 - Gama Goat

---

194 The Chaparral designated XMIM-72A/M48, was the U.S. Army's newest, mobile, ground-to-air missile arrangement. Based on the AIM-9 Sidewinder, the XMIM-72A missiles were transported on the M48 vehicle. This was developed by the Ford Motor Company and was based on one of the many versions of the widely used M113 APC.

195 Vulcan was a Gatling gun. Each of the cannon's six barrels fires once, in turn, during each revolution. The multiple barrels provide a rate of fire of 100+ rounds per second—which contributes to a longer life cycle by minimizing both barrel heat and wear-and-tear on any one of the barrels. The mean time between jams is in excess of 10,000 firings, making it an exceptionally dependable weapon.

196 MC 14/3, Plan B, was titled Strategic Concept for the Defense of the North Atlantic Area. This document was written to establish the required procedures for an in-progress invasion.

looking vehicle with a slightly lower profile than a typical Army truck. The M561 Gama Goat[197] was a six-wheel-drive semi-amphibious off-road vehicle originally developed for use in the Vietnam War.

Perfect for the terrain surrounding the Fulda Gap, this *goat* would provide a mobile re-supply solution for all the new players of the *Sparrow Hawk* strategy.

I was shown the operation order several weeks later by our S-3. "What am I looking at Carl?" I had asked.

"You're looking at OP Order 69-0712-15321."

"So, this is important to me, how?"

"These orders have the letters "DP"[198] printed in the upper left hand corner of the directive, directly above the DOI[199]."

"OK. So what?" I queried, holding up my hands with my palms up.

"DP means 'by the direction of the President' dummy. That's a big deal," Carl chastised.

"Oh, but if you remember, my orders had the letters DDCI on them."

"Your point being...?"

"My orders had more letters is all I can say."

Chaparral and Vulcan would be supported by a one-to-one ratio with the Gama Goat. Resupply on the fly was the order of the day. Each Squadron would be supported by eight Gama Goat vehicles. A ninth Goat would provide the eyes for Chaparral and Vulcan with an AN/MPQ-49 Forward Area Alerting Radar (FAAR).

Small, target-acquisition area radar, such as the FAAR[200], was

---

[197] Gama Goat was the military designation for the M561. The truck was a six by six tactical 1-1/4-ton truck with a pronounced two-attached body style. This allowed travel over exceptionally rough, often muddy terrain. It was equipped with a unique four-wheel steering arrangement with the front and rear wheels capable of turning in opposite directions.

[198] "DP" means by the direction of the president. Based on the CIA recommendation, one Battalion consisting of three Squadrons equipped with 33 vehicles of the categories stated above was created; and it was designated Sparrow/HAWK.

[199] Date of Issue

[200] The AN/MPQ-49 Forward Area Alerting Radar (FAAR) was developed in 1966 to support the Chaparral/Vulcan. The radar had a range of about 20

designed to provide aiming solutions for incoming targets long before a visual sighting was possible. This was made possible by a newly developed Bell Labs technology called *Data Link*[201].

"We just got a whole new set of teeth," I said to Larry as I walked up to RE-2. These would be the guys who would cover our retreat all the way back to the Rhine.

"Funny looking truck," said Larry as the driver of the approaching M561 Gama Goat pulled alongside RE-2 and stopped.

SPARROW HAWK
FARGO4 NATO HAWK 2 CR SQUADRON 3
1150 HOURS WEDNESDAY 5 NOVEMBER 1969

The project package I'd opened earlier that day had contained a sealed envelope. Printed across the front was "SOP: *Operation Sparrow Hawk*. Do Not Open Until Directed".

Bill Douglas, alias Major Carlstrum, had been riding shotgun in the Gama Goat that had pulled up to where we were parked. The contingent from Bravo Company had arrived in the same timeframe. They had pulled their seven vehicles parallel to RE-2 and parked nose-to-nose with the Goat.

I leaned in on the driver's side window and said, "Nice ride, Sir." Bill Douglas, in his Major Carlstrum persona, leaned across the driver to shake my hand. "How are you, Rick?"

"I'm fine, Sir. As you can see, the detail from Bravo Company just pulled in, so we are ready to go when you are."

"We're going to convoy to Fargo4," said the Major. "Follow us and stay close."

"Roger that, Sir," I said and turned and made a fist pump motion to all of the drivers to follow me.

It was amazing to see this rather strange looking but flexible

---

kilometers, contained the Mark XII Identification, Friend or Foe (IFF) system, and transmitted digital data to the target alerting data display sets (TADDS) located with each CHAPARRAL/VULCAN battalion. The FAAR section consisted of three men and one vehicle and trailer. A Tactical Data Link (TDL) uses radio waves or cable.

[201] Data Link was a radar interface that controlled the tilt and pan function of the hydraulics for each firing platform.

vehicle make a U-turn in such a small area. We made a left turn into the woods on the same trail that the Chaparral and Vulcan M48s had popped out of just minutes before.

We had followed what must have been an old logging road for several miles when the landscape suddenly dipped down at about a 15-degree angle. We crossed a streambed and started up the other side. At the top of the climb the trail opened into a large

Figure 33 - Fargo 4

clearing measuring at least a kilometer square. The forest surrounded the entire area on all sides.

In the exact center of the clearing, a large rectangular complex named Fargo4 could be seen. There was a five-meter high, double security fence surrounding the entire compound.

Large signs were displayed every 25 meters on the outer fence. Each sign was centered between the guard towers. They screamed in both the English and the German languages a central message. VORSICHT HOCH SPANNUNG/CAUTION HIGH VOLTAGE was printed in large black letters on a bright yellow background.

Three-story tall guard towers were tactically located every 50 meters. Each tower commanded a 360-degree view of the entire clearing. Each tower also had a backward internal view of the Fargo4 compound.

As we drove toward the main gate we could see guards walking with dogs, Belgian Shepherds, in the area between the fences. The guards were all carrying M14 rifles slung over their shoulders, plus each had a holstered 1911 45 ACP sidearm hanging from web gear.

The main entrance had a two-gate system. The gates could not be opened at the same time. It took a little extra time for our little convoy to complete the admission procedure.

There were service roads, both inside and out, that circumnavigated the entire complex. Lighting poles measuring 10 meters in height, with quad lamp fixtures were planted one meter just inside the internal fence line. These circled the entire complex and were pointed strategically outward. They would provide daylight characteristics outward for 150 meters during the hours of darkness.

The center of the compound directly across from the main gate had a horseshoe arrangement of what appeared to be above ground entrances to a series of 18 underground bunkers.

There was a triple helipad in the center of the horseshoe at the far end of the "U." An abundance of vacated concrete parking pads were positioned everywhere. Devoid of the current tenants, the base appeared to be manned only by a skeleton crew.

The Command Quarters was located 70 meters to the left of the main gate. It was a low profile concrete block structure that suggested some of the structure was below ground. This building housed the communications center. The backside of the building flaunted three 30-meter antennas that were spaced evenly, trailing off toward the southwest corner of the compound. The sandbags around the entrances and windows were a nice touch. The seriousness of the operation was becoming very apparent.

Directly across from, and to the right of, the main gate were the living quarters. These billets varied in size and shape. The largest, identified by a signpost, was the Mess Hall. All of the buildings were similarly constructed out of block and brick materials.

We were waved into the site unharmed and were directed to the parking area between the barracks and the Mess Hall. I heard the guard directing us at the gate tell Carlstrum to park by "chow down one".

The Major got out of the Goat and walked back to the RE-1 that I was riding in. The M48s that had been parked along the trail pulled in behind us. Both squadrons, Chaparral and Vulcan, pulled around our vehicles and continued deeper into the compound. I saluted at the Major and asked, "You want us to park here, Sir?"

He returned the salute and said, "That's as good a place as any, Rick. How are you Clark? It's been a while." He shook hands with Ken, who had walked up from RE-2.

"I've been good, Sir. Thanks for asking."

"Ken, go down the line and tell everyone, including Bravo, to stay put while I go with the Major," I said.

"Wait here a sec, Ken," said "Mr. D". "I want to go make my manners to Larry, Jack, and Von.

He walked on down the line of jeeps to where the rest of RedEye had gathered.

"What's that all about?" Ken asked me.

"I'm not sure, but I think Major Carlstrum has decided to let everyone know how important they are to this project. He's asked about all of you several times since he met you at the Battalion promotion ceremony."

Clark and I watched for a good five minutes while Douglas stood in the middle of Larry, Jack and Von -- plus several of the Bravo Company personnel who had walked over -- laughing, listening, and answering questions. When he walked back to where Clark and I were standing he said, "Let's take a walk, Rick."

"Yes, Sir," I said. "Ken, go tell everyone to wait here. I'll be back in a few minutes."

"We were glad to hear you survived your camping trip, Sir," I said as we walked to the side entrance of the larger of the two buildings on this side of the street. There was a sign next to the door labeling it as the Mess Hall.

"That was not for public consumption. Who told you?"

"Captain MacKennia," I replied. "He seemed highly upset when he sought me out. We decided not to tell anyone else."

"Please keep it that way." We walked on in silence for a few more feet. "Are you holding up OK, Rick?" I pulled open the side door that led into a rather large space that contained twenty to twenty-five large rectangular tables with benches that were arranged evenly throughout the room.

"Some days are better than others, but I'm managing. Thanks for asking, Sir."

There was a large serving line directly across from us constructed of stainless steel, and equipped for large quantities of steam trays. A great deal of activity was taking place directly behind a half height wall partition that separated the kitchen from the serving counter.

We walked to the far end of the hall through double glass doors into a private dining area. The tables in this room were round and had tablecloths and place settings for six to eight people. A table on the left was occupied by two officers and two senior NCOs.

Carlstrum walked over and said, "Gentleman, this is Sergeant Fontain. He is RedEye/*Sparrow6*. Rick, this is Major Gustafson, Captain Sager, CSM Houseman, and SFC Stebbins. They are the advance team for 3rd Squadron 2nd Armored Cavalry Regiment." I nodded my head but didn't say anything.

"The sergeant has hands-on experience with the terrain

between here and *Alpha*," said Carlstrum. He's also been briefed on the latest INTEL on the border situation."

"I'm glad to meet you," I said to the group. I saw Chaparral demonstrated at Bliss. It's a welcome addition to this operation."

"The projected invasion EVAC[202] routes through Fulda's blocking nodes, Chicago and Denver, are the key sockets being evaluated this coming week," said Carlstrum. "Sergeant Fontain and his team have a working knowledge of the types of aircraft that will be used by the aggressor force. This weekend's operation will..." was as far Carlstrum got before the sudden outburst.

"Operation?" interrupted a stunned Captain Sager. "You mean *exercise*, don't you, Sir?"

"Captain, the term *exercise* denotes that we are only going through the motions of playing a game. Games are played by children. *Operation Sparrow Hawk* has been sanctioned by our President. And believe me; we are not playing any games here."

"Yes, Sir. I meant no disrespect," replied Captain Sager.

"None taken, Sager; is this your first assignment in Europe?"

"Yes, Sir, it is."

"Most first timers are under the impression that all we do here is play war games. That could not be further from the truth. Isn't that so, Sergeant Fontain?"

"Yes, Sir. I've had two near-death experiences in just the last week," I answered with my most solemn look. The NCOs at the table started to laugh but stopped short. The officers seemed to be undecided as to the legitimacy of the comment.

Carlstrum ignored my remark and continued, "From this moment forward, you and your people will consider this operation TOP SECRET/*Sparrow Hawk*. Your CO, Lieutenant Colonel Kingston, has been delayed in transit and asked me to address your officers and NCO team leaders."

"Yes, Sir. He sent word this afternoon," replied CSM Houseman. "His ETA is Saturday, 1400 hours."

"I think the best way for me to address both your officers and NCOs is for me to talk to everyone in a group setting. Do you agree?" asked Carlstrum, looking directly at Major Houseman. Everyone, including Gustafson, replied with a nod of the head or a crisp "Yes, Sir."

---

[202] Evacuation

"Tonight, get all of your people settled in. From what I've been told, the facilities here are top drawer."

"Yes, Sir. That's been my observation also," said the CSM.

"Our NATO support is being provided by an HHC left here by the former residents. They will provide our security, mess[203], and S-4[204] services. From what I've seen, they also appear to be first rate."

"Yes, they've been both gracious and competent so far," said Major Gustafson.

"Let's do the briefing after chow in the morning. If you need me tonight I'll be in the CQ -- or they can tell you where you can find me. Do you have any questions before we break?" There were no questions.

I walked out into the larger dining room with "Mr. D."

"Rick, walk over to the CQ building and find a Staff Sergeant named Hoffenburger. Tell him I sent you and to set you up with accommodations. Once you get settled, bring everybody back here for chow."

"Roger that, Sir," I replied. "You're not going to the CQ?"

"No, Pezlola and Lawson are due in any moment by chopper. I'll meet you back here later."

"Yes, Sir," I said and walked out of the building and back to the parking lot.

TRANSLATING RIN TIN TIN
FARGO4 NATO HAWK 2 CR SQUADRON 3
1315 HOURS WEDNESDAY 5 NOVEMBER 1969

I walked to where Ken was standing next to RE-4. Jack Swanson was in the driver's seat, Larry and Von were standing around on the passenger side and the newest member of RedEye, PFC Fred Simpson, was in the passenger seat.

Fred was 21 years old and a native of Dayton, Ohio. He had arrived the previous week fresh from the RedEye course at Bliss. He was seated next to Jack because there wasn't time to procure the coveted Army driver's license for him before our latest excursion.

Barry Flax had called Bill Douglas to espouse Fred's exceptional

---

[203] Food Preparation

[204] Services and Equipment Supply

electronics aptitude. PFC Simpson would be able to handle any guidance and tracker upgrades in the field. "Sold" was the word Bill Douglas had used, and made arrangements for Fred to be sent to us.

All heads turned toward me as I walked up. "Larry you're with me. The rest of you wait here."

"Roger that," said Stockert.

"Everybody, if you haven't already, check your vehicle, weapons and gear. We're going to the CQ[205]. Ken, go up to the Mess Hall and ask when we should come for dinner."

"Specialist-4 Towson, better known as Glen the camera guy, was just up here asking for some direction," said Jack.

"The Bravo guys are huddled up in the second APC," added Von.

"Thanks, I'll stick my head in on my way by."

We walked through the main entrance of the CQ building. The interior was surprisingly well illuminated and all of the work areas were neat and clean and nicely furnished. The open office area had 12 desks, eight of which were occupied. There were private offices along the right and back walls. A counter, positioned ten feet inside the main entrance, was manned by a Staff Sergeant. "Good evening, Sergeant. We were told to see a Sergeant Hoffenburger," I announced.

"That's me. You must be the famous Sergeant Fontain," said Staff Sergeant Wally Hoffenburger.

"Guilty," I replied.

"Corporal Jenson," Hoffenburger called across the room to a soldier seated at a desk in the corner. "Take my jeep and show Sergeant Fontain how to get to the transient NCO barracks. Make sure the lights and water are turned on."

"Yes, Sergeant."

"You come right back here after that."

"Thanks for the help and the hospitality," I said to Hoffenburger.

"Anytime you need the S-4 clerk, dial 178. He can get you set up with any housekeeping supply issues you find lacking. Call me on extension 125 if you have any problems."

Larry got in the back and I sat up front on the short trip back to where we parked. Everyone was still gathered around RE-4. "Saddle up and follow us. Glen, go tell your guys to drop in behind Von and stay close."

---

[205] Command Quarters

I stayed in the jeep with our guide. We took the same service road that the Goats and M48s had disappeared on earlier. The road passed very close to the border fence on the north side before we turned left and headed back toward the center of the compound.

We had traveled for less than 100 yards when we came upon what appeared to be a large fenced kennel area configured in a mini compound. The single story concrete block building had 10 to 12 outside dog runs on each side of the building. Only about half of them seemed to be occupied.

There was a high fenced-in area off the backside of the kennel. A lean-to structure was situated in the center with a single dog chained to the main pillar holding up the highest part of the overhang.

A dozen feeding pans glittered around the animal in the sunlight. The metal pans were scattered about like so much wrapping paper on Christmas morning. The Shepherd lay despondent, with his head on the ground tucked between his paws. Even from where I sat I could see that his eyes were wide open. They say patience is a virtue and all good things come to those who wait.

"What's this place?" I asked.

"It's where the guard dogs are kept," said Corporal Jenson.

"And the big guy, the one in the back with the 200?"

"He attacked his handler. He's awaiting execution."

"Pull over a minute," I ordered. The entire convoy came to a stop.

Just as we stopped, one of the shelter staff emerged from the side door of the kennel building and proceeded to walk toward the condemned prisoner. He was carrying the same type of metal container that was on display in numerous quantities in front of the dog. The dog remained motionless.

"Why haven't the feed containers been removed after the dog eats? They must have an enormous supply of feed tubs."

"You're in for a real treat, Sergeant. Watch what happens after the dog finishes his meal," said the corporal as the food container was placed about five feet from where the dog was lying. The food deliverer backed away after putting the food down, and didn't turn his back on the dog until he'd reached the gate. He then left the stockade. The dog rose to his feet and stretched the chain to the limit in order to eat from the container. All of the food was gobbled in less than 45 seconds.

What happened next was truly amazing. After finishing the last bite, the dog picked the tin up by its edge and moved it back to a position in the center of all of the other empty containers.

Next, the crafty pooch walked back past the pillar where the chain was fastened. Once he had measured off five feet of chain the animal turned and trotted back to the same location he had occupied prior to dining. Everything was as it had been before, except there was now an additional feed pan in his growing inventory.

"I'll be damned. That is one clever, calculating K-9," I whispered.

"You got that right, Sergeant. The Lieutenant hopes the order to put the dog down arrives before they run out of feed pans" added the Corporal.

"Drive on, Corporal," I said and indicated that the other vehicles should follow.

Our new residence was located almost directly behind the huge horseshoe of bunkers we had seen on the way in. Hoffenburger had told me that the entire living quarters was ours for the duration.

The single story building was constructed out of the same materials as most others on campus. There was ample parking at the front, rear and on the right side of the main entrance. Lighting poles were helpfully located around the outskirts of the parking areas.

We followed Corporal Jenson into the building. There was a desk pushed up against a manager's counter in the lobby. The keys to the rooms were hanging on a wall rack that was mounted behind the desk. A floor plan was posted just below the keys. All of the rooms were situated around the outside walls. A large lounge area was located in the center.

Furnished with several sofas and chairs, the lounge could be accessed from the lobby. At the extreme rear there was a kitchen area with a laundry facility located in a utility room directly behind the pantry.

The hallway on the left side of the lobby had accommodations for twelve. These individual rooms were grouped in pairs with a shared toilet and shower between each two. The remaining six rooms were located to the right side of the lounge area. A common latrine was located to the right of the kitchen.

I sent the RedEye team down the hallway to the left and the Bravo men to the larger rooms on the right. Sergeant Hoffenburger's S-4 clerk arrived unsolicited to check the bedding and linen situation. We brought the last of our gear in and stacked the RedEye containers neatly in the center of the lounge area. *"So far, so good,"* I thought.

"What did the Mess Sergeant say about dinner?" I asked Ken, who was close by.

"The dinner meal is served from 1130 to 1400 and the supper meal from 1600 to 2000," replied Clark. "They rotate the menu every six hours but they pretty much stay open 24/7. The guard tours all overlap and demand constant service. Coffee and snacks are always available."

"I'm getting hungry. Pass the word that in ten minutes we'll drive up for dinner. One of us and two of the Bravo men need to stay here to watch over our weapons and equipment. Ask the others to flip a coin for the first watch. And find Glen and ask him to come see me."

"I'll take first watch," said Clark. "I'll go find Glen for you."

"Thanks, Ken."

I could hear the sound of an incoming helicopter off in the distance. There was a knock at my door. I had just finished making up my bunk and was putting my 1911 45 ACP in the small of my back as I turned to face the door and said, "Come."

"You wanted to see me Sergeant?" asked SPC4 Glen Towson.

"Hi, Glen. I haven't had much of a chance to greet your team. You guys find everything OK?"

"We did, and I must say these are exceptionally nice digs."

"I want you to assign two of your men to join Ken Clark from my team to watch our equipment and weapons while we go to dinner. As soon as your group finishes eating, send two men back to relieve them."

"Will do, but didn't First Sergeant Carstairs inform you that he assigned two E-5's[206] to this detail?"

"No, he didn't. How many Spec4s are with you?"

"There are four, counting myself."

"Ask the Sergeants to come see me. Tell them I wasn't aware that the First Sergeant had assigned them. There are six spare rooms over on this side for you and the other Spec4s if you want them. I'll tell the Sergeants when I see them".

"I'll tell the other 4s[207], but I'm fine where I'm bunked," replied

---

[206] E-5 denotes a Sergeant with three stripes

[207] Spec4s

Towson.

"Tell whoever you assign for the first shift to see Clark. Thanks, Glen," I said as he left the room.

MESS HALL
FARGO4 NATO HAWK 2 CR SQUADRON 3
1330 WEDNESDAY 5 NOVEMBER 1969

The chow was excellent. It was hot and the servings were generous. I was sitting with the two NCOs from Bravo Company. First Sergeant Jake Carstairs, Bravo Company, had assigned these NCOs to supervise the ten original volunteers previously assigned to RedEye during *Operation Synchronized Sparrow*. I looked up to see Jim Pezlola walking from the doorway of the rear dining room toward our table.

"Good evening, Sir. Sir, these are Sergeants Dan Elven and Stan Johnston. This is Lieutenant Pezlola."

"Glad to meet you. Thanks for supporting us this week," said the Lieutenant to Elven and Johnston.

"Sir," replied both E-5s.

"Rick, when you're done here we need you in the back."

"Yes, Sir. I'll be right there," I replied to Jim. He turned and went back into the rear dining room.

I turned back to Sergeants Elven and Johnston. "Hoffenburger told me that there's a makeshift club set up downstairs on the backside of this building. I don't see any reason why we can't take advantage of the facilities while we're here. But please impress on everyone to remain stoic and alert at all times. No one is to discuss anything about whom we are or why we are here. Order everyone to move around in groups of two or more. No one is to go off on his own. Understood?"

"Understood," said Johnston, who was the senior of the two.

"The first one won't be a problem," replied Elven. "We have no idea why we're here."

"Funny. And keep your 45s concealed. There's no point in getting the locals upset."

"Of course we will, but I wasn't being funny, and you being

evasive confirm my suspicions."

"Make sure the fire watch schedule is set up. We need eyes on the weapons full time. Get with Clark when you go back and set up a schedule that includes my guys. Do you have any problem with that?"

"No problem, I'll set it up when I finish here," said Johnston.

"Thanks. I'll catch up with you later tonight."

"This is beginning to feel like a script from a spy novel" commented Elven.

"You have no idea, Sergeant," I said as I got up and walked to the rear dining room.

Six of the tables were occupied with various members of the NATO support cadre and the recently arrived Hawk squadron leaders. Six more M48 crews had just rolled in from Bremerhaven[208]. Gary Lawson, who supervised the COMM[209] Center in the Bischofsgrun CIA listening post, saw me come in and motioned me over by raising his hand. He was seated at the largest table, located at the rear of the room. In attendance were the usual suspects I had met earlier, plus one new face -- a 1st Lieutenant. He was wearing the same shoulder patch as Staff Sergeant Hoffenburger.

"This is Sergeant Fontain," said Major Carlstrum. "Rick, this is Lieutenant Justin Gambeson."

"How do you do, Sir? I'm RedEye call sign *Sparrow6*."

"Rick, LT Gambeson's Headquarters Company will be providing compound security and a safe place to lay our heads at night."

"Yes, Sir. Thank you, Sir," I replied.

"Do you have any special requirements while you're here?" Gambeson asked.

"I've moved my weapons and handheld trackers indoors. Should we take any special precautions regarding where our vehicles are parked?"

"I've already posted two sentries around the front and rear parking pads of your building, plus there are roving patrols after dark, so that should be sufficient," said Gambeson.

"Yes, Sir. That will satisfy our requirements. I should let you

---

208 Bremerhaven is a city at the seaport of the Free Hanseatic City of Bremen, a state of the Federal Republic of Germany

209 Communications

know that all of my people are armed. Please instruct your people to announce themselves if they find it necessary to come inside our quarters at night."

"Armed? Our internal policies restrict the carrying of firearms to cadre only."

"Sergeant Fontain and his crew are authorized to use lethal force to protect themselves and certain material in their possession," said Douglas cum Carlstrum. "Am I making myself clear, Lieutenant?"

"Yes, Sir," Gambeson replied. All the eyes at the table were looking at me in a whole different light.

"So much for remaining inconspicuous," I thought.

The night before we had left Gelnhausen, CSM Bost and LT Key had summoned me to the Battalion S-3 office. A TWX had been received directing ten RedEye missiles to be transported and deployed in *Operation Sparrow Hawk*.

I excused myself for a minute and went back into the larger dining room. I looked around and spied Clark who had just arrived. He was sitting with Glen. "Hey, I'm going to be awhile," I said to them, "so leave one of the jeeps and catch a ride back with one of the others. Thanks for taking the first watch."

Pezlola met me halfway on my journey back to the table. "You need to read this," he said as he handed me a piece of yellow TWX paper. "And this." He handed me a folder.

"Congratulations! Good job, Rick," said Pezlola. The TWX was from Bost to Carlstrum. It directed the Major to give RedEye a heads-up as soon as possible.

Pezlola said, "Bost also indicated that he would make every effort to get back here to help wet your team down."

I had to open the folder to understand what Pezlola was talking about. I read the first page. It was a copy of a promotion order effective 1 November 1969. The first page listed my original RedEye team. Jack, Von, Larry, and Clark were being promoted to Sergeant E-5.

"This is good news, but Bost's idea of 'wetting down' is going to kill somebody."

"I think you'll also be interested in page two," said a smiling Jim Pezlola. "It seems your genius has been recognized yet again," he declared in a proud, father-like tone. My name was listed at the top of page two, and I was to be promoted to Staff Sergeant, pay grade E-6.

MESS HALL DAY TWO
FULDA COLD STRATEGY
FARGO4 NATO 2 CR SQUADRON 3
0515 HOURS THURSDAY 6 NOVEMBER 1969

We parked RE-1 in the same spot as we had the day before. We could see the bunkers across the way. Most all of them had their large concrete blast doors standing wide open.

The W52[210] was a thermonuclear warhead developed for the MGM-29 Sergeant short-range ballistic missile used by the United States Army from 1962 to 1977. The bunkers of Fargo4 now lay empty.

"Good morning, Sir," I said as I walked up to LT Pezlola. You're up early."

"Good morning, Rick, and I told you to knock off that "Sir" crap when we're out-of-pocket."

"Yes, Sir. Is we out-of-pocket, or just out of our minds, Sir?"

He laughed. "That depends on who you ask. Did you give the good news to your new sergeants last night?"

"No, I didn't. They were all asleep when I got back. I'm going to surprise them after the meeting this morning. Bost may not be back this way until tonight and, if we're lucky, we won't be graced with his presence until we are back in Gelnhausen and have better medical facilities."

"Medical facilities?" asked Pezlola.

"Drinking 16 ounces of Jim Beam in fifteen seconds is a problem for most new sergeants," I replied.

Lieutenant "P" laughed and continued to set up for the presentation that would occur after chow that morning. There was a small raised platform in the right rear corner of the dining area that was put there for just such occasions. He was in the process of running the microphone cable to the lectern at the center of the little stage.

"How do you feel about giving the *newbies* an overview of the

---

210 The W52 was 25 inches in diameter and 57 inches long, and weighed 950 pounds. It had a yield of 200 kilotons. A total of 300 W52 warheads were produced. A total of 103 warheads were redeployed from Fargo-4 to the newly positioned Enfield.

territory between here and *OP Alpha?*" Pezlola asked me.

"You mean brief these people on the terrain conditions?"

"That and what you found to be the most expeditious travel routes back through here from Chicago and Denver."

"OK," I said, "but why me? There must be a dozen guys at Division that study this shit full time."

"True, but those guys have probably never been outside of Frankfurt. You, on the other hand, have been running around up here in the woods for the past two months. Besides this new plan calls for a fading withdraw tactic that hasn't been tested since Korea. Every second saved on the march westward will save lives."

"No problem. Actually, we've found that the old logging roads provide good cover from the air. We should be able to maintain a constant flow of egress traffic from Denver. The more we can stay out of the open areas of the Gap the better protection from air attack. Is that the kind of info you want disseminated?"

"Affirmative, Rick. That is exactly what is needed," said the LT.

"Have you eaten yet?" My stomach informed my question.

"No. Let me get this set up and then we can go see if they'll feed us."

"I'll go get Clark. He's out by the jeep. You want to eat out here or in the back?" I asked as I pointed to my left.

"Right over there is fine with me," he said, pointing at a table right beside the podium.

MEETING—MESS HALL
SQUADRON 3 CRITIQUE FARGO4
0935 HOURS THURSDAY 6 NOVEMBER 1969

The projector held a map showing the node alignments of Fargo 2, 3 and 4. The presenter was Major Gustafson, the Commander of the newly arrived Hawk Squadron. He had just finished explaining how Fargo was positioned in the overall scheme of things. This unit was new to Germany but had trained together at White Sands for the previous five months. All of their equipment was practically brand-new and had been off-loaded recently at the nearby northern port of Bremerhaven. Squadrons One and Two were installed in Fargo 2 and 3 respectively. "We will be testing the Coms and the data link between these locations later today," said Gustafson.

"In closing, I want to direct all section leaders to get their screens calibrated and all hydraulics tested and working 100 percent. I want a net check with Hawk-ONE and Hawk-TWO by 1400. Our NET ID for this operation is *Hawk*. For example, my call sign will be Hawk43-6. The four being your node path, and the three identifying the squadron designation. We're fortunate to be co-located with the 1st/48th RedEye team, call sign *Sparrow*. Pay close attention to any traffic directed your way by them. They have been here living the situation for the last several months. They will be our eyes and ears during this operation. I have been promised by Sergeant Fontain that he will show us all of his favorite parking spots. Overwatch[211], gentlemen. That is our mission.

"Our main responsibility, our *only* responsibility, is to protect the traffic being funneled through Chicago and Denver as they fall back and leapfrog all the way back through here. Your training has prepared you very well for this exercise. Excuse me, I meant to say operation. It was recently pointed out to me that an exercise is for practice while an operation is run in real time. We will run this operation as if our lives depend on doing a good job. Colonel Kingston will be here Saturday. I expect everyone to be 100 percent by then," Gustafson concluded.

"Lt. Pezlola, do you have anything to add?"

"Yes, Sir. Thank you, Sir. Don Coover, Bell Laboratories, and Kelly Johnston of Lockheed, actually of the Lockheed Skunk Works, are flying in with your Battalion CO on Saturday morning. The key to our success in this operation is being able to quickly assimilate the newly developed interface to your weapons systems.

Pezlola continued, "Some of you trained on DATALINK at White Sands. Mr. Coover and Mr. Johnston are the ones who designed this technology. If anyone can fine-tune it for us, it's them. They've been here before and have been extremely helpful. This know-how was originally intended solely for line-of-sight communication between the radar interface and the hydraulics of the shooter. A daisy chain communications link will allow a unique target ID to be passed into the entire network -- allowing all of the *AN/MPQ-49 Forward Area Alerting Radar (FAAR)* [212] to coordinate their shots."

---

[211]   Overwatch: name of the Hawk ground-to-air defense

[212]   A FAAR was mounted on a boom that extended upward from the rear of the Gama Goat's trailer. It was a pulse Doppler radar that operated in the D band and had a range of about 20 kilometers. Data from the radar was generally not

"The textbook says this will provide Chaparral/Vulcan a sizable increase in effectiveness. We shall see how the proposed combat simulations affect this new type of communication."

"This new technology will not be an easy integration," Pezlola stated. "It would be difficult in a stationary combat position. What we've been charged with this coming week will be a shoot and move maneuver utilizing a bounding overwatch[213] procedure. The question before us: will DATALINK work in a highly energized and mobile environment?

"For the last two weeks we've been running a simulation gauntlet utilizing twenty-six F-4 Fighter aircraft out of Mildenhal as enemy aggressors. Your job, gentlemen, will be to bring their short term successes to a screeching halt."

Figure 34 - 104 Starfighter

Pezlola went on. "Eighteen German F104G Starfighters from JBJ 36 in Rheine-Hopsten[214], plus twelve UH1H Huey Gunships out of Hanau have provided the friendly umbrella thus far. JBJ 36 lost one of their Starfighters last week over Chicago. The pilot got out, but I mention this to point out that what we do is dangerous, and is not -- I repeat -- is not a game. We are attempting to make this as real as possible. We've been using the 1st/33rd and the 1st/48th to simulate the Russian fast attack force. The 2nd/48th and 14th CAV are our front line defense force."

"We've been simulating hit and run evasion and evacuation scenarios through Chicago and Denver for the last several weeks. This weekend we will add your lifeguard capability to the equation. There will be five Redeye fire teams embedded with you. Their responsibility will be to watch your backs while you provide convoy overwatch. They are very good at what they do. Their COMMs are also tied into DATALINK and will be an additional set of eyes on

---

used at the radar site itself, but broadcast over FM radio to the "Target Alerting Data Display Set" (TADDS), a small, battery-powered receiver and display unit. Field units, including the Chaparral, Vulcan and FIM-43 RedEye units, used the TADDS as an early-warning display, aiming their optically guided weapons in the general direction it provided.

[213] Bounding overwatch group of military vehicles performing movement tactics.

[214] Rheine-Hopsten Air Base is a closed German Air Force military air base located 9.3 kilometers northeast of Rheine in Westphalia, Germany.

your outer limits. If they speak to you, you should listen with great interest. Questions, Comments?"

Hands went up all around the room. Jim pointed at a Spec4 seated at a table in the center of the hall.

"Sir, it sounds like we're practicing to retreat."

"General Oliver Smith[215] once said, "We're not retreating; we're just advancing in a different direction." There were chuckles heard throughout the hall. "This is not a practiced retreat. We are perfecting an organized withdraw to the Rhein River. Your job is to kill any enemy aircraft that threatens our journey west."

"We will have four RedEye units embedded in HAWK3. One RedEye fire team will be assigned to cover the rear of the convoy: code name *rocking chair*. The egress will progress from Chicago to Denver and finally pass through here at Fargo. Before adding your Squadron to the equation, 60 percent of the attacking aircraft have gotten through." Jim let that sink in, then added, "We expect this will be greatly improve now that you are here. Next question."

More hands went up. "Yes, Sergeant?" Jim pointed to a table right in front of the podium.

"Sir, what happens to us when the last of our guys pass through here?"

"Good question. Did everyone hear the question?" Jim repeated it. "You won't be here when that happens. The plan calls for your deployment to a half a click from the rear of Chicago4. You will then fade behind the 11 CAV to a half a click behind Denver4 and so forth and so on. These are all good questions, but they will all be addressed in detail at tomorrow's briefing. Right now I want to introduce Sergeant Fontain. He is *Sparrow6*, the RedEye team leader."

"Good morning," I said. The response was a deafening silence. "Good morning!" I said again, with much more force. This time there was a loud response from everyone. With no real experience in speaking in front of a group, I continued.

---

215   Oliver Prince Smith (October 26, 1893-December 25, 1977) was a General in the United States Marine Corps and a highly decorated combat veteran of World War II and the Korean War. He is most noted for commanding the 1st Marine Division during the Battle of Chosin Reservoir. He retired at the rank of four-star general, being advanced in rank for having been specially commended for heroism in combat.

"I have the responsibility for RedEye in the 1st /48th. For the last two months we have run various configurations of ground-to-air combat operations in both the Chicago and Denver neighborhoods. I understand that most, if not all of you, have trained at Bliss. All of my shooters have had that experience as well.

"You may have noticed that the terrain here is slightly different." Muffled laughter could be detected throughout the room: White Sands was a desert and this part of Germany was forest and hills. "IR trackers and radar guidance systems use two different approaches in acquiring a target. Your systems will perform differently here than they did in the desert. Not poorly, but differently.

"The two scientists named by Lieutenant Pezlola are arriving this weekend. They are here specifically to help us marry two detection technologies with the sole objective to enhance our target acquisition and kill ratios. If you are approached by these individuals, answer their questions as best you can. Act as if your life depends on your cooperation, as indeed it will." Stillness settled over the room as I continued.

"The tracking radar and your mechanical targeting systems will utilize a new DATALINK technology developed by Lockheed. This is critical to the success of our mission and essential to our ability to perfect our fast train formation towards the Rhine. Finding out if this technology will function in this circumstance will be our first priority.

"I think I'm getting into information better left to tomorrow's briefing, so maybe I can answer some of your questions."

"Whoa...that was not smart, Rick." Just about every hand in the place went up at the same time.

I pointed at a Sergeant E-7 sitting right in front of me.

"The units we are supporting -- how are they equipped?"

"Good question. Let me repeat it for those in the back of the room. This forward-thinking sergeant has just asked how the units we'll be supporting are equipped.

"There are four combat components to *Operation Sparrow Hawk.* First, there are several different flavors of the newly developed anti-tank TOW, both land- and air-based platforms. Over 400 types of track vehicles will include tanks, APCs and self-propelled artillery.

"Second, there will be 175 traditional crew-served heavy weapons, such as Mortars and 50 CAL, utilizing a wide variety of jeeps and other types of utility vehicles for transport. There is also an engineering team laying smart-mine weapons on the tail end of the egress.

"Third, in RedEye, we have four Sections of us with five teams each and, now that you have arrived, three squadrons of Chaparral and Vulcan as well. The detail and logistics will be expanded upon in tomorrow's briefing. I'll take another question."

I called out to recognize a Spec4 in the rear of the hall.

"Will we have air support working with us? I mean that could cause some confusion working that close together, right?"

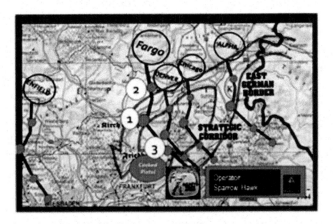

Figure 35 - Operation Sparrow Hawk

"Excellent point. I had the same concern when we were first briefed on the project parameters. Lieutenant, will you put up the first overhead image again, showing the position map?" I waited until the overhead went back up before continuing.

"Our air support has a restricted flight path that is fairly narrow. If the friendlies come down on the deck while mixing it up with the bad guys, let them have at it. In other words, hold your fire. One of the main purposes of this operation is being able to conduct our business with the entire support group.

"Enemy targets of opportunity will be here, initially." I pointed to a position on the overhead. "Any attack will come with little, if any, warning. RedEye embedded with the 14th ACR will take the initial hit. As soon as our friendlies respond, the immediate fallback through Chicago will start to take place. HAWK, that's you, will move to this area here." I indicated the area behind Chicago. "If we get lucky, only 60 percent of the enemy aircraft by this time will be coming down the Gap.

"If our guys stick to the plan, keeping to fire breaks and logging roads here, here, and here, our people will present a much smaller target. It is hoped that the enemy will expect us to use the main pathways out of Fulda.

"Sorry for the long, roundabout explanation, but we, you and me, will have a small, greatly focused, responsibility of keeping the bad guys off of people passing through the LODs[216] of Chicago and Denver."

I took several more questions, plus there were several positive comments made about how the dissemination of information was being handled. In closing, I promised to make myself available and to keep the facts flowing with the best information available.

"Major, would you like to close the meeting?" I had stepped off the stage and noticed that Bill Douglas had come in and sat down next to Jim Pezlola and Gary Lawson.

"Sergeant, you never cease to amaze," smiled Bill Douglas who, in this environment, would be known only as Major Carlstrum.

"It's a known fact that NCOs are much more conversant when addressing their parishioners -- much more so than their officer counterparts," contributed Gary.

Dr. Lattermire, Commanding Officer, Nuremberg Hospital Center, had walked up behind me. "Staff Sergeant in the pay grade of E-6 is not too shabby for a draftee."

"Sir, I'm glad to see you," I said, as my offered handshake turned into a somewhat emotional hug.

"You're a hard man to keep up with Fontain. I was in Gelnhausen a couple of weeks ago and I was told you were up in Hanau."

"Yes, Sir. I was invited to an awards ceremony for Gary. It was his third consecutive month without catching the clap."

Everyone laughed, even Carlstrum.

"Yes, Sir, that's correct," said Gary. "Fontain can't seem to get past the second month, so he wasn't eligible."

"Enough, you two," Carlstrum said, still laughing. "Rick, come to the CQ after you catch up here. Bring your weapon and side arm. We're going up to *Alpha*."

"Yes, Sir. How long before we leave, Sir?"

---

[216] Lines of Defense

"About an hour and a half before the chopper gets here. Have you told your guys about you-know-what yet?"

"No, I'll do that before we go," I replied. Carlstrum turned and walked out of the hall.

"How long are you going to be here, Sir?" I asked the doctor.

"I'll be in and out of here through Sunday. Perhaps we can grab some time to catch up tonight or tomorrow."

"I'd like that. Where are you staying?"

"There are apartments on the back side of the infirmary. I'll be there or in the CQ."

"If it's not too late tonight, I'll come find you."

"Good, I'll look for you."

TRANSIENT NCO QUARTERS
OPERATION FULDA COLD
FARGO4
1145 HOURS THURSDAY 6 NOVEMBER 1969

Gary handed me another envelope as I was leaving. "You owe me twelve dollars and fifty cents for the rank insignias. Pezlola gave me a heads-up before we left Nuremberg."

"Thanks, that was really thoughtful. My guys are going to be ecstatic about their rise in the ranks. Keep an eye on them tonight will you? Their Command Sergeant Major's idea of celebrating a promotion can be a little dangerous."

"I will, but I suspect you'll be back. Douglas is going to London tonight."

Clark was waiting by Redeye Jeep One. I got in the passenger seat and we drove all the way to our quarters in silence.

"You OK?" asked Ken. It amazed me how Ken always picked up on the smallest of mood changes.

In a tone that was not at all friendly, I said, "Ken, you go in there and tell Larry, Von and Jack to put on their web gear and fall-in out here in formation. Tell them that the CSM just reamed me a new one and now it's their turn. Go."

Ken was only gone 30 seconds when screen door was thrown open, banging against the siding of the building. As they were pouring out the door they were pulling on their alert gear.

"Fall-in, fall-in right here in front of this damned vehicle," I said in the harshest tone I could muster.

"Stand at attention and stop fidgeting. Sergeant Stockert, you sound winded. Are you not staying in shape on these relaxing outings the Army is providing you? Sergeant Boyd how about you? Are you not able to remain clothed in your alert gear, even though there may be an event needing your immediate attention? And, Sergeant Swanson, if you are not able to make it from the lounge to here without being winded, I suggest you stop smoking."

"Well, you're not going to believe this, but all of your hard work has paid off! Sergeant Clark, take this envelope and give each one of these new NCOs their new, much deserved, rank insignia. And, of course, take one for yourself.

"Now, please take notice that on my collar points are the rank and recognition bestowed to someone for superior leadership skills. We have been recognized by both the Army, and our dearly loved CSM Bost, as a group of exceptionally capable warriors. Congratulations to you all. Your promotions are very much deserved and your hard work and devotion to mission have been exemplary. Fall-out."

"Did you know this was in the works?" asked Von.

"No, but I did mention to the Major after our junket in Grafenwohr that we were all doing team leader level work and should be paid accordingly. So I suspect he made the suggestion to the Colonel."

I went to everyone and shook each man's hand. I cautioned them to be careful if Bost summoned them for a "wetting down". I grabbed my web gear and weapons and had PFC Simpson, without a proper driver's license; drive me over to the CQ.

Bill Douglas was coming out the front as we pulled up. He was wearing a flight jacket and I could see he was packing a 45 in a shoulder holster.

"Our ride is about five minutes out. You give the good news to the team?"

"Yes, Sir. I expect multiple re-enlistment signings by December. As for myself, I decided to attend medical school. I want to be a psychiatrist so I'll be able to better analyze my time here."

"I suspect Doc Lattermire will be able to help you with that," replied Douglas dryly.

The Huey was only on the ground for about 15 seconds. I settled into the center canvas seat and put on a set of cans[217] that were hanging above my head. I could hear Douglas over the intercom giving the coordinates of where he wanted us delivered. When he was satisfied with the direction he sat down next to me.

---

[217] Headphones

XVII

OPERATION SPARROW HAWK

"THE PIED PIPER EFFECT"

HALF A CLICK FROM OP ALPHA
BASE CAMP 1ST/48TH AND 1ST/33RD
1530 HOURS FRIDAY 7 NOVEMBER 1969

I was surprised that the chopper pilot shut down the aircraft. The announcement over the intercom was even more impressive. "We'll be right here, Mr. Douglas, when you're ready to go." We were at the base of the hill about a half a click directly behind the observation tower called *Alpha*. CSM Bost was sitting beside the LZ (Landing Zone), in one of three vehicles there to transport us. Douglas raised his arm to signal we would be over directly.

There was a large amount of vehicle traffic all around us raising a lot of dust. Two full battalions had taken up residence to prosecute *Sparrow Hawk*. We drove southwest to a cluster of command tracks nestled in a grove of very tall trees that completely surrounded the camp. "Mr. D" and I rode in the back of the open jeep with CSM Bost. Bost offered to ride in the back but Douglas told him the rear tires wouldn't support his bulk. Bost laughed and climbed back into the shotgun position.

All of the vehicles displayed at this location had removed their canvas tops, and the windshields were dropped and secured. We were driven to a tractor-trailer type structure. The room that we entered was set up as a conference/map room with a large, narrow, rectangular table in the middle and a dozen chairs surrounding it. There was a screen at the far end and a projector sitting on the table edge closest to the wall. Most of the chairs at this end of the room were empty.

Colonel Brogan, who was sitting across from the commanding officer of the 1st of the 33rd whose name I couldn't think of, had an older gentleman dressed in civilian attire seated next to him. He looked familiar, but I couldn't place where I had seen him before. A full chicken colonel from division was seated next to the civilian. Three 1st lieutenants and two captains were standing in conference at the doorway to the other part of the trailer.

"Uh, oh," I said to myself. The civilian had been at Fort Holabird when I was there for the DATALINK briefing. He had come in that afternoon, sat in the back and left before it was over.

Bill Douglas walked directly over to the other side of the room and said, "Good afternoon, Colonel, General. It's been awhile. It's very good to see you again."

We were introduced around the table. I sat down in a chair nearest the door. Both of the captains and one of the lieutenants also took seats, Two Spec5s entered and started to pass out folders marked *Top Secret: Sparrow Hawk*. The civilian, the one called "General" by Bill Douglas, spoke first.

"Sergeant," he was looking down the table directly at me, "you pressed the people in Holabird pretty hard on being able to tie the DATALINK information into the RedEye fire teams. Why?"

"Oh, shit." I knew there had been a reason Pezlola asked me to attend that briefing, but he had also told me to keep my mouth shut. *"Oh well, here goes nothing...."*

"Sir, RedEye has a distinct advantage if we can set up on a target with as much advance notice as possible. With all of the trees in this type of terrain, just a ten second heads-up would make all the difference in the acquisition and firing sequence. In most cases, because of the speed of the incoming aircraft, there isn't enough time to boot the gyro much less get a good tone lock. I inquired if DATALINK could be linked to our radio COMMS, Sir and..."

"And the briefing officer told you that it didn't make any sense to foul up the NET by disseminating information to a bunch of grunts with a missile launcher resting on their shoulders, running around in the woods looking up at the sky. Is that about what was said?" asked the General.

"Yes, Sir, that's about what was said."

"Except the part about calling the lieutenant a 'mother fucker' and threating to shove a pine tree up his ass."

"Sir, I apologized to the briefing officer. I thought it was a waste of a perfectly good tree." Bill Douglas was staring at me with a look, not of shock, but of resignation. This was obviously the first he was hearing any of this.

"Pezlola was right," the General continued. "He really doesn't like people who don't want to share, especially ones who might get him killed for not doing so. Sergeant, I passed your query to Lockheed and they say that they're already piggybacking the radio traffic between nodes. But no one had thought about how some of the peripheral systems like RedEye could benefit from DATALINK. So thank you for asking the question."

"So does that mean we get to listen in on the DATALINK traffic?" I asked. "Our S-2 has already set us up with ground-to-air COMMS to our friendlies. Perhaps we could provide some confirmation to our HAWK colleagues."

"Hawk and Vulcan are already equipped with the 77s. The DATALINK traffic will include RedEye for this operation."

"Yes, Sir. Thank you, Sir."

"There is a Bell Labs newly developed radar feature called *TRANSPONDER*. This will display the exact flying machine ID for multiple aircraft. We will be testing this feature on screen in real-time," said the Lieutenant who had taken the seat directly across from me.

"I can see where that information can be extremely useful, Sir."

The meeting went on for another hour. When it ended, the General walked around to where Douglas and I were sitting.

"Let's get a coffee somewhere," he said to Douglas.

"Yes, Sir," replied Douglas. "I'll inquire where we might find the Mess."

"I'm Gerald Bushman, by the way," said the CIA DDCI to me. "David James told me to tell you congratulations on your promotion. Let me add mine too. You seem to be everything you were described to be."

"Sir, if I've done anything to embarrass you or Mr. James I certainly apologize."

"Nonsense. You seem perfectly sane to me, despite the report that young lieutenant sent off to Army CID. You haven't said very much, Billy. Are you feeling alright?"

"I'm fine, Sir," replied Douglas. "I'm still pondering the giant pine tree scenario."

1ST/48TH COMMAND TRACK
BASE CAMP 1ST/48TH
1730 HOURS FRIDAY 7 NOVEMBER 1969

I stepped up on the metal cleat and entered the rear of the M1068 SICPS, (Standard Integrated Command Post). "Evening, Sir," I said to LTC Brogan, who was seated at a dropdown desk shelf located next to a bank of PRC 25s. There was a Spec5 I didn't recognize working on posting unit positions on the Plexiglas overlay. Lieutenant Key was at the far end, wearing a headset and talking on the radio.

"Hello, Fontain. Where's the Major? I wanted a word with him before he leaves."

"He went to see General Bushman off. He said he would meet me here, Sir."

"How are things working at Fargo?"

"It's an interesting marriage being arranged. Not sure if RedEye will be effective up here initially, but it should be able to fill in the cracks on the trip back west."

"You don't think RedEye belongs with Chaparral?"

"No, Sir, I didn't mean to suggest that. RedEye will work well in coverage on their peripherals. I was speaking of Vulcan and Chaparral working well together. They appear to be a good fit."

"Good evening, Sir," Douglas/Carlstrum said as he entered the CP. "CSM Bost said you wanted to see me before I take off."

"Yeah, I did. Let's take a walk. Fontain, you wait here. We'll be back in a few minutes," added the LTC.

"Yes, Sir. I'll ask LT Key if I can get word to the14th's ACR RedEye leaders about this weekend's scheduled events."

"Good idea. We'll be back shortly."

LTC BROGAN AND MAJOR CARLSTRUM
1ST/48TH COMMAND TRACK
BASE CAMP 1ST/48TH
1732 HOURS FRIDAY 7 NOVEMBER 1969

Brogan and Carlstrum walked down a footpath leading deeper into the campsite. It was pretty dark already and there wasn't much light coming from the encampment.

"We've had an increase in out-of-town visitors over the last month." It was a statement of fact by the Colonel.

"Yes, Sir, I've seen the reports. LT Pezlola has increased his activities into Czechoslovakia and north into East Germany. There's an increase in radio chatter but not any significant troop movements," added Carlstrum.

"One of the roving patrols between OPs Charlie and Dagwood had one of their people knocked unconscious," said Brogan. "It appears the bad guys did it on their way back out rather than on their way in. There wasn't any indication of how many had crossed over, but a large amount of blood was seen on the razor wire over near their outside fence line. Somebody needed a whole bunch of Band-Aids."

"It's a good bet that they know we abandoned Bradford. They probably have knowledge of Chicago, but not of its content," suggested Douglas.

"The General wants to talk to one of these out-of-towners, which is one of the reasons he came here. If your Lieutenant Pezlola would supply a talker then we could get on with more efficiently discouraging any un-solicited visitors. If you take my meaning?" said the LTC.

"Yes, Sir. I'll see what can be done."

FARGO4 INFIRMERY—BOQ #3
"IT'S A SMALL WORLD"
2245 HOURS FRIDAY 7 NOVEMBER 1969

Bill Douglas and I flew back to Fargo4 in relative silence. Upon landing he ordered the gunship shut down and steered me about thirty feet from the side of the aircraft's open door. "Bushman told me to tell you that you're doing a good job here. He wanted you to know that. I want to add my thanks. Jim Pezlola tells me all the time that I need to provide better feedback. However, we do need to discuss your knowledge of forestry and the way you threaten to harm certain species of trees. But I digress. You're doing a great job. I'll see you in Gelnhausen on Wednesday. Don't forget to go see Doc Lattermire. He's worried about you."

"I'll drop down and see him on the way back to quarters. Anything you need me to do this weekend?"

"Yeah, go talk to Pezlola if you find yourself in disagreement with any of the briefing officers or their subject matter. Let him address any issues you may have." He gave me a big grin, turned and made a winding up signal with his index finger while walking toward the chopper. I stood there until the Huey went light on the skids and disappeared into the night sky.

The infirmary building was a concrete block, single-story structure that was fabricated so that three quarters of its height was below ground level. The roof was constructed out of poured concrete and was at least a foot thick. There were a number of antennas that sprouted through at various positions along the three-foot high wall that outlined the entire roof area. Several empty, sandbagged structures were scattered around the perimeter, probably at one time equipped with all sorts of automatic weapons.

The front room was divided by a long counter in the center. There was only one person on duty when I walked through the main entrance.

"Good evening, can you tell me if Doctor Lattermire is here?"

"And you are?"

"Sergeant Fontain. He asked me to come see him."

"Yes, he expects you. He's in Apartment Three on the backside of this building. You can take the hallway to the end, turn left and exit the building into an enclosed walkway. The apartment numbers are on the doors."

"Thanks."

I found Apartment Three and knocked. I was told almost immediately to enter. The rooms were set up exactly how you would expect. I walked into a sitting area with a small kitchenette on the back wall. There was a breakfast bar in between the two. A hallway undoubtedly led to the bed and bath rooms. A voice called out, "I'm back here, Rick. Grab a beer out of the icebox and come on back."

Doc Lattermire was lying on the bed with a folded wet wash cloth placed over his eyes. "Sorry I didn't answer the door, damned migraine. I'm getting them more frequently lately."

"My Mom gets them every so often," I said. "Painful beyond description. Have you seen a doctor?" I asked, and chuckled.

"The Prasonio family was in Nuremberg last week. They asked me how you were doing."

"They're very nice people. I introduced myself to them at the church the day of the funeral. I could literally feel Janice's presence in both of them, especially her Mom. Her pain was sort of overwhelming. I'm kind of ashamed that I practically ran from the church afterward, but I knew that it was neither the time nor the place to add my heartache to theirs. Maybe someday we could...."

"Janice's mother would welcome that." The Doc finished the thought for me. "Mary sensed the very same feelings in you. She told me she understood why you left the church. She would very much like to share her Janice with your Janice -- when you're ready. No time constraints."

"That's very kind of her, but I'm not sure when that will be."

"Whenever you're ready," the doctor said simply.

"When someone that wonderful is ripped from your life...." I paused for a moment before continuing, "My mind hasn't been able resolve what I've been feeling. I'm not sure it can."

"When you decide that you need to try, there are people on my staff who can help you reason this out."

"Thanks, Doc, but right now I know I can't."

"A final piece of advice," said the good Doctor. "You'll need to talk to someone sooner or later about this. Sooner is best. Don't trap yourself here in 1969 with that one memory of her being killed. You have your whole life ahead of you. When you leave the Army next year, take all the wonderful positive memories of Janice with you, but leave her death here."

"How's your headache doing?" I asked. Doctor Lattermire knew the subject of Janice's death was now closed.

"I probably should try and eat something."

"The Mess is open. I'll bet we can get someone to fix us something," I suggested.

"Let me put my boots on and then we can walk over."

We walked along the path that ran parallel to the building housing the CQ. The illumination from the outside lighting provided the same amount of light as a full moon.

"I'm going to violate a confidence in telling you this, Rick, but I can't see what harm it can do now. Mary Prasonio is General Bushman's daughter. Janice was his granddaughter. They were very close."

"Jesus, Doc, I was just with the man. Why in the hell are you just telling me this now?"

"I'll tell you what Gerry Bushman told me when I called him to tell him that Janice was killed. He said he would call Mary and Walter and I was to have the young man she was involved with informed as soon we hung up. She had talked to him about you the week before, when he called to check up on her. She told him you were the one. I asked if it was OK to tell you about her family connections to the military and the company. He told me to do what I thought was best."

"Jesus, Doc," I said again. I had stopped walking for a moment. I needed time to process this. I took another couple of steps, "Jesus, Doc."

We walked on in silence, almost to the side door of the Mess Hall. I put my hand on Doc's shoulder to both steady myself and to halt our progress. "Doc, I still can't believe she's gone. I keep thinking I'll wake up and it will have just been a bad dream."

"Pay attention, because I'm only going to say this one time. You are one of those rare individuals who have a natural ability for the intelligence game. I know, because I use to do for Bill Colby[218] what

---

[218] William Egan Colby (January 4, 1920-April 27, 1996) spent a career in intelligence for the United States, culminating in holding the post of director of central intelligence (DCI) from September 1973 to January 1976. During World War II, Colby served with the Office of Strategic Services. After the war, he joined the newly created Central Intelligence Agency. Before and during the Vietnam War, Colby served as chief of station in Saigon, chief of the CIA's Far

Douglas does for David James."

"Who's Bill Colby?"

"Never mind that, it's not important. Bill Douglas confirmed your aptitude for the clandestine when he met with you in London back in February. You were identified from a set of imbedded questions in the aptitude testing conducted at Fort Bragg during Zero Week. You do remember Zero Week don't you?"

"Oh, yeah," I thought to myself. *"Answer the secret questions and wind up in the CIA."*

"Only .01 percent of the testing participants reveal a propensity for the skills valued by the company. They already know that you are going back to your civilian career with the Bell System when your tour is over."

I grabbed the door handle and held it open. "Yeah, I made that perfectly clear on the bus ride going from Holabird to Bragg way back when. What's your point, and more importantly, how do *they* know that I will decide to get out?"

"Janice told me, and I told Bill Douglas." We walked to the rear dining area and took a seat.

"Is Douglas upset?" I inquired.

"In case you haven't figured this out for yourself you don't need to be in the military for them to make use of your skills. You should also know that Janice told her grandfather that she would be requesting a state side assignment once you rotated out of Germany next year."

"I didn't know that. We didn't talk a lot about what we would do once I went back to the States. We both thought there would be more time."

A PFC who worked in the kitchen saw us walk in and came over to see what we needed. "Evening, Sir, Sergeant. Can I get you something from the kitchen?"

"Yes, a couple of coffees, if you please. Is it too early to get an order of bacon and eggs?" Lattermire asked.

"No problem, Sir. How about you, Staff Sergeant?" the PFC asked.

That was the first time I had been called by my new rank. "That sounds good. Please do it twice."

"I'll be right back with your coffee."

East Division

DOG GONE IT
KENNELS AT FARGO4
0615 HOURS SATURDAY 8 NOVEMBER 1969

"Hey, get away from that gate," said a voice from the doorway of the main kennel building. The fenced area located in the rear of the compound had a security gate latch, but it wasn't locked.

"Are you in charge here?" I tested as the SPEC4 walked over to where I was standing.

"Yes, Sergeant. And my orders are that no one is allowed near that animal. He almost killed Sergeant Jorgensen."

"I see. Have you worked here for a long time?"

"Yes, almost nine months."

"My name is Fontain. Can I ask you a few questions?"

"I'm not sure that Sergeant Jorgensen would approve."

I took a leather folder out of the chest pocket of my field jacket. Pezlola had given me the Army CID identification and told me to only display it when it was absolutely necessary. I held it up to within four inches of his face.

"You let me worry about Jorgensen, Specialist," I said, raising my voice and asking for his name.

"Farmer, Spec4 Jason Farmer."

"Is there somewhere we can go and talk, Jason?"

"We can go in the office."

"Good. You got any coffee, Jason?" I asked as we walked to the kennel building.

"Fred, wait there," I yelled across the compound. "I'll be out in a minute."

"OK R.... right, Sergeant," said PFC Fred Simpson.

The Belgian's name was Gustoff. He had been brought there originally by a private security firm run by a German National group about fifteen months prior. Since then, Gustoff had had four different handlers, the last assigned handler being Sergeant Jorgensen.

The file history of Gustoff showed no prior account of any anti-social behavior whatsoever. As a matter of fact, there were several handwritten notes in the margins from the previous caregivers praising his intelligence and dedication to the humans he worked with.

"What sort of person is this Sergeant Jorgensen?"

"I don't want any trouble. I'm going home in a couple of months and...."

"Answer the question, Jason. You're not going to get in any trouble but that guard dog out there has been marked to die because he attacked a human. So, I'll ask you again. What kind of person is this Jorgensen?"

Five minutes later we were standing out by the gate where Gustoff was watching us with interest, his head lying between his two front paws.

"You know, Jason, something tells me you knew, to some degree, that this dog is not to blame for what he has been accused. And, believe me when I tell you, this will not be the last time you will be intimidated by a psycho superior, but you should make up your mind that it will be the last time that you put up with it."

"Sergeant, he treats us worse than the animals boarded here."

"The next time you suspect something like this is going down, be proactive and get a second opinion. We clear?"

"Yes, Sergeant, I will. Sergeant Fountain, how is a mean son of a bitch like Jorgensen permitted in the Army, much less allowed to be around animals?"

"His CO will attempt to answer that question over coffee with his Colonel, but right now we need to go in there and explain all of this to Gustoff."

"Say what? No way," replied Jason, and gulped another cubic foot of air before continuing. "No, Sergeant, I don't think that's a good idea."

"Do you want to do it, or would you rather I did it? Do you speak German, Jason?" I inquired and continued without allowing an answer. "I'll do it. The problem as I see it is that Jorgensen didn't bother to read Gustoff's file. I, on the other hand, have," I said and pushed open the gate.

"None of this is his fault," I said as I headed into Gustoff's living quarters. "His temperament doesn't allow him to accept abuse. More importantly, Gustoff doesn't speak English." I walked to within five feet of where he was lying. All of those feed pans were at my feet. A low growling sound started as I took another step closer to him. As his head came off the ground, I said in the calmest voice I could produce, "Hallo, Gustoff. Guten tag. Ein braver Hund, Ja?" Gustoff's head turned from side to side at least two or three times

314

before his tail started to slowly wag back and forth. The growling had stopped. I turned to Jason. "Go get me his leash."

Gustoff was seated in the rear of the jeep as we approached the CQ building. Fred pulled straight in to the parking area located on the left side of the building. "Gustoff, bleiben," I ordered politely but firmly as I would with anybody with four legs. I would have said, "I'll be back", but Arnold Schwarzenegger wasn't famous yet.

"You speak any German, Fred?"

"No, Sergeant Rick, not at all."

"Well then, I suggest you not yell at the dog in English. I'll be in the CQ for just a second."

Jim Pezlola was walking out of the CQ with a large box and a map case hanging from one shoulder. "The railroad tracks[219] look good on you, Sir. Congratulations. I need a big favor, Sir, and I need it right now."

"Who's your friend?" asked Jim, looking over at the large K-9 now sitting in the passenger seat of RedEye One. Fred was scratching Gustoff behind his left ear.

"That's half the favor, Sir. I would also like to have someone transferred to us as soon as possible. Here is his information." I handed him a folded paper with the name Spec4 Jason Farmer written at the top.

"I'll explain everything when I get back from Denver."

"Go put your guys in position. I'll take care of it," replied just-promoted Captain Jim Pezlola.

HALF KILOMETER EAST OF DENVER2
1545 HOURS SUNDAY 9 NOVEMBER 1969

We finished the third and final go-round of *Sparrow Hawk.* Some parts of it went well, others did not. Coordinating 3,874 Army and Air Force ground personnel plus a combined 58 airplane drivers was a good trick on any day. The aggressor force was doing a good job. During the second trial run we found a pace that flowed well. Even with several enemy air attacks, we were able to travel

---

219   Refers to the rank of Captain

back through Fargo4 without any loss of force.

On Saturday at 1351 hours, we lost the second fighter aircraft in two weeks. A German 104 Starfighter went in[220] just 500 meters south of Chicago2. Thank God it had the new ejection seat technology installed.

The witticism going around Germany at the time specified that the cheapest way of obtaining a Starfighter[221] jet aircraft was to buy a small patch of land and simply wait. One would surely appear. The safety record of the F-104 Starfighter became high-profile news, especially in Germany in the mid-1960s.

The Rhine-Main accident investigation team didn't wrap up until 0255 hours Sunday morning. All attacking and defending forces were reset and were ready to go again at 0530 hours. The only snafu on the second run of *Sparrow Hawk* on Saturday afternoon was that one APC of the 14th CAV threw a track south of Chicago3 on its way west. The fire road that was cut through this part of the forest was on the side of a hill and too narrow to permit any further traffic to pass.

An ARRV (Armored Repair and Recovery Vehicle), was four back from the disabled M48. Had the balloon actually gone up[222] all four vehicles in front of the ARRV would have been pushed off the road so the rest could continue forward. But it was just practice, so thirteen vehicles backtracked, with a loss of seventeen minutes. If it had been real, more than just time would have been lost. Later on, engineers would be assigned to cut alternate passages for future use to minimize egress blockages, but today we were rerunning utilizing the same routes.

The mock invasion forces were represented by the 1st/33rd Armor and the 1st/48th Infantry Battalions. Their mutual job was to charge and take by surprise the defending forces of Chicago represented by the 2nd/48th and 2nd and 14th Calvary Regiments. The aggressors were evenly dispersed east along the now uninhabited Bradford LOD nodes. They were waiting patiently for the third and final attack order of the weekend.

---

220 Crashed

221 Robert Calvert of Hawkwind recorded an album called Captain Lockheed and the Starfighters. Nicknamed "Witwenmacher" ("The Widowmaker"), 647 F-104's were in inventory. The German Air Force lost about 30 percent of this aircraft in accidents.

222 A military term meaning that war has been declared.

Figure 36 - F4 Phantom

The first strike on Chicago would be the twenty-six F-4 Phantom fighter aircraft out of Mildenhal. FAAR went to full acquisition alert mode as the eight Phantoms coming from the north and eight from the south made their turn to the west, hugging the deck as they passed across the rear of *Alpha*. It would take them just two minutes and sixteen seconds to cross into the Gap at Bradford. The remaining ten enemy fighters would wait for the German 104s to respond. The snap count for the attacking land forces wouldn't begin for eighteen minutes, simulating the time a Russian advance would require traveling the distance from Eisenach east of *Alpha* to the old Bradford line-of-defense.

Our assignment that day was just north of Fargo4 on the edge of the steep, wooded hillside overlooking the southernmost edge of the Fulda Gap. We shot four F-4s and one Huey. I couldn't verify it was a gunship. Therefore, it may have been a friendly. DATALINK COMMS didn't offer any solution at all for the choppers at that time.

This, and several other gaps in the war plan, had already been uncovered -- not only by us -- but from the feedback received thus far from all of the participants in the first two episodes.

LTC Brogan and Major Carlstrum had formulated a plan that was sheer genius. Two goals had been accomplished in the last several months. RedEye and the 1st/48th were better prepared to go to war. Colonel Brogan now had under his command five, fully trained RedEye teams and, of course, the CIA had their ground level view of what to expect in the days ahead.

HANAU-FLIEGERHORST AIRFIELD KASERNE
SNACK BAR/COFFEE SHOP
1945 HOURS SUNDAY 9 NOVEMBER 1969

On Sunday, instead of providing cover from the rear of Chicago4, as we had in the first two assessments, we were ordered to be the last out of the Gap. We were ordered to provide rear guard *on the fly*, all the way down to the formal debrief in Hanau.

I hadn't been told officially, but from the briefing book I saw in the command trailer behind *Alpha*, the whole purpose of these maneuvers was to draw the enemy to a predetermined point just 15 kilometers east of the Rhine. What would happen next wasn't discussed. I hadn't decided whether or not to press Bill Douglas for additional information on the intent of this tactic.

"You look tired, Staff Sergeant," Jim Pezlola said as he walked up to the table I was using to write the updates to that day's activity log.

"Hi Jim. Are you all done with the debrief?"

"Yep. Gary said you were grabbing a coffee over here. We're catching a ride over to Hilversum in a few minutes. I just wanted to say goodbye."

"How's Gustoff doing?" I inquired regarding my new friend.

"He flew out direct to Hilversum yesterday afternoon. I'll be able to tell you more on Wednesday."

"And my request for Farmer?"

"It's in the works," said Pezlola.

"We have to get Farmer out of there before that asshole has a chance to hurt him."

"The asshole has been dealt with. Trust me." Then Jim asked, "Where are your guys?"

"I sent them on to Coleman. I kept the new guy with me. Fred Simpson is his name. We'll head back as soon as I turn in this after-action activity and route report into the Division S-2. It's been a long weekend. Did Doc get off okay?"

"Yeah. He drove back with one of the medics from the hospital early this morning. Did you two get together last night?"

"We did, and I need to run a few things past you, but not tonight. You said you're coming to Gelnhausen on Wednesday?" I asked.

"Yes. Tell you what, I'll come in Tuesday afternoon and I'll get a BOQ[223]," Jim said. "We can go grab dinner somewhere. There are also several things I need to talk to you about."

"Oh, has my request for an early discharge come through?"

"No, but I can get you a sizable reenlistment bonus if you want," Jim grinned.

"Unless it's for a million plus don't bother to bring the paperwork," I replied.

"Seriously, I do need to talk to you about a few things," Jim reiterated.

"It's a date. See you in G-town. Have a safe flight," I offered.

---

[223]   Bachelor Officer Quarters

"Thanks." Pezlola turned and left the coffee shop.

COLEMAN KASERNE
HHC 1ST/48TH
GELNHAUSEN
2415 HOURS SUNDAY 9 NOVEMBER 1969

I swung RE-1 into the service drive of the HHC. It had the bumper markings 1/48 INF/RE-1 in white block letters. Our trip back from Fliegerhorst had only taken half an hour. "Fred, did you bring the key to the team room?"

"Yes, Sergeant, I have it hooked to my dog tags."

"Good. And by the way, you can call me Rick when we're working by ourselves. Pull the radios, antennas, and the alert gear, and secure everything in the team room. I'll put our weapons back in the armory. Back the trailer over there with the others and return the jeep back to our space in the park."

"Yes, Sarg... Rick. You want me to come back here?"

"Only to take a shower and hit the sack. I'll see you tomorrow. Thanks for all the help. You did a good job this week."

"I want to thank you for making me feel like a member of the team," said Fred. "You wouldn't believe what it was like before I got here."

"Fred, I would believe it, and that's why you and I and the rest of the team are going to do extremely well together. Now get this done and get some shut-eye. And that's an order," I smiled, and gathered up our personal weapons and walked towards the Orderly Room.

I pushed open the door to the Orderly Room and saw Captain MacKennia, who was leaning against the door jamb of his office. Top (Bumpus) was seated behind his desk, and SPC5 Bernie Costa was in the process of putting a folder into a filing cabinet. Each one turned his head to see who had come in.

"Evening Sir, Top, Bernie. I need to get into the Arms Room. Can you let me in, Bernie?"

"You just getting back from Francois Kaserne?" asked MacKennia.

"Yes, Sir, we just got back, but I was diverted to Fliegerhorst for a quick de-brief by the Division S-2. Lieutenant Pezlola was present."

"Here, Bernie," Top handed him the keys to the Arms Room. "The rack keys are in the cabinet in Sergeant Kirtwin's office."

Rick, I'd like a word in private when you're done," said MacKennia.

"No problem, Sir. I'll be right back," I replied.

"Meet me out by my car," said MacKennia.

"Well, I'm out of here. I've had all the fun I can stand today," said the Top Sergeant as he walked to the door. "See you all bright and early tomorrow."

"Goodnight," everyone said at once.

Bernie and I walked along the sidewalk to the door to the Arms Room, which was located at the far end of the HHC just opposite the south stairwell.

"All my guys check in OK?" I asked.

"Yep, they rolled in here just after 1800 hours. Your equipment looked in good shape. Cushy assignment?" asked Bernie.

"We were assigned to drive the nurses from the hospital back and forth from the Mess Hall to the showers," I replied.

Bernie reacted with, "No shit."

Leaning against the driver's side door of his brand new BMW 2000 TSII, George MacKennia was smoking a cigar and blowing rings into the cool night air. We had had the good fortune of great weather for the entire outing and tonight was no exception. I had secured our weapons, thanked Bernie for his assistance and went to meet with the CO.

"Sorry to keep you waiting, Sir. We couldn't get the cable to unlock on the 45 locker."

"The Colonel called earlier. He said to tell you that you and your team did another outstanding job."

"Thank you, Sir, but you're the third or maybe the fourth person to tell me that. I keep expecting to be asked to parachute into East Germany next."

"I hadn't heard that. I heard it was Czechoslovakia," George chuckled and continued. "Seriously, from what I've seen on how you're conducting business, you can expect a lot of work sent your way in the coming weeks."

"Yeah, that seems to be how it works, Sir," I replied.

"Have you gotten any feedback on how *Sparrow Hawk* was graded?" asked the former gunship pilot.

"Nothing official, but your buddy Douglas seemed pleased when I ran into him at the airfield earlier today. The word on the street is that *Sparrow Hawk* will work well and can be executed with a minimal loss of life. There shouldn't be any problem pulling the invading force through the Gap to where they can be handled."

"You didn't hear this from me, but I think the correct term is disintegrated," added the CO.

"Yes, Sir. Mum's the word. Vaporized also comes to mind."

"You want to go get a drink?" asked MacKennia.

"Three bags full, Captain, Sir."

DAS GASTHAUS "ZWANZIG UND AUS"
GELNHAUSEN
0015 HOURS MONDAY 10 NOVEMBER 1969

"Gut Morgen, Herr Hansen," George greeted the older man behind the bar. "It's a good thing we have reservations."

I looked around the room. If you counted all of the people present, including Herr Hansen, you would count to three. We were, at that point, 15 minutes into the new day.

"How late are you open, Jimmy?" MacKennia asked as he guided us over to a booth toward the back of the room.

"I'll be here awhile. I'm waiting for a phone call from the States. My daughter is having a baby," replied the smiling barkeep.

"Congratulations. You ever been a grandfather before?" asked George, who went on without allowing an answer. "You know, when you become a grandfather, anyone present when it happens gets to drink for free for a month."

"No fooling! You prefer the water from the tap or the melted ice in the bottom of the bar sink?"

"OK, be that way. How about a couple of Gelnhausen's finest to start the celebration?"

"You got it." And with a couple of fast pulls on the tap handle we were served.

"How did you find this place? It's a couple of blocks off the main drag?" I commented.

"Bumpus knows him. He took his retirement here after he put his time in. The previous owner died about the time he was getting out. He's married to a German National. He liked it here, so he stayed."

"I've found the locals to be very good people. I like them," I shared. "Now I understand the name on the sign I saw when we came in."

"How so?" asked George.

"Zwanzig und aus translated means *twenty and out*," I replied and changed the subject. "Sir, what terrible news do you have for me that we needed to come all the way down here after midnight?"

"You ever read Catch-22, Rick?"

"Yep. Twice. I find myself regularly torn between the characters of John Yossarian and Nately's whore[224]. How about you, Sir?" I inquired.

"Carlstrum was right. You really don't like to make small talk. Call me George when we're not out saving the world from the Communist horde."

"Well, George, our mutual friend Major Carlstrum, who has about twenty aliases, has never revealed any information whatsoever to me, or anybody else, as far as I know. I would, therefore, have to classify him as the character Clevinger[225]. I wouldn't be surprised if he has one of those suicide pills hidden somewhere on his person," I kidded.

"You really don't know who Carlstrum is, do you." observed George. It was a statement more than a question.

"Why would I? I don't even know who you are."

"I'll drink to that," said George. "If you read the book twice, Rick, you probably know I'm more closely aligned to the character of the chaplain[226]."

"As long as you're not signing any of the HHC's Morning Reports

---

[224] Throughout the novel Catch-22, the protagonist's (Yossarian's) main concern is the idea that people are trying to kill him, either directly (by attacking his plane) or indirectly (by forcing him to fly missions), and he goes to great lengths to stay alive.

[225] Clevinger is a highly principled, highly educated man who acts as Yossarian's savior within the story. His optimistic view of the world causes Yossarian to consider him to be a "secret agent," and he and Yossarian each believe the other is crazy.

[226] Easily intimidated by the cruelty of others, the chaplain is a kind, gentle and sensitive man who worries constantly about his men. He is the only character in the book Yossarian truly trusts.

with the name Irving Washington[227] we should still be able to win this very cold war."

"Hank, could we get two more over here, please?" requested George. How would you like to go flying on Sunday morning, Sergeant Fontain?"

"Is this business or pleasure, George?"

BACHELOR OFFICERS QUARTERS
COLEMAN KASERNE
4TH FLOOR, ROOM 403B
1915 HOURS TUESDAY 11 NOVEMBER 1969

"How's my dog?" I enquired as I plopped myself in a chair in BOQ room 126B.

"Hello, Rick. I'm fine thank you. How have you been?" queried Jim Pezlola.

"How's Gustoff?" I persisted.

"Gustoff told me to tell you that you can handle all of his transfers. He was flown to the safe house in Hilversum. Max Gehnhas, head of security, says he has been incorporated into the guard cadre. Max has fallen in love with him. That was a wonderful thing you did getting him out of that place."

"Thanks for arranging to get everybody out of Dodge. I can't stand situations that mistreat animals and soldiers. And how did Specialist Farmer fare in all of this?"

"Bumped to E-5 and is presently a proud member of the 14th ACR. CSM Bost negotiated his transfer."

"Well, great. Jason's troubles are over. I hope he survives the wet down."

"Where do you want to have dinner?" asked Pezlola.

"If you're buying, I know some extremely expensive places in Nuremberg," replied Rick.

"I'll bet you do. How about if we just keep the selection to somewhere local?"

"Great! I'll just order two of everything on the menu."

"There's a very nice place down near the cathedral," said Jim.

---

[227] Yossarian had been abusing his duty of censoring letters sent home by the enlisted men, by signing them Irving Washington or Washington Irving.

"Yeah, I know the place you're talking about. I took Janice there."

"We don't have to go there if it will cause any...."

"No. Actually she really liked the place and the food was very good. Let's go. I don't want to be late for curfew."

DINIEREN IN PARADIES
ITALIAN/GERMAN RESTAURANT
0945 HOURS TUESDAY 11 NOVEMBER 1969

I pulled the green 1968 Porsche 912 into a parking space being vacated as we pulled up to the restaurant. The downtown area of Gelnhausen didn't have a whole lot of traffic this time of the evening. "This thing corners as if it's on rails. Are you thinking about selling anytime soon?"

"When you pass a competency exam and obtain a valid driver's license, we'll talk," Jim replied in a most solemn tone.

The name of the restaurant was Dinieren in Paradies. We were greeted warmly at the door by a woman in her late forties. Today, with a name like "Dining in Paradise", one would expect to be blown up while having dinner, but I digress. We were shown to a large table set for four in the center of the room. Two of the place settings were removed while the hostess handed us each a menu.

"Your server this evening will be Hanna," said the hostess. "May I get you something from the bar?"

"Yes, a scotch on the rocks please. *Pinch* if you have it," said Pezlola with a slight check of his eyes towards the hostess. "Rick?"

"Klang Gut. Zweimal, bitte."

"Your German is getting better and better," observed Jim.

"It's funny, in grade school I was force-fed Latin because I wanted to be an altar boy. In high school I never found it easy to learn a language from a textbook. I seem to do OK when living off the land, so to speak."

Hanna arrived with drinks a few minutes later. She looked as German as they come. She was drop dead gorgeous. The fraulein stood about five foot seven, with reddish brown hair and deep-chestnut colored eyes. "I'll be back in a moment to assist you with the menu selections," she said in near perfect English.

"Your Dutch is pretty near perfect. I heard you speaking on the radio to Sultan6. I suspect you didn't learn it here," I probed.

"No, my Mom and some of the servants taught me growing up."

"Servants. I always wanted my parents to get some of them. They told me that my brother and I were all they needed. Seriously?" I asked. "Servants?"

"My family, how to say it, is comfortable," replied Jim.

"Mine too, but that was just because our family room sofa was overstuffed."

"Do you have any questions about the menu?" asked the attractive
Hanna.

"I don't know about you, Jim, but I have found it best to ask for the recommendations of the house."

"Sounds good to me," replied Jim.

"Hanna, we place our palates in your delicious looking hands. That came out wrong. We would welcome your suggestions." She paused and looked at my face, trying to decide if I was being sarcastic or not.

"Of course," she smiled, and said, "You won't be disappointed."

"My newly acquired friendship with George MacKennia has presented an opportunity to go flying this weekend," I informed Pezlola in a tone that demanded his input. "Care to share what this is all about?"

"Haven't a clue, other than he likes you and probably thinks you would enjoy getting in a machine that has proven mathematically impossible to get off the ground."

"You're talking about the bumble bee. You know most chopper pilots are crazy and MacKennia is a good friend of our very own Bill Douglas. So, you're not going to tell me?"

"OK, I did overhear the two of them talking at the airstrip on Sunday. I only heard part of the conversation but MacKennia was suggesting that if RedEye was more mobile, a team could shield two to three times their usual coverage area."

"What did Douglas say?"

"Again, I couldn't hear everything being said but I suppose he told him to run it by you."

"Wonderful. The bright side in all this is that Captain George has access to some really neat toys."

Hanna didn't disappoint. Dinner was magnificent.

COLEMAN KASERNE
1ST/48TH INF BATTALION HQ
2ND FLOOR CONFERENCE ROOM
0915 HOURS WEDNESDAY 12 NOVEMBER 1969

The November 12 meeting was really a courtesy brief by the action team assigned by David James. Jack Swanson drove Colonel Brogan up to Division at first light. Brogan's assigned driver was still throwing up from something he'd been struggling with since coming off the previous week's operation.

I met both the Colonel and Jack at the side entrance of the Battalion HQ. They had their arms full of map cases and document folders. "Morning Sir, Jack." I was told to get the last box out of the back of RE-3 and to bring it up to the second floor conference room.

Jack was coming down the hall as I entered the second floor. "How come you're driving the Colonel around in RE-3?" I asked.

"His jeep has an expired trip ticket. Von renewed all of ours Monday morning under the pretext that we would be going back out this week."

"Be careful what you wish for. Oh, thanks for taking the call this morning."

"No problem. Our LTC is one of the good guys," said Jack.

"You been released?" I asked.

"Yep. I'm going back over to the company area. Larry's PRC77, ground-to-air COMMS, is on the fritz. Lieutenant Key said he would get one of his guys to look at it."

"OK, catch you later," I said in farewell.

The Colonel saw me come into the room "Put it over there on the counter Rick. Thanks for the assist."

"Did Sergeant Swanson take good care of you this morning, Sir?"

"Yes, indeed. Fine young man. When he speaks he sounds like a radio advertisement."

"Yes, Sir. Jack did the news for CBS radio in Chicago before his friends and neighbors got him this gig."

The Colonel chuckled, "I'll be damned."

Then my mouth got away from me. "Yes, Sir, we had an idea to sell commercial beer advertisements during air strikes." The LTC, who was leaning over an open document folder on the table, turned his head sideways to look at me and, with a straight face, said, "Division would never go for it. Hand me that map tube hanging on the chair back."

Apparently the 1st/33rd was also taking part that morning. I recognized their battalion CO and his S-3 from the meeting the previous week.

"Hello, Sergeant. It's very nice to see you again. Have you harmed any pine trees this week?"

"Yes, Sir. I mean no, Sir," I replied. He smiled. So did the Captain. They both went to the far end of the table and took their seats. The name on the Lieutenant Colonel's name tag was Peck. I remembered seeing a LTC Arthur J. Peck on the *Sparrow Hawk* distribution lists.

Jim Pezlola and Bill Douglas, both in uniform, came into the room and went immediately to the LTCs and made their manners. I had gotten a cup of coffee and made my way to my usual spot on the back wall. More people came in. Most looked familiar, but some of the officers I had not seen before.

Pezlola unrolled the map that the Colonel had brought back from Division. Douglas/Carlstrum was using his pen to point at several areas of interest on the overlay placed over the map.

They were all nodding their heads when our Colonel said in his command voice, "Gentlemen, take your seats and let's get started." The tone was the same as the voice you hear at the start of the Indy 500.

Colonel Brogan continued, "This is Major Carlstrum, and this is Captain Pezlola. They are here today as a courtesy follow-up to last week's activities. I know I speak for Colonel Peck when I say that we are all very proud of the way our people performed in *Sparrow Hawk*. "Major Carlstrum, if you would start the meeting with the results and observations from last week."

"Thank you, Sir. Good morning. *Sparrow Hawk* has been acknowledged as a solid solution strategy. The INTEL processed after *Synchronized Sparrow* continues to support the Fulda Gap as the primary invasion route.

"There are five other viable routes, besides Fulda, where the Russians could mount an invasion," continued Carlstrum. "Fulda has always been the favorite. It was just recently that we have realized why. We have identified their primary objective—the industrial complex at Offenbach[228].

Carlstrum flicked the switch on the overhead projector and a map of West Germany came slowly into view as the lamp reached full power. Spec5 Blubaugh entered the room and started handing out folders marked *RESULTS: Sparrow Hawk—10 November 1969*. "Please open your briefing document and turn to page 14," instructed Carlstrum. "This contains the traffic timing results."

The meeting went on for over an hour. Most of the material dealt solely with convoy formations and traffic patterns. None of the presentation, except for the opening remarks, revealed the true purpose of *Sparrow Hawk*.

I was receiving an education that normally would take most career NCOs years to gain. I was being groomed for something, but I wasn't sure for what. They knew I was getting out in a few months. Maybe they hoped I would change my mind.

There were worse ways to spend your life, I supposed. The acceptance of responsibility and the decision-making were becoming second nature. Truth be told, I was really starting to like this time in service. The company of soldiers was the strongest feeling of friendship I had ever experienced. I wondered if it was because the stakes were always so high, the trust so fragile, but so easily given. We counted on each other for everything.

POST MEETING
BRINKSMANSHIP
1ST/48TH INF BATTALION HQ
2ND FLOOR CONFERENCE ROOM
1225 HOURS WEDNESDAY 12 NOVEMBER 1969

The briefing documents and notes were all left on the table as directed. They would be collected and burned in the basement incinerator -- the same device that would be called upon if the balloon[229] went up. Captain Pezlola and Spec5 Blubaugh collected the

---

[228] Offenbach was the 1960s industrial complex for developing engineering and manufacturing technologies. It is the present day location for multiple graphic and industrial design companies. Today, the city hosts the German Association for Electrical, Electronic and Information Technologies.

[229] Notification of invasion

documents and left the room. Carlstrum asked me to stay while he gathered his presentation material. Colonel Brogan was the only one still in the room with us.

"Well, Sergeant Fontain, what did you think?" the LTC asked.

"Sir," I responded, "I'm not sure I understand the question."

"Go ahead Rick, tell him your impression of what was discussed this morning," ordered Carlstrum. With just the three of us in the room, Carlstrum seemed to be morphing back into his Douglas alter-ego.

"Yes, Sir. I thought it provided good feedback for what everyone was asked to do in making *Sparrow Hawk* a success."

"Now tell the Colonel what you really think," Carlstrum said.

I took a moment before I spoke. "Sir, I find it curious about what was not discussed as opposed to what was. The purpose of pulling the Russians to a predetermined point can only mean one of two possible choices. One, we will use the intrusion to bargain the exchange of land for a promise of peace. Or two, we want them in a certain place so that a more permanent solution can be enacted."

"You told me he has an exceptional grasp of the obvious," commented Brogan, as if I hadn't been in the room. "But it also seems he has the ability to extrapolate the unthinkable."

"Yes, Sir. That's been my observation as well," replied Carlstrum.

"With all due respect, Major Carlstrum," I said, "at this point, neither you nor the CIA has any idea what the Russians are thinking or what they will do. The terror I feel at this moment is the lack of INTEL that went into formulating MC 14/3 C. Please stop me if I start saying things you don't want in the open."

"Continue, Rick. But Colonel, none of this discussion is to leave this room, please," directed Carlstrum.

"Understood. Continue, Fontain," said the LTC.

"Yes, Sir. In the meeting at Eindhoven...."

"Where did you say?" Brogan interrupted.

"Eindhoven, in the Netherlands, Sir. The strategy changes that were discussed didn't mean anything to me at the time. However, it was apparent that the mutually assured destruction factor, the *MAD factor*, was being challenged by the Russians as being no longer viable."

"What did you make of the show of force at *OP Alpha*, Rick?"

asked Carlstrum.

"That demonstration of technology only provided proof that we were lacking the necessary boots on the ground to repel a larger opposing force," I answered.

"And, it bought us some additional time," reasoned Carlstrum.

"Why did you say what you just said, Rick?" asked the LTC.

"Sir, let me take that one step further, if I could?"

"Sure, continue."

"I've become friends with the General Dynamics representative, Barry Flax. He shared with me that we were willing to toss a whole lot of money at the problem. We're talking millions of dollars. Operation *Sparrow Hawk* involved even more dough. It should have been given a more descriptive project name."

"Such as," prompted Carlstrum.

"Pied Piper[230] is probably more appropriate. This phase involved more money than *Synchronized Sparrow*. The industrial complex at Offenbach was being used as the proverbial pipe, or lure."

"Why do you refer to it as Pied Piper?" asked Brogan.

"At first glance, *Sparrow Hawk* seemed like a well-financed solution to leapfrog our forces intact back to the Rhine."

"And at your second glance?" asked the LTC.

"It wasn't until I saw the map this morning that I realized the real purpose of a practiced withdrawal."

"And you put this scenario for *Sparrow Hawk* together how? From a conference in, what did you say the name of the place was, Eindhoven?" asked Brogan.

"No, Sir. *Sparrow Hawk* wasn't mentioned by name, but the required result was.

"Required result?" repeated Brogan.

"I stuck my head into one of the empty bunkers at Fargo4. One of the cleaners was coming out. I tested him by asking what was next. He said everything was to be recalculated for the view from Enfield."

"Enfield was dismantled, wasn't it, Major?" asked the Colonel.

---

[230] The Pied Piper of Hamelin is the subject of a German legend concerning the departure or death of a great number of children from the town of Hamelin in the Middle Ages. The earliest references describe a piper, dressed in pied (multicolored) clothing, leading the children away from the town, never to return.

But before Douglas was able to answer, I said, "The Saturday that we lost the second Starfighter, my team rolled through the old Enfield complex, four clicks east of Fargo. I spoke to one of the contractors. I questioned him if there were any problems getting reset at the new location. He said everything was already recalibrated."

"Recalibrated - what's that supposed to mean?"

"I wasn't sure myself until this morning's briefing. Our Battalion's new alert assignment is a defensive position 108 kilometers to the south of here. This is taking our Battalion completely away from the positions to which the Russians are being lured, by us. 108 kilometers south of here will undoubtedly be a good place from which to view the *ultimate solution.*

"Rick, you're speaking in tongues," said an exasperated Brogan. "Just what is this ultimate solution? You said 14/3?"

"MC 14/3 C, Sir. I suppose it could entail conventional measures, but moving the Battalion 108 clicks south, not east, suggests a harsher solution."

"Which is?" he prodded.

"MC 14/3 C mandates an immediate jump to DEFCON-2[231] as the invading forces emerge from the west end of the Gap. *Operation Cocked Pistol* will be launched, according to MC 14/3 C. The immediate execution of DEFCON-1 and *Fulda Cold* will proceed once the Russian attacking force reaches the prearranged set of coordinates we've drawn them to via *Sparrow Hawk.* That result, I believe, was the true purpose of *Sparrow Hawk.*"

"Extraordinary, Sergeant," said Carlstrum. "Let me add some recent INTEL to your growing repertoire. There is hard evidence that the recent global changes in technology, the ABM deterrent, plus nuclear weapons utilizing MIRV technology, have caused concern at the highest levels of our government.

"Multiple independent re-entry vehicles, MIRV, utilize one

---

[231] A defense readiness condition (DEFCON) is an alert state used by the United States Armed Forces. The DEFCON system was developed by the Joint Chiefs of Staff and unified and specified combatant commands. It prescribes five graduated levels of readiness (or states of alert) for the U.S. military, and increase in severity from DEFCON 5 (least severe) to DEFCON 1 (most severe) to match varying military situations.

payload that delivers 10 to 12 warheads. Mr. Flax from General Dynamics gave me his copy of a "Popular Mechanics" article on MIRV. A diagram of what was on the drawing board was included in the article.

"The Pentagon has gone on record saying that if the Russians utilize MIRV, it will be expensive to defend against," Carlstrum said and went to his briefcase. He pulled out a manila folder labeled with large red letters: TOP SECRET/Prague Spring. "There was a defection of high ranking officials from Alexander Dubcek's administration to the West in April of 1968 that has caused us to re-think the MAD counterbalance."

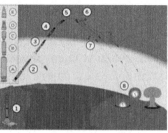

Figure 37

Multiple Independent Re-entry Vehicles

"Well named, don't you think?" I offered.

Carlstrum ignored me. "Documents brought out by these individuals detail the Warsaw Pact response to invasion from the West."

"It's illogical to assume that NATO countries would ever initiate a first strike against Warsaw Pact countries. NATO simply would not initiate an invasion into Eastern Europe," said Colonel Brogan.

"According to these men," Carlstrum explained, "the plan described in the documents they brought out was a hoax. A Western first strike would be faked. The Warsaw Pact's response would be the one outlined in the invasion document. One curious detail, however, was a list of places that would not be targeted. For example, France, in particular Paris, was cited, and all of Great Britain was also specifically mentioned."

"Holy shit," I whispered under my breath.

"Now that is interesting, and makes better sense of the logistics of *Sparrow Hawk*," said the Colonel. "In order for NATO to have plausible deniability of any invasion attempt, we will have to draw the Russians well inside the West German border so they can be addressed. Any claim by the Russians that NATO started an invasion would be proven false."

"Addressed?" I questioned the term. "Sir, that one word description could be interpreted as sarcasm."

"I agree," replied Carlstrum. "However, there are two other things to consider."

"Only two you say? We're just damn lucky that the show of force at *Alpha* didn't provide them the basis to claim aggression on our part," I exclaimed.

"No, it was too soon and too fast," said Carlstrum. "There wasn't enough time for them to get a consensus of their *Politburo*[232]."

"So what are we going to do?" I asked.

"During the Cuban missile crisis a new strategy term was created called brinksmanship[233]."

"Sounds ominous," I commented.

"What we're positing, Sergeant Fontain, is a strategy involving the threatened use of nuclear weapons against what the Russians believe to be a new and improved MC 14/3 C," Carlstrum explained. "The question *is it real*, is what we are asking them to consider. Our job is to convince them that it is, because it is."

"Great...the Russians have another name for it. It's called *roulette*[234]." I paused and just glared at the map board.

"What's wrong, Rick?" asked Carlstrum.

"I was just wondering."

"Wondering what?"

"How God feels about all of this."

TARMAC
"LUCY DOES" UNOFFICIALLY HUEY
35 MILES NORTH OF FULDA
0630 HOURS SUNDAY 16 NOVEMBER 1969

Figure 38
Bell UH-1D

The name on the nose of the ship read "Lucy Does". She was a Bell UH-1D Iroquois[235] (unofficially Huey).

---

232 The supreme policy-making body of the Soviet Union's Communist Party

233 Brinksmanship means to push dangerous events to the verge of—or to the brink of—disaster.

234 Russian roulette - A game where the missile eventually loses momentum and falls back into the atmosphere called reality.

235 A military helicopter powered by a single, turbo-shaft engine. It had a two-bladed main rotor on top, mounted horizontally, and at the rear of the fuselage a smaller blade mounted vertically, called a tail rotor. It was developed by Bell Helicopter to meet the United States Army's requirement for a medical evacuation and as a utility helicopter. Since being ordered into

"Is this one of the gunships that was in the show at *Alpha*?" I asked. Captain George MacKennia, sitting in the right seat of Army HA-C3476, was in the process of completing a banking maneuver just south of Brunswick. "Yep, it sure is, but you're out of luck today. All of the tubes are empty."

"Too bad, because I see a whole bunch of targets of opportunity down there."

"You like flying?"

"Yeah, I could get used to this. You must find it difficult to accept a paycheck."

"It's even better when someone is shooting at you. You want to take it for a while?"

"You mean fly it?" I had hoped my voice didn't reveal how excited I was by the prospect.

"A typical helicopter has three separate flight control inputs: the cyclic stick, the collective lever, and the anti-torque pedals," MacKennia explained. "Put your feet lightly on the pedals. Follow me with your feet. Feel the changes I make. They torque the tail and let you steer the bird."

"Left right, right left ... cool. Where's the turn signal?"

"The stick lets you change the angle of the rotor overhead. Put your hand on the stick and follow me for a few turns. Leave your feet where they are."

"Very nice... this will take some time to get used to."

"Ready for the third," George's voice came across the intercom built into my helmet.

"Sure. Does it have to do with this emergency brake looking thing?"

"That's the gas pedal. It lets you cut the air in big and small slices. Put your left hand on it and lightly pull up. Now push slightly down. Twist it slightly clockwise. You feel that?"

"Yeah, this is really something. How long do you have to train to get good at this?"

"Not long, Rick. Just how much bootleg time do you have in one of these things, anyway?"

"Sir?" I asked, not understanding his meaning.

---

production in March 1960, the UH-1 was the first turbine-powered helicopter; 16,000 have been produced worldwide. Like the Army's APC, it provides a platform for a wide variety of weapons systems.

"It usually takes about three months, both in the classroom and in the air, for someone to do what you just did."

"Really. This is my first time, George, but I hope it's not my last."

Forty-five minutes later we were flying at 2400 feet just west of Hoenffel's. "You seem comfortable with the controls," said MacKennia. "I'll take my hands off for a while."

"Are you going to tell me what's on your mind or did you just want the company on this beautiful day?"

"Give me my aircraft back." MacKennia paused and then continued. "I'm leaving soon Rick. I've been reassigned."

"You're kidding. You got here after me."

"I'm getting promoted. I've been asked to set up support to run LRRPs[236] in and out of Laos."

"What are *lurps?*"

"It stands for Long Range Reconnaissance Patrols. It's spelled L_R_R_P_S. They're the guys who take long walks in the woods."

"Oh, I know what you're talking about now. Gary Lawson, who works for Pezlola, told me about how that group works here in Europe."

"That's funny. Bill Douglas never mentioned anything about the program here. Douglas also indicated he's about finished here, or so he says."

"Yeah, there won't be much to do after WWIII starts," I quipped.

"How well do you know Jim Pezlola?"

"I'm on his short list to buy his car. That is, if he ever decides to sell. You do know that Pezlola is coordinating the LRRPs program in country for Bill Douglas." That comment was met by silence.

"Well, that certainly got your attention, didn't it, George?" had been my next thought.

I continued, "Did you also know that the *Long Range Reconnaissance* teams were actually established here for the first time in '56? The 11th Airborne Division in Augsburg, if memory serves."

"Are you playing with me, Rick?" MacKennia's eyes narrowed. "Did Douglas put you up to this?"

"No. Sorry. It's just difficult to have a friendly conversation

---

236 Long-range reconnaissance patrols or LRRPs (pronounced "Lurps"), are small, heavily armed, long-range reconnaissance teams that patrol deep in enemy-held territory.

these days without guarding everything you say. I just realized that one of Jim's people told me all about LRRPS and its origin when I was in Nuremburg. And you can bet your bottom dollar that he reported the conversation to Pezlola, who in turn, told Douglas. I'll deny ever saying this, but Jim Pezlola has several teams he runs back and forth across the Czech border. I understand that some are American, some are Czech, and some are actually East German. This is where *you* say, 'I had no idea, Rick.'"

"Well, that would be a true statement. And this whole conversation feels like a setup."

"The next question we need to ask ourselves is whose idea was it for us to get together today? Yours, or was it Douglas's?"

"This pisses me off." MacKennia pushed the talk switch to call the tower, then changed his mind and released it. "This really pisses me off."

"Nah, don't let it. You get used to it. Besides, you've known him longer than I have. You only know what you need to know. Look, once you come to grips with Bill Douglas's mind games you can just relax and enjoy the ride."

"What does that mean?"

"It means he trusts us well enough to share some down-time together. He knows how difficult it is to establish friendships. Probably your situation is even worse than mine. And, if you look real hard when he asks you what we talked about today, you will no doubt see him smile slightly."

"What were you doing in Nuremburg?"

"I was romantically involved with one of the doctors assigned to support Jim Pezlola. Bill Douglas only imparts information on a need to know basis. The only similarity of the two programs apparently is that they are spelled the same. LRRPS in Europe has no logistic similarity to the program in North Vietnam and Laos. That's probably why you weren't read in on the program here. Well, until just now."

"So you think this was all a set up?"

"No. You wanted someone to go flying with you and you wanted to hear what I thought about making Redeye more mobile. That's what today was about. Just remember, Bill Douglas probably can't help himself when it comes to this giant chess game he has going on in his head."

"I don't know whether to be upset or just laugh about this," MacKennia said after a moment.

"Be grateful. People like Bill Douglas are very necessary in the spy world. He gives each of us exactly what we need to do our jobs. Nothing more, nothing less, is given or expected. He's without a doubt the most patriotic, dedicated and focused individual I've ever met. Once you understand that, this journey becomes almost easy."

"I'm glad we had this talk." George took a deep breath and flicked the switch to radio. "Fliegerhorst, this is Army HA-C3476 coasting one mile south of runway 13 west. Request a straight in approach, over." George thumbed backed to intercom. "I think we should continue this R&R[237] at the nearest gasthaus."

"George, that's exactly what he would want us to do."

---

[237] Rest and relaxation

XVIII

A WHISPER IN THE CLEAR

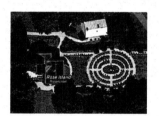

Figure 39 - Rose Island Conference

GARTENSAAL (GARDEN HALL)
ROSENINSEL—ROSE ISLAND
LAKE STAMBERG
26 MILES SOUTHEAST OF MUNICH
1130 HOURS SUNDAY 14 DECEMBER 1969

"Munich Riem, this is Army Rotor." MacKennia looked down at the plate mounted on the cockpit control panel, "HA-C2437 at 800 meters northwest of your location on visual flight plan out of

Hanau. 437Over."

"Roger, Army 437. No traffic at this time in your area. Do you need landing instructions?"

"Negative, Munich, we are just passing through your airspace. You have a nice day. Out," the Captain replied as he continued south to a place called Roseninsel—Rose Island.

"When is your last day, George?" I asked. I was riding in the left seat of the Huey gunship.

"I'm leaving on the big bird on Wednesday. Jim Pezlola called last night. He said it would be my last opportunity to talk to the boss before leaving. He also requested that I bring you along."

"Sounds like a plan. At least you know why you're here." Both George and I were wearing our Class-A uniforms. Mine was minus a name tag as per instructions from our fearless leader Bill Douglas.

The crew chief for today's flight was Spec5 Larry Anderson. Riding in the passenger bay were Captain Jim Pezlola and Sergeant First Class Gary Lawson. They were wearing civilian business attire.

Pezlola had arranged the chopper ride that morning in order for us to attend a hush-hush meeting being held on Roseninsel in Lake Stamberg. According to the map I held in my lap, the location was just southwest of the city of Munich. "How much farther, George?" asked Pezlola over the intercom.

"We're about ten minutes out, Jim. My ONC[238] doesn't show any landing facilities. You ever been here before?"

"No, but Douglas says there's a large open space near the Villa that will hold multiple aircraft."

"Roger that," replied MacKennia.

George put the Huey down at the far end of the open space located on the east side of the island. There were already four other aircraft parked around the perimeter of the field. Three were civilian, and one was a U.S. Air Force HH-3E Jolly Green Giant.

Four individuals in black leather trench coats, wearing sunglasses, and all brandishing Heckler & Koch MP5s, walked up on us as the rotors wound down. "Which of you is Captain Pezlola?" the tallest of the group asked in heavily accented English.

"Guilty," Jim said, raising his cupped right hand. Anderson was told to stay with the aircraft.

---

238 Operational navigation chart

We were being herded across the open field toward the lower roofed of two buildings. The people who had greeted us fanned out behind us. "OK, this is a little strange, people," I said. "George, are you sure we're still in West Germany and, if not, how long would it take to get back in the air if we ran back to the chopper?"

"Relax. These guys are German Security Service. The Germans are hosting today's meeting," said Pezlola.

"Oh, thank you, Sir. I feel so much better knowing the machine guns are German Secret Service."

"East or West?" I mumbled to myself under my breath.

We left the openness of the field for a stone-paved walkway that continued on through a garden. We entered the building through a side door that led into a long hallway that appeared to run the entire length of the building. There were four sets of double doors on the inside wall; each was manned by two individuals who must have been related to our tour guides.

We were asked to raise our arms as we were professionally patted down before being allowed access into the conference center. My 1911 45 ACP was under the left front seat on the chopper.

We entered a large room with an impressive cathedral ceiling. Wooden beams crisscrossed the width of the room in several places, while its height was supported by tapered beams fitted precisely into the side walls. A splendid display of carved woodwork decorated the entire room. The building gave the impression that it might have been a church at one time.

The floors were done in white marble with an eight foot black border of the same material outlining the entire room. There was a large, oval conference table in the exact center of the room with seating for over twenty individuals.

"Ah, here they are. We were getting worried," said the DDCI of the CIA.

"Good morning, Sir," Captain Pezlola said as our entire group walked to where General Bushman was standing. Along with him were David James, CIA Station Chief, London; Andrew Jackson Goodpaster, NATO's Supreme Allied Commander; Bill Douglas, resident spooky dude; N.G. Galaiologopoulos, Lieutenant General, Hellenic Army—Director, International Military Staff; and, Gustav Heinemann, outgoing West German President of the Federal Parliamentary Republic.

Everyone was introduced to everyone else, including me and

our chauffeur, soon-to-be Major, Captain George MacKennia. The General asked for a private word with Jim Pezlola. Pezlola, David James and Bill Douglas broke off to huddle in the corner of the room. As the General turned to follow them he made eye contact with me and nodded a silent greeting.

"I have been told you have a very interesting bird watching hobby," said Herr Heinemann, who had walked up after the others had left.

"Sir," I replied, as if I hadn't understood the question. "I'm afraid the people I work for don't allow much time for hobbies."

"Perhaps I misunderstood General Bushman. He seemed quite impressed with your ability to identify the many different species of birds, like the sparrow for example. This particular bird is common to this part of Germany."

"Well, I will admit to a certain admiration for the sparrow. However, I have always found it prudent to respect the versatility of the hawk." And I added, "The science of ornithology has only played a small part in our attempt to convince our neighbors as to why birds fly."

"That is so, Sergeant. Gerry was right." He was referring to Major General Gerald Bushman. "You are truly an unusual young man. Excuse me, the others are now arriving." He set his coffee cup and saucer down on the small table against the wall and headed toward the people who had just entered the room.

"Jesus, Rick, you haven't been here five minutes and you've already made a new friend -- or not," said George.

"I'm not sure, but he seemed well informed, don't you think, Sir," said Rick with just a slight touch of sarcasm.

It took another twenty minutes for everyone to filter in and take their seats. Installed around the table were representatives of NATO, the United States, and Germany, both East and West. At the head of the table was the newly elected West German Chancellor, Willy Brandt.

The meeting started with an outline of topics announced in German by Helmut Heinrich Waldemar Schmidt[239] that sounded

---

[239] Schmidt is a Social Democratic politician who was serving as West Germany's Minister of Defense at the time of this meeting. He later served as Chancellor of West Germany, from 1974 to 1982.

very much like a promise of free beer and bratwurst for everyone refusing to set off a nuclear weapon. The fortunate few who were not allowed at the table (and that included me) were directed to congregate in some small nooks evenly distributed along the back wall of the conference room. Gary Lawson moved his head to within a few inches of mine and whispered, "Douglas said to show this to you." With that he handed me a folder and walked over to refill his coffee cup.

The file contained a list of the day's attendees and a short narrative of their primary MOS's, or what we civilians would call their "hobbies". The one that gave me pause was number four on the list, Markus Wolf. Markus Johannes "Mischa" Wolf was head of the Hauptverwaltung Aufklärung, the foreign intelligence division of East Germany's Ministry for State Security, commonly known as the *Stasi*. He was the ministry's number two. Future intelligence experts would regard him as one of the greatest spymasters of all time.

Bill Douglas walked up as I closed the folder. "A penny for your thoughts," he prompted.

"Do they serve food at these functions? I missed breakfast this morning."

"You notice anything out of place about the guest list?"

"No, but I'll bet border security would shit a brick if they knew a certain someone was here."

David James walked up. "Yes, that's certainly true." He had heard what I had said. "But number two on the list works for number four."

"Well, that certainly is an interesting fact. You didn't answer me about dinner, Mr. D. Wait, does the Chancellor know?"

Bill Douglas, smiling slightly, shook his head from side to side. "You see what I mean, David?"

PRETENSE OF DECEPTION
GARTENSAAL (THE COUNTRY HOUSE CASINO)
ROSENINSEL—ROSE ISLAND
1430 HOURS SUNDAY 14 DECEMBER 1969

Bill Rogers (William P. Rogers, U. S. Secretary of State, 1969-1973) had arrived with the other latecomers. He had been invited to attend by President Heinemann. He'd brought with him a very personal message from the President of the United States to be delivered to Chancellor Brandt. Rogers was seated on the right side of the table, four seats down from Chancellor Brandt and next to Helmut Schmidt, who was very much familiar with what was being orchestrated at the meeting.

Rogers was not expected to speak at the gathering, but would, if asked, expound on the U.S. support commitment to NATO forces. This, of course, had little to do with the real purpose of the meeting.

In the minutes directly after the meeting officially ended, the Secretary would approach Chancellor Brandt (who was number one on the folder list), and would make *absolutely* sure that number two on the list, Brandt's aide, Günter Guillaume, was close by. He would ask for a private word and produce a personal letter from the U.S. President.

Dissemination of correct information is the intent of any meeting. In diplomatic circles, this is seldom accomplished. Remember Jack Webb in *Dragnet*[240]? "Just the facts, Ma'am," he would say. Well, in 1969 and probably in 2269, if you told a Russian what you intended to do if invaded, Ivan would automatically assume you were being deceitful. So, the decision was made at the highest levels of government to use "spy shit" to fix our resolve in the hearts and minds of our enemy.

In 1956, Günter Guillaume and his wife Christel immigrated to West Germany on *Stasi* orders to penetrate and spy on West Germany's political system. Rising through the hierarchy of the Social Democratic Party of Germany, Guillaume became a close aide to West German Chancellor Willy Brandt. It's unclear, even to this day, when it was that Willy found out about Guillaume's true colors, but it was one of the reasons given when Brandt resigned in 1974.

Bill Douglas had orchestrated most of the guest list for that day's meeting. He had even been responsible for the bogus agenda topics being discussed. He heard Guillaume offer to walk Wolf out to his aircraft, and after hearing Brandt's concurrence, Douglas turned and walked to the back of the room.

Guillaume's secret would be safe for at least another four years.

---

[240] Jack Webb was an American actor, television producer, director, and screenwriter. He was most famous for his role as Sergeant Joe Friday in the radio and television series "Dragnet".

But on that day he would be instrumental in completing a six-month secret operation called *Fulda Cold*. He was being duped into delivering select information directly from the inner circle of the West German government to the people he worked for in East Germany: namely, Herr Wolf.

It should be noted that the Russians were not aware that the East Germans had placed someone into Willy Brandt's inner circle. It should also be noted that when they found out four years later, they were highly pissed. It seems they were very much in love with Willy Brandt.

The Russians would receive the false information from Mischa Wolf, their *Stasi* representative. He would stipulate that he was present when a credible source related in exact detail that the policy outlined in MC 14/3 C was fully accepted by the United States and would become NATO's official response policy.

"Chancellor," Secretary of State Rogers said, offering the envelope to him. "The President and our Congress have agreed to the immediate implementation of MC 14/3 C. An immediate DEFCON-2 provision followed by the pre-authorized use of a nuclear response to an aggression has been approved."

"That was very quick, Herr Secretary. We thought it would take some time to gain your approval. We, like you, will not tolerate any Russian aggression against the West." Douglas was on the other side of the room, intently watching the expression on the face of Herr Guillaume as the letter and accompanying conversation set the hook deep into the Kremlin's military mind.

Herr Wolf's appearance at the Roseninsel meeting was under the pretext of the exchange of captured infiltrators, moles and spies. Our list of possible prisoners-of-interest was presented for exchange by Secretary Rogers. In turn, the East Germans presented their list. As bogus as the topic was, the negotiation to exchange people would have significant merit. Bill Douglas told me later that the list of those not selected for exchange was as important as the list of those who were.

When Rogers finished his post-meeting presentation, Douglas signaled with a slight hand gesture for us to remain where we were in the rear of the room. General Bushman left the table and walked over to us.

"Go with this gentleman next door to the Villa's library," he said and pointed to a staff person who had followed him over. "We'll be over after seeing our guests off." I asked Gary if he knew if they had any food where we were going.

The entire landscaped park was established in 1853 by the order of King Maximilian II. The villa was constructed much later on, in 1863. Sadly, it was abandoned upon the early death of the king in March 1864.

We entered the villa via the foyer. It was impressive. The entire entrance hall was opened all the way up to the full height of the mansion.

"What, no butler?" I asked.

A double stairway that originated on the second level landing came down both sides of the vestibule. "From what I understand about this entire island, no one lives here anymore," said Gary.

There was a huge, wrought iron chandelier hanging from a chain fastened to the ceiling three stories up. We were ushered into the library located to the immediate right of where we had entered. "Well, I hope someone brought their library card," I quipped.

It was a real library, complete with hundreds of volumes and several ladders strategically located around the perimeter that allowed access to a catwalk and the entire upper level of bookcases. Twelve four-foot wide windows took up the entire outside wall of the room. The panes of antique glass traveled the full height to the ceiling.

"Everyone grab a seat and make yourselves comfortable," said Bill Douglas.

"Gary, these places almost always have a hidden bar. You look over there and I'll check over here," I suggested.

"He's pulling your leg Gary," said Pezlola. "Librarians are almost always teetotalers."

"Will everyone please take a seat?" Douglas repeated. "The Secretary will be here in a minute."

"George, a word if you please," asked Douglas. "Thanks for bringing everyone here today," Douglas said as they took seats, not aware that I was within earshot. "Jim said you wanted to see me before you leave."

"Bitsy Canton, Captain Canton, was killed yesterday. It was in a hot LZ just inside the border. Automatic weapons fire knocked out his tail rotor. Everyone on board was killed. The second gunship reported he emptied the Gatling as it spun in. His loss is significant." MacKennia was clearly upset.

"Damn, he was the one who pulled me out last time. Is there anything I can do?" offered Douglas.

There was slight hesitation. "No, that was it. When can I expect you in country?" asked MacKennia.

"One week from today. Is that quick enough, George?"

"You have any suggestions for Bitsy's replacement?"

"See what you think when you get settled in," suggested Douglas. "Hell, if you want, we can ask Fontain if he'd be willing to help out for a few weeks, just until you get organized."

If I hadn't been fully paying attention before, I sure was now.

Douglas went on. "I know you've had him flying the last couple of months. Not that I'm suggesting he be allowed to fly, but he knows his way around a chopper and an S-3."

"You can't ask him to help with this. He only has two or three months left," said MacKennia.

"Let's see what he says. Hey, Rick, a moment of your time, if you please," Douglas called out to me.

"Yes, Sir." I took a seat directly opposite Douglas and MacKennia and played dumb.

"Would you be willing to go help George for a few weeks?"

"Sure..."

"It would only be a few weeks. I need somebody to get my office set up and running. My Exec was killed yesterday."

"I'm very sorry about that. I'll be glad to help. I assume you'll square my vacation with Colonel Brogan?"

"Done. George will fill you in on the arrangements," said Douglas. "Thanks for the assist. You can go join the others at the front of the room while I finish talking to George." I got up and walked to the front to sit next to Gary.

"I'll be damned," said Major-designate George MacKennia. "Where did you find him?"

"The testing center at Bragg last year," replied Douglas with a smug smile.

A FULL COMPLEMENT
THE ROYAL VILLA LIBRARY, 1ST FLOOR
ROSENINSEL—ROSE ISLAND
1640 HOURS SUNDAY 14 DECEMBER 1969

The door to the library opened and General Bushman, David James and Secretary Rogers entered, trailed by two of our friends in leather trench coats. The significance of all of these people gathered in that room at that moment didn't occur to me until decades later.

"Herr Douglas," said the taller trench coat, "this room has been swept as per your request. When you are ready we will be in the garden."

"Thank you. We will be as quick as we can," replied Douglas.

"There is no hurry. Please take all of the time you require," the German security man said, and closed the door to the library.

"If you all will gather here," Rogers said, pointing to the lounge area arranged in the center of the room, "I would like to speak to you."

George and "Mr. D" got up and walked to where everyone was gathered.

"General Bushman tells me you all have gone above and beyond in making today possible. This operation will allow us to continue this cold war in peace." I remember thinking how crazy that sounded at the time. It turned out to be the only truth God would allow us for quite a while.

Rogers shook hands with each of us. He held on to mine a good bit longer than the others. "I've been told you're getting out in a few months."

"Yes, Sir, my tour will end in April."

"Well, good luck to you. You've done a good job for us. I hope our paths cross again. David, if you would walk Gerald and me to the aircraft."

"Of course, Sir," said the London Station Chief.

"Gentleman," said the Secretary.

The door to the library was pulled shut as they left the room. "Jesus, what do you suppose '*I hope our paths cross again*' was supposed to mean?"

"State is always looking for a few good men to drop behind enemy lines," replied Gary.

"Seriously, what does "cross paths" insinuate?"

"A job, Dummy," said Gary. "Your employment in the Bell System may be their interest. Bell Labs would make a great international cover. I'll bet your friends there will give you a good reference."

Douglas interrupted. "Let me add my thanks for a job well done," he said. "George is leaving on Wednesday and I'll be following him this weekend. The rest of you will return to your normal duties. It'll be a few weeks before we get any feedback on the Russian acceptance or rejection of MC 14/3. But for all intents and purposes this "OP" is complete.

"George, David will be flying back with us," added Douglas. "We'll drop him at Rhine-Main."

"Roger that," replied George.

THE SPIRIT OF ADVENTURE
HUEY HEAVY
900 METERS—THREE MILES NW RHEIN-MAIN
1850 HOURS SUNDAY 14 DECEMBER 1969

"Fliegerhorst, this is Army HC_437 to your Southeast at 900 meters, requesting a straight in approach to 23 West. Over," said MacKennia.

"Roger, Army 437, no traffic at this time in your area. You are cleared for a straight in approach to 23 West."

"Roger, Fliegerhorst. Contact you again when I'm on the ground," said George, switching back to intercom.

"You haven't said much. Are you having second thoughts?" he asked me.

"No, Sir. It just dawned on me that we had a lot riding on today. Not today really, but getting to today," I said and turned my head to look into the rear passenger bay.

Everyone was seated with their eyes half-closed, taking advantage of the engine vibes. No one was wearing headphones. Spec5 Anderson was kneeling on the left side cabin floor near the door working on something. His helmet cable was not connected.

"I don't necessarily divulge to anyone that I like this job, George. I will admit to being attracted to this life. The company of soldiers and the people we serve command a loyalty that I can't explain. I realized when Rogers put words to the fact that my time here is coming to an end that I felt a certain... forfeiture is about to take place," I finished.

"You probably already know this but you don't need to be in the Army to be in the company of warriors, Rick. Whatever you decide to do with your life, you can always find the right company."

"Is that advice from the heart, or from personal experience, Major, Sir?"

"Both," replied George.

"Anyway, what do I need to do before we go? Or do we just go?"

"Douglas will arrange your TDY[241] tomorrow with Bost. I'll get another seat laid on for Wednesday. I can't tell you how much I appreciate you coming with me."

"I guess it's too late to get some Kung Fu lessons before we leave?"

"You want to land the bird?"

"Yes, Sir! I placed my feet and hands on the controls. "I have the aircraft."

---

[241] Temporary duty assignment

XIX

THE LAST HOORAH

Coming Home

QUANG NAM PROVINCE
1015 HOURS THURSDAY 22 JANUARY 1970

The C-141 Starlifter touched down at Rhein-Main at 1005. Bill Douglas had arranged my transportation from Saigon through Bahrain. It would be years later that I would use the King Fahd Causeway, linking Bahrain with the Saudi Arabian mainland, to attend to a matter for Ambassador David James.

From Bahrain we flew directly into Germany. The Air Force crew was very gracious. They let me use one of the long-range crew bunks located in the rear area of the upper deck. It had been a fifteen-hour trip from wheels up in Saigon.

My six-week assignment in Vietnam had started immediately upon my arrival in Saigon. Major MacKennia believed in hitting the ground running. Bill Douglas had arrived a week later to be greeted by the five UH-1D Hueys, complete with crews. "Everybody ready to

350

go to work?" he had asked.

The second week we moved the entire operation from Saigon to a place thirty-five clicks west of Da Nang, in the Quang Nam Province. I knew better than to ask questions about the mission, but I was working in a makeshift tent office with maps of North Vietnam piled halfway up the one of the walls. The main point of interest had been a place called Son Tay.

Son Tay was indicated by the initials IGJP[242] marked on the map overlay with a red grease pencil. It was located straight across the border from a village called Sam Neua in Laos. Of course, the only reason I knew this was because I had access to the plot board located on the back wall of George's hooch[243].

The entire OP had been considered to be Black,[244] and was in the very early planning stage. I was present on more than one occasion when Major MacKennia read the riot act to the air crews before take-off. He warned them repeatedly about removing all identification and personal items from their pockets. I don't think any of them knew the purpose of their flights up north.

I had only been able to sneak one ride up north when one of the crew chiefs had become ill. Major MacKennia chewed me out but good when I got back. Bill Douglas just sat in the corner of Major MacKennia's hooch with an expression of pure amusement. I figured George was just pissed because Douglas didn't want him flying any of the missions into northern Laos.

A Colonel named Simons visited us twice. There was one half of an A-team with him that went up north to get a first-hand look at the terrain of the entry point at the border and of the topography surrounding a nearby POW prison. They referred to their outing as a "feasibility study".

The day I left, MacKennia walked me out to the chopper that would take me to the air base at Da Nang. "You don't know how much I appreciate your help over the last six weeks. Put this on your uniform when you change into your Class A's in Saigon." He then handed me the much-coveted CIB.[245] "That's the one Douglas

---

242 Information gathering jump point

243 Hooch is a slang term for quarters

244 A Black Operation or Black OP is a covert operation by a government, a government agency, or a military organization.

245 Combat Infantry Badge

gave me when we walked out of the jungle last year."

"I don't know what to say George, but thanks. Where is Douglas, by the way?"

Ignoring the question, George said, "I had your 201 updated to reflect the award, as well as the other things. Wear it with honor. You've earned it."

The engine of the Huey started its journey to perform another miracle of vertical flight. "Tell Douglas I'll see him when I see him," George said. I saluted and jumped aboard the gunship. I shouted out the side door, "Three bags full, Major, Sir."

"Blood and Guts, Sergeant," he yelled, and we saluted each other one last time.

The Arrival

RHEIN-MAIN AFB
TARMAC IN FRONT OF HANGAR BUILDING 538
1035 HOURS THURSDAY 22 JANUARY 1970

Spec5 Carl Blubaugh was waiting on the tarmac when I walked out of the cargo ramp at Rhein-Main Air Base. Captain Pezlola had given the heads up the previous afternoon to my S-3 after it was confirmed that I had departed RAF Muharraq[246] earlier that morning.

"Yahoo, Soldier Man, looking for a good time?" asked Carl in an exaggerated, high-pitched voice.

"Hey, Carl. How come one of my guys didn't come to get me -- not that I'm not glad to see you," I said and threw my duffel into the back seat of the jeep with the bumper marking S-36. I extended my hand as I got into the passenger seat.

"There have been some organizational changes since you went AWOL, old boy."

"Like what for instance?"

"Well, let's start with MacKennia's replacement. A grade A,

---

[246] Muharraq airfield is a military base located adjacent to Bahrain International Airport.

number one prick named Lieutenant Walter P. Janzen[247]." Janzen thinks the people he is appointed over, especially the enlisted swine, should be treated as simple children, and they are not to be trusted. How someone with his mindset is allowed to pass through the Academy is hard to understand.

"Now that he's been promoted to first Lieutenant," Carl continued, "he's made it his mission in life to mold the 1st/48th Headquarters-Headquarters Company into a stupendously tuned machine of organizational efficiency. Becoming Captain Janzen seems to be the goal. Or, that's what was promised to him by those who sent him here."

"Come on, it can't be that bad, can it?"

"His first order of business was the centralization of all HHC vehicles, assigning them, driverless, to the newly created duty pool."

"How will the scheduled maintenance and trip ticket certification work if the drivers aren't assigned their own vehicles?"

"Oh that," replied Carl facetiously. "You don't seem to have the global view on how an HHC functions in peacetime Germany."

"I guess I don't." The former policy requirements for the NCOIC[248] and OD (Officer of the Day) personnel required that the person assigned would be supported by the driver-assigned vehicle. Drawing a vehicle from the vehicle duty pool would only work for a short timeframe. The very nature of the road certification process required the constant attention of an assigned driver. This was due mainly to the present age of our entire inventory of equipment.

"Didn't you and the First Sergeant work this out when you first took over RedEye?"

"Yeah, I helped Top put it together when our five, previously unassigned, vehicles were assigned to RedEye. The reason for their mutual failed condition was no-driver-assigned. Well, Janzen cancelled the policy like a stamp. He just changed it without even talking to Bumpus."

"What does Lieutenant Key have to say about this departure from good order and sanity?" I questioned with mock seriousness.

---

[247] Walter Person Janzen, born September 17, 1943; recent graduate of WestPoint, class of 1967; 143rd in his class; was strongly opinionated and sought promotion through recognition of his ability to organize and manage men and materiel.

[248] NCOIC = Noncommissioned Officer in Charge

"My boss went over to talk about the readiness requirements for a Battalion HHC. He came back about twenty minutes later and went directly into his office and slammed the door. So, this new procedure is put into practice and goes on for several weeks. Three of the RedEye and four other vehicles fail inspection on somewhat minor technicalities. Six others, mostly trucks, are failed on major component failures. That's thirteen vehicles without road status or, as our beloved S-36, LT Key, calculated, a twenty-seven percent vehicle outage."

"Jesus, if an alert is called in the next few weeks HHC would fail combat readiness on vehicle status alone. Nine percent is the limit," I recalled.

"Today, your number five was put on notice for brakes and will not receive a trip ticket in the coming week. So, here I am only because Bumpus likes you and went to Lieutenant Key and asked if I could pick you up. I personally went to Jacobs, the new maintenance supervisor, and he walked me through the entire trip ticket checklist. So, you're welcome. Our new CO wanted you to take the train."

"Of course, all of the former drivers were blamed for not maintaining the vehicles?"

Carl ignored the question. "Meanwhile, Colonel Brogan's ride blows a head gasket yesterday. So, Bost asks Bumpus to get Clark to drive the CO and EXEC to Hanau for a command appearance with the Division Commander. But Clark wasn't available because Janzen has him, Larry and Jack assigned to Denver2 NATO guard duty."

"Go on," I said, laughing. "You better hope Jack doesn't have a loaded weapon. Where's Von hiding?"

"Von is in Hohenfels driving a deuce and a half for the new S-4, a Lieutenant Guffersen, who just happens to be an asshole buddy of Janzen," Carl said, letting out a deep breath.

We were waved through the main gate by an Air Force MP. "Where are Simpson and the other newbie, Zimmerman, being held? They're under arrest, right?"

"Oh, Von got Fred bumped to E-4, but Zim is on whatever crap detail, mostly KP[249], until such time as he can be assigned up the hill[250]. It seems that RedEye is only needed during an alert."

---

[249]   Kitchen patrol
[250]   1*st*/48*th* Line Company

"Fantastic. Does the Colonel know what's going on?"

"Yeah, he does, but Bost was told to let it play out. Brogan said the man will figure it out or hang himself in the process. Not a very comforting response from management."

"It sounds like we need to keep our POVs in good shape. We may need them to escape across the Rhine. When's the next alert scheduled?"

"Not anytime soon, I hope," replied Carl. We rode on in silence for over ten minutes. "You know, I've never seen you get flustered."

"The day is young, Carl."

"How long has it been since you came into my office? Was it March of last year?"

"That's classified, Carl. I've never been to your office. By the way, I never cry in public but you will probably hear me whimpering in the dark up on level five most every night from here on out."

"Well, good luck with your meeting with your new CO. He wants to see you as soon as you get back to Coleman."

"How did he know I was coming back today?"

"I just told you. He controls all of the vehicles."

"Why does he want to see me?"

"This is just a guess, but right after you left he sees your name being carried on the morning report. So, he tells Top to get it off of there, like it was some blemish on his permanent record. Top tells him he can't do that because you're still assigned to the Battalion. The TDY is open-ended per the Colonel and until further notice you must remain on the rolls of the HHC."

"Remind me to thank Top for putting me in Janzen's good graces."

1ST/48TH INF HHC
ORDERLY ROOM
1205 THURSDAY 23 JANUARY 1970

My uniform wasn't in too bad shape, and I'd been able to wash my face and shave before landing that morning. I had also managed to remove my uniform to keep it fresh and to get about five hours of sleep on the way back. With a little bit of luck the new CO wouldn't be in his office. Carl pulled the jeep to the front of the HHC directly in line with the entrance to the Orderly Room.

"Thanks for the ride, Carl. You should be very careful when you park this."

"Why's that?"

"According to you, this is one of the only 'fit for duty' vehicles on Post. You may get mugged."

"Don't worry about that, son. As soon as I get back to my desk this jeep will be Lieutenant Key's responsibility. See ya when I see ya."

I got out of the jeep, walked to the OR entrance, and entered the office.

Bernie Costa was seated with his back to the door, typing away, when I entered. "Hi Bernie, how've you been?" He turned in his chair and motioned with his head toward the CO's closed office door.

"I've been OK. We've missed you around here." I was walking over to shake hands with him when the door to the office was abruptly opened and out came the new CO.

"You're Fontain." He said it almost as if it was an accusation.

"Yes, Sir," I answered.

"In my office, if you please, Sergeant. I'll be right with you."

"Specialist Costa, have you heard from your First Sergeant?" asked Janzen.

"No, Sir. He said he was going to the MP to see the maintenance sergeant, Sir."

"MP?" Janzen asked.

"Motor pool," said Costa, then quickly added, "Sir."

"Let's skip the initials when you're talking to me."

"Yes, Sir. I can call down to the motor pool if you want, Sir."

"No, that won't be necessary. See that I'm not disturbed." At that, he turned and came back into his office and closed the door.

"Stand at attention, Sergeant, until I tell you different."

"Yes, Sir." I went from parade rest to a position of full attention, my heels clicking a little louder then I intended. Janzen's head jerked up at the sound.

"You think this is funny, Sergeant?"

"Sir, if I have done something to displease you?"

"Quiet. Your type thinks you can carry on any way you want. I've asked around about you and I've been told that you consider yourself something special. Well, that ends right goddamn now. Do you understand that?"

I just stood there at attention in silence.

"I asked you a question, Sergeant. What do you have to say for yourself?" His voice was becoming more agitated, and louder, with every syllable.

"Sir, no, Sir," I replied.

"No, you don't understand, or no you aren't going to comment?"

"Sir, I haven't the foggiest fucking idea of what the Lieutenant is talking about." With that his jaw dropped about seven inches and banged soundly on the top of the wooden desk. At this point in our conversation I was almost assured that his mind was preparing the paperwork necessary for court martial. Suddenly the door to his office was pushed open and banged into the wall behind it.

"Costa, I told you I didn't want to be disturbed," Janzen snapped.

LTC Thomas Brogan entered at a fast pace interrupting Janzen's train of thought. "How are you Rick, you just get in?" he asked.

"Yes, Sir."

"Please wait for me. I was going to say by my jeep, but my jeep is broken. Wait for me in your team room."

"Aye, aye, Sir," I said, did an about face that would have made Audie Murphy[251] proud, and marched out of the office, pulling the door shut behind me.

"Bernie, if you have a moment," I requested, and held the door open for us to leave the Orderly Room. We walked two doors down and entered the hallway where the RedEye team room was located. I unbuttoned one of my shirt buttons and pulled out my dog tag chain holding the key to the room.

"What the fuck was that all about?" I said, as I inserted the key and let us into the room. "I thought we left all of those guys stateside."

"He showed up here the weekend after you left. There are only four or five of us who know where you went. He has a stroke at the mere mention of your name."

"He doesn't know where I was?"

"No, and we were told not to tell him or anyone else for that matter."

"Do you know where I was"?

---

251 Audie Leon Murphy (June 20, 1925-May 28, 1971) was one of the most famous and decorated American combat soldiers of World War II. He was awarded every U.S. military combat award for valor available from the U.S. Army, and was also decorated by France and Belgium.

"No, but judging from the CIB you're wearing, I can guess."

"But why wasn't he told when he took over?"

"You met him. Does that answer your question?"

"Jesus. Why is the Colonel here?"

"I called over there when Janzen took you in his office."

"Well, I guess I'll pay you back those ten dollars I borrowed from you. Thanks." There was a knock on the door. "Jesus! Now who the hell could that be?" I said as I pulled the door open.

"Are you Fontain?" asked a Major who was standing in the hallway.

"Yes, Sir. Please come in." I closed the door and turned to find an extended hand.

"I'm David Hamadan[252], Colonel Brogan's EXEC. One of the drivers out front said he saw you come in here. I was told to wait with you while the Colonel has a word with your new CO."

Bernie later told me Hamadan had just finished a tour in Vietnam. He came to us with some experience as an S-3 and was on the fast track to learn how a Battalion is run. The scuttlebutt described him as smart and very well motivated. He was here, as we all were, to make our Colonel Thomas Brogan successful.

"I'm very glad to meet you, Sir. This is Specialist Bernie Costa, our very proficient HHC Company Clerk."

"Ah, yes. I was there when the phone call came in. You all seem to be a very close-knit bunch."

"Yes, Sir. I hope you will consider yourself in that membership."

"What's the advantage to that?" he asked.

"Staying alive for one, Sir, and more importantly providing the Colonel with the best damn support group possible," I responded.

"I see why the Colonel dropped everything when he heard you were back. Things haven't been running too efficiently over here."

---

252 David John Hamadan, DOB 6 June 1941, promoted to major 12/12/1969; married to Mary Jackson Hamadan; age 27; educated and graduated from Norwich class of 1962.

1ST/48TH INF HHC
REDEYE TEAM ROOM
1255 HOURS THURSDAY 23 JANUARY 1970

A short while later, there were three knocks on the door as I was folding the *Sparrow Hawk* Operations map. I handed the map to Bernie, who put it back in the wall locker. "It's getting crowded in here. Can you ask the CO if he can assign us a larger meeting area?" I joked as Hamadan laughed and I opened the door to a smiling Colonel Brogan.

"Well, you look like you came through OK. How in the hell are you, Rick?"

"Very well, Sir. I'm sorry for whatever caused the confrontation today. I'm not sure what everyone was told when I went on TDY status."

"Are you and David getting along alright?" asked Brogan, ignoring what had transpired with his new CO.

"Yes, Sir," Hamadan spoke up. "Fontain was kind enough to brief me on *Sparrow Hawk* while we were waiting."

"Sir, has it been decided when I'll be executed?"

"No, but it was decided that there was a bit of a misunderstanding about your absence. That, as they say, has all been cleared up."

"So, I won't have to hide in here until April?"

"What happens in April?" asked Hamadan.

"Sergeant Fontain's illustrious career comes to an end, right Sergeant?" asked Brogan.

"Good Lord willing and the river don't rise, Sir."

"Tell you what, your pal Pezlola told me about this restaurant downtown that's supposed to be pretty good."

"Was it Dinieren in Paradies, Sir?"

"Yeah, that was the name. Meet us there at 1930 hours and bring Bernie here. Lord knows he deserves a break after the last several weeks of all this chicken shit."

"Yes, Sir. Thank you, Sir," both Bernie and I said in almost perfect harmony.

DINIEREN IN PARADIES
ITALIAN/GERMAN RESTAURANT
DOWNTOWN GELNHAUSEN
1925 HOURS THURSDAY 23 JANUARY 1970

"Guten Abend, Hanna," I said as we entered the lobby of the Restaurant Paradies.

"Sergeant Fountain, so gut zu sehen wieder," she said as she walked up to us. She placed her hand on my arm for just a brief moment and then said in perfect English "Please come in. Your friends are already seated."

"This is my colleague, Bernie. Bernie, this is Hanna. He writes for a gourmet dining magazine."

"I do not, but I'm very glad to meet you."

Hanna laughed and turned to guide us into the dining room. The table was set for six. Major Hamadan stood and introduced his wife, Mary. The Colonel, still seated, presented his wife, Ellee. I took a seat between Major Hamadan and Mrs. Brogan. Bernie, who looked like he was having second thoughts about his last meal before the dawn, sat down next to Mrs. Hamadan.

"May I get you something from the bar?" inquired Hanna.

"Did the gentleman I was here with last time leave any of the good scotch?"

She laughed. "Yes, of course. Pinch was the brand, yes?"

"Yes. I would like it straight up with water on the side, please."

"I'll have one of your good draft beers, please," Bernie said in a slightly subdued voice.

Hanna returned with our drinks. "Would any of you like another round before ordering or would you like to hear our specials?"

"Well, I'm getting hungry so I would like to order. What do you recommend this evening?" asked Ellee.

"When I was here last, we placed our trust in Hanna and the specialty of the day," I said.

"That sounds like a wonderful suggestion, Rick," said Ellee.

"Well, if everyone agrees," Colonel Brogan said, looking around the table. "Yes? Hanna, we place our appetites in your capable hands."

"Sehr Gut," she replied.

"Tom tells me you just returned from a temporary duty assignment," Ellee said addressing me.

360

I glanced at the Colonel's face before speaking, "Yes, I did. Sorry it took me a moment to recognize the name. Only the Mess Hall sergeant is allowed to address the Colonel by his Christian name."

Everyone laughed. "It's the other unholy names uttered behind my back that provide the insightful feedback on how the Battalion is really functioning," offered Brogan.

I asked, "Sir, how could the name 'old lead bottom' possibly provide you with any worthwhile feedback?" Major Hamadan, who was in the process of taking a sip of water, sprayed the table in front of him. Everyone laughed at that.

"How's your dog doing?" asked the Colonel.

"Fine, Sir. How did you hear about that?"

"I'm not without my sources." Looking around the table, Brogan continued, "Rick found out that one of the NATO guard dogs was scheduled to be put down. So he went into a NATO Guard Dog compound and demanded to see the charge record and the history file on the animal."

"How in the world did you get access?" asked Hamadan.

"Rick has a special club ID card that gets him in most everywhere."

"Oh my, this isn't going to end well", I thought.

"He then went out into the fenced in area where the dog was being held, ordered the Belgian Shepherd to get into his jeep, and the rest is history. That about it, Rick?" asked the Colonel.

"Yes, Sir," I replied.

"Except," said Bernie, who was speaking for the first time since ordering his drink, "the new guy, Simpson, told me he heard the kennel supervisor tell you that the dog had attacked and almost killed his handler. The dog was super clever and had amassed two weeks of dinner bowls arranged around where he was chained up. He left just enough slack in the chain hoping to draw in the person delivering his dinner."

"True," I said, "but Gustoff -- that's the dog's name, didn't speak any English. The handler, whom I will limit my description of to being a despicable human being, had mistreated Gustoff, and had caused the dog to defend himself. I merely went into his kill zone or, in this case, his living quarters, to ask him a question."

"Which was?" asked Ellee.

"I asked him if he would like a new home. He's now working for Captain Pezlola in Holland."

"Well dear, you said dinner would generate some interesting

conversation," said Ellee, smiling at her husband.

"Rick, may I call you Rick?"

"Yes, ma'am, you sure can."

"How on earth did you know that the dog would not attack you?"

"It wasn't all that hard to figure out what the dog expected of his humans. You see, I use to work for someone just like Gustoff's handler. Once I understood *that*, I knew just what to say to him. It turns out that Gustoff is a sweetie pie."

"Are you going to tell us what you said?" asked Mary Hamadan, who had spoken for the first time.

"Sure. I requested that he should consider two simple questions. First, I asked him, 'Gustoff, Was ish los?' and then, 'Sind Sie so weit?' ['What is happening'? and 'Are you ready to go'?] "While he tilted his head to almost 90 degrees and was thinking that over, I clipped his leash to his collar and made a motion to proceed to the gate. When he got to the jeep he wanted to drive but I told him to get in the back."

There wasn't any conversation for a full fifteen seconds. Everyone was just staring at me. "Come on, now, you know I couldn't let him drive one of our vehicles. The dog had enough problems without getting busted for driving without a license."

"Pretty insightful for such a young man, wouldn't you agree, Tom?" Ellee observed.

"That's why I invited him to dinner," replied the LTC.

The food was served by Hanna and two waiters. This allowed everyone to be served almost at the same time. My first bite screamed delicious. I wondered what George MacKennia was having for his supper. In the years ahead I would have hundreds of dinners just as delicious as this one, but none would ever capture the same feeling that one gets by being around real soldiers and their families.

Hanna offered everyone coffee, but only four of us accepted. When she returned, she had the coffee plus six bubble glasses with a shot of the house's best cognac in each.

"Please accept these after dinner drinks with our thanks to you for dining with us this evening."

"This calls for a toast," I announced, "but wait here one second, Hanna."

I got up and went to the bar and retuned with an additional

glass and handed it to Hanna.

"Bitte, ist es Zeit Hanna! [Please, it is time Hanna], for good friends to raise their glasses," I said and took a stance next to Hanna. "To delicious food and drink and good friends to share it with, and, to all of those who couldn't be here," I said, and then added, "To absent companions[253]."

The Major and Mary were the first to leave. Then the Colonel, Ellee, and Bernie got up and walked out to the street together. I went to say goodbye to Hanna and thank her again for taking very good care of us that evening.

"Your friends are very nice," said Hanna.

"Yes, they are, and they seemed to really enjoy themselves this evening."

"I overheard someone say you will be leaving soon."

"Not for a few months yet," I replied.

"Well, please come again soon."

"I will," I replied. "Thank you, again." I kissed her lightly on the cheek, squeezed her hand slightly and went to find Bernie outside on the sidewalk.

As I left the restaurant, I saw the Colonel and the others down by the corner, near where they had parked. A match was struck by someone standing in the shadows behind me.

"Guten Abend, Sergeant. We have a mutual friend -- Herr Pezlola."

"I should have known when he suggested this place for dinner that it would have valet parking. And... you are?"

"Max Gresonine, a friend of the family."

"What can I do for you Max?"

"Nothing, I just wanted to say hello. If you need anything you can always find me here, or they will know where I am."

"Thanks, Max, but who's 'they'?"

"Oh sorry. I meant to say Hanna and her mother. Hanna's mom is my sister-in-law. Captain Pezlola's mother is a cousin."

"I can't think of anything right now," I answered, not sure how to take the related information.

---

[253] To absent companions - Honoring the military fallen in the wars of the United States.

"Then I'll say Good Night," he said, and turned to reenter the restaurant.

"Do I know you from somewhere? Your name sounds familiar."

"I arranged for your room and meals the night of your near electrocution."

"Huh. You know, the bacon was crispy just the way I like it."

"Well, we were all glad it was the bacon and not you. I'm Jimmy's father-in-law by the way. Hanna is my brother's daughter. She recently lost her husband. I thought you should know this. When two people are experiencing similar emotions, as you both certainly are, I thought perhaps an awareness of your situations may be helpful."

"Thanks. That explains the sad eyes behind the marvelous smile. I see the same expression when I look in the mirror. Perhaps you could share my situation with her. It might explain feelings that we're having but aren't yet ready to deal with. Good night, Max," I said and walked down the block to where the others were waiting.

"Who was that?" asked Ellee.

"The owner. Apparently he wanted to know if everything was satisfactory with our dinner, and why the Colonel took the silverware off the table."

Ellee laughed as I turned to the Colonel. "Sir, I would appreciate just one more moment of your time?"

"You see, Dear, he doesn't call me 'old lead bottom' when he wants my advice. Bernie, could you walk Mrs. Brogan across the street to our car? I also require a quick word with Sergeant Rick."

"Yes, Sir," replied Bernie.

"Good night, Rick. It was very nice to meet you," said Ellee.

"Yes, ma'am. It was very nice to meet you also." Bernie and Ellee walked across the street.

"I would like your guidance on how to solve the immediate transportation problems, Sir. I'm not asking for myself. There were reports today that a Lieutenant Colonel was seen hitchhiking to Hanau."

"What did German intelligence want with you this time of night?" asked Brogan.

"I'm not sure I know, but he admitted to being Jim Pezlola's father-in-law. I suspect that's how we wound up in this particular restaurant the last time we had dinner. You recognized him, Sir?"

"I've seen him before at Division. Starting tomorrow morning, I want your focus entirely on vehicle situation readiness. Get it under control as quickly as possible. There's an alert coming that will test our egress to the south. Your people have been summoned from near and far so that they may assist you with this task."

"Sir, this assignment will include a larger scope then just the RedEye vehicles?"

"You're not listening, Sergeant. You're being appointed NCOIC for Battalion Vehicle Readiness. You'll have a much broader opportunity for decision-making."

"Yes, Sir, and how will my new duties be positioned with my new CO?"

"You'll find him extraordinarily enthusiastic, or not at all, if you take my meaning."

"How much time do we have, Sir?"

"Not much, I'll stall Division for as long as I can. Two weeks at the outside, maybe."

"Yes, Sir. Thank you for dinner. I'll see you on campus tomorrow."

"No, actually you won't. I've ordered all officers to an all-day off-post exercise conducted by Major Hamadan in Hanau, commonly referred to as a boondoggle. All officers will be told not to return to the Kaserne until Monday at 0700. I'll be in Frankfurt. If you need to get in touch, see CSM Bost."

"Good night, Sir." I called across the street, "Good night, Mrs. Brogan. Let's go Bernie."

The Colonel walked across to his car, opened the door for his wife, and got in the driver's seat.

DEPENDANT HOUSING AREA
BUILDING 203
GELNHAUSEN
2245 HOURS THURSDAY 23 JANUARY 1970

I pulled into the dependent housing area located just outside the fence on the west side of the post. "Wait in the car, Bernie. Which building is it?"

"Two-zero-three. His name is on the mailbox. This is a good idea, right?" Bernie asked anxiously.

"Wait here."

Apartment 2A was on the second floor. I knocked twice and waited. The door was opened by an attractive woman in her early forties.

"Mrs. Bumpus, my name is Fontain. Is the First Sergeant available?"

"Please come in and have a seat." She pointed to what appeared to be a den located just to the left of the hall entrance.

"Ernie, you have someone here to see you," I heard her say as she got halfway down the hallway.

I heard Top's footsteps coming down the hall. "Hello, Fontain. How was your vacation? I'm sorry I wasn't there for your welcome home party." He laughed at his own humor and continued. "What brings you to my humble abode at this hour?" he asked.

"Top, I need your advice and I decided it shouldn't wait until tomorrow morning."

"Bost said you might be stopping by. Did Brogan drop your new responsibilities on you tonight?"

"Yep, he did, but he was kind of vague as to what can be done to get us back on track with the upcoming alert."

"There's nothing that can't be fixed in a normal maintenance cycle. The problem to address is the amount of time we have before the next alert is called."

"The Colonel thinks he can buy us two weeks on the outside. What is this really all about, Top? The only transports affected thus far are assigned to the HHC. Our combat readiness is still intact, yes?"

"The game being played here is decided at the higher levels."

"Higher, like Division?"

"Higher, a lot higher," replied the Top Sergeant, "and the building they live in has five sides to it."

"No way," I said.

"The promotion list is out for full Colonel. Brogan is on it. If the alert was held tomorrow our company would fail to field the necessary percentage of working vehicles and our battalion commander would ultimately take the hit."

"So, you think our new CO was sent here to block Brogan's promotion?"

Top shrugged his shoulders. "Maybe, maybe not. More than likely, Janzen was sent to this assignment by those who expected him to act because they knew of his prior behavior."

"What type of prior behavior?"

"I called a buddy of mine at Knox. It seems Janzen pulled this same stunt in a line company, as a second lieutenant, on his very first assignment after graduating. The company commander found out and put a stop to it. His next assignment was -- you'll never guess where."

"To the Pentagon," I answered.

"Yes, and more than likely it's the WPPA that got him the assignment," said Top.

"Could you repeat that?"

"The WPPA: The West Point Protective Association. Janzen was promoted and assigned here by someone who knew full well he would launch the same failed set of policy procedures that got interrupted at Knox."

"Well, First Sergeant, I would like to hear your advice on how to fix this. I have several ideas, but none of them are for the faint of heart."

1ST/48TH INF HHC
ZERO HOUR PLUS THREE
MESS HALL
0455 HOURS FRIDAY 24 JANUARY 1970

Steam rose from the mugs of coffee sitting on the table in front of the six NCOs seated at the rear of the room. The First Sergeant had called all four of them the night before and asked three of them to be there before 0500 this morning. The fourth was simply notified of the meeting and had opted to attend.

"What in the hell is a forty-eight hour full court press[254], Fontain?" asked Command Sergeant Major Bost.

"The line company vehicles are in pretty good shape. Ours, the HHC vehicles, are not. My suggestion is that a pre-readiness alert inspection be ordered for today at 0800 hours."

"Just how you came up with this idea is probably a fascinating story," said Jacobs, who was in charge of the motor pool. "Not to

---

[254] A full court press is a basketball term for a defensive style which takes a great deal of effort, but can be extremely effective.

burst your bubble, but Division has issued a moratorium on the distribution of repair parts."

"Yeah, Blubaugh showed me the TWX last night. Sergeant Ralston has agreed to help us out by making the 1st/33rd spare parts inventory available to us. Isn't that right, Sergeant?" I asked. He nodded "Yes".

"The engine and the two APC transmissions you said you'll give us will allow us to get three APCs back to full combat status," I continued.

"Now wait one goddamn minute," said Summering. Staff Sergeant Malcolm Summering was our S-4 NCO. "We waited three months for those parts to be delivered. The vehicles they were intended for need those parts."

"True, but at the moment all three of ours are still operational, and both Battalions need to be ready to travel intact by week's end. Sergeant Major Bost, your call, but there are nineteen out of forty seven HHC service vehicles without road certification. We don't need one hundred percent but we can't have more than four out of service" I explained.

"Unless the 1st/33rd has the largest spare parts locker in history there isn't any way to fix nineteen plus vehicles," stated Bost.

"That's true, Sergeant Major, but we don't need to fix all nineteen. Let me tell you my idea to get us off the dime."

1ST/48TH INF BRAVO
ORDERLY ROOM
0845 HOURS FRIDAY 24 JANUARY 1970

SPC4 Glen Towson, camera guy, was standing out in front of Bravo Company's Orderly Room when we pulled up. A jeep with the bumper marking 1/48 INF B-36, which earlier this morning had the bumper marking 1/48 INF HHC 61, exactly matched the vehicle parked directly in front of it.

"Hey Glen, long time no see. You remember Jack Swanson? Is your First Sergeant in his office?"

"Yeah, he walked in a few minutes ago. Hi Jack, how's it going?"

"So far so good," replied Jack with his best announcer voice. "But the day is young."

"Thanks for meeting me, Glen. I'm going in to make my

manners. Keep an eye out for Ken and Larry will you? They should be here any minute now. They will swap their vehicles for those two vehicles," I said and pointed to the two jeeps parked down at the end of the service road.

"Sure thing," replied Glen.

Ken, Larry, and Jack had gotten back from Denver LOD[255] the previous evening around 2000 hours. Von was due in this morning. The S-4 Lieutenant, whom he had been driving around in Hohenfels, would have a de-briefing with the Battalion EXEC in Hanau that very morning. I went into the Orderly Room. It was virtually identical to that of the HHC.

"Good morning, First Sergeant. I need to ask you another favor. We need some assistance with our vehicle dilemma."

"The scuttlebutt is that the HHC has really got itself in a bind," he said.

"Oh, good grief. I think this isn't going to go as well as I was led to believe it would," I thought.

"Yep, we sure are. If there was any other way to get ready for this alert, I...."

"Relax, Sergeant. You're somewhat of a celebrity with my guys around here. We'll be glad to help out."

"You have made my day, First Sergeant," I said with some relief. "The three jeeps we're dropping off need to be recertified for trip ticket status. If the drivers of the ones we're trading with will run the checklist on them, get the trip tickets issued, and call us when they're ready to be swapped back, we will be most grateful".

"You got it. Everyone understands what's at stake here."

"Thanks," I said. "Can I expect the same cooperation all the way up the hill, First Sergeant?"

"You can, and if you don't get it, you call me," said the Top Sergeant of Bravo Company.

---

255   Denver - NATO blocking position located in the Fulda Gap.

1ST/48TH INF HHC
REDEYE TEAM ROOM
1345 HOURS FRIDAY 24 JANUARY 1970

I had returned from my last kidnap swap with Charlie Company. The HHC vehicles selected for the *witness protection and certification program* were all in position.

Seated around the table in the team room was the complete NCO cadre of RedEye. "Thanks for doing the templates," I said. "It made the transition go really smoothly."

"You're welcome, but we charge $1.00 a stencil. So you owe us $48.00."

"How much if I just have you sent back to NATO guard duty?"

"Forget it, no charge," everyone said at almost the same time.

"You may wish you were back in Denver after this weekend. By Monday morning we need three of the remaining nine vehicles to be certified for trip tickets."

"Why only three?" asked Larry.

"Two of our five assigned vehicles lost certification over minor infractions. They were cleared this morning. That's the good news, gentleman. The bad news is the headcount that needed to be recertified remains at nineteen.

"Three of the twelve we took up the hill have already been given trip ticket status. We hope by Monday to be ready to take the Battalion down south with 97% of our equipment combat ready.

"Ken, you and Jack position an overwatch in the motor pool and coordinate between the line companies and the HHC maintenance people. Work on the ones that have the best chance of being readied with the parts we have available."

"Who has the list?" asked Jack.

"Spec4 Gordon," I said.

"It is a short[256] list. So, Von and Larry, I want you to coordinate with the S-4 to make sure the engine and the two transmissions get delivered to the 1st/33rd. Joe Gordon has also made a list of the parts we need. See Staff Sergeant Ralston and cross reference what we

---

[256] A short list denotes missing working items and features necessary to receive road certification and trip ticket status.

can liberate from their inventory. Sometime on Sunday afternoon we'll make a decision as to which vehicles can be cannibalized to get the maximum remaining downed vehicles roadworthy."

Spec4 Joe Gordon was one of our more gifted mechanics. His abilities ranked right up there with Robert Fulton and Henry Ford.

"Gentleman, for unspoken and not so obvious reasons, there will be no interaction with our officer cadre. If you are approached by an officer and solicited for information about this weekend's exercise, you will refer them to me. That stays in effect until Monday morning at 0600 hundred hours. Are there any questions?" There were a few questions and zero complaints about having to work the weekend.

SPEC5 CARL BLUBAUGH AND CSM DAVID BOST
1ST/48TH INF
BATALLION S-3
1520 HOURS FRIDAY 24 JANUARY 1970

Seated at his desk pondering when the MPs from 3rd Armor would show up, Spec5 Carl Blubaugh placed the last MSR—88 form[257] in his typewriter. Before he pressed the first key, he analyzed his remaining strength. He didn't think he was going to have enough oomph to walk across the street to get some chow. He had just finished reallocating seventy-nine individual vehicle records and four complete inventories for each of the Battalion's Company record jackets.

"Blubaugh, you look really tired," said a smiling Command Sergeant Major Bost.

"Yes, Sergeant Major, I was jerked out of bed at 0300 by an insane man on a mission from God."

"God didn't send us Sergeant Fontain. It was the devil himself, the mysterious Major Carlstrum," said the CSM.

"His real name is Bill Douglas and we may owe him a great deal if this operation succeeds," said Blubaugh.

"You're not permitted to say that name out loud," replied Bost.

"Whoever it was, someone was really watching over us. It was a real education watching Fontain go through our 88s. It only took him

---

257   Vehicle Maintenance Status Record

an hour and a half to discern the bad from the good. He then generated a matrix of the bad that could be good, and the sequence best used to get it done in forty-eight hours. Then he took twelve of the nineteen HHC's failed jeeps and trucks and drew up a mini OP order to re-stencil, reassign, and swap a predetermined line company vehicle. He did all of that just in case the alert was called in the middle of all this."

"Let's keep all of these unusual maintenance housekeeping procedures just between you and me," said CSM Bost.

"That'll be no problem, Boss. I'm not sure I believe what I've seen and heard in the last twelve hours anyway."

"Go get something to eat Carl, and then take a nap. Get with Fontain later this evening and see if he needs anything. I don't want the Colonel or any of the other officers entangled in this. Call me and let me know how it's going."

"Yes, Command Sergeant Major," replied Carl. "Rick said that when Sunday evening comes along we can put all of the records back the way they were."

1ST/48TH INF
HOUR 58.75 COMPLETE
MOTOR POOL TRACK BAY#3
2245 HOURS SUNDAY 25 JANUARY 1970

Track bay number three was on the extreme right side of the maintenance building. Each bay had its own set of rolling door panels that offered some relief from the outside elements. There was a three and a half foot wide trench stretching fifteen feet to the rear of bay, with a set of concrete steps providing easy access.

An APC with markings showing ownership by 1/48 INF B-107 was resting comfortably with its tracks straddling each side of the pit. The engine compartment was wide open, and two pairs of hands were struggling to position one of the newly replaced 48-volt batteries back into its retaining bracket -- a feat that was easier said than done.

"The son of a bitch came out of there, Joe. Why in the hell are we having so much trouble getting it back in?" I grumbled.

"Besides the fact that I've lost the feeling in most of my fingertips, and we are the only two assholes left in the park, I haven't the foggiest fucking idea, Sergeant," said Joe Gordon, mechanic extraordinaire of the 1st/48th HHC.

I heard the footsteps first, but I couldn't turn my head far enough around to see who had entered the bay. "Such language gentleman," said the owner of the footsteps. "Maybe you should get some better mechanics down here to fix this vehicle."

Not letting go of the back of the precariously balanced battery bracket, Joe said, "Why don't you get your fat ass in here if you think you can do any better?"

"Ah, Joe, I wouldn't be making that kind of demand. That voice sounds very similar to our beloved battalion commander," I said. "He prefers to be called '*old lead bottom*'."

Twenty minutes later the APC was completely healed. Specialist4 Joe Gordon, Lieutenant Colonel Brogan and I were seated around a desk in a semi-circle with our hands wrapped around various size mugs of piping hot coffee. All three of us were staring silently through the window of the Maintenance NCOs office looking down through the track park.

"Sergeant Gordon, when you get the feeling back in those fingers of yours, why don't you get a shower and something to eat. I understand Sergeant Thomas has kept the Mess Hall open until 2400 hundred hours," said the LTC.

"Yes, Sir, but I'm only an E4, Sir," replied Joe.

"Not anymore. Goodnight Sergeant. I thank you for all your efforts today."

"Thank you, Sir, Rick!" Joe exclaimed as he made his way to the door.

"That should be a happy walk back up the hill for him, Sir."

"You want to go get a drink somewhere?" asked Brogan.

I was a little worried, though. All of the vehicle records should have been put back to their original assignments by this point; the methods and procedures utilized in the full court press would cause concern if examined.

"I haven't been to confession in a very long time, Sir," I said, not a little sheepishly. "I'm not sure the Colonel wants to know the extent of all of my sins against man and machine."

"Oh, but the Colonel does want to know. Your creativity will make an interesting chapter in my memoirs of this time in service."

PHONE CALL:
LTC TOM BROGAN AND GENERAL GERALD BUSHMAN
1ST/48TH INF
BATTALION COMMANDERS OFFICE
0740 HOURS WEDNESDAY 28 JANUARY 1970

The office was of good size, located in the corner of the building with a southern exposure overlooking the pond. It was modestly furnished with a large desk that was well organized with everything a commander needed to do his job. The phone rang as Lieutenant Colonel Brogan entered his office and was rounding his desk. He plucked the phone from its cradle on his way to his overstuffed leather desk chair.

"This is Colonel Brogan. Oh, Hello Gerald, you must be keeping some late hours? What can I do for the DDCI?" Brogan listened for almost a full minute. "Interesting, but thanks again to our mutual acquaintance, everything here is shipshape. We are officially combat ready as of 0800 hundred hours on the 26th."

He listened again and finished the conversation by saying, "Thanks for calling, General. I'll pass your message to him as soon as I hang up."

General Bushman, instead of his usual hang-up at the end of a telephone conversation, said, "Blood and Guts, Colonel." This, of course, was the required salutation of anyone in the 1st and 48th Infantry and all those who respected its members.

The Colonel reached over, depressed the switch hook, and immediately released it. He then dialed extension 8234.

"Carl, call over to the HHC and ask someone to find Staff Sergeant Fontain. Ask him to come see me. If they can't find him ask them to call you back."

"Yes Sir," said Car, but the CO had already hung up.

1ST/48TH INF
BATTALION COMMANDERS OFFICE
0755 HOURS WEDNESDAY 28 JANUARY 1970

I had received a call from Carl Blubaugh, requesting my immediate presence in LTC Brogan's office.

I announced myself, "Sergeant Fontain, reporting to the Battalion Commander as ordered, Sir."

"At ease, Rick, take a seat," said Brogan. "You want a coffee?"

"No thank you, Sir."

"Gerald Bushman just called and fed me an interesting piece of info."

"Yes, Sir. I hope the General is in good health."

"He is, and he asked me to pass along to you that all of your jungle buddies are doing well."

"That is good news, Sir."

"Did you know I was on the promotion list for Colonel?"

"Yes, Sir. Well deserved. Congratulations," I said.

"When did you come by this information? The reason I ask is that I only found out about it on Tuesday."

"Sir, I'm not entirely comfortable answering that question."

"It's a known fact, and I know this because I have been in the Army longer then you have, that First Sergeants have an undeclared telepathy amongst themselves."

"Yes, Sir, that seems to be true in this case as well," I said, confirming my source.

"What General Bushman called to tell me in part was that the people who were conspiring to upset my chances for promotion has been found out and dealt with. Also, he's very certain that your CO, Lieutenant Janzen, wasn't involved."

"Yes, Sir. It looks like someone was using the Lieutenant's previous behavior at Knox to cause us a problem."

"That information is disturbing. I cannot tolerate one of my officers being investigated behind his back."

"Sir, there was no investigation. There was someone at Knox who offered the information to us because he had served in the same unit as our CO."

"Our CO?" inquired the LTC, "Do you still plan on being loyal to the man after all he has done?"

"Sir, as I understand it, the role of a commanding officer is to command. Although misguided, I believe his policies were not done to harm us, but were his best approach to make the HHC successful."

"Hmm" was the sound from the LTC. "You believe that?" He continued, "Well, he's already been counseled by a senior officer, and will henceforth gain a better understanding of how to run an HHC," said the LTC.

"That's good news, Sir," I said. "And Sir, I would agree that listening and talking to one's field first before issuing orders is good advice."

"Is there nothing private on this base, Sergeant?"

"Sir, he had employed the same policies at Knox as he was in the process of implementing here. My guess is someone in the Pentagon found out about his beliefs and got him sent here hoping he would use the same processes."

"All is well that ends well even if it kills the patient?" mused the LTC. He continued, "The Battalion was placed on full combat readiness status as of 26 January."

"Well, Sir, that is really good news," I replied. "Thanks for passing the info about the Majors MacKennia and Carlstrum. I'll let you get back to work." I stood and asked, "With your permission, Sir."

"Sit down, Rick," said Full Colonel-Designate Thomas Brogan. "I want to talk to you about your CIB. And more importantly, about you getting, how did the General put it? 'Dinged' in Southeast Asia."

"Well, Sir, there really isn't much to tell. One of the crew chiefs got a tummy ache and I raised my hand to take his place on the mission."

"MacKennia swore to me you were not going to be put in harm's way. He sat right there where you are now and promised me."

"Well, that probably explains why he got so mad at me after I got back, Sir."

"You mean from the hospital, don't you?"

"Well, yes, Sir. Since I've been in the Army, I seem to spend a considerable amount of time in Army hospitals."

"Except in this case it was a Navy hospital," corrected the Colonel.

"Sir, Colonel Simons had me taken aboard the *Coral Sea*[258] and then got me a ride back to base three days later."

"Bull Simons is who you're talking about?"

"Yes, Sir, I believe I heard him being addressed by that name."

"Well, you certainly have led a full life during your time with us,

---

[258] USS Coral Sea, a Midway-class aircraft carrier, was the third ship of the United States Navy to be named for the Battle of the Coral Sea. She earned the affectionate nickname "Ageless Warrior" through her long career. She was classified as an aircraft carrier with hull classification symbol CV-43.

haven't you?"

I was silent. I didn't have the words to respond.

"Nothing to say? Cat got your tongue?"

"Sir, what George, Captain MacKennia, is doing is very important. He wasn't in camp when I took the flight. The second LZ we dropped into was hot. If I hadn't jumped out of that chopper, they would have had to leave that man there. I couldn't let that happen, Sir."

"Christ, Rick. You were shot."

"Yes, Sir. Everybody on board that day, except the pilot, got shot at least once, some of the guys two or three times."

Brogan pushed back in his chair and was silent for a moment.

"Blood and Guts, Sergeant. You are dismissed."

"Yes, Sir. Thank you, Sir," I said, and turned to leave.

"Rick." I turned back toward the desk. "Thanks for saving that man."

"He didn't make it, Sir, but at least he got to go home to his family."

1ST/48TH INF HHC
ARMORY
1040 HOURS WEDNESDAY 28 JANUARY 1970

The sidearm locker contained a large selection of the M1911 45 caliber pistols. There were several personal weapons that were stored here also. A Mauser C96 termed "Broom handle belonged to Ernie Bumpus. Several 38 S&M[259] revolvers with different barrel lengths and a German Luger were owned by Staff Sergeant Kirtwin who ran the Arms Room.

I had just finished cleaning my assigned weapon and was returning it to the locker when I heard someone come through the main entrance. Sergeant Kirtwin had gone to drop off two recently tweaked M14s to Bravo's Arms Room.

"Sergeant Fontain," called 1st Lieutenant Janzen.

"Yes, Sir. I'm over here."

"I would like a moment of your time," he said.

---

[259] Smith & Wesson

"Of course, Sir. Is here okay, or should we go elsewhere?"

"Are we alone?"

"Yes, we are," I replied.

"Here's fine."

"First Sergeant Bumpus told me I have you to thank for getting our vehicles back on road status."

"Sir, the entire Battalion pitched in to make that happen."

"The Colonel communicated to me to get it together or find another home. He also expressed concern about my leadership abilities."

"I'm not sure what I'm supposed to say to that, Sir."

"Perhaps what I need to do is start over. Sergeant Fontain, welcome back from your TDY assignment. I'm First Lieutenant W. P. Janzen," he said and stuck out his hand. "You'll notice I've started to make better use of abbreviations."

"Yes, Sir. Glad to meet you, Sir," I said.

"Because I've gotten off on the wrong foot with just about everybody here, I've decided to request a transfer."

"Sir, I wouldn't recommend that at all, especially if you're expecting to make a career out of this life."

"Have you decided to stay in Sergeant?" he asked.

"No, Sir. I'm getting out in April. I was drafted twenty months ago."

"You made Staff Sergeant in twenty months?"

"Actually, it has only been in the last five months that my superman-like abilities have been recognized," I said with a grin. "Seriously Sir, I would not recommend that course of action. Sir, may I offer a suggestion?"

"You may."

"You went to West Point, right?"

"I did. How did you know that?"

"Lucky guess or maybe it was your ring. My gut tells me that the Academy is big on teaching policy and procedure for use in commanding everything from the squad right up through the Division levels."

"I get the feeling you know more than just the gist of my meeting with the Colonel."

"I do. Your transfer from the line company at Knox to the Pentagon may have set you up for failure on this assignment."

"How do you know all of this?"

"Sir, it is a very long but worthwhile story. Sergeant Kirtwin will be back in a few minutes. Why don't you and I take a ride?"

"OK," replied Janzen.

"Give me a minute to lock up and I'll meet you out by my car. It's the Porsche camouflaged as a '56 Volkswagen," I said.

DOWNTOWN GELNHAUSEN
DAS GASTHAUS "ZWANZIG UND AUS"
0045 HOURS WEDNESDAY 28 JANUARY 1970

"Guten Tag, Herr Hansen," I said, as we walked into the Gasthaus "Zwanzig und Daraus."

"How is the grandson doing?" I asked the rugged looking ex-NCO keeping busy behind the bar.

"Very well, Sergeant Rick. Thanks for asking. What can I get for you?"

"You got any coffee made? If so, how about two cups at the table over there," I pointed toward the rear of the room.

"You got it." Janzen and I took a seat in the back of the room.

Herr Hansen brought the coffee immediately. "Here you go. I just made it. Can I get you anything else?"

"No, this is good for the moment. This is Lieutenant Janzen, my CO."

"I'm very glad to meet you, Sir. Let me know if you need a refill. And, before I forget," he said to me, "I wanted to thank you for telling your guys about this place. We really appreciate the business."

"Nothing I did. They talk about coming down here all the time. You got a winner here, Jimmy." Hanson thanked me again and returned to what he had been doing behind the bar.

"Is there any part of your day that you keep for yourself, Sergeant?" asked Janzen.

"Please call me Rick, Lieutenant. I try to set aside at least an hour every night to cry myself to sleep, Sir."

"Well, Rick, it has been strongly suggested that I apologize for our first meeting."

"None needed nor expected, Sir. But you could shed some light on why you were so pissed at me when I came back from TDY."

"There was another Lieutenant. One who reported in at the same time I did."

379

"You're talking about the S-4 Lieutenant?"

"Affirmative, how did you know that?"

"Begging your pardon, Sir, never mind that now. Sir, please continue. What about the LT, Sir?"

"What's LT? Oh, you mean the lieutenant, right?"

"Right."

"Anyway, he told me that you were off partying with some of the chopper pilots in Hanau. He said they had arranged it with your former CO before he left."

"Interesting, did he say who he got that idea from?"

"No, but he said his source was some buddy of his stationed in the Pentagon."

"Ah," I said. "Well, listen to this and maybe you'll feel a little less trusting of your buddy's INTEL."

It took me over fifteen minutes to outline what I knew.

"So you see, once the Top NCO found out Brogan was on the promotion list, it looked like what you were doing, specifically the driverless vehicle program, was an intentional act to hurt the Colonel's chances for advancement."

"I can quote you chapter and verse that a centralized equipment approach in a HHC increases its efficiency by 20 percent."

"Well, Sir, configuring an HHC that way may work stateside. Now I'm just an E-6 civilian at heart, so you can take what I think with a grain of salt, but what you tried to implement for our HHC would only work if we were in a peacetime setting, had a complete inventory of fairly new vehicles, and a fully staffed Battalion. The 1st/48th is 24 percent undermanned, and our motor pool is working on equipment that is well over ten years old. The availability of parts is OK at times, but the usage requirements mandate constant TLC."

"What's TLC?"

"Well, Sir, when you take the driver away from vehicles, living under these circumstances, the equipment will stop working in a short period of time. TLC stands for tender loving care."

"Jesus, I really got played, didn't I?"

"Sir, these old soldiers are completely loyal to their officers, all of their officers. They don't have to like you, but they do need to be able to trust you not to get them killed. What you did made them not trust you. And, by the way, this isn't a peacetime assignment. What we do here is damned dangerous."

"Christ, what a mess," replied the Lieutenant. "I feel like such an ass."

"It's not your fault entirely. We had just come off a fully involved field exercise just before you reported in. However, an important question to ask yourself is why you didn't ask First Sergeant Bumpus for the lay of the land when you reported in. Once you come to terms with that one issue, everything else will fall into place for you."

"OK, you're right. That makes sense. But how can I gain back the Colonel's trust?"

"Short answer is you never lost it. As a matter of fact, the Colonel didn't even know about the list until yesterday. And for your information, regarding our commander, it wouldn't have mattered if he did."

"How do I get back in everyone's good graces?"

"Become a team player. The Colonel knows what happened. He doesn't blame you. Have you met the EXEC?"

"Yes, an introduction was made when I reported in."

"With your permission, Sir, a re-introduction is warranted."

XX

A FOND FAREWELL

NATO ALERT AD-0202703
MAIN GATE COLEMAN KASERNE
0504 HOURS
MONDAY 02 FEBRUARY 1970

Figure 40
Track Park Alert - 1969

The alert notification had come at 0435 eleven days after what had become known as the "Miracle on 1st/48th Street"[260]. Our Headquarters and Headquarters Company had followed Bravo Company out of Coleman at 0504. All of our vehicles had made the trip with the exception of two. These were being held out of service for capital component repair items, which meant they would probably be written off as junk.

The 1st/48th Bravo and HHC were the lead groups and the first to park at the assembly point on that morning. Rally Group Area (RGA) 34B was an oval-shaped meadow surrounded by woods on three sides. Across from where we were parked were the combined combat support elements of the 1st/33rd Alpha and Charlie companies. They had arrived on scene twenty-two minutes after us.

---

[260] "Miracle on 34th Street" is a 1947 Christmas film written and directed by George Seaton and based on a story by Valentine Davies.

That morning, Alpha and Charlie Companies had been entrusted with both the moral and spiritual guidance of the 2nd/6th Artillery and 123rd/ Ordnance combat teams. RE-3 was embedded with them for the duration of this readiness exercise, an alert courtesy extended by the management of the 1st/48th Infantry Battalion.

Only eleven of the sixteen M110s, 69 percent, made it out of the gate that morning. The M110s were having major engine and transmission difficulties. This had been the main reason most of the 2nd/6th Artillery's vehicles had not participated in Operation *Sparrow Hawk*.

Figure 41
Nicknamed Bad News

A Howitzer toting a 155-millimeter tube makes a big difference in the mindset of an approaching enemy. The Colonel had emphasized on more than one occasion the importance of self-propelled artillery.

When I had been scrounging vehicle parts the previous weekend I had made the acquaintance of Master Sergeant Thomas of the 123nd/Ordnance Combat Support Group. He told me about their maintenance dilemma of the 2nd/6th Artillery.

The previous week, five track mechanics from 1st/33rd, courtesy of LTC Peck, Commanding 1st/33rd, and a phone call to 3rd Armor Division Maintenance from our own CSM Bost, had resulted in both men and parts being sent to the 2nd/6th Artillery's maintenance sergeant. Their efforts added four additional M110s to the morning's alert.

The Howitzers had a really neat nickname: "Bad News". The radio chatter in Grafenwohr requesting to give the "Bad News" to whoever needed it was usually followed by a specified set of map coordinates.

"Well named," I thought. One look at this weapon system and you just knew more was better.

The morning's rally point would be used to realign and reshape the convoys that would be going south. Had this been an actual alert condition, the exit from Coleman would have been conducted in a 'first ready, first to leave situation'. Because of the recent field exercises, another large expenditure of fuel would be a major factor in the decision to extend our convoys south. Engines were shut down while we waited for orders to proceed or terminate.

Remarkably, the entire mass exodus from Coleman only took

fifty-four minutes. The 1st/48th cleared post in the first twenty-nine minutes of the notification. If Brogan had suspected that our equipment had been preloaded and combat-stacked he would be providing that observation at the after-action briefing.

The next morning at 0800, the German military, in conjunction with the Polizei (German police) and local governments in the surrounding 400 square mile area, including Gelnhausen, would conduct the recently re-activated IAWS[261].

Pamphlets had been distributed throughout the previous month describing what to do if the air raid type siren was sounded. The next day's exercise had been advertised as a test. However, it was hoped that when an evacuation procedure was called, the possibility of impending Russian citizenship would result in a mass exodus. Disintegration was not mentioned in the brochure.

RedEye Jeep Number One (RE-1) was the ninth vehicle in line.

"Fred, shut down the engine. Wait here while I go up front. Run a check with all the REs and let me know if there are any problems."

"Roger that," he said and reached around to pick up the mike for our battalion COMMs. I heard him say as I left the jeep, "Sparrows two through five, this is Sparrow one/one, radio check, over."

I found Janzen and First Sergeant Bumpus standing next to their vehicles, which were the third and fourth in the lineup. "Blood and Guts, Sir, Top," I said as I saluted. "Did everybody make it out OK this morning?"

"Everybody did," said Top with a touch of pride in his voice. "It remains to be seen whether the Colonel will be pleased or show up here breathing fire."

"Why would he be upset about this morning's exodus?" asked Janzen.

"Sir, in spite of realizing that we may have set a new world record for alert response, he may be slightly concerned with how we gleaned our intelligence."

"Oh, no," said Janzen.

"This will turn out to be another career-ending situation exemplifying the frying pan into the fire scenario," offered Top.

"I'm sure glad you're on our side, Sergeant," replied Janzen.

"Me, too, Sir. I don't speak very much Russian," I said.

"Heads up," said Bumpus. The EXEC drove up next to where we were standing. We all saluted as we turned to face Major Hamadan's

---

261 Invasion Alert Warning System

jeep.

"Blood and Guts, everyone," said the Major, but he remained in the jeep. "We're still on hold. The Colonel asked me to find you, Lieutenant, and you, Sergeant Fontain. I'm to direct you to these coordinates," he said, handing a clipboard to Janzen. "If you want, we can all ride over in my jeep," said the Major. "It looks to be about five clicks from here, as the crow flies."

"Very good, Sir. Let me go tell my driver where I'm going. Top, will you look after Fred and see that he gets to where he needs to be?"

"No problem. Take off," said Top.

NATO ALERT AD-0202703
16.5 CLICKS S. OF BAD ORB
0650 HOURS MONDAY 02 FEBURARY 1970

When I returned to RE-21, Fred told me about a positioning issue with RE-23 that needed my attention. I grabbed the mike. "Sparrow23, Sparrow61. Over," I said and un-keyed the mike.

"Sparrow61, Sparrow231. 235 is on the job. 231 Over."

"Roger that, 231. Call Sparrow61 upon return. Over," I replied.

"Roger that, Sparrow61. This is Sparrow231. Out."

"Fred, hand me the combat stacking list from last night's projected slant report." I sat in the passenger seat to examine the list.

"I can't tell from this what Jack is wrestling with back there." I reached over and picked up the mike, but before I keyed it I said, "Fred, pull out of line and drive up behind the Major's jeep. We're going to follow him to a meeting point with BG66."

"Roger that," replied Fred.

I hopped out and informed them that we would follow in RE-1. Lieutenant Janzen got in the rear seat of BG-5 and I remounted RE-21. We had gone only half a click when the radio came to life.

"Break, Sparrow61. This is Sparrow25. Over."

"Roger, 25. Read you five by five. Over," I said. The spring-corded mike was stretched over my shoulder all the way to the front passenger seat from its mounting on the rear fender well.

"Sparrow6, be advised convoy is being split. Request that Sparrow25 be repositioned to accommodate reconfig. Over," said

Jack Swanson, who was managing Sparrow23.

"Negative. Let's leapfrog Sparrow24 for the coverage. Break-break. Sparrow24, contact 25 for a reposition. Over."

Almost immediately there was a response from Sparrow24.

"Roger that. 6 out," I replied.

"Break, break. Sparrow25, this is Sparrow6. Over."

"Sparrow6, this is 25. Go."

"Sparrow25, you have the rocking chair until further notice. Out."

"Roger. 25 have the chair. Out."

MAJOR DAVID HAMADAN AND LIETENANT WALTER JANZEN
JEEP, EN ROUTE TO BAD ORB
0655 HOURS MONDAY 02 FEBURARY 1970

Major Hamadan, who had been listening to the radio exchange being conducted by the RedEye teams, turned to face the passenger traveling on the rear bench seat.

"You recognize Fontain's voice on that exchange?"

"Yes, Sir, I did. He seems to know what he's doing, doesn't he?" said Janzen.

"Lieutenant, you can listen to radio chatter for your whole career and never bear witness to the voice of a natural born combat commander in action. The Colonel refers to him as the battalion sportscaster." They rode on for a few more minutes in silence.

"Walter, Sergeant Fontain has led me to believe that my support and orientation for you when you reported in was lacking. He also said that your approach to HHC equipment management, without any guidance from management on the lay of the land, was text book."

"Sir...." Lieutenant Walter Janzen started to speak.

"Wait one," said the Major, holding up his hand. "Lieutenant, you and I will start over with a proper introduction and a comprehensive reorientation."

"I appreciate the restart, Sir."

"Blood and Guts, Lieutenant. Welcome to the next revolution" replied the Major.

"Yes, Sir. Thank you, Sir. Blood and Guts."

NATO ALERT AD-0202703
SACHENBACHER FORST
LZ CHARLIE/VICTOR
27.8 CLICKS SOUTH OF GELNHAUSEN
0720 HOURS MONDAY 02 FEBURARY 1970

The coordinates led us into a clearing being used as an LZ. The Colonel was standing by the right side of the closest of three helicopter gunships. He was talking to the pilot through the open window. We pulled our jeeps in behind the motor vehicle with bumper markings showing BG-6.

"David," called Brogan. "A word, if you please."

"Yes, Sir," Major Hamadan replied and walked out toward the silent aircraft. Lieutenant Janzen and I stayed with the vehicles.

The conversation between the two lasted only about a minute. Colonel Brogan waved at the pilot and then both he and Major Hamadan walked back toward us.

"Good morning, Colonel," said Janzen.

"Good morning, Janzen, Rick," replied Brogan as he returned our salutes.

"Lieutenant, you and I are going for a chopper ride down south," said Hamadan to Janzen.

"Rick, you still have a driver's license?" queried Brogan.

"Yes, Sir," I answered.

"Carson, you ride in Fontain's jeep. Sergeant Fontain needs to have his driving skills evaluated."

"Yes, Sir," said Jake, smiling. He was the Colonel's driver and bodyguard, and would keep close behind during the driving test.

"Have a good trip, Gentleman," said Brogan to Hamadan and Janzen. Both saluted.

Spec4 Jerry Wilson was driving BG-Five. "Drop in behind RedEye and stick to the Colonel for the rest of the alert," ordered Hamadan.

"Roger that, Sir," said Wilson.

Hamadan and Janzen then walked briskly to the chopper. The turbine began to whine immediately as they entered the aircraft.

"Jake," I called. He was in the process of getting into the passenger side of RE-1. "You want your weapon?" It was an M3A1, known as the Grease Gun. He had obtained the firearm by trading a

German Luger pistol that he'd won in a poker game to a tank crewman from the 1st/33rd.

"You know how nervous the Colonel gets around loaded weapons," I said in the most solemn tone I could muster.

I leaned across the driver's seat and picked up the weapon and the pouch containing several 30 round magazines which had the same design as the clips used in the British Sten gun.

The Colonel smiled broadly at this exchange. "You think it's safe for us to drive around unarmed, Sergeant?" asked Brogan.

"Sir, besides the 357 Ruger Blackhawk in your concealed shoulder holster, we have this." I unzipped my field jacket and, reaching for the small of my back, pulled my M1911 Colt 45 ACP from its skeleton holster and laid it down between the seats. "We should be able to repel the first fourteen borders. Where do you want to conduct my driving test, Sir?"

"Let's go back to Coleman," said the LTC. He looked at his watch, turned, and picked up the mike cord. "BG Five-five, BG Seven-Seven. Over."

"BG Five-five, Go BG Seven," was the instant reply from CSM Bost.

"BG Five-five, exercise complete, oh seven five zero hours. Start graduated withdraws to home base. Acknowledge. Over."

"Roger BG. Exercise completed 0750. Returning to home base. Blood and Guts. Out," replied the Command Sergeant Major.

"I'm sending Hamadan down to the southernmost rally point to close out the exercise and to put his eyes on the physical features of the area surrounding the RP[262]," Brogan revealed to me.

"Yes, Sir. No one from our group has been down there before?" I asked.

"No, the RP was established just a few weeks ago," said the Colonel.

"We're sure to wind up down there sooner or later," I said.

"What do you mean by that? You know something I don't?"

"No, Sir, I merely meant it seemed like a good idea to physically see the land around the rally point."

"And, what else?" asked Brogan.

"Well, since none of us are going down there today, perhaps I

---

[262] Rally Point

can drive down there next week and take note of any roadway issues between here and there."

"Not necessary. Lieutenant Janzen will volunteer later this morning to do just that."

"Yes, Sir," I said. "That will work."

"David James called me on Tuesday. He said to tell you that your suspicions were correct and that it has been corrected," said Brogan as if starting off any old casual conversation.

"Sir, I'm not sure I understand the message context."

"Come now, Rick. Didn't you ask Jim Pezlola to check out an officer assignment made recently to us in order to verify if said assignment had anything to do with the recently announced promotion list? A list of those eligible to receive a silver chicken?" asked Brogan.

"You're speaking about the new S-4 Lieutenant, Sir? Sir, I spoke to Lieutenant Pezlola about the recent situation facing the 1st/48th's combat readiness status. A subsequent conversation with my CO made me curious."

"Curious in what way?" asked Brogan. "And why didn't you come to me with that observation?"

I described to the Colonel what I had discussed with Captain Pezlola. "Sir, the equipment situation was the immediate concern. I also asked him if he thought it possible for the assignment system to be manipulated."

"You lost me. How do you connect the dots between recent officer assignments to our HHC to a critical vehicle maintenance issue?"

"I didn't at first, Sir, but Pezlola said it would be interesting to find out if this particular problem had occurred before."

"And, had it?"

"Yes, Sir. It sure had. A serving 2nd Lieutenant at Benning, a recent graduate from the Point, was implementing the same approach, but on a much smaller scale, obviously. The remarks entered into his efficiency report were, and I'll paraphrase, 'Vehicle maintenance policies that were implemented to bolster efficiency did not work. In fact they were counterproductive.' The policy was canned for equipment availability issues by his commanding officer. The cross reference of the assignment led to a certain group in the Pentagon."

"So, why didn't you just have him terminated?" Brogan paused for a second and quickly added, "Strike that. I was trying to put a little levity into all of this, but I forgot who your friends work for." I acted like I didn't understand what he meant and continued.

"Sir, there were six other occurrences of similar policy implementation over the last two years."

"So, what's your point?"

"One occurred in a unit where a full bird was to be selected for BG[263], two more units had LTCs selected for promotion, and there was one unit that had a Major on the list for LTC. All units had been sent recent graduates who embraced the same centralized pooling policy doctrine."

"That's pretty thin," replied the LTC.

"Yes, Sir. We weren't able to connect the dots at that point. Sir, I wanted to have a conversation with our Lieutenant Janzen before any of this went any further."

"And did you have a talk with the Lieutenant?"

"I asked the EXEC to set up a meeting. The Lieutenant and I had a good long talk. It turns out what he was attempting to implement here and at Knox is still being taught at the Point."

"No way," replied Brogan. "We are talking about West Point?"

"Yes. Specifically, it is presently part of the curriculum being taught by the Department of Behavioral Sciences and Leadership. The course in question is designated as CE490, Infrastructure Analysis and Protection. I think the TWX said it was either Chapter 20 or 22 that describes in detail the most efficient policy approaches for managing equipment in the Company environment."

"You're pulling my leg," said the LTC.

"Unfortunately, whoever designed the course assumed 100 percent staffing, all new equipment right off the factory floor, and a company being operated in a peacetime environment."

"Textbook application!" replied Brogan.

"Pezlola told me that General Bushman asked the CID to conduct a look-see inside the Pentagon. A certain Major General was found to be responsible for several influenced assignments."

"Influenced?" asked the LTC.

"Contrived is a better word," I said. "Stacking the deck is even more accurate. Once the promotion list for full bird was configured, certain assignments were manufactured. It was quite a complex operation, requiring a rather complex intelligence gathering

---

[263] Brigadier General

mechanism." We rode in silence for almost a full minute.

"Apparently this procedure had been run successfully in the past," I continued. "Our own LT Janzen was the one who was meant to affect us, but...."

"But your First Sergeant found out about the policy thwarted at Knox and the rest, as they say, is history," said Brogan.

"Yes, Sir," I replied. "Except for the fact the CID discovered a file folder with a copy of a term paper that was written by Walter in his senior year at the Point. The title was *Centralized Vehicle Management in the HHC Environment.*"

"I'll be damned," said the Colonel.

"Yes, Sir. That's probably true for most of us. Lieutenant Janzen will make a fine officer and a solid addition to our merry band of warriors."

NATO ALERT AD-0202703
6.4KM SOUTH OF GELNHAUSEN
0840 HOURS MONDAY 02 FEBURARY 1970

The Colonel rode on in silence for a few miles. "There's something else you should know before we get back to Coleman, Rick. Division is sending us ten RedEye trained Spec4s, one Staff Sergeant, and a 1st Lieutenant."

"That's great news, isn't it, Sir?"

"You know, Rick, it's been my experience that when manna drops from heaven it is anything but a godsend."

"Yes, Sir," I answered, not fully understanding the comment.

"The first RedEye allocation directive came in October of '68 -- unsolicited, by the way. I found out through a friend of mine in Division that the request was made by the CIA. David James confirmed the assignment in March of last year."

"That's about the same time I finished the RedEye training. Bill Douglas told me I was selected for assignment from one of the tests I took at Fort Bragg, Sir."

"He admitted to me the same set of facts right before we executed *Sparrow Hawk*. It didn't occur to me until right now that your assignment here had very little to do with RedEye."

"Sir, I'm not following you."

"The original plan was for you to attend OCS. Apparently, you had a change of heart. However, the wheels of progress had already turned. The FBI had already completed your background check and the rest was played by ear."

"Bill Douglas's list of things he wants to do before he dies would be an interesting read, Sir."

"That would be the understatement of the year, Sergeant. Your service here in the Battalion has been exemplary. We, I, owe you a personal thanks for your dedication to your duties here."

"No, Sir. It is I who owe you. Being allowed to participate here has been the best set of experiences I've ever had."

"If I had my way I would offer to put bars on your collar and send you to back to school for completion of your degree. You're one of those rare individuals who have a natural ability to command men. Unfortunately I have been told not to interfere with you ending your service in April. And that, as they say, Sergeant, is a damn shame," said Lieutenant Colonel Thomas Brogan.

"Sir, I don't know how to respond to that. I do know that it was you who gave me the opportunity to contribute here. There is no doubt my military experience would have been quite different if it were not for your leadership."

"I'll say this, Rick, I can't pressure you to stay in, but you certainly are welcome to continue on."

"Thank you again, Sir, for your confidence. I've already been told that the next evolution in my service will best be fulfilled as a civilian."

"Understood, but I would have been remiss if I didn't thank you personally and make it known that you are more than welcome to stay."

"Yes, Sir. Thank you," I said. But in that same instant I already knew my decision. I would select the more dangerous of the two.

"Your immediate assignment, when we get back to Coleman, will be to transition this new RedEye group into your existing teams," said Brogan.

"Yes, Sir," I said. The conversation on my future was now closed. "These additional personnel may be a blessing in disguise."

"How so?" asked Brogan.

"Sir, it was proven in the operation at *OP Alpha* and again during *Sparrow Hawk* that the fire teams functioned more efficiently when assigned a third person."

"You know Rick, out of all of the people who I've served with, you are without a doubt the most, and I'm searching for the right word, *centered*. Yes, *centered*, I think describes you very well."

BATTALION HQ
3RD FLOOR—ROOM 307
NCOIC PROCESSES & SCHEDULING
0640 HOURS THURSDAY 12 MARCH 1970

Command Sergeant Major Bost entered the small windowless office on the third floor carrying two mugs. He slid into the chair placed beside the small table pushed up against the far wall. He placed one of the steaming mugs of coffee onto the desk, within my reach.

"You're here nice and early this morning, Fontain."

"Good morning, Boss. Thanks for the coffee. You're a lifesaver. Lieutenant Berkline and Staff Sergeant Covel asked me to check their route plan this morning before they left for Hohenfels."

"And, was everything copasetic?" asked Bost.

"Everything looked good. I told Boyd to keep an eye out."

"How is the new management getting along over there?"

"They seem to be adjusting well, Sergeant Major."

"Then the reports of mass suicides are ill founded," said the CSM.

"We'll see. I'll touch base again when they return," I said, and chuckled.

"Good, you do that. You have a nice day, Rick," said Bost.

I walked out of my office and down the hall. Carl Blubaugh stepped out in the corridor just as I was about to enter the stairwell.

"Hey, guy, I got your note. I was just coming down to see you," I said.

"Here you go," he said and thrust a half-inch thick stack of mimeographed papers into my hands. Bernie Costa killed an entire tree preparing this for you."

"What's all this?"

"That, my friend, is your ticket home."

"Already? I still have about six weeks left, or so I thought."

"Not anymore, Sergeant. You are scheduled on a MAC flight out of Rhein-Main on the second of April."

"Well I'll be. I didn't think it would come so soon. And, I didn't figure it would feel like this."

"Feel like what?"

"You'll think I'm crazy, but I felt a little sad watching them drive off without me this morning."

BATTALION HQ
3RD FLOOR—ROOM 307
STAFF SGT R. FONTAIN - S-3 PROCESSES & SCHEDULING
1640 HOURS FRIDAY 13 MARCH 1970

I was sitting at my desk staring at the telephone. Carl had gotten me the local number and had shown me how to access an outside line. The phones here were connected differently than the ones in the company areas.

I had just returned from the HHC and had received the bad news that no one wanted my car. Go figure. Why no one wanted a hardly restored multi-colored 1956 VW with gazillion miles on the odometer was perplexing. The good news was that Bernie would take back the keys and the responsibility for keeping it safe in the junkyard. I had already given the tools to Joe Gordon for all the work he had done for us during the alert prep.

I picked up the handset and dialed the number from memory. "Guten Tag. Dinieren in Paradies," said the female voice that answered.

"Guten Abend, this is Rick Fontain, I...."

I was cut off mid-sentence, "Hello, Rick. This is Hanna. How are you?"

"Hanna, I'm fine. It's good to hear your voice. You've been well, I hope?"

"Very well, thanks. You must be calling to say goodbye?"

"Well, yes, I mean, it won't be for a few more weeks...."

I was cut off again. "I was hoping to see you before you go, if you have time, I mean."

"Of course, that's why I was calling. I wanted to know if you would like to get together and have dinner somewhere."

"I would like that. Would you like to do it tomorrow night? I don't have to work."

"That would be great. Where should I pick you up?"

RINGSTRABE 3004
63589 LINSENGERICHT
1940 HOURS SATURDAY 14 MARCH 1970

Linsengericht is a municipality only an eight-minute drive to the south of Gelnhausen. Hanna had given very detailed directions to her home. I knew I had heard the name Linsengericht before, but I could not for the life of me remember where. Her street offered parking on both sides. I found a place almost directly in front of her house. I walked up the three steps to the front porch and rang the bell.

Hanna Gresonine Schmidt, 24 years old, reddish brown hair and deep-chestnut colored eyes, stood five feet eight inches tall and weighed only 56 kilos. She and her mother ran the restaurant, 'Dining in Paradise', in Gelnhausen. Max Gresonine, her uncle, owned the hotel located near Nuremburg that Jim Pezlola had been using for CIA surveillance operations.

She had attended the state university at Heidelberg, graduated with honors in Social Economics, spoke four languages, and played piano and violin. She had a fourth degree black belt in one of the unpronounceable martial arts. Widowed at age 23, she had been married to Karl Guntur Schmidt, an agent for the West German organization known as the Bundesnachrichtendienst. This was the German Federal Intelligence Service, the BND as it is sometimes called -- a successor to the Gehlen Organization[264]. Karl had been killed in the line of duty.

"Hello, Hanna," I said as the door was pulled wide open.

"Hello, Rick. Did you have any problem finding the house?"

"No, your directions were perfect," I said and handed her a bouquet of flowers. I had gotten them from a vendor cart at the market that afternoon.

"Why, thank you. They are beautiful. Please come in and let me hang up your coat." I walked a little further down the hallway to a

---

[264] Gehlen Organization or Gehlen Org was an intelligence agency established in June 1946 by U.S. occupation authorities in the United States Zone of Germany, and consisted of former members of the 12th Department of the Army General Staff (Foreign Armies East, or FHO). It carries the name of Reinhardt Gehlen.

closet door Hanna was opening. "Put your coat in here while I put these in some water. Go into the living room and make yourself zu hause," ["at home"], she said as she walked further down the hallway.

"Thanks, I'll do that," I said and waited until she disappeared before removing my 1911 Colt 45 ACP from the small of my back and sticking it into the inside pocket of my leather jacket.

She returned to the living room holding a bottle of Highland Park in one hand and a chilled bottle of Riesling in the other. She was wearing a black pullover sweater with a single strand of pearls, and a short, pleated, cream-colored skirt with matching fleece lined boots.

"Which would you prefer?"

"You choose. All three look wonderful," I said. It took her just a second to realize that she was one of the three desirable choices.

"Scotch over ice, would that be OK?" she cocked her head to one side when she made the suggestion. "Uncle Max buys it by the case for his high end clients in Nuremberg," she said as she retreated back into the kitchen.

I looked around the comfortably furnished room. There were a couple of overstuffed leather chairs and a sofa facing the fireplace. Although it was not as cold outside as it should be for this time of year, the fire felt good. A large number of photographs were hanging on the walls. Smaller ones were on display on the fireplace mantel. I recognized her mother in some of them from having met her at the restaurant. There were several of Hanna and, I supposed, her deceased husband.

"That is Karl, my husband. He was killed last year," she said, walking up behind me with one of the glasses.

"Max told me. I'm sorry," I said.

"We were separated at the time. We were probably too young when we decided to marry."

"How long were you married?"

"Three years. We got engaged when I graduated from the University. His job never really allowed us much of a life together."

"I'm sorry for not calling sooner. I found myself thinking of you quite a bit lately and I didn't want to leave it unsaid any longer."

"Verlassen was unsagte?" ["Leave what unsaid?"] She asked. "Oh, you mean not talking openly, yes."

"Or, as we say in America, beating around the bush," I said. "If I'm being too presumptuous, I apologize."

"Oh please, I'm grateful for your clarity. Did you know I met Dr. Prasonio? I met her when I was visiting Uncle Max in Nuremberg. I'm very sorry," she said as she stepped very close to me.

"A wise man told me recently that life is for the living," I whispered.

I lifted my glass and touched hers, "Guten freunden, die nähere freunde sein wollen." ["To good friends who want to be closer friends."]

She took a sip and stepped up so close that her breasts were pushing ever so lightly into my chest. "Somehow... I knew you would know exactly what to say. Cheers," she whispered, leaning in very slow motion, her lips almost touching my right ear.

RINGSTRABE 3004
63589 LINSENGERICHT
0705 HOURS SUNDAY 15 MARCH 1970

I awoke to the smell of freshly brewed coffee, "Guten Morgen. Schlafen Sie gut ich stoße," ["Good morning. You slept well, I trust,"] she said with a slight smile on her face.

"Wenn Sie unverbindlich Schlafen Ich habe nicht gewusst, dass sie waren unehrlich." ["When you suggested sleep, I didn't know you were being dishonest."]

"Was für tun Sie meinen, Art Herr?" ["Whatever do you mean kind Sir?"] She asked, half laughing.

"I mean, sleep was the last thing on your mind last night. I could have been killed," I said with as much sincerity as I could fake.

"Mein Gott, Ihr schrecklich," ["My God, you're terrible,"] Hanna said while picking up one of the pillows to hit me over the head and giggling the whole time. It was the first time I had seen her really laugh.

COLEMAN KASERNE
1ST/48TH INF HHC
MESS HALL
0605 HOURS THURSDAY 19 MARCH 1970

"How was the field trip, Ken?" I asked as I pulled a chair up to the table, making eye contact with both of my favorite RedEye NCOs.

"We're still alive. Actually, it wasn't all that bad..." said Ken, not making any attempt to hide his disappointment.

"Yeah, we went to exactly the point marked on the map, made camp, played with trainers, and drove back here," said Jack Swanson, also in a not so thrilled sounding voice. Five days in the boonies...."

"Completely uneventful, really," added Ken.

"You sound disappointed. Is everybody playing nicely with each other? I was asked to check on you by the CSM."

"Neither Lieutenant Berkline, nor his assistant, Staff Sergeant Covel, were RedEye-trained at Bliss. The Spec4s, however, are all fresh from the course at Bliss."

"You didn't answer my question. Not being RedEye qualified shouldn't be a problem in the long term."

"The Lieutenant has taken a hands-off approach. Staff Sergeant Covel has been told to whip us into shape. The problem is that he has the organizational skillset of a first grader. He thinks PFC Zimmerman, who's been with us since before *Sparrow Hawk* and worked his ass off to get his and everybody's vehicle alert ready, is his personal go-fer."

"What's your take Ken?"

"Covel isn't behaving as he should."

"Right you are, Sergeant Clark....So, other than that, Mrs. Lincoln, how did you like the play?" I commented.

"What's that supposed to mean?" asked Jack.

"Nothing. Hang tight. I'll have a word with Bost."

COLEMAN KASERNE
NCO CLUB
1815 HOURS THURSDAY 19 MARCH 1970

CSM Bost was seated at a remote table in the rear of the NCO dining room. Seated with him was the First Sergeant of Bravo Company, Jake Carstairs.

"Sergeant Major, Top," I said as I walked up to them. "I didn't see your note until I got back to my desk," I said, addressing Bost.

"Sit down, Rick. What will you have?" asked Bost.

My mouth ran away from me. "I almost said, 'whatever you're having', but I can't handle a half gallon of Jim Beam. A beer, please," I said to the waitress while I was taking a seat next to Carstairs, who was shaking his head and laughing.

"How many of your new NCOs have been killed by that promotion ritual?" I asked, looking directly at First Sergeant Jake Carstairs.

"The Sergeant Major was just telling me about his plan to switch the refreshment of choice from bourbon to the less expensive *Linsengericht firewater.*"

"That's where I heard that name," I said. "The stuff you drink while it's on fire, right?"

"Yeah, they've been making it around here for a very long time."

"Great, if the new NCO doesn't set himself on fire, the homemade brew blows a hole in the back of his head."

"How did your RedEye guys make out on their first camping trip under new management?" asked the CSM, getting us back on topic.

"They made it back alive. Have you met the E-6 assigned?"

"No, but you probably already knew that. Aren't your kids getting along with him?"

"Those kids are four and five years older than I am. The NCOs are dealing with it. PFC Zimmerman, however, is having a bit of trouble with his new role as a personal valet. If you remember, he's the one who drove all the way to Bremerhaven, round-trip, the weekend before the alert just to pick up the wheel bearings for your command vehicle."

"Your point...?"

"PFC Zimmerman needs a new job or a promotion, or both. And even then, you'll still only be postponing the problem you'll have down the road unless you nip it in the bud now."

"Enlighten me, Sergeant," said the CSM in a tone that commanded an explanation. "Specifically, what is the problem?"

"It's the same familiar story, Sergeant Major. Someone has promoted their problem and sent him to us. Sometimes we can fix them; sometimes we shoot them. In either case, Private Zimmerman shouldn't have to attend the goat rodeo that started when Lieutenant Berkline turned that clown loose on a well-trained RedEye team."

"What do you suggest?"

"Transfer Covel. I suggest a position that is shaped and overseen by someone in a supervisory capacity. An E-7 or higher should do the trick."

"That's feasible. I'll talk to the EXEC so that he can have a word to inspire the participation of Lieutenant Berkline in a more pronounced leadership role."

"I just had a thought," I said. "Our new company commander has recently been born again, if you will. Let me see what he suggests before you get Major Hamadan involved."

"Better make it quick. The word on the street is that you are getting very short," said Bost.

DINIEREN IN PARADIES
ITALIAN/GERMAN RESTAURANT
DOWNTOWN GELNHAUSEN
2005 HOURS THURSDAY 19 MARCH 1970

"Hallo, Hanna. Es ist so gut Ihr lächelndes Gesicht zu sehen," ["Hello Hanna. It is so good to see your smiling face,"] I said as I entered the lobby of the dining establishment.

"Schober hoffte ich, dass Sie kommen würden. Wir sind dabei, früh heute abend zu schließen." ["Rick, I was hoping you would come. We are going to close early tonight."]

"Great, what time can I pick you up?"

"Nine thirty should be good."

"I need to run an errand. I'll be back here a little after nine," I said and kissed her lightly on the cheek. I caught sight of her mother out of the corner of my eye, looking at us from the bar area at the rear of the room. She was smiling.

I left the restaurant and started to cross the street.

"Hi, Rick," a voice called from a parked car located directly across from the front entrance. "Have you got a minute?" called Max Gresonine from his driver side window.

"Hi, Max," I said and started over toward the car, pulling the zipper of my coat all the way open as I approached.

"Please be careful with that. Jimmy has warned me -- you carry it cocked, yes?" Max asked, only partly teasing.

"No, not cocked, but there is one in the tube. What can I do for you, Max?"

"Come around and sit with me for a minute."

I went around and got in the passenger side of the Mercedes.

"What's up?"

"I'm going to offer Hanna a job in our embassy in Washington DC. I want to know if that is going to pose any problems for you."

"Actually, that's rather good news, but is this job going to be a problem for my friends in Virginia?"

"Absolutely not. She will be handling the COMMS and some of the crypto for our Ambassador. This is someone you have met recently -- Herr Gustav Heinemann."

"Interesting...then there will be no *Jane Bond* exploits? Was this already decided when the meeting took place at Rose Island?"

"I'm not sure if it was discussed then.... Jane Bond? Oh, it is a reference to the British MI-6, yes?"

"Well, it sounds like a good opportunity for Hanna."

"Please don't say anything until I talk to her. I'll speak to her tonight before she goes home."

BACHELOR OFFICERS QUARTERS
NEAR COLEMAN KASERNE
GELNHAUSEN
2045 HOURS THURSDAY 19 MARCH 1970

"Hello, Sergeant. I'm looking for Lieutenant Janzen. Do you know if he's in?"

"Hello, Sergeant Fontain. Yes, he is. I recognize you from the NATO Denver4 infirmary during *Sparrow Hawk*. Your Sergeant Clark got me transported there and stayed with me until I was treated."

"Oh, sorry I didn't recognize you. How's your leg?"

"I got the cast off last week. My First Sergeant got me this gig until I can return to full duty."

"What Company are you with?"

"I'm in Bravo."

"First Sergeant Carstairs seems like a good guy to work for. Clark never told me how you hurt your leg."

"We were changing a tire in the mud. The jack slipped out. The jeep came down on my leg. Your guy Clark saw it happen and took charge and got me out. After he got me help he went back and made sure my guys got back to base. You're lucky to have someone like that."

"Well, I've got to tell you we've given him extra training for just such emergencies. I thank you for bringing this to my attention. You're right. We are very lucky to have Sergeant Clark.

"The Lieutenant is in 207. He came in about thirty minutes ago."

"Can I just go up and bang on his door?"

"You sure can. Let me know if you have any trouble finding him."

"Thanks," I said, and took the stairwell up to the second floor. I found room 207 at the end of the hallway. I knocked twice.

"Sir, it's Sergeant Fontain."

The door was opened almost immediately. A smiling Lieutenant Janzen said, "Well, to what do I owe this unexpected pleasure?"

"I would like your advice on a situation that has developed with your RedEye team, Sir."

"Come in and have a seat. Would you like a beer?"

"No, thank you, Sir." I took a seat on one of two chairs that were placed on each side of a large window located on the back wall.

"You and the EXEC have a good trip down south?" I asked.

"I think he phrased it as a complete re-start. I have you to thank for that. As a matter of fact, all of the NCOs have come forward and asked if I needed anything."

"That's great, Sir, but it was First Sergeant Bumpus who figured everything out. These older NCOs are always our best "go to" source for guidance." I changed gears. "Have you met Lieutenant Berkline? He was assigned by Division to take over the RedEye group."

"He reported in the weekend before the alert. He lives here on the third floor."

"What was your impression of him?"

"He seemed a bit reserved. He was polite but I could tell he didn't have much field experience."

"Quiet and shy like me in other words."

"Yeah, right. Why the questions about this officer? I take it that things are not as they should be?"

"I'll let you be the judge. He has apparently given over control of the operations of RedEye to the Staff Sergeant who came in with him. The Sergeant's name is Covel."

"Are you saying that's unusual?"

"No, not the order itself, but his leadership position requires him not to relinquish his responsibility to those he has been appointed to lead. He needs to know and understand the mission of RedEye and all of what it takes to manage its success. And, it goes without saying; he needs to ensure that his people are being treated fairly."

"What do you suggest?"

"Unfortunately, neither the lieutenant, nor this new E-6, has a clue as to how to manage an existing fire team. This particular RedEye team has been trained to perform a function within this Battalion. These new people will be of assistance only if someone takes the time to integrate them into the existing fire teams. To do anything less would be counterproductive."

"I take it the reason you're here is because things are not going smoothly?"

"Covel's only focus so far has been to assign the only PFC in the group as his personal valet."

"Would you like me to have a word with the Lieutenant?"

"I would, and I humbly suggest that you allocate the Lieutenant time to work alongside Sergeant Boyd for the next several weeks. That way he'll get to know everybody, learn how the weapon system works, and learn the necessary protocols in case we get involved in an invasion."

"What about Sergeant Covel?"

"He'll be too busy with his new S-4 duties to be concerned. The Lieutenant needs to take part in every activity. He needs to understand all of the nitty-gritty details about vehicle road certification, generating the required reports to our S-3, and the basic logistics for operating a RedEye combat team."

"I get the general idea."

"Yes, Sir, I'm sure you do. Understanding the basics of any job here will help save our Company and our lives down the road. Don't spend much time worrying about Covel. I have it on good authority he will be receiving a new vision in the short term. Thanks for your time, Sir. Blood and Guts."

"Anytime, Rick. Our time together is always...educational. Blood and Guts."

MASTER BEDROOM
RINGSTRABE 3004
63589 LINSENGERICHT
0135 HOURS FRIDAY 20 MARCH 1970

"Do you want me to go downstairs and bring the rest of our clothes up here?"

"Mein Gott, Sie ist verrückt." ["My God, you are crazy."]

"I think you really scared your cat."

"Cat, I don't have a cat."

"Well, I guess we lingered too long on the staircase before closing the front door," I said with my most serious voice inflection. "The poor animal seemed terrified, by the way. While you were attacking me, ripping off my clothes, and screaming those wild obscenities, it sent him screaming into the night."

"Obscenities, whatever are you talking about?"

"Don't you remember repeating the word 'Oh god, oh, oh' several hundred times between the front door and the foot of this bed?"

"That's not very funny," said Hanna, trying very hard to suppress her laughter.

"You know, speaking in incomplete sentences can be a sign of a more serious problem. It's called *lackanookie*."

"What is... what did say: lac a nuky?"

"Yes. Come here and I'll explain."

MASTER BEDROOM
RINGSTRABE 3004
63589 LINSENGERICHT
0540 HOURS FRIDAY 20 MARCH 1970

I awoke at a little after five. Hanna was cuddled up close with her back snug against my chest. My mind was still trying to justify the pure joy I was feeling at this moment versus an emptiness deep down inside that would belong to me for the rest of my life.

"Are you awake?"

"Just barely," she whispered. "Do you want to go down and make us some coffee and let the cat in?" she asked with a giggle.

"So, you do admit to owning a cat and your sentence structure is much better this morning. You must have been cured last night."

"Mein Arzt ist sehr gut; er hat eine wunderbare Kopfende-Weise." ["My doctor is very good; he has a wonderful bedside manner."]

"Well, I think one more treatment should help prevent any relapse."

"You're the doctor," replied Hanna and threw the comforter towards the bottom of the bed.

THE KITCHEN
RINGSTRABE 3004
63589 LINSENGERICHT
0650 HOURS FRIDAY 20 MARCH 1970

I needed to be in the office by 0800. I got up and took a shower and went down to let the cat in. I was sitting at the kitchen table waiting for the coffee to finish perking.

"Did you find everything?" Hanna, dressed only in my tee shirt and white panties, asked me as she came around the table and sat in my lap.

"I think the cat is not coming back."

"Max asked me last night to take a job in Washington, D.C. He said he talked to you right before he came in."

"He did," I said. "What do you think of the offer?"

"I want to say this first. I never in all my life ever expected to feel this way about anyone. These feelings...."

"I know." I placed my hands on both sides of her face. I think you should take the job. But only if leaving Gelnhausen won't cause you and your family, your mother in particular, any hardship."

"My mother thinks it would be good for me."

"Then you should take the job. But beware, things are not always as they seem."

"Does that mean you are having second thoughts?"

"Not at all," I said. "You are aware of what your uncle does for a living?"

"Meaning?" she asked.

"Meaning, you were married to someone who was in the same line of work. Living inside a secret causes problems for both parties. All I'm saying is that you may be assigned other duties as time goes on."

"Like what?"

I looked her straight in the eye for a good 30 seconds. "Are you telling me you were never involved with what your husband was doing?"

"Of course not," replied Hanna. "I never knew about anything he was involved with. I swear, Rick."

"I believe you, Hanna," I said. "All I'm saying is that we should remember this conversation going forward. I doubt if you will be asked to do anything dangerous, but if and when that day comes, I want you to promise to tell me."

"I'm not sure I understand what you mean."

"Your uncle is an intelligence officer. The games in Washington are played at a very high level. You and I will probably be involved in that world from time to time."

"Are you an intelligence officer?"

"I can't answer that," I said. "I could tell you, but then I would have to kill you," I said, trying to make a joke.

"What?" she said in a very soft voice.

"That was a joke," I said. "But promise me you will tell me when that day comes."

"I promise".

"Right now I feel happy, alive, and in love. You and I will do very well together. I'm so very glad we've found each other."

"Oh, Rick, I feel the same about you."

"Job or no job, we are still going to need a new cat!"

S-4 WAREHOUSE
COLEMAN KASERNE
0940 HOURS FRIDAY 27 MARCH 1970

"Thanks for the ride, Ken. I'll see you and the rest of the guys at the club for dinner, right?" I reminded him.

"Yep. Larry asked for the private dining room for us. Don't be late. I hear the 1st Sergeant may attend."

"Sounds good. I'll be there with bells on," I said.

"See you down there," replied Ken.

I hoisted one duffel bag onto my shoulder and put the clipboard with the checklist for clearing post under my armpit. I grabbed the strap handle on the other duffel and climbed the concrete steps next to the loading dock.

The door was pushed outward and held open as I reached the top.

"I saw you drive up. Can I give you a hand with that?" asked Sergeant First Class Malcolm Summering.

"Thanks. By the way, congratulations on your promotion. It's much deserved. My guys always raved about the support you provided us. I can't tell you how much safer it made our jobs in the field."

"Glad to hear it," Summering replied. "Are you here to turn in your alert gear?"

"I had no idea there were so many steps to clearing post. Blubaugh gave me this copy of the TOE[265] that I signed for when I reported in."

I handed Malcolm the paper and he pulled his copy out of the file cabinet. "I'll initial both copies and sign off on your checklist. Hand me your clipboard."

"Don't you want to check the equipment?"

"Nah, we trust you. Besides I have people who do that for me now. What's your next stop?"

"I guess I should have packed the 45 ACP. Finance is the last one," I answered.

Ignoring the first remark, he suggested, "Ask them to get you to a zero balance. It will speed up your experience at McGuire."

"Thanks. I will," I said.

"Oh, by the way, I was told I have you to thank for the additional help to conduct the annual inventory. Some Staff Sergeant named Covel has been assigned as my new assistant."

"Please do me a favor and do not repeat that to anyone, especially to the Staff Sergeant. And you're welcome!"

---

[265] Training/Operation Equipment

THE DINNER—NCO CLUB
COLEMAN KASERNE
1225 HOURS FRIDAY 27 MARCH 1970

The trip through the land of Finance only took 45 minutes. The good news was I was granted the much-coveted zero balance. I walked the short distance around the pond to the parking area in front of the NCO Club. It was unusually packed, with parked vehicles strewn everywhere like life-size versions of toy cars. There were two jeeps with Military Police markings parked close to the main entrance. A late model black Mercedes sedan with a General Staff flag on the bumper displaying two stars was parked to the left of the main entrance. There were four fully outfitted MPs standing in various positions beside them. The tallest of the four was a Captain. I saluted and said, "Good evening, Sir. Blood and Guts." He smiled and returned the salute, but didn't speak. I pulled open one of the double glass doors and went inside.

There were three Sergeant E-5s milling around the lobby as I entered. They were dressed in Class As. I noticed that their unit patch was not a local one. I walked on into the main dining area and was surprised to see that the room was almost completely full. Most soldiers were dressed in fatigues but there were more than the usual number dressed in their Class A uniforms. A hush fell over the room; everyone seemed to turn their attention toward me when I entered. I remember thinking it was a good thing Larry had reserved the private dining room.

My attention went immediately to the rear of the room where there was a long table staffed with very high-ranking NCOs. As I got closer, a Major General seated in the center stood up and motioned for me to approach.

"Holy shit, what the hell is going on here?" I asked myself.

I walked up and saw that all three of the battalion commanders were arranged on both sides of the general. There were two Command Sergeant Majors, one of who was my very own, and, of course, my beloved First Sergeant, Ernie Bumpus. They were seated at the far end of a very long table. This had to be the fanciest court martial I had ever attended.

Major General Marian Roseborough commanded the 3rd Armor Division from August 1969-May 1971. I learned later that he was present at the request of Lieutenant Colonel Brogan.

"Sir, Sergeant Fontain," I introduced myself. My eyes shifted to Colonel Brogan in search of some indication as to what was going on. He just smiled.

"Sergeant, why don't you just take a seat there," suggested the General, pointing to a table directly front row center. I turned my head and I saw the entire RedEye group consisting of Ken Clark, Jack Swanson, Larry Stockert, Von Boyd, and our new company commander, 1st Lieutenant Walter Janzen. He was seated between Ken and Jack.

The table directly behind them included Lieutenant Key, Spec5 Carl Blubaugh, newly-promoted Sergeant "camera guy" Glen Towson and Spec5 Bernie Costa. The last seat at that table was filled by Sergeant First Class Malcolm Summering, who had just processed my alert gear at the S-4 warehouse. He had walked in behind me and was smiling from ear to ear.

"Jesus," I said, as I looked around the room. Every NCO on Coleman had to have been in attendance. I found out later that it was not mandatory for any one of them to be there.

The General moved to a lectern situated on the tabletop. He tapped the microphone a couple of times to both test it and get everyone's attention.

"Gentleman, please join me in reciting the pledge." Everyone stood and faced the flag that was prominently displayed directly behind the Major General. This was the first time I had recited the "Pledge of Allegiance" since high school. The entire room rose up at the same time and in one voice said;

> *"I pledge allegiance to the Flag of the United States of America and to the Republic for which it stands, one Nation under God, indivisible, with liberty and justice for all."*
> (Over three quarters of the audience added "Blood and Guts" at the end.)

"Please be seated. That, gentlemen, is the most perfect mission statement ever written."

The General continued, "It applies to our Division, to our Battalions, our Companies, and, on a personal level, to us as citizens of the greatest country the world has ever known. Every time I hear it I want to re-enlist." The room was completely silent. You could have heard a pin drop.

"Years from now, when someone asks you what you did in the military, you will tell them that you stood on the brink and successfully defended Western Europe from invasion by the Russian communists. And you will go on to tell them that no blood was shed because you were here. But you should make it known to whoever asks that what we did, what we do, and what we will continue to accomplish here was and will continue to be damned dangerous.

"Our worst enemy, as I see it, is the possibility that the discipline we practice each day could become humdrum, or that we could become complacent about it. But our very lives depend on it. Our jobs call for twenty-four hours a day, seven days a week of dedication. Not just at the top, but at every level of decision-making right on down to the individual soldier. It will be you, our NCOs, who will instill that dedication of purpose to everyone you are assigned to manage and support. Let me see a show of hands of everyone who knows why we have gathered here today," commanded General Marian Roseborough.

Every hand, as if rehearsed, went up at almost the same time. I, however, had no clue.

"OK, put your hands down. Sergeant Fontain, why is it you don't know why you are here?" interrogated the General.

I got to my feet and stood at attention. There was laughter erupting from all parts of the room, including my own table.

"Sir, it appears that you and I are the only two who don't know why we are here."

There was more laughter. Colonel Brogan cupped both hands over his face at that remark. I looked back at the General who was laughing along with the others at his table. "I had heard that you are indeed a silver-tongued devil, especially on your RedEye radio broadcasts," the General said. "Attention to Orders and Decorations", he announced loudly through the room's sound system.

I immediately reconfirmed the position of attention. The General referred to the document placed on the lectern in front of him.

"Attention to Orders and Awards," again boomed Major General Roseborough. "On March 13, 1970, the Office of the Commanding General, 3rd AD -- that's me, Sergeant Fontain, in case you were wondering who I am. You see, as it turns out, you are the only one here who is in the dark, so to speak," said the General with a broad smile.

He continued, "The subject being discussed is the promotion

and award for Staff Sergeant R. Fontain, US51672681, with promotion to Sergeant First Class, E-7 pay grade, with an effective date of February 17, 1970. Pretty good so far isn't it, Rick?"

3ᴿᴰ ARMOR DIVISION

Date: March 13, 1970

From: Office of the Commanding General, 3ʳᵈ AD
Subject: Promotion and Award

Staff Sergeant R. Fontain, US51672681, is promoted to Sergeant First Class, E-7 pay grade, effective date February 17, 1970.

Awards to be presented: The following decoration(s) of the Purple Heart [first occurrence] and the Bronze Star Award.

Description of Circumstance: While on TDY with a third party agency; Staff Sergeant Fontain was wounded while substituting as a crew chief on a UH-1D [Huey] Gun Ship. Attempting to land in a hot LZ; several members of a combat team were off loaded and were immediately taken under heavy fire from automatic weapons.

All four of these team members were hit. Only three were able to get back into the aircraft. Sergeant Fontain seeing the fourth member was down assisted the wounded man back to the waiting gun ship.

Due to the secrecy of the mission, all additional details have been removed.

Figure 42 - Attention to Orders

"Sir," is all I could say.

Maj. Gen. Marian Roseborough smiled again and went on.

"The following decorations of the Purple Heart (first occurrence) and the Bronze Star Award are also being made at this time. When I first became aware of these actions I asked your Colonel Brogan if I might come and present them to you personally. Your actions reflect well on our unit, as they do on you as an individual."

"Yes, Sir. Thank you, Sir," I said.

"Now pay attention. This is the good part."

The General cleared his throat. "While on TDY with a special operations group, which shall remain nameless but everyone can guess who."

"Ut oh, I said to myself, *"Bill Douglas is not going to be happy about that tidbit of information being exposed."*

"Staff Sergeant Fontain, in case you were wondering, it was General Bushman who provided us with these details."

"Why am I surprised? You don't get to be a Major General without being able to read people's minds."

The Division Commander continued, "Fontain was wounded while acting as crew chief on a UH-1D Gunship. While attempting to offload one half of an A-team of Green Berets in a hot LZ, the aircraft and the Special Forces members who had left the chopper were immediately taken under heavy automatic weapons fire."

The entire room had gotten very quiet.

"All four of the Special Forces team members were hit by gunfire. Only three were able to get back into the aircraft. Staff Sergeant Fontain, seeing the fourth member was down and unable to get back, helped the wounded man back into the aircraft."

With that announcement there was an immediate outbreak of whispered conversations going on throughout the hall.

"Just so everyone in attendance today knows, there is the unofficial version of what really occurred in that LZ."

"Oh, boy, what now," I thought.

"An eyewitness, in this case the co-pilot, states that Staff Sergeant Fontain jumped from the helicopter to assist two of the four soldiers in climbing back into the passenger bay. It was at this point he was shot in the back of his upper left leg. He then limped across 35 yards of open area to where the fourth team member was down."

"If anyone deserves a medal it's the two pilots. CWO Oden took two shots to his flak jacket and one to his right arm. How they kept that aircraft in position for that length of time was a miracle," is what was running through my head as the General spoke.

"He then, not without great difficulty, pulled the injured man to his feet and slung him across his shoulders and limped back across the open area to the waiting aircraft," the General said.

At that point, I was reliving the experience. *"I can still see the smile on his face as we were pulled into the chopper. Then he just closed his eyes."*

"Unfortunately, that man later died of his wounds in a Navy infirmary, but that solider is at rest in our Arlington Cemetery, where his family can visit him. Blood and Guts, Sergeant," concluded Major General Roseborough.

CLOSING REMARKS—NCO CLUB
COLEMAN KASERNE
1250 HOURS FRIDAY 27 MARCH 1970

"Colonel Brogan, will you do the honors, please?" asked General Roseborough.

"It would be an honor, Sir," said Colonel-designate Brogan.

The rank insignia was changed, and the awards were attached to the pocket of my fatigue blouse. Colonel Brogan took a step back and saluted. "Congratulations. Blood and Guts, Sergeant," he said.

I returned the salute, shook his offered hand and whispered, "If I had known this was going to happen I wouldn't have worked so hard on the alert prep."

"Yeah, you would have."

The audience of my peers began to chant, "Speech, Speech," and the General, being an accommodating fellow, ordered me to the lectern.

I double tapped the microphone and took a deep breath. "Thank you all for coming to celebrate this truly great honor." I paused and collected my thoughts.

"I started this journey as a boy hoping to survive the experience of being drafted. That's right, I was drafted. I was fortunate to be selected to receive the RedEye training, and even more privileged to have been assigned with you in the 3rd Armor Division." Cheers and clapping erupted throughout the room.

"We are unique. We are the United States Army, and our battalions collectively are *"us."* Our Division is, and will always be, molded in my mind as *"we."*

"Hear, hear," voices proclaimed from the table beside me.

"It will not be easy moving from my home of the last fifteen months back to the land where I spent my childhood. I almost said where I grew up." I paused.

"But that couldn't be further from the truth. That's not where I grew up; Gelnhausen is where I grew up -- becoming a man, a soldier, a warrior.... has been an experience I will cherish forever," with that said my throat tightened slightly.

"As you may know, my time here is just about over. I thank you for allowing me to say goodbye to most everyone all at once. Some of you I know on a first name basis, most of you I've have met during my time here."

There was complete silence and every face was pointed directly at me. I took a deep breath and continued. "I will forever carry a special place in my heart for all of you. God bless 3rd Armor and God bless the United States of America. Gentlemen, Blood and Guts."

EPILOGUE

MAC FLIGHT X240
CHARTER FLIGHT—SATURN AIR
FRANKFURT/MCGUIRE AFB
0950 HOURS THURSDAY 02 APRIL 1970

Figure 43
MAC Flight X240

The Saturn Airlines 707 took the second taxi-exit turnoff from the main runway. It proceeded to park in between the two National Guard C-141 aircraft. An Air Force service truck equipped with a set of steps pulled up to the plane. The door swung open as the PA system directed us to exit through the forward cabin door.

A bus pulled up at the base of the stairs to take us the quarter mile to the transit terminal building. An NCO, who was holding a clipboard by his side, had just departed the bus and had taken up a position at the foot of the stairs.

I was halfway down the steps when a 1968 Black Chevy Biscayne with government plates drove up and parked head-in to the front of the bus. Both the driver and the passenger exited the car and walked to the foot of the stairway. The two men were wearing dark colored business suits and sunglasses. The taller of the two removed what looked like a wallet from his inside jacket pocket and showed it to the Staff Sergeant.

As I got closer, I recognized the shorter of the two. It was the smiling face of Bill Douglas. The good news was that I was probably going to be given a ride out of here. The really bad news was that *Wild Bill* had found out about the references to the CIA in the General's presentation at the awards banquet the previous week.

I stepped down onto the tarmac and extended my hand, which to my surprise, was ignored in favor of a genuine hug.

"Sir, I don't know what to say. What a surprise," I said.

"Au contraire, Sergeant, your exploits as the silver-tongued devil of Gelnhausen will live forever in the halls of 3rd Armor. Colonel Brogan talked to the General yesterday. I was in town for a conference at Meade when I got the word that you were coming in today. And the rest, as they say, is just a coincidence."

"So, nobody's mad at me? You're not here to perform a hit?"

"Ed McCall, this is Sergeant First Class Rick Fontain, soon to be known as just plain old Rick," said Douglas. Ed McCall, in his mid- to late-twenties, was six feet two inches tall and about 220 pounds. He looked very, shall we say, capable.

"Ed, I'm glad to meet you. Are you assigned to guard Mr. Douglas while he is in country?" I asked. Ed laughed at the thought of that.

"No, Sir. Joe Wilson didn't want any more of our staff cars destroyed while Mr. Douglas was visiting."

"You're kidding?"

410 DUNLOGGIN ROAD
ELLICOTT CITY MARYLAND
FONTAIN FAMILY RESIDANCE
1650 HOURS THURSDAY 02 APRIL 1970

My Mom and Dad had just excused themselves and left Bill Douglas, Ed and me sitting at the bar in the downstairs family room. The bar was constructed out of solid cherry switchboard panels that had been rescued by my Dad from a recent renovation of a C&P Telephone Company Central Office.

"Please thank your Mom for the best dinner I've had in a very long time," said Ed. He then politely excused himself and went out to the car.

"You grew up in a very lovely home," said the assistant head spook from the London office.

"Thanks. Are you going to tell me why you came to pick me up?"

"No mystery. We just wanted to make sure you got home safe and sound. We want you to relax for a few weeks, notify your employer that you are back and ask when they want you to start back to work."

"And...." I said, waiting for just a little more information.

"We'll play all of that by ear as the day's progress. Again, relax because there is absolutely no rush."

"You know Hanna got a job here," I said.

"Oh, yeah. Old Max thinks she'll be a great help to the Ambassador. That reminds me, I almost forgot." He lifted his briefcase from beside the stool he was sitting on and placed it on the bar. He spun the wheels of the combination on both locks and pushed open the lid.

"Max asked me to give you this," and handed me a wooden, walnut I guesstimated, gun case. The lid had the Walther company name inset into the finish. I opened it and found a Model PP Zella, 9MM KURZ, with a three inch barrel and leather *inside the belt* holster. I pulled it out to examine it, and under the holster was a small cutout of a newspaper clipping. I quickly scanned the first few sentences. It started out: Nuremburg, Germany, March 12, 1970. The recently convicted 39-year old truck driver committed suicide today....

"It came via embassy courier a couple of days ago," Bill said.

I looked up at Douglas to ask what this was all about but something in his eyes told me not to bother.

Nuremburg Germany March 12, 1970. The recently convicted 39 year old truck driver committed suicide today...

Figure 44 - News Clip

Some things are better left alone.

"Jesus, I miss her," I thought to myself.

"What, no silencer?" I asked jokingly, referring to the pistol.

"We use the smaller caliber pistols, like the Ruger 10-23, which is manufactured with that capability."

"No shit," I said. "I actually miss the comfort of my 1911 in the small of my back. This is really an expensive gift. If you see Max before I do, please thank him profusely for me," I said.

Douglas went back into the brief case. "This is from the General." He handed me a chrome plated model 1911 ACP.

"He said that you would probably feel naked without one." He then placed on the bar two charged clip cases attached to a shoulder strap of the skeleton holster.

"I'm speechless," I said.

"David James told me that this was the General's personal weapon he carried throughout his service."

"Will I have a chance to see the General any time soon?"

"Yes, you will."

"You were going to comment on Hanna's new employer. What do you think?" I asked.

"Well, new job, not really a new employer. As you might expect, her Uncle Max may have a hidden agenda. Be that as it may, I think she'll do really well with a change of scenery."

"Are you telling me she is, and has been, in the intelligence game?"

"No, but indirectly her entire family has ties to the BND[266]. I knew her husband. She deserved better. I hope you two find happiness with each other. You both really deserve it."

"Thanks, Bill that means a lot coming from you. What aren't you sharing with me about her husband and Uncle Max?"

"Nothing that will affect the two of you in the short term," replied Douglas, but I guessed that wasn't entirely true.

"How long are you going to be in town?"

"'Until this weekend," he replied and reached into the briefcase again. "And, this is also for you. The same rules apply as before." He handed me a leather ID wallet. "A gift from Joe Wilson, who was told by David to replace the one you had left in the safe in the 1st/48th's S-3. Don't buy any more dogs with it."

"And just why does David think I'll need this?" I opened the leather wallet, revealing a silver and blue badge on one side and a plastic laminate shield with my picture on the other. I read the inscription.

---

[266] The Bundesnachrichtendienst (Federal Intelligence Service) also known as the BND. CIA code name CASCOPE, is the foreign intelligence agency of Germany, directly subordinate to the Chancellor's Office.

"I have been transferred from the CID[267]." I glanced back down at the credentials. "The identification of a deputy U.S. Marshal?" I said, asking for some guidance.

"You'll find it difficult to get on a commercial airliner with your newly obtained gifts that Max and the General have showered upon you."

"Marvelous," I said. "Why do I get the feeling that yours and my idea of the word 'relax' are worlds apart?"

"You are a very suspicious fellow, Rick."

I walked around to the business side of the bar and took the bottle of Johnny Walker Black from the top shelf. "You want one more for the road?"

"No thanks. I've got another stop to make on the way back to D.C."

"I'll ask this again: just what is expected of me in the short term?"

"Rick, you're going to be invited to play an important role for us in the private sector. What General Bushman has asked is that you come and see him in few weeks to discuss your options. When is Hanna arriving in Washington?"

"She told me she has a flight on Thursday the 16th, coming into Friendship International[268]."

"Great. The General is hosting a polo event on the 18th. It's located just off the Washington Beltway by way of the River Road exit. He keeps a house here now to be near his office at Langley."

"Polo?" I asked, somewhat surprised. The request for information went unanswered.

"You can bring Hanna. I believe her Uncle Max and General Bushman are already acquainted."

"What do you think I'll be doing in the short term?" I tried again.

"Not sure, but my guess is you'll go back to work for the Bell System and then do a tour of duty at Bell Labs -- an international assignment I expect. You'll be encouraged to finish your degree, of

---

267   Criminal Investigative organization and Department of Defense's premier investigative organization. The CID is responsible for conducting criminal investigations in which the Army is, or may be, a party of interest.

268   Located in Anne Arundel County, Maryland next to the site where Friendship Methodist Church stood until 1948. Friendship International Airport was dedicated on June 24, 1950 by President Harry Truman. Today it is known as Baltimore/Washington International Airport, or BWI.

course, and in your spare time you'll be sent to the Presidio[269] for language training. And, there are several methods and procedure courses held in and around Langley that are to die for, figuratively."

"Spare time," I commented in my best sarcastic tone.

"Rick, you're being asked to belong to something that is important to our country's wellbeing. You are a natural for this life. I hope you decide to stay with us."

Bill Douglas stood and offered his hand. "You did a great job for us. The country owes you a great deal." And with that, he drained his glass. "I'll say goodnight. Please thank your Mom again for dinner," said the ever-smiling Douglas. He turned at the door.

"In either case, whatever you decide to do, I want to thank you for all you have done already. I'm personally very grateful for your service. No, that's not at all what I meant to say. It's your friendship... is what I meant to say, and I hope to have it for a good long time."

I didn't know how to reply to that statement so I didn't say anything.

I walked him across the patio and watched him cross the driveway. It seemed like a very long time since our first meeting in London. Ed McCall, in the government car, started the engine. Its lights came on as Douglas approached the waiting vehicle. We would not meet again for almost a year.

www.billfortin.com/book

---

[269] The Presidio, located near San Francisco, serves all branches of the Department of Defense and other select government agencies. The Defense Language Institute (DLI) is the Defense Department's primary center for foreign language instruction. The center constitutes the principal activity at the Presidio.

WHAT'S NEXT!

Figure 45- What's Next from Cold War Publications